BY MARIEKE NIJKAMP

This Is Where It Ends

Before I Let Go

Even if We Break

At the End of Everything

The Oracle Code (art by Manuel Preitano)

Ink Girls (art by Sylvia Bi)

Unbroken: 13 Stories Starring Disabled Teens

VOX MACHINA
KITH & KIN

VOX MACHINA
KITH & KIN

MARIEKE NIJKAMP

NEW YORK

2022 Del Rey Trade Paperback Edition

Published in the United States by Del Rey, an imprint of Random House, a division of Penguin Random House LLC, New York.

DEL REY and the CIRCLE colophon are registered trademarks of Penguin Random House LLC.

Originally published in hardcover in the United States by Del Rey, an imprint of Random House, a division of Penguin Random House LLC, in 2021.

LIBRARY OF CONGRESS CATALOGING-IN-PUBLICATION DATA
Names: Nijkamp, Marieke, author.
Title: Vox machina: kith & kin / Marieke Nijkamp.
Other titles: Kith & kin | Critical role (Television program)
Description: New York: Del Rey, [2021] | Series: Critical role
Identifiers: LCCN 2021036347 (print) | ICCN 2021036348 (ebook) |
ISBN 9780593496626 (hardcover) | ISBN 9780593496633 (ebook) |
ISBN 9780593496657 (international edition) |
ISBN 9780593496640 (trade paperback)
Subjects: LCGFT: Fantasy fiction.
Classification: LCC PT5882.24.I38 V29 2021 (print) |
LCC PT5882.24.I38 (ebook) | DDC 839.313/7—dc23
LC record available at https://lccn.loc.gov/2021036347
LC ebook record available at https://lccn.loc.gov/2021036348

Printed in the United States of America on acid-free paper

randomhousebooks.com

1st Printing

Book design by Alexis Capitini

To siblings in all shapes and forms,
whether by blood, by choice, or by shared stories.

And to my sisters. With love.

VOX MACHINA
KITH & KIN

PROLOGUE

Twelve years ago

The people of Byroden rarely ever left their town. Travelers who passed through on their way to glory, riches, or certain death in the Rifenmist were welcomed with warmth and sent on their way with good wishes, but seldom was their example followed. Most people who made their home in Byroden didn't feel the call of curiosity or the need to traverse untrodden paths. They carved out their lives between the Gladepools to the north and the endless plains and rolling hills to the south, and they were happy. They caught fish in the pools and worked the land of their ancestors, while their homes and hearts held the history of the town: from the notches in the walls that showed generations of children growing taller, to the stories told around the hearth with mirth and merriment, to the small but tenderly cared for cemetery at the edge of town. Life in Byroden followed the cycles of nature and life.

On rare occasions, younger townsfolk who were cursed with wandering feet did leave to find their fortune in the cities. To far-off Emon, to take to the Ozmit Sea or to study at the city's temples or academies. To Kymal, if their desires were of a more questionable nature. But those wanderers were few and far between, and more often than not, eventually, they returned.

It was a simple life and, according to the adults who lived there, it was a good life.

But the children of Byroden played at adventure. They ran after travelers until they couldn't keep up with the horses anymore. They used sticks for swords and staffs and reenacted every bedtime story ever told to them. They pretended the ore being extracted from the mines outside of town was not simply metal but pure magic, far stronger than that of Mistress Fara, the gnomish healer, or that of Old Wenric, the musty halfling owner of Byroden's Bliss, the local tavern with its single guest room that thrived on foolhardy wanderers. They saw mystery and wonder in every corner of their hometown.

And whenever a traveler passed through Byroden, word among the children spread like wildfire. Regardless of chores, lessons, or bedtime, they immediately gathered to see what was happening.

So on that day, when a well-dressed elven man with long dark-brown hair and heavy bracelets around his wrists rode through the town with the setting sun at his back, glancing curiously at the houses around him, Feena was the first to see him. She dumped the oats she was carrying into the goats' trough and looked around until she spotted Tym, working in his parents' hayloft. She curled her fingers around the copper wire flower hanging from her necklace, pointed in Tym's direction, and let him know they needed to gather. Tym shouted down to alert his younger brother. His younger brother raced across the street to collect the farrier's daughter, and the farrier's daughter threw a crumpled note through the open window of the butcher's attic, where his eldest son sat practicing his letters. So the word rushed through town, weaving through muddy streets, echoing from one person to the next.

Until it reached a pair of wayward half-elven twins, who'd escaped their mother's notice and had spent the afternoon tracking near the Gladepools. They both had dark-brown hair, fine features, and simple but well-made clothes. They were not yet ten and were convinced they were invincible. Two days ago, the boy had overheard Old Wenric mutter about a boggle—a mischievous creature—near the pools, and so he'd talked his sister into tracking down the creature and capturing it. After all, a trophy like that was sure to impress the other children, and perhaps they could even entice the boggle to play some act of mischief on Padric, the town's grumpiest farmer.

But despite the boy's quiet feet and the girl's piercingly keen eyes, they'd run around in circles for hours feeling for all the world like they were the ones on the wrong side of the creature's mischief now.

With dusk settling in, the boy kept glancing around at the rustling undergrowth, shivering at the yawning wind around them. Although he and his sister were alike in many ways, he appeared far less at ease amidst the trees and their lengthening shadows, and while he had been the one to bring up the boggle, that was miles on muddy ground ago.

"Are you *sure* it exists?" asked the girl. She wore her long hair bound back in a braid, and she absentmindedly tugged at the leather cord that held it in place, causing a few strands to slip out. With her feet planted firmly on the marshy soil, she looked at ease. She looked like she belonged here.

"I'm sure I heard Wenric talk about it," the boy replied, sullenly but unable to back down. The boggle and the opportunity to play pranks still outweighed his discomfort, even if they did so barely.

"*Fine.*" The girl rolled her eyes. "We'll keep looking."

She pushed a stray strand of hair out of her face and crouched down in a narrow clearing, where she thought she'd last seen the boggle's tracks. The ground here was uneven, with gnarly tree roots digging through the earth like fingers clawing for purchase, and a dusting of leaves everywhere. A nearby twig had broken off at an odd angle. Something had disturbed the dirt underneath.

After a moment, the girl reached out and traced her fingers over the nearest root, leaving a thin oily coat of ooze on her fingertips. She smelled at it and grinned—the boy gagged—when a branch snapped. Then another. The leaves around them rustled and heavy footsteps came their way.

The girl lurched to her feet, while the boy grabbed the small knife he'd stolen from the kitchen that morning.

"Vex! Vax!" A third person stumbled into the clearing. Neither boggle nor marshland creature, it was the baker's oldest boy, Duncan. With his bigger-than-most halfling stature, he made enough noise to scare every animal and creature in the vicinity away from them. Duncan came to a halt in front of the twins, putting his hands on his knees and trying to catch his breath.

"Visitor," he breathed. "Come quick."

The boy called Vax tilted his head, the boggle already half forgotten by the promise of mysteries back home. "Someone interesting?"

"You scared away everything around us," the girl called Vex snapped, folding her arms and accidentally smearing some of the ooze on her light-blue sleeves. "I had a trail! I was close to finding that boggle."

"Were not," her brother immediately shot back.

"Were too."

Duncan straightened but still sounded winded. "An elven man," he said. "Looks like royalty or something, all fancy robes and sparkling bracelets and his nose in the air. He was on his way to Old Wenric's when I ran out here."

"What does someone like that want in Byroden?" Vex demanded crossly.

Vax put the knife back in his belt. "I don't know, but we're going to find out." He reached out, brushed the ooze off his sister's shirt, and offered her a crooked smile. "Unless you want to keep walking in circles."

"We *weren't* walking in circles. I *know* these woods." She slapped his hands away.

Vax shrugged. The knowledge that they'd soon be out of here made it easier to be nonchalant. "I've seen this tree at least three times, so unless it up and moved we were."

"Next time, you can track if you're so clever."

Duncan cleared his throat. "Are you coming or are you going to argue all day?"

"We're coming," Vax said, while at the exact same time his sister snapped, "Both."

"I didn't see any weapons or supplies on him," Duncan said—entirely too used to the twins' bickering and far too preoccupied by the stranger. "He looked like he dressed for market day and not for survival."

"Maybe he knows magic?" Vex suggested, despite herself. The travelers who passed through Byroden to the Rifenmist usually fit the same pattern. Armed to the teeth, a peculiar kind of restlessness, and more supplies than sense. No one entered the Rifenmist without preparation.

"If he does, he must be very powerful," Duncan said. "He wasn't in a hurry either. It looked like he was trying to find something here, and I want to get back before he finds it."

With that, he set a firm pace out of the shadowy marshlands, having fulfilled his duty as a friend to warn the twins of the strange goings-on in town but not wanting to risk missing another moment of this break in the daily monotony. And perhaps—not wanting to linger too long amidst the trees' shadows and the whispers of a boggle nearby. The twins might see the creature's presence as a challenge, but the baker's son preferred life to be calmer and slightly less complicated.

Still, the oddity of the traveler was quite enough to lure both twins away from their quarry. Vex cast a lingering glance at the clawing roots where she'd been inspecting the curious ooze, then shrugged and turned to her brother. She knew, with all the confidence of a nearly-ten-year-old, that the boggle was out there, hidden in the darkened corners, laughing at the two of them. She also knew, with that very same confidence, that there would be other days. She wouldn't have wandering feet, like the adults sometimes grumbled about. As long as she could play at adventures with her friends, get into mischief with her brother, and at the end of the day go home to her mother, she was content here. She was happy, and nothing could ever change that.

So while dusk covered the marshland like a blanket, she let the tracks be the tracks, grabbed her brother by the hand, and charged after their friend. And somewhere in the shadows, a small creature laughed.

ALL THE CHILDREN OF BYRODEN had gathered in the stables of Byroden's Bliss, where most of the stalls had been converted to storage. Just as there was only one guest room in the inn, there also was only one hay-covered corner for a horse left, and the traveler's blue roan stood comfortably chewing her hay.

There had been more, once. Bliss used to have three guest rooms and enough space to keep at least half a dozen horses. Until some fifteen years ago, when Old Wenric's father broke his shoulder while working his land, decided to stay with his son for a few days, and simply never left. Three years later, a cousin from far-off Drynna showed up at Wenric's doorstep, her infant daughter in tow. She refused to share what brought them here, but she begged for a few nights' rest. She, too, never left. Old Wenric grumbled it was for the better, when anyone asked him. Those few and far-between travelers foolish enough to brave the Rifenmist could brave a night together in a single room too, and with no children of his own to follow in his footsteps, his cousin's daughter became his apprentice.

Iselle was fourteen now. Quite too old—according to her uncle—to spend her time playing, but fortunately she was clever enough to know better. She left the shutters open so the other children could spy more easily.

And the strange traveler was still there, illuminated by the soft glow of half a dozen candles. He sat on one of the raggedy wooden chairs, his back ramrod-straight and discomfort written clear across his face. With one hand he held on to a cup of some hot drink or other. No one had seen him take a sip yet.

By the time the twins clambered into the stable, the whispered theories were flying back and forth. The traveler was in fact a powerful mage, on a quest so secretive he could not speak to anyone about it—or speak to anyone at all. He was a nobleman in disguise, or a traveler from places so distant they might as well be imagined, like Westruun or Stilben or the cities beyond the Ozmit Sea.

Vex climbed onto a bale of hay next to Feena so she would have a better viewpoint of what happened inside, but Vax stayed in the shadows near the entrance to the stable. He leaned against the wall. He wasn't sure what held him back. Perhaps it was a lingering discomfort from the boggle hunt, perhaps it was the all-too-familiar way in which the traveler arched his eyebrows, but he could see fine from here. Some days, he was far more comfortable being hidden.

It was this angle that allowed him to see the traveler's face when the door to the inn opened and the last light of dusk filtered in. Briefly, the man's discomfort melted and made place for a sense of wonder. The lines around his eyes softened, and his shoulders dropped. But it was only a moment and then it was gone, the man's aloofness firmly back in place. He got to his feet and bowed slightly to a person just out of their collective line of sight, and while they were all too distant to overhear him, the gesture sparked another round of whispers.

Vax stole a glance at his sister, who had pulled her knees up to her chest and was biting at her lip. Her eyes flicked in his direction, as always acutely aware of his watching her, but she didn't move. Not until the other person stepped into the candlelight, and Vex gasped.

The person on the other side was a slender human woman with thick dark hair, kind eyes, and gentle hands. Byroden's seamstress, Elaina. The twins' mother. She held herself proudly, her face a mixture of concern and defiance.

But before either of them could do or say anything—though Vax had no idea what to expect, exactly—the grizzled face of Old Wenric swam into vision. He leaned out the window, glared at his dumbstruck audience, and pulled the shutters closed.

Immediately the twins were covered under a barrage of questions.

"Did you see that? Why would your mother meet with a traveler like him?" Tym demanded.

"That's obvious, isn't it?" Feena shoved him with her foot and immediately turned to Vex. "Do you think he's family? Do you think he's your *father*?"

"He looks so rich. Did you see his jewelry? He has more gold and gems than the whole town put together," Duncan put in.

From there the suggestions continued:

"Maybe you're elven royalty."

"Maybe you were hidden away here to protect you from a curse or enemies or . . ."

"*Maybe* he's coming to bring you home." A short pause from Feena, and then she continued, "Wouldn't that be something?"

They all said it like it was a good thing, and Vax felt the air constrict around him. Like his sister, he only played at adventure. Of course he was curious, some days, at what lay beyond the Gladepools. He loved to hear the stories travelers told and the trinkets they brought from distant places. And some nights, he dreamed of being a hero with all the ferocity of a nine-year-old boy. But he always dreamed of coming home here. He didn't want to be anywhere else.

Before anyone else could suggest they were better off somewhere else, he snapped, "We're good here, the three of us. This *is* home."

He pushed himself away from the wall and stalked out into the courtyard past the inn, where dusk deepened to night, and a lone owl took to the sky. On warm summer nights, when the days were long and the harvest plenty, the townsfolk would gather here to tell tall tales around a campfire, to drink and dance. But on days like these, when the weather was turning and change was in the air, the place felt lonely and cold and far too big for his boots.

Mere moments passed before another set of footsteps echoed against the walls, and Vex quietly came to stand next to her brother. Her eyes showed the same confusion and worry and fear.

"It's not real, is it?" she asked softly. "Vax?"

Vax set his jaw, though his hands clenched. Neither of them actually knew much about their father, but they'd never needed to know. They had a family. They had a home. "No. It can't be."

"He won't take us away, will he?"

"Of course not. He can't." His lips trembled. "This is where we belong. Don't you know what Mistress Fara always says? The people of Byroden might as well have roots for feet, because no one truly leaves."

She offered him a weak smile. She slipped her hand in his, and she noticed his fingers were far colder than the night air warranted, so she pulled him closer until she realized they were both shivering. "And whatever happens"—the girl whispered the words fiercely, because they both needed to hear them—"we'll always be together. Right?"

The boy didn't have to think about that. He swallowed past the tremor in his voice and believed the words hard enough to make them so. "Always and no matter what happens."

CHAPTER 1

The spider crashed into the undergrowth with a dagger buried into one of its eyes, its claws still twitching and its jaw clicking. A large brown bear immediately leaped on top of it, his paws crushing the spider's legs, like branches that snapped underneath his weight.

Vex'ahlia Vessar shuddered at the crunching sound. "Ugh, gross. How about a cleaner kill next time, brother?"

"At least I brought one of them down," her brother Vax'ildan shot back, his eyes on the two other spiders that were still circling them. "Besides, who led us straight into their nest in the first place?"

"*Trinket* brought one of them down." Her bow fully drawn, Vex tracked one of the spiders with her arrow. Half-elf twins, they'd stumbled upon a nest, hidden away in the thicket, as they'd crossed into Bramblewood Forest on their way to Westruun. The trail they'd followed from the river to the city got swallowed up by the trees. Three spiders, concealed by the greens and browns around them, had scurried out of their burrow—and attacked before they'd been able to back away and change course. "And *you* wanted to take a shortcut."

"I'm fucking tired of trees," Vax said, like that was a better reason to walk into a spider's nest. He took a new dagger from his belt. "And Trinket only *helped*."

"That spider was still moving."

"Twitching. It would have died eventually."

"Because Trinket killed it."

Still on top of the spider, Trinket growled and looked around the narrow clearing in the woods for the other arachnids, ready to jump on another one if the need arose.

Vex breathed out and focused on her target. One of the spiders scuttled up a large tree—dashing around the thorns that covered the bark, lending the forest its name—and circled the trunk. Like the first, it was the size of a large dog or a wolf, its hairy legs at sharp angles and its eyes focused on the twins. The four smallest eyes tracked their every movement, while the larger eyes on top reflected the speckled sunlight, giving them an eerie glow. It rounded the tree and when it reappeared, it darted across an overhanging branch and made to leap at Vex.

As soon as the spider jumped, Vex let her arrow fly. The bowstring reverberated next to her ear, and the wooden shaft of the arrow curved through the air. For the briefest of moments, no more than a heartbeat, both the spider and the arrow sped toward each other—then the arrow hit, with a satisfying *thud,* directly underneath the creature's jaw. Its leap interrupted, the spider crashed to the ground like the first one had.

Unlike the first one, this one fell and remained motionless, its legs broken and askew.

Vex raised an eyebrow at her brother. "*That's* how you kill a spider."

"Luck," he smirked. She elbowed him.

"Skill, thank you very much." She grabbed a new arrow from her quiver and placed it against the string, keeping an eye on the trees around them for the last spider and the largest of the three.

To anyone who might observe the half-elves and give them no more than a cursory glance, the two looked exactly the same. Dark-brown hair—messy from their time in the woods—slender physique, practical clothes, and deadly weapons. All angles and raw edges. To full-blooded elves, they might appear too young to be this weathered and wary, but to any perceptive observer, it was clear they came by their caution honestly, and they moved with a grace brought on by years of traveling around together.

Vax held blades in both his hands, and kept his back toward his sister as the remaining spider circled them. Back-to-back, they scanned the forest, ready to attack if the spider jumped at them.

To Vex's left, something crackled in the undergrowth. A twig snapped, and she reacted immediately, swinging her bow in the direction of the sound and letting an arrow loose. It hurtled through the air without a target and struck a tree.

A large shadow clambered into the trees and disappeared between the leaves. They could hear the spider rustle overhead. It was stealthy and cautious. The scarring along its thick legs indicated it had seen and survived its fair share of fights.

Vex twisted toward the movement, grabbed another arrow, and sent it toward the large arachnid. She heard it impact, but the spider kept prowling the trees overhead, seemingly unbothered by a meager shaft. She narrowed her eyes as the spider skittered up higher, until it disappeared from view. "Careful."

Vax held his daggers at the ready and squinted up at the trees too. He winced at the size of the creature. "Looks like we woke Mama Spider," he said.

Trinket ambled closer, snout pointed up and hesitation in his gait.

When the spider shifted and dashed to one of the lower branches, Vax weighed his dagger and threw it with precision. The weapon cut through the arachnid's outer shell and stuck there, right next to Vex's arrow. The creature hissed sharply and reared back, front legs stretched out toward Vax, and in that instant it was easy to see how much larger it was than the other two spiders had been; when it stretched out, it was nearly the size of the brown bear down below.

Vex let another arrow fly. "Get out!" she whispered at her brother and her bear. She reached for her quiver once more, backing away to the edge of the clearing, keeping the trees behind her and her eyes on the spider.

Vax held on to his dagger and held his ground, clearly trying to uncover the spider's weakest points. "I've got this."

"She's Trinket's size. She'll—"

Before she could finish the sentence, the spider overhead screeched loudly, the sound echoing against the trees. It pushed off the branch, and *fell.* There was no grace to the attack. The spider let itself fall toward Vax, using the same tactic Trinket had, trying to crush its prey underneath its legs—and presumably to sink its fangs into a convenient midday meal. One of Vex's arrows sped past it. Vax brought his dagger up in an attempt to strike—

And the spider crashed into him. Its legs caved. Its head snapped forward, large fangs digging into Vax—and then it collapsed on top of him.

"Vax!" Vex dashed forward, while Trinket leaped toward the spider too.

"Got it," Vax grunted. "M'okay, I think."

Vex breathed a sigh of relief as her brother tried to roll out from under the spider, but the weight of the creature kept him down. One of its fangs tore along his collarbone.

And before Vex's eyes, Vax began to lock up. His shoulders and arms tensed, and he couldn't push the spider's jaws away anymore. As the venom from the bite spread through him, his hands clawed into fists. The spider's body rolled back on top of his chest, and he cursed. "Ow. Fuck."

But he leaned his head back on the mossy ground, stared at his sister, and grinned. "Definitely brought that one down."

IT TOOK THE BETTER PART of an hour for Vax to regain use of his arms, and it took until they set up camp in a quieter clearing, several hours later and far away from any spiders' nests, for the dark lines around the wound to fade. He rolled his shoulders and inspected the wound through the puncture hole in his shirt. "Did you use the antivenin we got in Kymal?"

Vex leaned against Trinket, who napped comfortably near the campfire she'd built as dusk crawled through the trees and the first owls took to the sky. "Well, your shoulder was turning blue."

With more than a little help from her bear, Vex had pulled her brother out from under the spider, and she'd used what was left of a small, near-empty vial of a viscous green liquid on the puncture wound. They'd dealt with spiders like these before, most recently at the behest of a wine merchant who'd had an infestation in his cellars, and she was glad she'd held on to the last remaining bit. Vax's wound hadn't been a bad one—a clean cut, not too deep—but by the time she'd gotten him free, the wound's edges had been darkening and vicious lines were crawling across his shoulder. Not much longer, and he would've been completely unable to move.

"I'm glad it worked," he said. "Blue looks far better on you than it does on me."

Vex removed her bracers to clean them, and she picked at the thread that she'd used to mend the fraying buckles. "What *exactly* possessed you to stand underneath that spider anyway?"

"I needed to get through its armor," he said reasonably.

"Oh, well, that explains that then." Vex tied the thread in place again and turned the bracers around. Though they bore the wear and tear of previous fights, they'd made it through this confrontation mostly un-scathed. The leather was cracked and torn, and a large gash ran down the middle of her right bracer, the result of fending off a rabid wolf. But they had a little while left in them if she was careful.

She had to be. With the two of them getting closer to Westruun, she was going over what they needed and what they could afford. She'd al-ready added a new vial of antivenin to her endless list of supplies, along-side the tally of what everything would cost. They had coin enough for maybe half of it.

At least they would make it to Westruun by the next day. That's what had brought them here in the first place: a bit of work ferrying a message from a spice merchant to her girlfriend in the Westruun Shields—the local military force. They'd be able to deliver it without the sort of delay that usually caused people to complain about paying. And she'd har-vested the venom from the spiders as best she could. She hoped she could make a good deal with the apothecary.

Across from Vex, Vax dug out a piece of cloth and set to work pol-ishing his daggers. He tested one of the blades out on his thumb, before slipping the weapon into his boot and moving on to the others. He seemed lost in thought for a while, and she knew he was thinking about the city too. He glanced at her. "I will need to get these sharpened prop-erly when we get to Westruun."

She added it to the tally and grimaced. "We'll need to restock on supplies. Get antivenin. And a coat that doesn't look like it has more holes than fabric." She would also need a new set of bowstrings. She could make her own bows, arrows, and fletching, but good string was harder to come by. "We can stay in town for a day."

It was her opening offer.

Vax stretched against the lingering stiffness of the venom, and his shoulders cracked. He leaned back. "You know it won't kill you to spend the night in a comfortable bed in a decent inn?"

She looked at the clearing around them and raised an eyebrow. A generous clearing in the forest surrounding a stream that found its way down from the mountains, and a good distance away from Westruun's hunters and loggers. She'd be more than comfortable right here. The woods could provide for almost anything. Food, protection, a place where they didn't have to worry about anything or anyone else. It was simple and peaceful—most of the time.

Vax rolled his eyes. "Well, it certainly won't kill me. I know you like to pretend otherwise, but we're not woodland creatures, and I wouldn't mind a bit of comfort."

Vex gave her brother a withering look. "We were in Kymal three weeks ago. And it's coin we don't need to spend."

"If you're being thrifty, it means we're running out of funds, so staying in the city for a few days will give me time to scrounge up a bit of work. It's not like we're going to stumble over bags full of gold out here in the middle of nowhere." He pulled his whetstone from his belt to get rid of a blemish on one of the other daggers and purposefully didn't look at her. "A week. A week of soft beds and good food. I'll find us a decent, cheap-but-no-bedbugs place to stay, and we find a bit of work to raise enough funds until Winter's Crest."

Vex crossed her arms. Behind her, Trinket grumbled. He knew this dance as well as the two of them. "We don't need a week. One night at most. A day to gather what we need and a day to ask around."

They had variations on the same argument every time they neared a new city. It was perhaps the main difference between the two of them. She understood the wilds, while he thrived in city streets and their accompanying shadows.

"I can't find decent work in a day. I'm very good, but I'm not *that* good," Vax said.

"Fine." Vex knew he was right, though she wouldn't admit that. Finding enough work was how they could afford to survive on their own, and plenty of people could use hired hands for all sorts of odd jobs. They had protected travelers, sought out monsters that endangered farmers' flocks or hunters' prey, and run messages from town to town. "Two nights."

Her brother took a dagger and sent it spinning into the air, catching it as it came down. The light of the campfire reflected off the metal, and the spinning blade resembled an oversized firefly tumbling through the clearing. "Have you considered you'll be in a much better bargaining position with merchants if you have time to walk away for a day?"

Vex grabbed her bow. "I'm going to find us dinner." She scratched Trinket's ear. "Are you coming, buddy?" If they stayed in town for longer than a night, he'd have to stay behind. Though at least this was a perfect location for a bear who'd attract far too much attention in the city.

At the edge of the campfire's glow, she turned around. "Three nights. Not a day more. And only if you can find an affordable place to stay."

Vax grinned. They somehow always settled on three nights.

CHAPTER 2

Voices rang through the Market Ward of Westruun. Merchants praised their wares, every one of them trying to drown out the others. A group of street children ran after a ball, weaving through the crowds, across the cobblestone roads, and laughing uproariously. A young girl—perhaps the one with the nimblest fingers—managed to cut a purse or two along the way. Outside a dodgy-looking tavern, a gray-haired dwarven bard gathered a small audience while he drunkenly belted an ode to Zan Tal'Dorei, and two patrons appeared to be in the midst of a heated argument.

The city was, Vex decided, obnoxious and loud compared to the woods. It wasn't just the noise either. It was the stench of the place. Muck and manure mixed with ale, sweat, and rotted food. Even the comforting smell of fresh bread from one of the bakers couldn't mask the grime underneath, and it clung to her.

Cities always got under her skin when she came in from the wild. But where she raised her hackles, Vax thrived. His shoulders dropped and his awareness sharpened. He walked with the gait of someone who expected trouble and would in fact welcome it.

"You look like you'd rather step into another spider's nest than hang about here, sister," he teased. He'd snatched an apple from a cart and tossed it high up into the air before taking a bite. "Don't worry, I'll find us something fun to do."

She rubbed at her forehead. "Why does your idea of fun concern me?"

Vax sidestepped one of the children running across the street, and as a result nearly collided with a brash half-orc who immediately swung around, hand on ax. "Hey, asshole! Watch where you're going!"

The half-orc, who wore patched-up leather armor and had an impressive array of tattoos snaking up her arms, had at least a couple of inches and quite a bit of muscle on Vax, and he raised his hands in a soothing gesture, letting the apple drop to the ground. "Sorry, friend. Didn't mean any harm."

She scowled, her hands high and her stance tense, but her dwarven companion reached up to grab her by the arm and steered her away in the direction of an armorer's workshop. As soon as she was out of sight, Vax let a small coin purse tumble out of his sleeve, the sleight of hand made effortless by many years of practice, and weighed it in his hands. "This should cover at least an extra night in town."

Vex rolled her eyes. "You're insufferable. Why do I put up with you?"

"Because you love me. And I help pay the bills." Vax emptied the purse into one of his pockets and tossed the pouch itself into the shopping bag of an elderly gnome woman. "Plus, I'm your favorite brother."

"You're my *only* brother," Vex said coolly.

He grinned. "So what you're saying is I'm right."

"What I'm *saying* is you should deliver that letter and earn us some honest coin."

"You like coin regardless of where it's from."

When she didn't reply, he turned to her, and she shrugged. "I'm not going to deny that."

They made their way to a large square, where stalls and shops and side streets tumbled over one another, with awnings and cloths in vibrant colors, all the metalwares gleaming in the afternoon sun. Outside an apothecary, a young halfling girl juggled half a dozen vials in different colors, sparks of light glinting off them, and praised the quality and potency of the concoctions on offer. A young man in a sleek gray coat, wearing a pair of stylish boots, stood in front of a jeweler's shop, haggling over a silver bracelet.

Here too the sound cascaded around the twins. And while Vax's attention was drawn by the bladesmith's stall tucked away in one corner, Vex took a moment to plot her approach, determined to find the best places to get their goods, the right balance between quality and reasonable prices. She'd made a mental list of errands. She'd counted and re-counted their coin before they entered Westruun, figured out the lay of the land, and knew which supplies were most necessary. The apothecary was a must. A new vial of antivenin would be expensive, but she didn't want to travel without, and she had the harvested venom to trade and bring down the price. They also needed a new supply of dried herbs for poultices.

Then her eye fell on another storefront, where the shutters were opened to show an entire cabinet full of copper and tin figurines, as well as some wooden carvings. Birds of all shapes and sizes, wolves, bears, little cats and ferocious dragons, intricate trees too, and houses. Inside the shop, a shadowed figure sat whittling away at a dimly lit table.

Vex gasped. Without stopping to think, she wandered over and picked up a small copper bear. She turned it this way and that, letting the figure catch the bright sunlight. In the interplay of light and shadows, the rough scratches that crossed the copper animal became fur, and the lines around the head were full of emotion and character. It was no big-ger than an inch or two.

"Hello?" The craftsman inside the shop stood and walked into the light. He had a heavily stained apron tied around his waist, and his thick glasses magnified sharp eyes. He wore his long black hair with strands of silver tied back in a braid, and the shorn sides made his pointed ears stand out. He took in Vex's scruffy appearance, and his welcoming ex-pression made way for an icier one. He folded his arms and narrowed his eyes. "Can I help you?" The words were blandly polite, while his tone was full of suspicion.

"Never mind." Vex put the figurine back, nearly knocking a few oth-ers from their place, and she turned before the shopkeeper could say another word. She slammed past another customer who'd stepped up to the shop and registered someone muttering behind her. Someone else laughed.

This was why she didn't take to cities. Life was simpler out in the wild. She didn't have to prove herself to anyone. Here, she did. She wanted to be able to walk up to any of the shopkeepers and be seen as someone worthy of attention, but that bastard's glare and his tone of derision were proof that she couldn't, and it poked at a bruise that wouldn't fade.

Vax, who was still at the bladesmith's stall, glanced her way and frowned, so Vex shook her head and rolled her eyes. She straightened her shoulders. They needed to focus on what they came here to do and nothing more. If Vax could find them some decent jobs, at least that would be one fewer worry.

She pushed across the square, passing half a dozen gnomish girls who were sharing a bag of sweets and giggling loudly. A halfling man carried an infant girl on his shoulders and pointed out the juggling vials and a string of magical lights around a baker's stall. A group of young men wearing the familiar trappings of the Shields of the Plains were discussing the size of their swords, presumably.

By the time Vex reached her brother, he was flirting with the pale-haired young woman minding the wares, and she was blushing furiously. Vax pulled at the collar of his shirt, no doubt to indicate where the spider had bit, and Vex groaned inwardly.

She stepped in, grabbed him by the sleeve, and pulled him away from the stall. "Excuse us for a moment."

"I was in the middle of doing business," Vax protested.

"I'm sure you were having a lovely discussion about sharpening your blades, O slayer of spiders. But we have more pressing matters." Vex reached into his pocket and pulled out the letter they were hired to deliver. It was wrapped up in waxed paper and sealed, its name written in a careful though slightly uncertain hand. She held it out to him. "This, jobs, and supplies."

"But I *do* need to get my blades sharpened," Vax tried in a tone of utmost reason.

She glared at him, and after a moment's hesitation, he snatched the letter from her hand. He grinned at her. "*Fine.* Meet me at the Temple of the Changebringer when you're done here. I'll take care of everything."

Her brother exchanged a few more words with the bladesmith before wandering off, a challenge in his step and his hands flexing by his side. Vex watched him go. He'd scope out work as comfortably as she could follow tracks when they were out in the wild. He'd probably also steal enough to cover the next few nights on the way to whatever dodgy inn he located. They teamed up, on occasion, if needs were dire or people were awful or they were exceptionally bored. She would distract shopkeepers while he snatched what they needed. She'd become good at charming even the roughest and gruffest types. But it was always a means to survival for her. Her brother seemed to get a kick out of it all, as easy to him as breathing.

She glanced back at the elven craftsperson with the figurines, who was now in the process of helping a human man with blond hair and a stylish hat, and a treacherous voice in the back of her mind wondered what her father would say if he could see the two of them now. Presumably they lived up to all his prejudices about half-elves and their impunity.

She pushed the thoughts away with a snarl, startling a human woman carrying a braided basket full of vegetables. With one look at Vex's frown, the woman dashed out of the way, grumbling something about those fighting types.

Gods. She needed to focus. Vex set her jaw and told herself to set to work. Concentrate on her errands, tick off as many things as possible on her list of necessary goods, and haggle for every last copper piece. So she did. She had to threaten to walk away from one of the apothecaries and take her gold to his competitor before he agreed to lower the prices for her. She winked at and sweet-talked a willowy, green-eyed bowyer with an easy smile, who refused to budge on the price of bracers, but who gave her a good deal on strings and wax and invited her out to drinks later.

While Vex didn't plan to take the bowyer up on that, she promised herself to come back for the bracers the next day, if she couldn't find anything else. She relaxed into the familiar push and pull of bargaining. This, too, was a necessary skill, and one she was good at. She loved making every copper count.

By the time Vex had finished two-thirds of her list, the sun was low in the sky and the majority of the shops were shuttering. Dusk crept through the streets. A handful of carts and stalls still kept their wares spread out, and the most stubborn would remain in business for as long as there was light, reminding her now of another market she once frequented, in what felt like another lifetime. But there was no magic in the air here, no song or starlit charms. Merely loud voices and barking dogs and screaming children. The day wrapping up, and the rhythm of the city turning to a softer pace. At nightfall, the energy of the day dwindled and everyone went home or to the tavern.

She took her bearings and was making her way to one of the tailors when the high window of a narrow shop, wedged deftly between a butcher and a weaver, caught her eye. The glass panes were cracked in places and dirty, and a soft orange light glowed inside. It illuminated stacks and stacks of books and scrolls. On tables, on shelves, even randomly placed across the floor. Next to the entrance stood a raggedy table, only half sheltered by the store's awning, and on top of it were yet more books. A scruffy gnomish individual sat next to them, his chair leaning back against the wall and a pipe in his mouth. He had a book on his lap and gestured at her to take a look at his wares without taking his pale-green eyes off his reading. He had no intention of closing for the day.

And with Vax off to find his own inevitable trouble, she hesitated. She couldn't resist a look. If her brother scrounged up a few jobs, perhaps she would be able to treat herself to a book—if the gnome had anything worthwhile. It wasn't necessity, but it was need all the same.

She pushed her bag higher on her shoulder and reached for a tome at random, a thin volume bound in cracked red leather. It showed the title—*The Beast of Wildwood*—in stamped letters on the cover. When she leafed through, many of the pages were yellowed and torn. Another book showed similar wear and tear, as did a third. It appeared the gnome didn't mind or didn't care. He simply kept reading his book.

Vex walked around the table until she stood in the door opening to the store, picking up and discarding books at random. A book full of drunken rhymes. A thin volume on birds and bird-watching. A battered tome on the architecture of temples. All of them looked well used and none of them were what she was looking for. There might be nothing of interest here, but it went against her better judgment not to try.

"Excuse me?" She had to repeat the words once more before the gnome looked up. He squinted at her.

"Yes?" He kept his pipe in the corner of his mouth while he spoke—though it didn't appear to be lit—and as a result his words were slurred. "Looking for something?"

Vex plastered on a polite smile and wondered how susceptible the bookseller was to a well-placed wink. "Do you have anything on the biology of dragons?"

"Nursery tales inside. Fiction too. Might be a work or two of ancient history, but nothing recent and nothing good," he replied, his interest rapidly waning and flicking back to the book. He chewed on the pipe. "Nothing that is worth your time. Best be off now. Thank you for your interest." The words were spoken with such cheerful finality that Vex was taken aback for a second.

Before she could gather her thoughts and reply, another voice cut in. "Perhaps I might be of assistance?"

She turned and found a human man with a pale complexion standing a few paces away. He wore a sleek gray coat trimmed with gold, and his ash-blond hair fell above the shoulder while his eyes were piercingly blue. He carried a hat and his purse in one hand and showed no visible weaponry. Executing a perfect, gallant bow, he reached out a hand to Vex. "Allow me to introduce myself, my lady, my name is Lord Berin Abenard, officer of the court of law and your faithful servant."

Fuck. Just what this day needed.

CHAPTER 3

Lord Berin held out his hand to her, and Vex considered him. She realized she'd seen the gentleman in front of her around the Market Ward several times during the day, always in her periphery. He appeared to be some years older than she, in his late twenties at most, and he carried himself with the confidence of a man who believed the world to be his. It was a confidence bought by gold or titles, and in Vex's experience people like him didn't simply offer assistance. If there was one thing Vex had learned scraping by with her brother these past few years—and in her father's house before that—it was that there was always a catch to such offers. A cost or a cruelty. There was always someone who wanted something, whether it was to impress her or to degrade her. She wasn't in the mood for either.

But whether intentionally or not, he effectively blocked her exit, so she had no alternative but to play his game.

She let the lordling take her hand and held her head high. "Charmed."

"A pleasure, my lady." Lord Berin smiled. He straightened and placed his hat and his purse on the table with books, next to the one she'd just returned—an otherwise interesting volume on poisons. "If you'll forgive me, I couldn't help but overhear your conversation."

Next to Vex, the bookseller harrumphed, though whether his disapproval was targeted at this man's smooth words or at the continued interruption of his reading was entirely unclear. He kept his focus on his book, but his ears had pricked up.

"You were following me," Vex suggested casually.

"Nothing of the sort, my lady. Though I'll admit to noticing you in the market today. It would be impossible not to." Lord Berin tugged at his sleeves as if nervous, and a blush spread from his neck up to his cheeks. "If it's information on dragons you seek and this fine gentleman can't help you"—the gnome muttered something, turning a page with force—"I could guide you to the Scholar Ward at your leisure."

"The Scholar Ward?" Vex kept her voice light. She put on a smile like armor.

Lord Berin inclined his head. "I have contacts at the Cobalt Reserve— at the library—who are not usually open to consultation, but I'm sure with the right introductions they would be more than willing to make an exception for one such as you. They could aid you with any inquiries you may have. Their collection is awe inspiring."

Vex took a measured step back. "One such as me?"

"A beautiful young woman in the pursuit of knowledge, of course," he said, without hesitation. "A lack of contacts should not get in the way of your interests." He twisted one of his gold bracelets. He'd perfected the look of bashful naïveté that might have put other people at ease, but Vex saw the hint of shrewd calculation in his eyes, and his words were as slick as some of the concoctions the apothecary sold. While he talked a good game—and despite her better judgment Vex found herself intrigued by the suggestion—she didn't trust that his benevolence came without strings attached. And she refused to become tied up in them.

"What would you get out of it?" she asked.

He frowned. "What do you mean?"

"With your wish to escort me? Or to connect me with your contacts?" She winked at him, as if amused by the suggestion. "It can't all be for the pursuit of knowledge and the betterment of your fellow people?"

Lord Berin smiled a smile that never reached his eyes. He flexed his fingers, purposefully showing off a number of rings and gems. He indicated the emptying street around them. "I would gain the pleasure of your company, my lady," he said.

"As I would gain the pleasure of yours?"

"Of course," he said, like that went without saying. "I'm sure you'll understand the value of my company. As yours is clear to me. I saw you standing here, in all your radiance, and I could not simply keep walking."

Vex snorted at that. She couldn't help it. She considered what he must see when he looked at her. A half-elf with dirty clothes, a fraying cloak, and hair that hadn't seen a bath in too many days. In hindsight, that would've been the only argument her brother needed. If he could find them an inn that would provide hot water for a decent bath, she would be entirely content. But right now, she had dirt beneath her fingernails and bear fur on her boots. There were bloodstains and mud stains on her clothes, and as far as she could tell there was nothing beautiful or radiant about her. Contrarily, the lordling's air of importance was as finely tailored as his coat. He seemed all too aware of his own appearance, all too comfortable with using his wealth and position to entice those around him to do his bidding.

He raised his eyebrows, as if taken aback by her reaction. "Do you mock me, my lady?"

"No more than you me," she said. She managed a polite rejection through clenched teeth. "No thank you. I don't need any assistance. I am perfectly fine on my own. Now if you could be so kind as to step aside so I could go home, I would appreciate that too."

"Best be off now," the gnome muttered viciously. He'd closed the book and put it and the pipe into a pocket of his coat, after which he climbed on his chair and began stacking the books on the table to prepare for the night as well.

Lord Berin didn't move. "But I insist," he said. His frown deepened. The calculation in his gaze made way for something sharper, and his charm bled away. "Perhaps you do not know who you're dealing with, but I assure you, you do not want to say no to me." By the sound of it, very few people ever had.

Vex had expected no less, and her patience was running thinner and thinner. "I assure you, I do. And I insist you step aside."

"Foolish girl, you think too highly of yourself." Instead of leaving like she told him to, Lord Berin crowded her, one hand reaching for her arm, another for her face. His eyes flashed. "Come now, don't be so shy. I'm a gentle man. I could show you a side of the city that you could never afford on your own."

Vex reacted without hesitation. She ducked under his arm, and when he overstretched, she spun away from him. She used his momentum to drive him forward while twisting herself around him, and she reached for the knife in her belt. With all her strength she braced against him and dug the point of the knife into his side. Deep enough to show she was serious, not deep enough for lasting damage.

Lord Berin yelped.

"You piece of shit, I said *go*," Vex hissed, leaning as close as she dared before stepping back out of the corner he'd pushed her in. In front of the table with books, she reevaluated her possible escape routes. She could leave now, but she didn't want to turn her back on him. And while she wished she could pull out bow and arrow, she knew how to look menacing with a blade too. She only had to channel her brother. "Now."

Lord Berin was bright red when he turned to her, and he pressed his hand against his side. "Do you have any idea what a mistake you're making? Or who you're threatening?"

She held the belt knife loosely, the blade following his every movement. She placed her feet more firmly on the ground and grinned her teeth bare. Her expression conveyed no amusement, only threat. "I don't know, and I don't care."

He breathed in hard and seemed to take stock of his options, so she did too. He didn't carry a weapon, or he would've reached for it already. Presumably magic could have given him the upper hand in an instant too. Since he'd used neither of those, she didn't mind pushing him a bit further. She made a shooing motion with the blade and pointed in the direction of the square, where lanterns were being lit to brighten the streets and different-colored lights illuminated the second-story living quarters above many shuttered shops. "Best be off now," she said, mimicking the gnome's earlier advice.

Lord Berin snarled, and for the first time since he'd addressed her, he took no care to hide his anger and his disdain. "Who on earth do you think you are, to deny me like this? You're nothing. You're no one." He spat at the floor and reached for her, only to be driven away by her blade again. "Better watch your back from now on. I'll see that you pay for this." And with that, he spun around and marched off.

She watched to make sure he left the square, instead of changing his mind, before she put the knife away. Her hands trembled, and her head pounded. The lordling's threats repeated themselves over and over, and his oily words clung to her. She hated how he thought he had a right to approach her like this. That those rich bastards *always* thought they had the right. There was *always* a cost or a cruelty.

This was why she hated cities.

"Dangerous type," the gnome commented. He took the last three books and placed them on top of the pile that now towered over him.

With near-impossible balance, he picked up the stack and ambled in the direction of the shop, as though the standoff had only been a minor inconvenience to him. "Good night."

Vex blinked. "Thanks?" She shook her head. *Thanks for the help too.*

She pulled her bag up on her shoulder again and noticed Lord Berin's hat and purse still on the book table. In his anger and frustration, he'd left them behind. After a moment's hesitation, she took a step closer.

She made sure the few wanderers around the square were busy when she pushed the hat to the side and snatched up the purse. She recognized the familiar weight of gold and silver coin, and she kept her face carefully neutral, though something unwound inside her. At least the lordling's carelessness would pay for her bracers and a good winter coat for her brother.

She needed to get back to Vax. With twilight blanketing the city, he was probably worried now that she was running so late. She had to keep her mind on that—on getting back to her brother—and avoid walking in the same direction as Lord Berin. She glanced across the street once more before she set out for the Temple Ward.

"SO LET ME GET THIS straight: You threatened a nobleman claiming to be an officer of the court in broad daylight and then stole from him," Vax summarized, staring at the coins on the bedspread. He'd found the two of them a room in a shabby little inn near the edge of the city, where the half-orc innkeeper had served them a surprisingly decent meal of soup with cream, vegetables, and unidentifiable lumps, as well as a cut of roast meat and a few pieces of freshly baked bread. The room itself looked like it might fall apart in a stiff breeze, with its wooden walls and roof all at slightly odd angles.

But it was clean enough and private, and as soon as she'd closed the door behind them, Vex had thrown a bundled-up cloak at Vax then emptied out a purse full of coins on one of the beds. She sat counting them now. "It was dusk, actually."

"I'm so proud of you." Vax unwrapped the cloak and ran his hands along the garment. The fabric was of a rich and lasting quality. A long cloak for colder weather, made of a deep dark leather that felt both sturdy and supple, with dark-gray fur lining, trimmed with a lighter gray, softer than anything he'd felt in years. The leather still smelled faintly acidic, like it had been cured but never been worn before. On the inside lining, he saw smudges of chalk that the tailor must have used to take measurements. When he reached out to brush it away, his fingers lingered for a heartbeat or so.

Meanwhile, the purse had been filled with coppers, silvers, and even some gold coins. More by some measure than he got for delivering the letter. And that was *after* she'd found the fur-lined cloak.

What with the coin, the supplies, and perhaps an odd job or two, this could easily tide them over until Winter's Crest, perhaps longer.

Vex sighed. She scooped up the gold coins and put them in a hidden pocket in her belt. "What if I got us in trouble because of this? Fucks like him always find a way to get what they want."

If that was the case, Vax knew exactly what he *wanted* to do: find the nobleman and impress upon him—with the sharp end of his daggers—that no one threatened his sister and got away with it. She'd refused to tell him *exactly* what he'd said to her, but when she'd walked up to the temple, she'd been angry and weary, and he could still see the lines of tension around her shoulders.

"Sounds like he's got his head so far up his own ass, he'll need a map to find his way out. We'll be long gone by then."

Vax peeked out the window and found the expected images of a city at night. Outside the entrance to the inn, a handful of dwarves were drinking and singing. Two city guards walked the streets. Across the road, a person in a long maroon cloak squinted up at the inn as the Shields passed him by. He lingered for a moment longer before he too continued his walk. Vax turned away. "Besides, I'm an expert at trouble. If you got us in, we'll get ourselves out again."

Vex grumbled but smiled. "Next time, I'm sticking to giant spiders."

CHAPTER 4

When Westruun woke up around them the following morning, loud voices, the clattering of cart wheels, and birdsong filling the air, some part of Vex was still tempted to pack up and skip town. Choose the solitary wild over judgmental cities. But she'd made herself a promise once that she wouldn't let anyone hurt her again. So she wouldn't.

Instead, while Vax returned to scouring for new jobs, she resolutely continued gathering the supplies they needed, with enough coin for once to not have to worry about running low or choosing between necessary provisions.

She visited one of the other apothecary stalls in the Market Ward to add a few more healing herbs to her collection. Enough for simple poultices that she could use both for her brother and herself, and for Trinket. She eyed the glass vials with different-colored liquids, all of which promised the most wondrous effects, and all of which were out of her price range—even with the lordling's purse. The apothecary's assistant—a young man with a shock of red hair and laughing blue eyes—did offer her a jar of root salve, a foul-smelling herbal concoction that helped heal cuts and bruises. After a few minutes of intense haggling, she got a bundle of herbs and a jar the size of her palm—and a hearty wink from the assistant, after she'd tried to sweet-talk him into dropping the price further.

Still, she was restless. Midway through the morning, a gentleman with blond hair and a familiar hat passed her by at a distance, and Vex tensed. Without a second thought, she ducked behind a cart full of soaps and perfumes. When she showed herself again, he was nowhere to be seen. She held her head high and kept walking.

Sometime after noon, she thought she saw a figure in the same sleek gray coat, but when she leaped out of the way and tracked him, it turned out to be someone else entirely.

As the sun arced high over the Market Ward, Vex returned to the bowyer, who perked up when she saw Vex. She pushed her dark hair behind a pierced ear and produced the bracers she'd set aside. "I was hoping you'd come back."

Vex smiled, something about the way the bowyer fidgeted with a leather archer tab disarming her. The spark in the bowyer's eyes was one of genuine delight. "I had to come back for those bracers, didn't I?"

The bowyer's pink cheeks darkened and she bit her lip. "I'm sorry you missed drinks. The bracers are still seven gold." She held them out to Vex.

It was expensive for a pair of leather bracers. Vex reached for the pair and turned them back and forth in the sunlight. She'd fallen in love with them the moment she'd laid eyes on them. They were of a high quality, and the decorations were spectacular. The bowyer, who looked young to be a master craftswoman, had carved out an intricate design of branches and leaves that wrapped around the curve of the leather. They weren't enchanted, but they were beautiful.

"This is stunning work," Vex said sincerely.

The bowyer's smile deepened, and briefly Vex wondered what it would be like to have a friend to go shooting with, to compare skill and strategy with someone who loved bows and arrows not simply as weapons—like her brother did—but as pieces of art.

Still, archery wasn't the only art form. "Five gold," she countered.

The bowyer grinned, and she leaned forward over her stall, her face close to Vex's. "Seven," she said softly.

"Six and my everlasting admiration for your fine work," Vex tried.

"I already *have* your admiration," the bowyer said, and her emerald eyes danced. She considered Vex carefully. "Seven, and I throw in the tab." She held up the archer tab she'd been toying with, made from an uneven piece of leather, with tiny flowers carved along the edges. She tilted her head.

Vex hesitated. She could find plain bracers for a gold piece if she asked around, and with the gloves she wore, she didn't need tabs. They could put the coin to better use. Maybe she should accept something simpler.

But she loved pretty things. Before she could talk herself out of it, she counted out seven gold coins from her purse and slapped them down in front of her.

The bowyer snatched up the coins with one hand and held out the tab with the other. When Vex reached out to grab it, the bowyer's fingers gently brushed against hers. "The offer for drinks still stands too."

The haggling and the conversation would usually have lifted her spirits, but today the unease remained.

The late afternoon passed in a blur of shopping and haggling. At the edge of dusk, she was sure someone followed her, but when she turned around to check, she saw nothing untoward, just a group of three girls who played with a small cluster of kittens, all of which were focused intently on a piece of string with a feather tied at the end of it.

Vex watched the chaos that ensued before she continued on her way, and as day bled into night, reminders of Lord Berin's threats lost their sharpest edges, easing instead into becoming simply another part of the city life she hated and yet still longed for. Deep down she knew it wasn't—necessarily—the cities she hated, but being made to feel like an outsider. While life in the wild was simple and free of scorn, it was lonelier too. It didn't hold the riches and the vibrancy of the city. She wanted a part of that. Somehow. Even as it scared her to be denied it.

Perhaps that was why, when everything else disappeared to the background, Lord Berin's suggestion to visit the library still piqued her interest. And it stuck with her, like a burr. It stuck with her when she returned to the inn with new supplies, when she and her brother shared another meal of questionable ingredients, and all through the night when sleep wouldn't come.

When the streets around the inn emptied but for the occasional drunkard stumbling home, and bats and barn owls took to the skies, Vex did the only thing she could do. She sneaked out. She'd pulled on her brother's darker cloak so she wouldn't draw attention to herself.

And she walked.

The tall spire of the mountain Gatshadow loomed over the city like someone had cut out a slice of sky and stars and all that was left was a triangular void. Vex kept the strange outline as an anchor to walk in a northwestern direction. Toward the Scholar Ward and the library of the Cobalt Reserve. She didn't know the way exactly, but the past two days had given her a solid understanding of the layout of the city, and she didn't easily get lost. She could retrace her steps if she needed to.

As she wound down streets and through squares, making her way across Westruun, she found she liked cities better at night. The rats only concerned themselves with the day's waste, and those random few passersby kept their hands on their weapons and their eyes firmly on the road. This deep into the night was not a place for pleasant conversations or curiosity.

She saw the city change around her. The buildings near the ramshackle inn all showed some level of dilapidation. In the interplay of light and shadow, the cracks in the walls looked like ivy, and the boarded-up windows were unmistakable. The roofs all leaned against each other, making the whole block a precariously balanced pile of bricks and beams.

Somewhat closer to the city center, the houses grew more stable and bigger too. They were decorated with neatly painted shutters and doors that locked and kept all the worries of the world out.

Near the library, crammed residential areas all made way for erudite consideration. The streets were wider. Framed by the outline of Gatshadow against the night sky, a tall gray tower overlooked a number of well-kept buildings that could be schools or other places of learning, and there were even spots of green here. Some grass and flowers. A handful of trees scattered around the buildings. Finally, beyond the tower, the magnificent library of the Cobalt Reserve stretched as far as the eye could see. Underneath its vast blue dome, it held an unimaginable wealth of knowledge.

Vex placed a hand on the outer wall and stared up at it. It *did* look awe inspiring. She could find her way in, if only to prove to herself that she could. She wouldn't let the slick words of some self-important, conceited creep stop her from visiting if she wanted to.

She didn't.

Besides, why would they welcome you? that treacherous voice in the back of her mind asked her. Tonight, it sounded remarkably like Lord Berin. *You're nothing. You're no one. Never good enough. Never smart enough. Never enough. All you know is how to run away, and you've never stopped running.*

Vex scraped her fingers over the rough stone of the outer wall, before she turned away and shut that voice down. She wasn't a scholar and she had no desire to be. She researched dragons for what they ultimately were—prey. Her studiousness belonged to another time and place. Where knowledge wasn't stored between the walls of a library, but where tall redwood trees encompassed as much history as the books in this building did, and countless scholars worked to preserve the memory of their home.

Her home was on the road, with her brother.

She stepped back from the wall and stilled when, in her periphery, something shifted. Everything around her grew quiet, and she reached for her belt knife. Vex had brought her survival instincts out from the wild into the city, and quiet meant danger. Quiet meant a predator nearby.

She turned slowly so she could pinpoint where she'd seen the movement, but both the street and the rooftops across the street were empty. Only a handful of rats had followed her as if hoping for crumbs. She cursed and kept turning, making sure to take in the whole of her surroundings.

The moons overhead were bright enough to illuminate the cobblestones and to color the world in dim shades of gray, even as the buildings cast their shadows and the street corners made for deadly hiding places. She disliked how angular and hard cities were. In the wild, she knew how to read her surroundings. She knew how to trace others and how to get rid of her own tracks. She knew the various tricks to disappearing. Here, she felt closed off.

Shit. She shouldn't have come here on her own. She needed to get back to the inn.

She held a firm grip on her knife and began to walk away from the library. With her back to an open street, she felt painfully exposed, especially when she realized the silence followed her. She glanced over her shoulder once, twice, and saw nothing. A third time, she was sure she saw the same flicker of movement: there and gone again.

She picked up her pace. From carefully to casually to determined. Her heartbeat increased. Every other time she looked over her shoulder, she felt that glimmer of a presence. No weapons, no immediate threat yet, but impossible to avoid. She'd been so preoccupied with proving that obnoxious lordling wrong, she hadn't stopped to think about the dangers of the city by night.

The streets in front of her tapered and twisted, and Vex made a split-second decision. She avoided going back to the quiet residential areas, and instead chose the city center with its taverns and bars. It was late enough that she didn't expect the place to be bustling, but at least she wouldn't be on her own.

Suddenly, she spied something moving over her left shoulder. A discordant shadow on the edge of a roof. Then: a glint of metal.

She did the only thing possible: she ran. She widened her stride, swung the knife back and forth, and dashed through the alleys as quickly as possible.

She rounded the corner and flung herself out of the way at the last moment when something small and metal zoomed past her ear.

Desperately, she tried to keep her balance. Before she could find her footing, a rat ran straight into her path. A second followed the first. Vermin crawled her way from all corners, not scurrying away in panic, like they were supposed to, but flinging themselves at her legs and feet.

She kicked one of the rats off her boot, sending it flying into the wall, where it disappeared from sight. Before she could take another step, a new rat had already appeared in front of her. They didn't squeak and they certainly didn't behave the way rats normally would, but she wasn't planning to stop and study them.

"Go away, go away, *go away*." She swung her knife at them, nearly dropping it once when she overextended her balance, and pushed through. In the distance, she could hear the off-key tones of a drunken shanty and she could see the faint glow of lanternlight mixed with the moonlight from above.

Another buzz. Something snagged on her cloak, and this time the knife went flying. It clattered on the stones a few feet away. She grabbed at it, but a trio of rats immediately crawled on top of it, and shy of stopping to fight them off, she couldn't do anything.

She rounded another corner, the maze of streets an unexpected blessing, and caught her breath. She reached for her bow, nudged an arrow from the quiver on her belt, and in one fluid motion nocked the arrow and pulled the string back. She leaned around the corner and tried to calculate where her assailant was. When she saw the same flash of metal she'd seen before, she released and immediately sent another arrow flying after the first.

She didn't wait to hear if either of them hit. She only needed the distraction. She reached for whatever had snagged on her cloak and found a long needle, the size of her palm. Careful not to touch the pointy end, she flung it against the far wall and picked up her pace again, toward the tavern lights and the sound of laughter—the few remaining rats still trailing her.

VAX LEAPED FROM ONE ROOFTOP to the next, keeping an eye on his sister from a distance. After her worries yesterday, she'd been restless all evening today too, so he'd let her think she could sneak out on him, but there was no way he'd let her wander the streets of Westruun on her own. Not with that creep threatening her. He knew she could take care of herself, but that didn't mean he wouldn't also take care of her.

He'd spotted the shadow slightly before she had. He'd seen the hooded figure darting across the rooftops with an ease that could only come from intimate familiarity, and he'd immediately begun to trail them both, ready to leap on top of the figure with his daggers out if they got too close to his sister.

But while he knew how to stay close to Vex without being seen, it was harder to do that with her shadow present. The figure kept weaving in and out of sight, scurrying between rooftops that seemed to have no connection whatsoever, and Vax constantly felt two steps behind. When the chase lasted beyond the first narrow, empty alleyways and grew closer to the city's nighttime revelry, he became convinced this wasn't a chance robbery.

Cold fury settled inside him. The shadow moved with purpose and a kind of determination that only came from a decent quantity of gold or favors or a personal grudge. If someone had put a target on his sister's back, Vax wanted to know who, where to find them, how to get rid of it, and how to get rid of them.

When two arrows suddenly arched over the rooftops, the shadow dropped and pushed themself flat against the ridge of a narrow roof to avoid them. Across the street, Vax saw his opportunity. He clambered up to the highest rooftop, ran, and launched himself across the emptiness between buildings. He landed on the edge of the ridge, his hands clinging to the rough stone and half dangling above the street. He pulled himself up at the same time that the figure crawled to their feet.

The shadow—a young man—was roughly the same size as Vax, dressed in all black, a cloak running from his shoulders to his ankles, with a hood low over his face and a piece of cloth in front of his mouth, bright-silver eyes awash with confusion. "There's *two* of you?"

Refusing to dignify the obvious with a response, Vax grabbed two of his daggers.

His adversary reached inside his sleeve.

Before he could attack or escape, Vax leaped forward, both daggers out. The shadow took a step back to meet him, and they collided with each other, a tangle of limbs and weapons. Vax felt one dagger cut through fabric and flesh, while something sharp jabbed at his leg. The hooded man blocked another strike, and the ridge beneath their feet creaked.

The last thing Vax thought before the roof gave way from under them was that this would at least allow his sister to get away. Then they both went sprawling and tumbling toward the street.

CHAPTER 5

The ground rushed up to meet them. In those few instants before colliding, Vax and the hooded man clung to each other, tumbled over each other, and both tried to get the upper hand, though it was far more chance than skill. The world and the starry sky traded places and traded places again. Pieces of roof and ledge slammed into the street first with a clattering loud enough to wake those asleep in the adjacent houses.

A heartbeat later, they both crashed into the stones. The hooded man first, arms and back smashing into the cobblestones. Vax immediately after, landing askew across his quarry while he cracked one shoulder against the stones. Breath whooshed out of him, and the edges of his vision blurred. His ears were ringing. It felt like the world was still twisting and turning, and briefly he wondered if they were still falling.

Bit by bit, his senses settled. The tangy taste of metal filled his mouth, and he smelled muck and mud. He spat on the ground and cursed. Sharp pain spread through his leg, from his outer thigh to his knee, and a dull ache throbbed within his right shoulder.

One of his daggers had fallen out of his grasp and lay a few yards away from him. Vax tried to push himself upright with one hand on the hooded figure's chest. The man grunted but didn't fight him off.

When Vax's vision sharpened, he realized his other dagger was still sticking in the man's shoulder. Vax grabbed it and used it to propel himself forward to the fallen blade. His adversary screamed.

A few houses away, someone slammed open a window, the shutters bouncing against the outer wall. "Sod off if you can't be quiet! People are trying to sleep here!" The shutters and window closed again with force. On the street below, vermin squeaked and scattered.

Vax groaned. He had to fight to keep himself steady and semi-upright, especially when underneath him the silver-eyed man writhed and tried ineffectively to push him away. Vax let the momentum carry him forward and reached for the dagger. He could feel the grip underneath his fingertips. He managed to curl his fingers around the cross guard, and pulled it closer. When he had the familiar weapon safely in his hand again, he took stock of the situation.

A needlelike dart stuck in his leg. The area around it grew numb, but the discomfort didn't spread. His right arm tingled but was usable.

He still held the man who'd attacked his sister pinned to the ground with his body weight, but reaching for the dagger had allowed for a bit of wiggle room. The man was muttering curses while trying to twist free, though he held himself precariously and one of his arms bent at an odd angle.

They were, for the moment at least, alone in the street, and Vax's anger could keep him going.

"What the fuck do you want with my sister?"

The silver eyes settled on him, and his assailant clamped his mouth shut.

Vax wrapped his fingers around the dart in his thigh, clenched his teeth, and pulled the weapon free. The wound immediately began to bleed, the faintness from a moment ago returning. He tossed the blackened dart out of reach and shifted so that he sat across his adversary's chest again. With one foot, he pinned the man's good arm to the ground. He struggled and tried to break free, while Vax used his dagger to cut off a piece of cloth from his shirt, and tied it around his leg.

When no answer came, Vax reached back and rattled the dagger still stuck in his assailant's shoulder. "What *the fuck* do you want with my sister?"

"Shit," the man groaned, shifting and arching back from the blade. He breathed hard. "No one told me there were two of you. This was supposed to be easy."

Vax reached out and pulled the hood and mask away, showing a disgruntled young man whose skin had gone pale. Harsh silver eyes flicked back and forth, and drops of sweat formed on his brow. A thin scar ran from just below his right eye to his chin.

Vax leaned in closer, hand curling around the dagger. "Don't make me ask you again."

"There's a contract on her," the other man said through clenched teeth.

Vax shifted his weight, everything inside him growing cold. "What kind of contract? Who hired you?"

"Can't say." The man's breathing was labored. He kept glancing to Vax's hand and the dagger, but he set his jaw in a foolish attempt at courage or stubbornness. "If you don't let me go, others will come."

"That's not the wisest threat right now, friend." The ache from the dart and the fall left Vax impatient, and if others were trailing Vex—or worse, if they found their way to the inn . . . The night was still young and too full of dangerous opportunities. He casually flashed his other dagger, turning it around in his hand, but he never took his attention off his foe. "I'm not interested in games when my sister's life is at stake, so you should consider your next words very carefully."

The man blanched further and shook his head. Underneath Vax's foot, he twisted his hand. "I was bluffing. I'm sorry." He sounded winded, and beads of sweat pearled on his forehead. He kept glancing down the street, no doubt looking for a way out. Vax knew the type. He was the slippery sort, as much of an escape artist in conversation as he was on the rooftops. Presumably he would say whatever he thought Vax wanted to hear. "Contract was to bring her in. Alive, if that makes you feel any better."

It didn't. "Whose contract is it? Who's after her?"

"I don't know. I never saw the details. It was only an assignment."

"An assignment from whom, precisely?" Vax pushed his foot down harder, and the man's nostrils flared.

"I can't tell you!" he insisted. "I can't break my bond. It's my skin if I do." His voice trembled, and his hair clung in strands to his face, but underneath the layer of fear he remained watchful, following Vax's every movement.

"It's your skin if you don't too." Vax changed his position slightly, and as soon as he did, the silver-eyed man underneath him twisted. He pulled his arm free and in the same motion grabbed a dart from a leather cuff and jammed it through Vax's boot into his ankle. He shoved Vax off him and rolled away, scrambling to his feet as soon as he could.

Vax cursed. While the second needle wasn't deep enough to harm, he was beginning to feel bruised and annoyed. He dug it out and clambered to his feet too.

The man was half a dozen steps ahead of Vax, swaying heavily. He held one arm close to his chest and with the other he weakly grabbed at the dagger still buried in his shoulder.

Vax's footing felt unsteady, the floor rolling underneath his feet, but he followed. He would if it meant doing so by sheer willpower. He would not let his sister's stalker get away. He didn't even plan to let him get far.

Once the other man reached the corner where Vex had disappeared into the night, he was swaying heavily. He nearly collided with the wall, and he reached out an arm to steady himself. A rat ran out of the shadows and scuttled away.

Vax weighed his dagger in his hand, took aim during that sliver of hesitation, and threw.

The second dagger buried itself in the back of the man's arm, below his other shoulder, and the force of the impact—and his own precarious balance—sent him to his knees with a soft cry.

Vax covered the distance between them and yanked the dagger out. Before the other man could so much as cry out, Vax placed the blade along his jawline, breaking skin and pressing down hard enough for blood to trickle down the folds of the hood. "A word of advice: you need to get a healer to look at those cuts." He struggled to keep his voice calm, when worry and anger burned cold inside him. "And I'm not going anywhere until you tell me who put a contract out on my sister." If it had been that creep she met in the marketplace, he'd track him down next. With Vex by his side if she wanted.

The man swallowed against the blade and his shoulders dropped, the fight draining away. "I told you, it was only an assignment."

"Then take me to someone who can tell me," Vax growled. "The person who gave you the assignment. The person who negotiated the details. There must be *someone*."

The man didn't answer for what seemed like forever. He arched back, resting his head against the wall and considering his remaining options. When Vax leaned in, he breathed out hard and shook his head. "Patch me up and I'll take you to the spireling who gave me the assignment." He sounded younger when he spoke the truth. He turned his head slightly to face Vax. The calculation had made way for feverish despondency, and he was still growing paler and weaker.

Vax considered the words. "Spireling?"

The young man groaned. "You're not from around here, are you? Gods. Why couldn't one of those hapless halfling brothers have taken this contract? Spireling Gideor is the one in charge. The one who agreed to the contract. He's also the only one with the power to break it. So maybe you can convince him. For your sister's sake."

"For *your* sake, you better be right," Vax said. "And you better not try to run again."

"So you can poke more holes in me?" He wheezed. "No thank you. They might just kill me anyway, if you can't convince them why they should listen to you. Not—not fulfilling a contract is one thing, but this—this is signing my own death warrant."

"You'll die out here too." It was clear the other man was slipping now, in more pain than he tried to show. Vax eased up on the pressure. "So take me to your spireling." He picked up the edge of the hooded cloak and tore off another sizable chunk of fabric, using his dagger to cut it into strips that he tied around the man's arm wound. With the same efficiency as before, he knotted the bandages around the weirdly angled arm, careful not to jostle it too much.

He spun his new friend around, pushing him against the wall, and stuffed some of the bandages into his mouth.

"This is going to hurt," he said, by way of warning, and he pulled the other dagger out. The blade snagged on bone, and the young man looked as if he might faint, his head lolling backward. With one steady hand, Vax kept him pushed up against the stone. With the other, he cleaned the dagger on his shirt and sheathed it before pressing a bundle of fabric against the gaping hole the weapon left.

Vax tied the bundle tight against the wound, and he felt the blood seep through and stain his fingers. He cursed. He needed to keep the man alive for now. He needed to know exactly who or what was after Vex and why. "I don't know how long this'll last."

He took a step back and gestured for the other to take the lead. "Let's go." There was too much night left, and too many opportunities for this to still go wrong.

The young man reached out a hand and curled his fingers around Vax's wrist. He looked at him with a feverish glow that made his silver eyes even paler. His sharp nails dug into Vax's skin. "I warn you: oath breaking doesn't come cheap in this town. You are playing a dangerous game mingling with the Clasp, and you'll need solid arguments to convince Gideor to renege on a bond. I hope you're prepared for that. Because if you're not, they'll kill us both." With that, he turned around and with unsteady step began walking back to where he came from.

Vax straightened his shoulders and kept his daggers ready. He followed. He'd had his answer ready from the moment he'd considered leaping from the highest rooftops on top of the hooded figure to protect his sister. And many such times over many years before that. "I'll do whatever it takes."

CHAPTER 6

The hooded young man guided Vax through the back alleys of Westruun, swaying back and forth and mumbling incoherently. He sounded sad and defensive, though it was impossible to make out what he said, exactly. Every time someone passed them, Vax hid his daggers and pretended to be worried about his drunken friend. As soon as the coast was clear, he grabbed his weapons again. He didn't think the wretch would be much of a threat in this state, but he also didn't want to underestimate him. Especially when they entered a maze of narrow streets, where the man guided him through a set of double doors into a basement underneath a small, unappealing flower shop.

The shop itself was closed up for the night. The cellar doors were unlocked. When Vax climbed down the stairs, he found a dimly lit basement that spread out underneath the building and far beyond.

"Be quiet here," his unwilling guide murmured. "Being watched."

Vax ran a thumb along the cross guard of a dagger and scanned the room. If anyone else was here he couldn't see them. On either side of the basement, alcoves were hewn into the walls, and most of the storage space was filled with wooden crates and casks. Globules of soft, magical light drifted near the arched roof, and while they illuminated the space with enough light to walk by, they also created deep pockets of shadow where others could easily hide.

They went deeper into the basement, down another set of steps, into another room, where the air became colder and slightly damp. It smelled of mold and sewage, and the light from above didn't extend past the first few yards. The stone under Vax's feet felt smooth and slippery, and he had to walk gently to keep from falling.

"What is this place?" he hissed.

"Hush." His wounded foe walked with his hand along the wall, slightly leaning into the touch and leaving traces of blood behind. It wasn't just a matter of support. His fingers were also tracing the stones—or counting. The stonework was rough and uneven, and although it was too dark to see color, it was clear there were various shades here on the walls.

They passed two narrow openings that might have been alcoves or perhaps tunnels, but the young man kept walking, disregarding them. Vax peeked inside both times, semi-convinced he'd find onlookers there. That part, at least, had fallen into place once the other man had mentioned the Clasp. In the years of traveling around with his sister and doing odd jobs in all sorts of places, he'd come across many stories and legends about the organization: a powerful guild of thieves, smugglers, assassins, and spies that spread out all across Tal'Dorei. Some of the fences he worked with were sure to be members too, though up until this point he'd simply tried to keep his distance and not encroach on their territory too much. With his sister's safety in mind, it seemed like the best of all possible options. They were better off on their own than bound to anyone.

Ironic to think that was what brought him here now.

After a handful of minutes and a continuous walk deeper into underground rooms and tunnels, the silver-eyed man paused and seemed to hesitate. The same interplay of light and shadows made it hard to get a decent look at the room they were in now. It was big enough that Vax couldn't see the walls. And it was cold enough that they were likely a fair way underground.

Next to his guide, there appeared to be a third narrow opening, and with a soft groan the man reached higher on the wall. His fingers curved around a stone ledge, and Vax took a step back, ready to fight if the other pulled a weapon on him.

The moment he did, two sharp points poked into his sides. "No farther, stranger," a deep, resonant voice said. "Best let go of those blades. Lyre, what is your play here?"

Half a dozen possible scenarios echoed through Vax's head. He'd known from the start that asking his adversary—Lyre—to do this might mean he was walking into a trap. What if they were simply both killed? What if Lyre claimed he'd thought Vax was his target all along? He'd seemed genuinely surprised his mark was one of a pair.

Vax knew it had been the right play to let Vex get away—he would never want to bring his sister right to this den of thieves targeting her— but he felt vulnerable and exposed without her by his side, and he tightened his grip on his daggers.

"Visitor for Spireling Gideor," Lyre managed. He swayed and a smaller figure moved out from the shadows toward him. A halfling woman with brown skin and hair that lay in waves across her shoulders. She wore the same inconspicuous clothing that Lyre wore but for the mask and hood. She used a slender wheelchair in shades of midnight blue.

She sighed. "One night without anyone doing something ridiculous. Is that so much to ask?" She reached for his hand, and when they touched her own hand glowed bright copper for a moment.

Lyre stumbled. "M'sorry."

The woman looked around. "Can someone bring this hapless excuse for a thief to Elisen? He needs to get those wounds looked at before we decide what to do with him. And clean up his blood."

"Of course, Ro." A third figure walked past Vax and toward Lyre. She grabbed him by the arm and not-so-gently offered him aid, marching him through the narrow opening and up a flight of stairs.

Vax leaned forward to get a better look when the weapons in his back dug deeper.

"Not so fast," the halfling woman said. She turned around to face him. "Don't expect you can walk up there without an explanation and with weapons. Hand over those blades." She looked him over as if to determine any other hidden weapons.

Vax met her gaze. He didn't want to hand over his daggers, but he expected he wouldn't get in until he did. He flipped the weapons over and held them out to her, hilts first.

She kept waiting, and with some hesitation, he also took a dagger from his boot. "Will I get them back?"

Ro tilted her head and grinned. "If you're very good."

She snapped her fingers and the pressure of the blades against his back eased. A figure the size of two men stacked on top of each other reached for Vax's daggers, smiling broadly to show a row of sharp and pointy teeth.

"Now, Lyre mentioned you're a visitor for our Spireling Gideor, eh?" Ro asked. "It's not often that visitors are brought in through the back entrance. Does the not-very-esteemed gentleman know that you're coming?"

Vax straightened. He felt naked without his blades, but he was determined. "I've come to find out who put a price on my sister's head, and to make sure no one else will try to take that contract."

"Oh, it's like that, is it?" Ro sniffed, as if she had her own feelings about people who came to bargain for the lives of others. "It's been a while since we had someone come in here looking for charity. Well, I'm sure Gideor will be thrilled to see you. He always takes a special interest in the hopeless cases. Besides, if Lyre gave you his word, who am I to renege on it?"

"What will happen to him?" Vax asked.

"Why do you want to know?"

Vax considered his words, not entirely sure himself. Then he settled on the closest thing he had to the truth. "I forced him to come back here." He didn't regret it, but he was curious.

Ro shrugged. "That foolish boy would've been in far more trouble if he'd tried to disappear. His luck was going to run out one of these days. What happens to him is up to the spireling to decide."

"So Spireling Gideor is the one in charge of everything here?" Vax pried.

"Gods, no. Not the only one. There are three of them on good days." Ro patted his arm. "But nights like tonight? It's only Gideor. So keep that in mind when you meet him and act accordingly, stranger. I'm just sorry we can't offer you the scenic route."

She snapped her fingers once more, and the world around Vax went dark.

He came to in a comfortably lit office, propped up in a tall, leather chair. Around him, the walls were covered in paintings in all sorts of styles, and all the shelves and cabinets were lined with trinkets. From gems to jewelry to gaudy-looking boxes. On the mantel above the fireplace stood a small silver wolf, the craftsmanship exquisite.

In another chair, one that looked like a throne with all its riches and carvings, sat a stout dwarf with deep-set untrusting eyes and a braided blond beard. He wore a finely tailored blue coat with golden embroidery and emerald decorations that looked as gaudy as some of his collection of curiosities. He had his fingers tented as he smiled at Vax. "So you are the one who outsmarted one of our fine trackers. A remarkable feat, if I do say so."

The fact that the dwarf didn't have weapons visible on him didn't make him any less dangerous. He was all edges. Sharp words, sharp smiles, sharp knives. He exuded power.

"You must be Spireling Gideor," Vax said. He cracked his neck and reached for his daggers out of habit, before remembering he'd had to hand those over.

"I must be," Gideor said. "And you go by the name Vax'ildan, or so I've heard. A pleasure to make your acquaintance. Would you care for something to drink?" Without waiting for the answer, he took a large glass carafe and poured an amber liquid into two glasses. He passed one to Vax and kept the other for himself. On his left index finger, he wore a gold signet ring with—Vax assumed—the symbol of the Clasp etched into it. It looked like a stylized rapier with a crescent shape in front, and it was also pressed in gold filigree on the spines of several books on a shelf behind the spireling.

The dwarf saluted him with his glass. "To your continued good health. Tell me, what can I or the Clasp do for you?"

Vax set his glass aside without taking a sip, thrown by what the man seemed to know about him. "I want to know who put a contract out on my sister," he said, without preamble. "And I want to know how to break it."

"I will give you an answer to your first question," Gideor said. "As a gesture of goodwill. The man who offered the contract is a minor noble-man who has requested our services before. He thinks himself impor-tant, and unfortunately he has a habit of acting on that instinct. It's a foul business, I admit, but he is a good customer. You may have met him. Or if not you, then perhaps your sister? Regrettably, I cannot tell you his name." It was only a half answer, and Vax was in no position to demand more. After Vex's tale the night before, he could venture a guess. Perhaps the lordling hadn't been entirely incompetent, but he certainly was full of himself.

"And my second question?" Vax insisted.

Gideor smiled and it sent a shiver down Vax's spine. He held his glass in one hand and swirled the liquid back and forth. "You must understand, we are not in the habit of breaking contracts. It's terribly bad for business. But," he continued, before Vax could interrupt, "we might be in the business of amending them. For the right price, of course."

Vax folded his arms. "Such as what?"

"Well, since our friend Lyre was so kind as to bring you to me, and it is clear to me you fight for a good cause, you present me with an interesting opportunity. Say, a simple assignment on my terms." The glow of the fireplace and the soft crackling of the fire created a comfortable, pleasant atmosphere in the office, but it did nothing to dull the spireling's edges. He studied Vax carefully to see how he would react. "A casual heist, nothing more. You've been asking around for work. Consider this a job offer."

Vax hesitated. "You seem to know a great deal about me." The disparity in knowledge was keeping him on his toes and he hated it. This was something Vex was far better at.

Gideor raised an eyebrow. "I make it my business to know what goes on in my town. Or who, as the case may be. Information is as valuable as gold in my profession."

"And yet you didn't tell Lyre that my sister and I come as a pair," Vax countered.

The spireling considered that. "Much like gold, information must be earned. I expect my people to be able to handle their jobs with a certain sense of . . . shall we say, flexibility and creativity, even when they don't have all the details. It's good to know how people handle the unexpected and whether or not they can turn unforeseen circumstances into opportunities." He nodded at Vax to underscore his point.

Vax clenched his jaw. "So what's the job?"

"I would like you to retrieve by any means necessary a ring from Jorenn Village, a small town at the foot of the Umbra Hills. It's an easy matter. As it is a few days' worth of travel, it will also get you and your sister out of Westruun while we handle the contract—and your nobleman friend." Gideor emptied his glass, and his eyes sparkled with a dangerous sort of humor. "Additionally, if you prove to be valuable assets in the long run, the Clasp can provide for you and your sister. We have plenty of other contracts for you to fulfill, and I promise you we pay better than whatever petty jobs you can cobble together."

Vax pushed his glass in the direction of the spireling. Tendrils of worry snaked through him. "What's the catch? What are you not telling me?"

Gideor smiled. "How delightfully distrustful. Why would I withhold anything?"

"Because information must be earned." Vax shifted in his seat. "And you have no reason to trust me."

"But I do. You'll swear your allegiance to the Clasp, of course," Gideor said, like it was a foregone conclusion. "And we know where to find your sister if you don't."

When the full extent of his impossible position became clear, Vax swallowed. Lyre had warned him that oath breaking didn't come cheap, but he hadn't thought beyond the immediate danger. Still, it was the immediate danger that needed solving, and he'd find a way to deal with whatever would come next, later. "How?"

"How what?"

"How will you handle the contract? How do I know someone else won't come after my sister the moment we leave to go find that ring for you?"

Spireling Gideor set down his glass and got to his feet. He straightened his rich coat and smoothed his beard. And though Vax physically towered over him, it was the dwarf whose presence dominated the room. "Come, I'll show you."

SPIRELING GIDEOR LED VAX OUT of his office. Next to the door stood a half-orc in equally colorful attire, picking at his nails with a dagger. He looked up when the two of them exited. "Need anything, boss?"

The dwarf waved generously. "Carry on."

The walk through the building was the complete opposite of sneaking down the city under the cover of night. Everything was brightly lit and colorful here. The walls were covered in rich tapestries and wooden paneling, with light fixtures on either side of every door: some lanterns, but more often than not decorative gems that were imbued with bright magical light that flowed through the hallways. A decadent use of magic, and a none-too-subtle reminder of the Clasp's wealth—and power.

Although the hallways weren't crowded, Clasp members were scattered about. Few wore the rich, hooded cloaks that Lyre and Ro had worn, with most instead preferring the rich, tailored outfits that Gideor showcased, while others dressed in simple yet elegant traveler's gear. Everyone stepped aside when the spireling walked through, even if some of them—distracted, it seemed, by sensitive business deals—had to be convinced with sharp nudges or hissed reminders.

Down two sets of stairs, the spireling guided Vax to a door that was guarded by a tall human man on one side and a distractible halfling on the other. The man carried a morningstar on his belt while the halfling was juggling with fairy lights. He wore a bright-blue shirt that fell loose around his shoulders and revealed the edges of a branding scar curving between his shoulder blades, showing the same stylized Clasp symbol that Spireling Gideor wore etched in his ring.

"Is Culwen back from his assignment?" Gideor asked the halfling, tossing him a small pouch of something or other. The halfling caught it and kept up juggling.

"Not seen him yet, boss. Probably still in Turst Fields or wherever that assignment took him."

"Good." Gideor passed them and pushed open the door, a wave of sound cascaded out, and the dwarf nodded. Something in his stance relaxed as if, despite all the fineries and appearances, this was where he felt most at home.

He stepped through a back door into a wide tavern, filled with two dozen tables, patrons around them all, a crowded bar, and a trio of halfling women singing in the corner. The sound lulled for a second when the spireling entered, but immediately picked up again.

The tavern looked like any other tavern in Westruun, except that the patrons all seemed to be preternaturally attentive. Half a dozen people were playing a card game at one of the far tables, and they all kept their weapons within hand's reach. A dwarf emptied out a small pouch of gems on a table while a human woman in front of him investigated every single one of them carefully. A halfling boy, seemingly too young to be this drunk, swayed to the sound of the trio's singing. But the second another patron bumped into him, he had his knives out. In any other place, a move like that would've led to a brawl, but the other patron laughed and said something Vax couldn't overhear and the boy simply went back to dancing without any sense of rhythm whatsoever.

The relaxed atmosphere of the room and the pleasant buzz of voices wrapped around Vax as he followed Gideor, as if to remind him that perhaps the Clasp wasn't so bad an ally to have. That perhaps there was something to the spireling's words after all. Vax regarded it all warily, recognizing how the tavern functioned as both a lure and a mask for the dangers that lay underneath.

"We take care of our own, my boy," Spireling Gideor said, like he could read Vax's thoughts. "Our organization would be a poor one indeed if we didn't. Hold your duty to us, and we'll hold ours to you."

"And if anyone fails to do so?" Vax asked.

Gideor nodded toward the far end of the room. "Come, follow me."

At the bar sat Lyre, a large tankard of ale in front of him, and his head on his arms. His shoulders and arms were bandaged up anew, while tension rippled down his back. He sat on his own, with empty chairs on either side that stood out compared to the crowded place. He glanced behind him and immediately buried his head in his arms again, clearly trying to will himself to be invisible.

Undeterred by this, Gideor walked up to him and slapped his shoulder, causing the young man to flinch. "Our friend Lyre here will be the answer to all of your questions."

Lyre turned to face him, one hand clinging to the tankard and the other trembling fiercely in his lap. "Spireling Gideor, sir, I can—I *will* do better with my next contract. I nearly had the girl too. My rats were on her. If I hadn't been interrupted, if my darts had been properly spelled, but I . . . I thought you should hear what her brother had to say."

He cringed away from Vax's angry scowl, and the hand that was holding the tankard was now trembling so hard that the ale inside sloshed over the rim.

Spireling Gideor offered Lyre the same casual smile he'd shown Vax, and again it didn't convey any sort of humor or amusement. "Unless I lost count, this isn't the first contact you messed up. Did I lose count, Lyre?"

"No, sir." Lyre's voice was barely a whisper, but it was audible in the room, because all the conversations around them had fallen quiet.

"Feel free to jog my memory, but wasn't there the business with that young girl in the Shields some time ago? And a sizable sum of gold owed by a certain bookseller?"

Lyre shrank in on himself, and he looked to be on the verge of crying. "I swear I can do better."

"I know, I know." Spireling Gideor patted Lyre's back and sounded entirely reasonable. "That's why you're going to help us with this bit of nasty business. Walk with us."

Behind the bar, a young woman was cleaning glasses with a disinterested look on her face. The spireling nodded at her and tapped the ring on his finger. When he asked her something in a guttural language Vax didn't understand, she reached underneath the bar and pulled some kind of lever, which opened up a door to a back room.

"Thanks, gorgeous," he said.

His charming attitude dropped the moment he closed the door behind Vax and Lyre, and the three of them were alone. A triangular table was set up in the middle of the room, with three high-backed chairs all draped with moss-green covers showing the Clasp symbol embroidered in shimmering gold. There were thick curtains in front of what Vax assumed was a window, and cabinets on two of the walls.

This must be a meeting room for the three spirelings, like Ro had mentioned. Three powerful—and likely power-hungry—figures in charge of a guild of thieves and smugglers. Vax wondered what those meetings looked like.

Gideor opened up two lanterns to light up the room and softly traced a finger along the back of one of the chairs until Vax heard the faintest of clicks. The spireling nodded. He took a key from a necklace and opened up the tall cabinet on the right side of the room. He reached in and took out a short staff, roughly the size of his forearm. He held it for a moment, looking at it in rapt fascination. The staff, which appeared to be made from leather or skin or flesh, twisted and coiled in Gideor's hand like it was a living thing.

"Vax'ildan." The spireling turned to Vax and held out the staff. From closer up, it wasn't flesh but entirely made up out of tongues that were shivering and curling, and Vax stared at the staff in mute horror. "I owed you an answer as to how I plan to fulfill my deal with you while not antagonizing our previous contractor. I believe far better than to tell you is to show you."

Gideor ran a fingernail along the staff and shifted his attention to the third person in the room. "You know that the Clasp—*my* Clasp does not suffer failures, Lyre."

Lyre trembled all over and dropped to his knees. "I'm sorry, I'm sorry, I'm s—"

"Shhh." Spireling Gideor held out the staff toward the sobbing figure in front of him, and before Vax could wrap his mind around what was happening—before he could *do* anything—Lyre's form began to shimmer. He clawed at his face and his protests became louder—

Until his voice broke and changed.

His features twisted, warping perversely. His shoulders narrowed and his arms snapped like they were breaking. His torso crumpled and unfurled. His messy hair grew out, falling in long brown strands around his face. His terrified silver eyes gradually darkened.

In front of Vax, Lyre was turned into a perverted copy of his sister and lay on the floor clutching her throat, moaning in that exact same voice Vax would always recognize, no matter where they were.

When Lyre opened his mouth to cry out, his voice—*Vex's* voice—cracking at the edges, Gideor reached out, grabbed the thief's tongue, and yanked. With a nauseating snap, the tongue came loose, and Lyre roared helplessly. Tears streamed down his face and mingled with the blood that coated his chin and chest.

Vax stumbled toward the table because his legs threatened to give out. He was going to be sick. He was going to claw out his own eyes and find a way to undo what happened.

Spireling Gideor still held on to the staff, and he held the bloodied tongue up to it. The other tongues immediately lapped up the blood, and the staff shivered and expanded to make room for a new addition to its collection. Gideor studied it curiously. "What a marvelous thing indeed."

"It's horrifying," Vax managed. He had to stop himself from putting his hands over his ears to block out Lyre's broken cries. He couldn't even look at him.

Spireling Gideor raised his eyebrows. "You asked me how I would handle our nobleman, and this is my answer. We provide him with a decoy."

"How long?" Vax asked, fighting to keep his voice steady.

"For as long as our gentleman contractor has use of him." Gideor walked over to the cabinet and returned the staff, locking the doors carefully. He looked down on Lyre. "I could have and should have demanded your life, Lyre. Instead you'll have one last chance to serve the Clasp. Wouldn't you consider that merciful after those many mistakes you made?"

He didn't wait for a reply before he walked up to Vax. "You see, I prefer working together based on mutual agreement." He spoke comfortably. "But please understand that I consider us to be in contract now too. And while I have shown myself flexible because I believed it to be in both our interests, do not think I make it a habit of accepting anything but the results we've agreed upon."

Vax felt his stomach twist and turn inside him, and their inn's terrible lumpy food threatened to crawl up his throat. If he didn't find a way out of here soon, out of this room with a cursed copy of his sister and the unmoving demands of the dwarf in front of him, he was going to be sick.

"Do we have an understanding?" Spireling Gideor asked.

"We do," Vax croaked.

"Wonderful. I'm so pleased to hear that. Come, I will see to it that you get your weapons back and that you have all the information you need." The dwarf straightened his coat, and the twinkle in his eyes was lethal. The tight-lipped smile he threw Lyre's way was the first true smile Vax had seen since he met the dwarf.

When Spireling Gideor reached out to him to take his arm, Vax had to fight not to flinch away.

CHAPTER 7

"It's just a job, Vex'ahlia." Vax rubbed his face. It was disorienting to try to convince his sister, because every time he looked at her, he saw Lyre change into her again.

When he'd returned last night, she'd already been asleep, her blanket pulled tight, and her bow within reaching distance. He'd almost been grateful for the reprieve, because he didn't have the words to tell her he'd seen her stalker changed into a shitty, messed-up copy of her, only to be given to the man who put the contract out on her.

But it didn't make this morning's conversation any easier. She was tired and snappy, and he was unsuccessfully trying to get the image of Lyre and the staff of tongues out of his head.

"It's *not* just a job," Vex said, her worries drawing deep lines across her face. "A job is running messages or protecting travelers or returning people's lost property. You've always told me to keep an eye out for the Clasp and to stay far away." She wrapped her new bracers around her forearms, tightening the straps with fierce determination. "Why the fuck would you say yes to them?"

Vax sat down heavily on the bed. Part of him wanted to let her believe that it was just a foolish decision like so many he'd made. Let her be angry at him if it meant she didn't have to worry about the Clasp and their illicit work. But he couldn't. It had always been the two of them against the world, and he didn't want anything to come between them.

He couldn't let her think he'd be so careless with their safety when there was nothing more important.

"Because I didn't have a choice." He couldn't lie to her, not even to protect her.

She stilled immediately in the midst of lacing up her boots. "What happened? Are you in some kind of trouble?"

"No." He grimaced at the irony of it. "I trailed you last night. I was there when that guy attacked you."

She frowned. "Oh. I thought I'd handled that."

"You did, but I jumped him. I wanted to make sure he wouldn't follow you when you escaped. We got into a fight, and . . ." He considered his words carefully. "In doing so messed up a Clasp mission."

Vex paled. She finished tying up her boots and leaned against the broken-down cabinet, her arms wrapped around her waist. "What did the Clasp want with me?"

He made a split-second decision and forced himself to meet her gaze. He could protect her from this part, at least. "You were in the wrong place at the wrong time, Stubby. And apparently so was I."

Something passed across her face. Concern. Relief. Both. "I was worried it had been—" She stopped and shook her head. "So you got into a fight with them, and then what happened?"

"Well, they're dangerous. And they don't take kindly to anyone getting between them and a job. So we negotiated a deal. For me to fulfill a job for them, in payment for the failed mission." None of it was technically a lie, and he could convince himself it was kinder than to tell her it *had* been about her, and that some poor bastard now wore her face and was at the mercy of her stalker. She didn't need to carry that weight.

Vex bit her lip. She glanced past him, toward the window. "Or what, they'd kill you?"

"Something like that, yeah." He crossed the room and came to stand in front of her. "Look, I wanted to stay far away from them too. But maybe it isn't all bad. We have some coin for now, but it won't last us forever. Good jobs are hard to come by, and what we find is hardly enough to sustain us. They pay better than anything I can scrounge up."

Spireling Gideor's words left a bitter taste in his mouth, but everything else aside, there was a core of truth to them. After sharing the details about this job, the spireling had told him about some of the other jobs the Clasp brought in, and while some of the work was similar to what he and Vex had been doing over the past five years, the pay was at least double what they earned. The Clasp's fences paid better, and the taverns they owned were decent and affordable for members. They had healers who'd patched up Vax—dealing with the wounds left by Lyre's darts, and the cuts and bruises from the tumble across the rooftops—no questions asked.

"Does that mean you're a member now?" Vex demanded.

He rolled his shoulders. "Not yet. It's only one assignment. But people don't just walk away from the Clasp." Spireling Gideor had casually told him there was no need to brand him yet. Not until after he returned from Jorenn Village, at least. He felt Vax would be in a better position there without any identifying markers.

And Vax had decided he didn't need to know the full details about branding there and then, because his head had been spinning and everything inside him felt wrong. It still did.

"They'll demand your loyalty, you know they will. Fuck, Vax. What if they also demand something you can't give? What if they get between us?"

"They won't," Vax said, instantly and with force. "Nothing and no one will ever come between us. But I have to do this. I've given my word. And I don't want to get on their bad side."

He reached out to her and held her, despite her protests. "Do you trust me?" he whispered.

"Always." She squeezed his hand before she disentangled herself and she rubbed her arms. "I don't trust *them*."

"Me neither," he admitted. "I still have to do this." And it wasn't just because they'd already demanded the impossible. It was because some part of him, some small part of him, had latched on to the improbable. A way to make something better out of a bad situation. Better jobs meant a sense of security, of safety for the both of them. He'd go wherever his sister did, and if that meant they would continue to run around for the rest of their lives then so be it, but some days he wondered what was beyond that.

She hiccuped a laugh. "They're probably not even paying you for the contract, are they?"

"Well, there's the whole letting-us-live part." He gently tugged her braid, relief coursing through him at her words.

She walked to the window and looked out at the city that was waking up around them. She sighed heavily. "We'll go. We'll get that ring. We'll leave this bloody city behind us. I'm sick and tired of people threatening us."

V EX HAD MORE MISGIVINGS ABOUT this plan than arrows in her quiver. When she'd gotten back to the inn the previous night, her brother had been gone, and she'd assumed he'd been on some kind of sneaky business or other. By the time she'd managed to sleep, she'd spent hours trying to convince herself that the hunt through the city was nothing and that she'd simply crossed the wrong person's path. After all, her assailant had left her alone once she reached the busier side of Westruun, and the rats had scattered and disappeared too, as though whatever caused their interest in her had also vanished. She still felt a bit uncomfortable, but it was nothing. Really.

Except it hadn't been nothing. She knew that now. She hadn't missed Vax's slip that fulfilling the assignment would mean the Clasp would let them both live.

But once outside of the city walls, on gentle horses provided by the Clasp, she breathed easier.

The Bramblewood Forest that embraced Westruun stretched out toward the mountains, and the air smelled fresher here. A stillness came from the forest that she could find nowhere else. A sense of life and endlessness, of gnarled roots burrowing deep into the ground and tall trees reaching ever higher. Even the jagged thorns that crawled up the tree bark added to its strange beauty. She preferred woods that weren't innocent.

She felt better here, and more like herself instead of the person other people wished her to be. If only she could carry that feeling everywhere.

And if she kept her eyes on the road in front of her, she didn't have to look up to where the misty outline of Gatshadow loomed, larger still than it had inside the city, like it was observing the two of them. She wondered what it saw and what it had seen. They'd gone into the city with such different expectations. More finding simple work, less getting conscripted by the Clasp. At least they left with a full purse and stocked up on all the necessities.

Other travelers were leaving Westruun with the rising sun too, and the crossroads around the city were an anthill. Chaotic. Constantly in motion. Few travelers turned north toward the Black Valley, and the road that stretched out in front of them, past the forest and parallel to the peaks to the west, was thankfully quiet.

"Tell me about that shitty ring again," she said when she was certain no one could overhear them.

Vax picked at a spot on his leg. She knew she wasn't the only one worried about the Clasp; he looked as tired as she felt. "It's an heirloom of a Westruun family that somehow made its way to the hands of the Shadewatch of Jorenn," he said. "According to my contact, it's very recognizable. An intricate silver band with dark cloudy gems and shards of bone. Affectionately known as Fracture."

"A ring with a name. Sounds great," she said flatly. "So it's magic?"

"I don't know. I've only been told that the Clasp wants it, badly. It's only one ring, Vex. It's supposed to be easy. I've stolen rings before."

She shook her head and focused on the path in front of her. "I don't trust things that are supposed to be easy. And if we're going back to stealing trinkets again, I want my own by my side."

She expected Vax to point out that they'd be far more noticeable with a giant bear by their side. When he remained quiet, she turned to him, one eyebrow arched up. Her brother was staring out into the forest pensively, his fingers tight around his horse's reins. "Good call."

She snorted. "I wasn't asking for your permission, brother. But I'm glad you agree."

He rolled his eyes.

They followed the road until they were out of sight from the city and any fellow travelers, until they found a small trail that led deeper into the forest where sunlight dappled the leaves around them. Vex had to stop herself from pushing her horse harder.

When the trail widened in front of her, Vex slid off her horse, walking the last couple of yards to the clearing where they'd made camp before entering the city. There Trinket stood in the middle of the stream, staring intently at the water in front of him. His large paws were dark and muddy, and she laughed when she saw purple stains around his snout. It wasn't hard to spot the mauled blackberry bush on the other side of the stream.

"I wouldn't have minded some blackberries too," Vax commented from a little way away.

She snorted. "We'll find you some along the way."

At the sound of voices, the bear looked up, the fish around him immediately forgotten. He stood on his hind legs and splashed into the water again, momentarily looking exactly like the young bear cub she'd helped raise. Vex laughed. "Oh, Trinket."

Trinket ambled toward her and she crossed half the distance, until she could wrap her arms around the bear and push her face into his fur. The bear grunted and nudged her with his head and she scratched his neck and breathed in the familiar scent of fur and mud and safety. "Buddy. We're traveling again. Are you coming with us?"

"I love how you *tell* me what to do, and you *ask* your bear."

She winked at him, and he shuddered. "Gods, don't do that."

Trinket snorted. He nudged her again. He always seemed to understand more than she thought was possible.

With the two of them by her side, she didn't need anything else.

"You know we could leave," she suggested, knowing that there was no one around who could overhear but her bear and her brother. "Keep traveling east and go toward the coast or the forests there. No one will ever know."

Vax had grabbed both horses by the reins. "You know we can't."

"If it becomes too dangerous, we'll walk away, all right?" she asked, suddenly needing that reassurance. Trinket butted her gently with his head, and she leaned into him tightly. Somehow, her bear always knew what she needed.

"It's a simple heist. We'll be back in Westruun in a couple of days, and we can follow our own path from there," Vax said, with a sense of determination Vex wished she could feel.

"And?" she pressed.

He looked at her, *really* looked at her, and nodded. "If it becomes too dangerous, we'll walk away."

THE LANDSCAPE CHANGED AROUND THEM as they traveled northward. The Cliffkeep Mountains remained a steadfast visage on the western horizon, like jagged edges around every sunset. They spent one night in the forest, and once they left the Bramblewood behind, peaks began to arise on the northern and eastern horizons as well, like they were slowly being surrounded by hill creatures and stone giants.

In the morning, they crossed paths with a messenger who was making her way east. She carried missives to Turst Fields and though she didn't want to break bread with them, they did exchange a few words while she watered her horse. Because, as she said, "Those of us who share the same roads have to mind each other."

She pointed at the road that wound its way northward. "There's a group of merchants about a day's travel ahead of you. Their cart is slow and cumbersome, and the two men in charge keep quarreling, so if you keep a comfortable pace, you'll catch up with them. You may want to consider that."

"Why?" Vex asked, with a worried glance at Vax, who was busying himself with his saddlebags.

The messenger pulled out a handful of green-brown cubes from a container and fed them to her horse, making sure the animal was in good shape for the rest of the long ride. Better shape than the messenger was, Vex realized quietly. The young woman had circles under her eyes and she kept rubbing her neck, her long auburn braid dancing over her back. "The Blackvalley Path is safe enough, but from what I heard in Jorenn, they have problems with dead things coming down the Umbra Hills." When the horse had finished the food, she brushed her hands on her tunic. "That whole area is supposed to be haunted. Strange magics, and all that."

"Oh," Vex managed. "Great."

The messenger flashed her a grin that lit up her whole tired face. "I recommend getting out before the trouble starts. It makes life a whole lot easier."

"I'm sure we'll do that," Vex said, emphasizing the words, even though Vax didn't appear to be listening.

He wrapped a piece of bread and some of their other supplies in a piece of cloth. He walked up to the messenger as she was getting back in the saddle. "I noticed your bags were empty. You should have something to eat on the way east."

Her nostrils flared, and Vex saw a flash of pride. Briefly, she thought the messenger wouldn't accept the offered food. Then she nodded. "Thank you for your kindness. Changebringer guide you."

When the messenger nudged her horse into a trot, Vex mounted too. She narrowed her eyes at her brother, who was still staunchly avoiding her gaze. "*Dead* things?"

"Coming down the hills, apparently," he said after a moment, mounting up and nudging his horse into a trot. He made sure he was out of punching distance before he turned back to her. "Don't tell me you're afraid?"

"Tell me you didn't know about those strange magics either."

"We'll keep an eye out for the merchants. And we only need the ring. In and out. We'll be careful."

"Are you *sure* this was supposed to be a nice and easy heist?"

"It'll be far better than dealing with the Clasp." Vax glanced northward, and the shadow of a grin crept over his face, as if the idea of there being a strange type of danger in Jorenn Village made it more appealing instead of less so. "Besides, the two of us against strange magics and a haunted town? Where's your sense of adventure?"

"I think someone dropped you on your head when you were a boy," Vex groaned. "I should've stayed in that clearing with Trinket."

Trinket, who heard his name, looked at Vex and grunted.

They made their way northward regardless, and the day passed around them. The valley that spread out in front of them was one of glowing hills and endless rolling plains. The grassland allowed for some hunting, but the natural resources were scarce and very few people tried to use this land for farming. The sides of the hills were covered in heather of all different types of greens and purples.

On the first night they made camp in the valley, the merchants were nowhere to be seen. Vex found a good campsite near the banks of a river that meandered along the northernmost edge of the Bramblewood. They dined on freshly caught fish and whatever autumn berries they could find, and the nights outside were quieter without fear for any shadows and stalkers.

An endless blanket of constellations and stars spread out over them, and when the first moon rose, Vex leaned against Trinket, her head resting on his back. The nights were growing colder, and Trinket's presence was warm and reassuring. This was something no city could ever hope to emulate. The feeling of freedom and space and the solid earth under her feet. Even if they were—apparently—on their way to a town with undead dangers.

Vax came to sit next to her, cleaning one of several daggers with a polishing cloth. At least the new cloak looked good on him, and strangely, that mattered. Being able to provide him—them—with good supplies was a tangible form of protection.

He worked in silence for a moment, and then he stopped.

She raised an eyebrow but didn't say a word.

He reached into his pocket and pulled out a small bundle, wrapped up in a square piece of linen, tied with twine, and handed it to her, not meeting her eye. "You know I'm sorry I dragged you into this, Stubby."

"It seems I dragged you into it first." She nudged him with her shoulder. "And you know I'll go anywhere with you."

With careful hands, she untied the twine and opened up the linen, only to find the small copper bear she'd admired in the elf's workshop in Westruun. It was tied to a long leather necklace. Her breath caught. "Vax . . ."

"I didn't pay for it," he admitted, with the barest hint of a challenge to his voice. "I saw how much you loved it, and you shouldn't be afraid of loving something just because some elves are assholes."

Her fingers tightened around the little copper bear, and she grinned. "We met the worst of them, didn't we?"

"The absolute worst," he acknowledged. "Come here, let me help you with that." He took the necklace out of her hand, and when Vex lifted up her hair, he tied it gently around her neck.

CHAPTER 8

Eleven years ago

They were comfortably ten and the city that rose up in front of them was that of a dream—or a nightmare. Neither twin was entirely certain yet. On the one hand, this was everything the stories they'd begged for talked about and more. The verdant city in front of them was magnificent and awe inspiring, with spires and citadels that towered over the jade-green walls, and such finery and power that the trees themselves seemed to bend and give way to it. The buildings nestled securely in the embrace of the mountains, as though they'd been hewn out of the rocks or were grown from them. It was full of magic and full of grace.

On the other hand, it wasn't home.

Their fellow travelers straightened in recognition of their imminent arrival, but all the twins could do was to reach out to each other and entwine their fingers.

These last few days, they'd seen more of the world than they knew existed, and neither one of them knew exactly how to deal with it. Vex withdrew further within herself, speaking only with her brother and even then barely. Vax contemplated all the ways he knew how to escape this company, grab his sister, and bring them both back to the only world they needed.

"Syngorn is a wondrous place," the elven guard to Vax's right said quietly. "You'll find a home here, even if it may take some getting used to."

Out of the three guards that showed up at their doorstep with a letter from their father, Tharyn had been the youngest and the only one to initiate conversations with the twins. When they camped together on their way here, Tharyn had sat down next to them by the fire, comfortably quiet and whittling away at a small wooden horse. They answered the twins' questions with a ready smile and nothing of the distance that the other two guards showed. They told the twins about the beauty of Syngorn, new stories about the Gladepools, and scary tales about the dense, dark part of the forest they passed, where all the trees seemed knotted and twisted and hungry.

"Your father is a well-respected man," they continued. "And being part of his household will offer you opportunities that you may never have found back in your village home. He'll make sure you have the best education Syngorn can offer, and connections far beyond your wildest dreams."

Vex's hand twitched inside her brother's, and Vax peeked up at Tharyn. The elf spoke with sincerity, as best as Vax could tell. They'd tied their long auburn hair back in a single tail and they stared up at the city with a reverence so intense it made Vax's stomach ache, because it was the sight of someone who'd left to see the world a hundred times—if their stories were to be believed—but never saw a sight so perfect as their first glimpse of home again.

The two other guards rode on ahead of them, leaving Tharyn with the twins, while they announced their arrival at the imposing gates, warded with deep blue sigils.

"Will there be others like us?" Vex asked quietly.

Tharyn looked at her and furrowed their brow. "Children? Yes, some, for our lives are long and our Dreamweavers take great care in selecting the right parents for our next generations. But you'll find others your age, I'm quite certain."

Vex bit her lip, leaving Vax to ask the question he was sure his sister had meant. "Will there be other half-elves like us?"

A shadow crossed over Tharyn's face, and for the first time they looked uncomfortable. They threw a glance in the direction of the other guards, who were not quite out of earshot, and their hazel eyes were guarded. "Not many. You will be the only ones that I know of."

"Why? Are there no other people than elves in Syngorn?"

"There are a few with the High Warden's leave to stay inside our walls, so long as they respect our customs. They are visitors, and they keep to themselves. None but elves are citizens of Syngorn." It was quite clear that there were other things Tharyn couldn't say—or wouldn't say—and frankly, the idea that they would be the only ones was disturbing enough. Byroden may look like a scruffy village compared with the might and glamour of this place, but they'd never been alone. Feena's father was a half-elf too, and she had pointier ears than any of her brothers. Though it had never been spoken out loud, everyone in town was convinced Duncan had not just halfling but gnomish heritage. No one batted an eye at mixed family trees, because they all considered one another neighbors.

When the guards in front of them turned and beckoned them forward, Vex sat up straight all of a sudden and she looked at Tharyn intently. "Does that mean we'll be considered visitors too?"

Tharyn grimaced at that. They nudged their horse in the direction of the gates and their shoulders dropped. They didn't look back at the two of them when they answered. "You have the High Warden's permission to stay, at the bequest of your father. You are welcome here."

When the eldest guard—a gray-haired female elf with broad shoulders and proud eyes—announced them to the watchers at the gate as "Ambassador Syldor's *half-elf* children" and those words were met with frowns and disgust, Vax doubted every single word of that welcome. But all he could do was tighten his grip on his sister's fingers and follow their guards into the city and to the home of their father.

INSIDE THE WALLS, SYNGORN WAS as beautiful as Tharyn had promised it to be. The houses and other buildings showed a level of craftsmanship that every farmer in Byroden would eye with jealousy and, perhaps, a hint of practical suspicion as well. The grace of the buildings was that of the forest around them: ageless and unconquerable.

But it wasn't the buildings that took Vex's breath away. It was the vastness of it all. With the sun high overhead, the white citadel in the distance shone like a beacon and the city stretched as far as the eye could see. The sunlight also refracted on the lake in the center of the city, causing the calm waters to sparkle vibrantly. The occasionally blinding light didn't stop elves from wandering along the lakeshore, or traversing it in small, colorful boats. A family of three—two sharply dressed, darkskinned elves and a girl a few years younger than the twins—stepped into a narrow boat with violet flowers strung on the side, using some kind of magic spell to propel them onto the lake. Vex could hear their voices and laughter echo across the water, as though no one here had a care in the world.

Syngorn was a place of promise, and above all else that was why she and her brother had followed their father's instructions. The promise of a better life and a future far beyond what Byroden could offer them. But with every elf they passed who looked at them with sneering contempt, that promise morphed and twisted into something far less palatable, and all she wanted to do was run home again.

"It'll be better once we get to our father's home," Vax whispered, so quietly Vex doubted anyone but she could hear.

"He'll accept us," she said. "It's why he invited us to come in the first place, right?"

"He said so in the letter he sent Mother. We'll want for nothing." Vax's voice took on an edge of determined desperation.

But when their traveling companions guided them to the eastern side of the city, where the houses were large and imposing, meticulously crafted to mirror the proud, tall trees, their unease grew. As with every enterprising child in Byroden, there were times when they'd played the wrong prank, angered the wrong person, and were made to feel small. They felt smaller here and more vulnerable than ever before.

Especially so when Tharyn pointed out Syldor's house to them: a mansion easily three times the size of their old home, with cracked white marble walls and a jade-shingled roof. Ivy climbed up every wall and circled the high windows, and a handful of large red trees were placed around the building like ancient sentries. Small, strawberry-colored birds darted between the branches.

"This will be your new home," Tharyn said. "Your father will have been informed of your arrival."

If that was the case, there was no sign of it. The door remained closed when they rode up to the building, where the twins dismounted and the three Verdant Guards remained in the saddle.

"We'll leave you here," the gray-haired woman said, with no hint of kindness or consideration. "The horses are the ambassador's. He'll see to their—and your—care."

"We can wait until they're inside," Tharyn argued, with little force behind their words.

"Our duty was to see them to the ambassador's home safely. That ends here. We have other duties to see to, Tharyn." The last words held a note of warning.

Tharyn colored slightly and straightened. They adjusted their uniform and nodded once in the direction of the twins. "Goodbye then. I wish you well here."

"Thank you," Vex whispered, her throat clenched tight. Next to her, Vax had pressed his lips together in a thin line, and he turned away from the guards. She reached for him. "Let's go."

Vax clung to her hand. He tightened the traveling cloak their mother had made for them around his shoulders and flinched at the sound of horseshoes retreating on the road. "Let's go back."

It was an alluring option, and she imagined it for a moment—turning around and giving in to her inclination to sneak back past the gates and find a way home through the forest. "We can't. We should try to stay here, right? It'll be good for us. It's a chance for a better life."

It was what Tharyn had told them. It was what their father had written. It was what their mother had said, when she'd wrapped her arms around them and whispered she wanted only the very best for them.

"I don't want a better life. I want our life," Vax said. He pulled away, and lines of tension still crawled along his shoulders and spine.

"We'll have to make this ours. At least for now." Vex breathed in deeply, the air as potent and powerful as everything around them, and stepped up to the door.

Before she could knock—or before her brother could stop her—the door swung open and a young man stepped aside to reveal the same elven traveler they'd seen in Byroden so many months ago.

Syldor Vessar looked different here. He'd traded in his practical traveling gear for heavy brown robes with golden embroidery. The long sleeves were cut open to show fine gold silk underneath, and the garment's high neck made him appear taller. Sterner too, if that was at all possible, for the way he looked at his children was nothing like the way he'd looked at Elaina. He regarded their travel-worn appearance with distaste and snapped his fingers to the other elf—who appeared to be a servant of some sort. "See to their horses and whatever belongings they carry. Discard their clothes and find them something more suitable. Son, daughter, come in."

It wasn't so much a request as an order, and Syldor turned, clearly expecting it to be followed. The servant took the horses from the pair of them and led the mounts away. The door stayed open, reminding the twins to follow their father.

Vex swallowed her hurt, even as she felt her brother's anger radiate. She took a step back, purposefully aiming to land on top of her brother's foot, and she hissed, "We have to *try* to make this life ours. Mother expects it of us."

"I hate him already," he bristled.

"Maybe he's just not used to us yet. He didn't even know we existed. Give him time."

"He's had six months. He could've chosen to keep out of our lives."

She reached for his sleeve and tugged him in the direction of the building. "It'll be fine."

"You don't know that," he threw back.

She didn't answer. She didn't know that. But it had to be, because it was the only reason this trip and leaving everything behind was worth it. Besides which, he was family. Did that not count for something? This wasn't supposed to take them away from their home, but be a home too.

But when they walked through the wide hallway, with light filtering in through the overhead windows, the walls paneled with wood, and the comforting smell of cedar wrapping around them, it felt like they were trespassing.

At the end of the hallway, past a number of closed doors, Syldor stood in the opening to a large office. With his arms folded and his eyebrows quirked, his impatience was palpable. "Get in. Sit down."

He closed the door behind him and took his place behind a large wooden desk. It was as artfully made as any of the buildings they passed, with the legs carved like branches and the handles to the countless small drawers like leaves inlaid with emeralds. Two of the walls were covered in bookshelves, with tomes and scrolls from ceiling to floor. The wall perpendicular to the door boasted a long and narrow window, equally as tall as the shelves, with stained decorations along the edges and a view of a forgotten herb garden, while the last wall had a large painting of a beautiful lake, shimmering in the pale light of the moons. On one of the shelves, in front of a row of books bound in red leather, stood two charcoal drawings of elves, without any markings or names to identify them.

Everything about this house could be beautiful, Vex realized. Instead it was as cold as the reception they got.

Syldor rested his hands on the desk and leaned in their direction. "I appreciate that your mother chose the wiser path in sending you here. Your existence came as a surprise to me, or I would've acted sooner, but you are still young enough that all hope is not lost."

Vax cleared his throat, his expression defiant. "What does that mean?"

"Your education is abysmal, even for ones such as yourself," Syldor continued, as if Vax hadn't spoken at all. "I've already seen to it that you will be given the finest tutoring and schooling in the land, until such time that you can learn among others your age and not bring shame upon my name."

"Wouldn't that be *our* name?" Vax pressed. He'd raised his chin, and only Vex could see how hard his hands were trembling. Although neither of them had known what to expect from this meeting, they'd surely not expected this.

Syldor's mouth thinned. "Of course. Our name."

He twisted the bracelet around his wrist and stared past his children. "Once Alin has seen to your horses, he will show you to your rooms. Your tutor will arrive in the morning. You will not leave the house unless you have my express permission. You will not dress in those peasant clothes anymore. You will not disturb me during my meetings or my work." His gaze snapped to Vex, and she could only imagine how she must look to him. Dirty, unworthy, and on the verge of tears. All her thoughts were tangled together with hurt and confusion and contempt at the small part of her that had been cautiously excited about meeting her father. She'd wanted him to be pleased to meet them, to realize how much he could care for them, and what a wondrous thing it could be to become a family together.

She pressed her fingernails in the palms of her hands and did the only thing she could do: tilt her head like her brother and refuse to blink.

He sniffed and took a scroll from the case next to him. "You are welcome here. Now leave me."

CHAPTER 9

They caught up with the merchants when the Black Valley narrowed and the flatlands rose into hills. Over the course of several hours, as they neared the end of another day, Jorenn Village had ebbed and flowed in the distance, its vague shape showing on the horizon if they crested over hills, then disappearing again behind the undulating landscape.

It was far enough and the landscape treacherous enough that Vax didn't think they'd make it before nightfall, but at least the town was visible, and it looked like any other frontier town. Small and determined. He wondered what its strange magics looked like.

The hillside behind it, however, was quite another matter. While the valley around them was a lush but empty green, and the hills were spattered with pink and purple heathers, the rolling hills beyond the town were scarred and gray. They seemed to be covered in ashes, and all the plants were burnt or otherwise colorless. It was a slice of the mountains where color had simply ceased to exist. It gave the place a desolate appearance, and a hopelessness that Vax tried hard to ignore.

He could easily imagine dead things coming down the hills.

They traveled until the sun dipped behind the Cliffkeep Mountains and the temperature around them dropped. The horses were struggling with the uneven terrain, and Vax's stomach was growling. He was about to ask Vex if they should make camp when she raised her hand to silence him.

She listened intently for a second or two, placed a hand on Trinket's head to quiet the bear too, then motioned him to wait as she slid from her saddle and scouted the trail ahead.

Knowing that she must have heard something, he listened too. At first he only heard the normal sounds of nightfall around them. The chirping of crickets in the grasslands. The howling of wolves or coyotes at some distance, and birdcalls high up in the sky. Trinket grumbled, and one of the horses blew spit from his nose. Then another, discordant sound. The rise and fall of voices, at the edge of his range. An argument of sorts, perhaps?

Not long after he recognized it, Vex returned, a frustrated expression on her face. "It's those merchants the messenger told us about," she said. "They set up camp too, and they're being loud and obnoxious."

"I don't think the rocks mind," he said.

She grunted. "They're drawing attention to themselves."

"We can stay here, if you want," Vax said. He glanced in the direction of the hills. So far, they hadn't come across anything. "But . . ."

"We should join them," Vex said, and she followed his gaze. She continued before he could interrupt her. "Don't say I didn't warn you when you realize that they are bickering constantly, all right? They're already giving me a headache."

Most of the time, the two of them avoided other travelers, setting up camp on their own. But they both knew to heed the messenger's warning. They'd be noticeable in this valley, and for tonight Vax *did* prefer joining them, for all sorts of reasons. Information. Protection. Strength in numbers. The part of him that wanted to surround Vex with an armed guard, if she'd let him. "If I can get them talking about those strange magics in Jorenn, we'll be better prepared."

Vex mashed her face against her horse's flank before mounting up. "*If* they know anything."

"Besides," he said, with an innocent smile he knew she hated, "I'm used to bickering."

"You're going to regret that," she threatened.

He scratched Trinket's ears. "Probably. And you did warn me and I didn't listen, so we have that out of the way too."

Vex rolled her eyes. She nudged her horse in the direction of the merchants and led her brother and her bear to a sizable camp a mile or so northward.

A small campfire lit up a large cart that had been pulled to a flat area off the road, near the river. Two dwarves were taking care of the horses and cleaning tack. A female half-elf in the sensible greens and browns of a ranger or a scout sat on a protruding piece of rock, keeping an eye on the chaos and on the road. She was rubbing at her temple.

In the midst of an open area amidst three canvas tents, two human men were sitting on either side of the fire, arguing bitterly over the appropriate care and use of ancient manuscripts and other historical artifacts.

The half-elf got to her feet when the twins approached, and her brown eyes widened at the sight of Trinket. She whistled sharply. The dwarves looked up and reached for their weapons, while the two men kept quarreling. They'd locked on to each other like the world might end around them and they'd still keep fighting.

The half-elf placed an arrow on her bow but didn't draw. She nodded in the direction of the twins. "What do you want?"

Vax raised his hands. "We're on our way to Jorenn Village. We're looking for a place to spend the night. May we join you?" It wasn't all that uncommon for travelers to share camps out in the wild, but every such encounter was a balance between potential danger and perilous trust. Not everyone liked having strangers close by, for a multitude of reasons.

"You two and the bear?"

"My sister, my nephew, and I," Vax said blandly.

The half-elf didn't falter. She turned back to the men, who'd at least stopped talking when one of the dwarves had pointed out the situation to them. The taller of the two, a dark-skinned man in his late thirties, with a long practical cloak, gloves on his hands, and a pair of glasses on a chain around his neck, waved them forward. "Of course, come in. The more, the merrier, right?"

"That entirely depends on the company," the other man snapped. His tanned skin was slightly lighter than his adversary's. He held on to a staff made from three pieces of wood braided together, and at the top the braid expanded to envelop a gleaming blue stone. "You're welcome if you must join us."

"Gee, thanks," Vex muttered.

"We have food enough to spare!" the first man said. "Come, make yourselves comfortable, for tomorrow we'll all be in Jorenn and our research continues."

The half-elf managed to keep a blank expression and gestured them in, but when the twins passed her, they both heard her soft, "Moonweaver give me strength."

Vax grinned.

With permission to join the camp, they picketed the horses near those of the sturdy mountain ponies of the other travelers. The two dwarves had already carried in fresh water from a nearby stream, and they had enough pellets to share, so all they needed to do was brush the horses and clean their tack. The dwarves reacted with some suspicion toward Trinket, but when the bear didn't immediately try to maul the horses, they settled.

"Been through a lot with my horses," said one, a gruff dwarven woman with her hair tied back in a tail that fell far past her shoulders. She carried hand axes on her belt and wore a constant frown that crowned gentle eyes. "I don't want to see them hurt."

Vex patted Trinket's nose. "I know that feeling well. Trinket won't harm your horses. You have my word."

"What constitutes *a lot* in these parts, anyway?" Vax asked.

"Anything from shadow demons to obnoxious travelers," the other dwarf said, by way of explanation. He was half a head taller than his partner, with mocking brown eyes and short-cropped black hair. Once his animals were cared for, he took out a small zither and settled down in front of one of the tents.

Vax trailed him curiously. "Who are those two?" he asked, indicating the men who had either continued their argument or started up a new one.

"Master Simeon, a retired bookbinder from Emon, and Lord Willan, a scholar of history. They've been traveling together for the better part of a year and I don't believe they've stopped fighting since we joined in their service. You haven't heard a bloody argument until you've heard them going off on the proper use of gloves. *Gloves.*"

"You've been with them for a year?"

The musician cackled. "Gods, no. Just from Turst Fields to Jorenn. We guide travelers back and forth on a regular basis, especially if they want to go into the Umbra Hills for shadegrass. There's always some fool who wants to see it, study it, sell it. And every trip allows us to run some mail and supplies back and forth too. At least this way, my love and I make a decent living." He looked in the dwarven woman's direction with a soft smile on his face and began to pluck at the zither, playing a cheerful rendition of a well-known drinking song, that provided a mocking counterpoint to the arguing.

Vax found himself relaxing into the music and the knowledge that they were protected if only for the night. He settled down near the campfire, where one of the scholars was cooking dinner. Vex and Trinket joined them, and his sister toyed with the necklace. With music in the background and the smell of good food wrapping around them, life seemed so much simpler.

Once they'd eaten, one of the scholars retreated to a tent while the other climbed onto the cart.

Vex took out her bow and wax for the bowstring. "So what's Jorenn like?"

The two dwarves shared a look. "Frontier town. Folk as tough as the shadegrass around them. Some right bastards. Some kind folk once you get to know 'em," the musician said. "Don't take it personally if they're not very welcoming, it's life in these hills, gorgeous."

"So what about these hills? Strange magic?" Vex insisted, with a faint blush and a look in Vax's direction. "We heard stories."

"Dead things," he supplied.

The woman nodded in the direction of the town and the hills beyond it. She was using sturdy pieces of leather to braid a bridle of sorts. "By day, Jorenn is like any old town you'd find around these parts. He isn't wrong about life in these hills being harsh and depressing. It's no different from anywhere in the Cliffkeep Mountains. But Jorenn has access to mines, and riches make even the harshest life bearable."

"And by night?" Vax asked. "You said it's a normal town by day. What happens by night? Do the monsters come out?"

She leaned in, indicating to Vax that he should come closer. Both he and Vex scooted forward. The dwarf glanced around, toward the scholar on the cart and the half-elf scout who had gone back to keeping the first watch. She leaned in farther and lowered her voice. "By night, the town is haunted. Undead creatures prowl the streets, and they'll attack anyone who's foolish enough to show themselves after nightfall. They are one with the shadows, invisible to the untrained eye, and those poor bastards who get too close are never even aware of what's coming. They'll think themselves safe and then they'll feel the caress of a finger along their jaw, the softest touch of breath across their neck. A whisper, no way out. And then, *suddenly,* they attack."

Taking his cue from those last words, the musician strummed his zither, and even though he had an inkling it was coming, Vax jumped. Vex startled, and even the bickering pair—who'd leaned in over the course of the tale—straightened. The dwarves laughed.

"No, nothing of the sort. There are ash creatures that come down from the hills," one of them acknowledged. "Cursed dead things. Bandits too, on occasion. We'll be quiet. We're still far enough away from Jorenn that we should be fine."

WHEN VEX CURLED UP NEXT to Trinket, Vax sat down next to the scout—who'd introduced herself as Nera—and stared out over the ashen hills, feeling the push and pull of an unfamiliar landscape in front of him. He wondered how to get out of the trap of branded loyalty and demands, and he worried about what Jorenn would bring them. But he knew he could manage a heist like the one the Clasp demanded, especially with his sister's life at stake. And dead things coming down the hills or not, he was curious about the town in front of him. He longed to see it. He longed to keep exploring with his sister by his side, beyond the camps they set up in the wild, beyond even the cities they visited, because at the end of the day, all those places were fleeting and they only ever passed through. Something inside of him kept tugging him onward.

He glanced sideways at the scout, who also stared into the distance thoughtfully.

Neither of them said a word, until Nera cleared her throat.

"Your sister doesn't like me," she said, by way of observation. She'd rather unsuccessfully tried to make conversation over dinner, but she'd retreated to her lookout immediately after. She kept an eye on their surroundings while mending a tear in her cloak, her slender brown hands graceful and skilled.

Vax felt his defenses rise. "She's cautious. That isn't the same thing. It's nothing personal."

"Neither is my comment. Merely an observation." Nera shrugged. "It's not uncommon, especially in those who come from Syngorn."

Vax breathed out hard, the words landing like a gut punch. Few people connected him to the elven city, and he didn't like to be connected.

Nera put needle and thread aside and smirked. "What, do you think you're the only one who is observant? You may dress like you've been traveling for a while, but you still sound like one who was educated by the bloody Dreamweavers, and you walk like it too." Her voice was scathing. "It's an easy place to learn how to hate yourself."

"Did you grow up there?" Vax asked quietly.

"Gods no, they shipped me off to one of the outposts." She managed a grin at that. "I rebelled by going to live in Kraghammer."

"I like that," he admitted, with a hint of jealousy. "It wasn't an option for us."

Nera drew breath to speak when something distracted her. Clouds filled the skies overhead, obscuring the light from the moons and the brightest stars. The shadows of the clouds danced macabrely across the campfire and the tents, and the hair on Vax's neck stood on edge.

"What's going on?" He got to his feet at the sound of a slight rustling of burnt heather, the tumbling of a few rocks. Then something fell into the campfire and a cloud of sparks swept through the camp. At the same time, something sharp slammed into him, and it sent him flying to the ground.

"Fuck," Nera breathed. "Attack!" She whistled sharply and Vax scrambled to his feet, daggers in hand, before he fully realized what was happening. "We're under attack!"

"Wake up, we're under attack!"

At least half a dozen strange, shambling creatures spread out through the camp, their movements jagged and uncoordinated. In the flickering glow of the campfire, they could be mistaken for travelers, but when they came closer, Vax could see they were in various states of decay, their skin and bones as gray as the hills around them. Dead things. Like the one who'd slammed him to the ground. The creature—the man?—was half a head taller than Vax, with his rib cage exposed and bones sticking out through his skin. His eye sockets were burning like embers, and every inch of his corpse, from his exposed flesh to scraps of what may once have been clothes, was covered in a layer of dust—or soot. Ash, one of the dwarves had said.

The ashen man titled his head slightly, as if considering Vax, before slashing out with clawed fingers.

Vax ducked out of reach and dashed away. He held his daggers at the ready, and he glanced back toward the tents. "Vex!"

She was already up and reaching for her bow. Next to her, a sleep-weary Trinket growled. She looked up at Vax, and their eyes met. She nodded. "Be careful!"

"What's going on?" one of the dwarves called out.

"I don't know, are corpses supposed to move?" Vex shot back, exasperation in her voice.

She stood with her bow in hand, barely awake, as a skeletal figure leaped toward her, claws out, teeth sharp. She sent one arrow flying and it ricocheted off its exposed shoulder blade. Vex immediately reached for the second arrow and tried to back away, to put distance between them. Two other crumbling corpses converged on one of the scholars, who tried to crawl behind Trinket. From behind Vax, Nera was loosing arrows into the fray as well.

"Those fucking ash creatures!" she shouted. "Watch out!"

Vax leaped out of the way of another creature—this one small enough to be a child. Her arms were narrow and thin, but her exposed bony hands were sharpened to talons, and she snarled ferociously. Vax stabbed without hesitation. He caught the creature once in the side and once in an empty eye socket. Both times, when the daggers hit, a cloud of soot and ash emanated from her, like these dead were made from the same dust that covered the hills.

Vax dodged out of the way when the creature retaliated. A second one slammed into him from his side and slashed into him. Pain radiated through his arm and back.

A third attacked him, and drove him deeper toward the pack of the ashen dead. Vax stabbed at the ones coming too close, but every time his daggers connected with bones, soot and dust rose up from the corpses. Ash wrapped around him and tore at his lungs. Vax coughed and fought.

Past the first wave of the dead, others appeared, wandering through the camp. Two were drawn to the horses, while a third was wrestling with Trinket. One of the creatures, its teeth razor-sharp, made its way over to one of the ponies and tore into its flank, feasting while the animal tried desperately to get away.

Vax took a second to find an escape route toward his sister. The cloud of ash and bones threatened to enclose them all, and for every creature they fought and killed, there came another and another.

"Vax! Get down!" An arrow zoomed over Vax's shoulder and drilled itself into one of the wretched creatures looming over him. Vax sprang forward with his daggers, determined to keep going. His first blade tore at the figure's arm muscles, and the other went straight through its gut, covering him in another layer of soot.

Killing one ashen corpse only meant that two others appeared in its place. One of the cursed dead slammed into the side of his head with such ferocity that he saw stars, while the other hit rattled his teeth. He would've sworn he heard rushed footsteps around him and horns in the distance.

A tall figure with patched-up clothes leaped past him, sword out, and into one of the creatures. The light of the campfire reflected on new blades and insignias of a kind.

Then sharp claws raked deep across Vax's back, and ash swirled up to cover him. A chill spread through him. His muscles locked up, his daggers tumbled from his hands, and he fell forward. The last thing he saw before the darkness claimed him was another arrow bringing down the looming corpse in front of him.

CHAPTER 10

"Vax!" Vex couldn't see her brother anymore. She'd seen him dodge out of the way. He'd been in the fray around the campfire seconds ago, but when a group of soldiers came thundering in, she lost track. She reached behind her for the steady presence of Trinket at her back, then scanned the camp for a way to get closer to where she'd last seen her brother. "*Shit.*"

She called Vax's name again, to no response.

Everywhere she looked, she saw those dead things fighting. Three had converged around the dwarves. Two were as tall as the dwarves were, and it looked like they were fighting wretched copies of themselves. Axes tore through bone and sinew, while zither song wrapped itself around the creatures. Cursed dead, they'd called them. The creatures all looked like they had been people once, but no longer, as though the ash that covered ate away at them.

An ashen corpse, taller than the dwarves or anyone in the camp, lurched in Vex's direction, its movements wild and uncoordinated. She brought up her bow, took aim, and shot the tall, lumbering creature in the knee.

But no matter how hard she—or anyone—fought, the corpses slammed through horses and travelers alike. The camp would've been entirely overrun if it weren't for the group of riders that had come barging in, swords at the ready. And now . . . now they weren't alone, at least. Vex counted six riders, slashing their way through the creatures. She thought she saw others too, in more practical gear, but she couldn't be sure.

She sent another arrow into the thick of the fight, where it glanced past the bookbinder to hit an ash creature in the eye. It only stalled the creature for a few heartbeats before it continued to swing wildly with bony arms, its rotting hands dripping with blood.

She still couldn't see Vax anywhere. She called out again before she nudged Trinket. "Come on, Trinket, we've got to find him."

Growling, the bear slammed one of the corpses out of the way, causing a cloud of soot to cover his fur. With an affronted shudder, he shrugged it off. Before he could follow Vex to help, another one of the dead creatures leaped at him. They were everywhere, with sharp claws and sharper teeth. The clouds of dust obscured other figures drawing closer.

Trinket slammed at the shambling cadaver until Vex could hear the sickening crack of bones breaking.

She circled the encampment as best she could, trying to make sure none of the dead could come around her, keeping uneven ground and rocks at her back. Trinket followed to the best of his abilities. On the other side of the camp, Nera, the half-elf scout, did the same, though she clutched at one leg that was badly bleeding. She reached into her tunic and threw some pieces of paper into the campfire, causing sparks to shoot up into the sky.

Soldiers and horses cut their way through the cursed dead, and for a moment Vex thought she saw her brother lying on the ground, his hair spread out around his head and his cloak trampled. Before she could be certain, her line of sight disappeared. A lanky ash creature stumbled her way. It wore sooty tangles of hair like a shroud around its burning eyes, and maybe it had once had another facial expression, but now all that remained was hunger. Behind it, another creature dropped whatever it was eating and focused on Vex too.

She aimed for the first creature, drew her bow, and sent an arrow straight into its hip. The other arrow she aimed at the second creature. Both continued walking unimpeded.

Withdrawing farther, a sharp rock formation at her back, she pulled and shot again, causing one of the ambling corpses to stumble. One of her arrows buried itself deep into its half-protruding spine, while the other skidded harmlessly off a skeletal shoulder.

Her heart rate picked up. She put a new arrow on her string. Before she could aim, something thundered past her. Strong arms wrapped themselves around Vex and pulled her out of the path of the creature and sideways onto the saddle of a chestnut mare. "We're withdrawing to Jorenn," the rider shouted, though her voice was barely audible over the chaos of the fight around them. "We need to get you behind the barriers."

Vex struggled, her heart still in her throat. She tried to push herself into a more comfortable position. "My brother is there!" she called out, pointing in the direction of the camp.

"One of the others will get to him," the rider replied. "We've been sent to evacuate all of you, and it's my duty to get you into town as soon as possible."

The horse's hoofbeats created a discordant rhythm with her own heartbeat, and she tried to slide off, but the rider wouldn't let her. "My bear!"

"Shademaster's orders! I need to get you behind the palisades!"

Vex twisted and fought, and the rider cursed but never budged. The best she could do was raise her head far enough to see an angry bear thundering after the horse, shaking off crumbling corpses left and right. He roared when he saw Vex and kept struggling.

Behind him, other riders picked up travelers. The scholar got scooped up from the horses' trough, where he'd barricaded himself and flung streaks of vibrant blue light toward the creatures. Another rider rushed toward Nera and dismounted to help her into the saddle. They were all gathering travelers as effectively and efficiently as her rider had.

She breathed out hard, overcome by relief and shock, and let herself be carried, still clinging to her bow and the arrow she'd grabbed. It was far from comfortable like this, but it was far better than being murdered by cursed dead.

The horses' hooves thundered across the ground, and the sound of it echoed in her ears. The screams and snarls of battle, the pounding of blades on undead flesh and bone, disappeared in the distance.

After a couple of miles, the rider slowed the horse to a trot and helped Vex sit up more comfortably. When Vex could finally see her well, she viewed a scarred human face with crow's-feet around her eyes and a determined grimace underneath a battered mail coif. Before Vex could even ask or say anything, she shook her head. "I'm sorry, we keep going until we're inside. The Shademaster kept the gates open and the whole town is exposed."

"What the fuck *are* those things?" Vex managed. She reached out to

Trinket, who'd caught up with her and threw an affronted look at the horse for carrying her off without warning.

"Ash walkers," the rider answered. "Bloody bane of our existence."

She nudged the horse forward once more, and the animal shuddered but picked up the pace. Trinket ran too. Other riders did the same thing: they helped their quarries to sit comfortably before making their way toward the town that appeared on the horizon. One of the riders held two empty ponies by a rein, though the poor animals looked half frightened to death and exhausted. She tried to spot Vax.

But they kept going before she could get a good look around. They all did, until Jorenn Village rose out of the hills in front of them. The town was walled on all sides, wooden palisades strengthening its natural defenses, and large torches on either side of a set of open gates lit up the path. A dozen archers covered the entrance, their bows at the ready to give the riders cover or to protect themselves, while another group of archers patrolled the makeshift battlements.

When the riders approached, the archers jumped aside. Vex and her guard were the first to storm through, past the gates and down a wide unpaved street that led them to a large square in the middle of town. Trinket followed at a short distance, undeterred by the strange looks from the guards around them.

Inside its walls, Jorenn Village looked like a small town in chaos, but it was a structured chaos. Teen messengers ran around from the palisades to the streets to the large town hall adjacent to the square, stopping only to jump out of the way of the horses. A dozen or so people busied themselves with boarding up doors and windows of predominantly wooden buildings, while others collected weapons from their houses and from guards in the same uniform as the riders. A healer busied himself with herbs and bandages near the entrance to the hall.

Other than the stars in the sky and the cold night air that crept through the streets, Jorenn looked and acted like it was the middle of the day, and the lanterns that were set up on every street corner bathed the town in a deep orange glow.

"Does this type of thing happen often?" Vex asked. "Everyone seems to know exactly what they're doing."

"None of this is new to the people here. It isn't a matter of *if* those cursed creatures will attack, but *when*." The rider patted her horse's neck and slowed the animal down. She sounded winded too. "But they know what to do, and they also know Shademaster Derowen will protect them."

"She's the leader of the guard?" Vex guessed. "Your guard?"

"Leader of the Shadewatch. She's the one who gave the order to take in all travelers caught amidst the ash." She pushed her mail coif back, and a mane of curled gray hair appeared. "She's a hero to most here."

Other riders thundered through the gates and a cry went up around the town. "Close the gate! Raise the barrier!" And just like that, everyone's positions shifted again. Messengers ran toward the palisades. The townspeople who'd armed themselves managed tight smiles. The wooden gates were closed with a dull thud that echoed through the dusty streets, and Vex thought she felt a sigh of relief around them, in the knowledge that while the danger hadn't passed, at least there was another obstacle between them and the dead.

Vex glanced around to see if she saw her brother yet, but the riders were still making their way toward the square.

The one who'd helped her ran a hand across her forehead, wiping away beads of sweat, and the rush of the fight visibly made way for exhaustion. She rattled off everything Vex needed to know. "Come, there are rooms set up for you in The Scattered Bar. You'll be safe here, and in the morning one of the Shademaster's people will help you find your way in town. If you left belongings behind, we may be able to retrieve those. If you need assistance, the Shademaster can help too."

"Thank you. I don't know what we would've done without you." It wasn't false flattery. Vex was certain the night would've looked far different without the help of the Shadewatch.

With the rider's aid, she slid unceremoniously down the chestnut horse and onto the stamped ground. Her legs trembled, and she fought to keep her balance when Trinket rushed over to her and nudged her with his head, sniffing her to make sure she was all right and pushing his nose into her face. She clung to him and tried to brush the layer of ash from his fur. "I'm okay, buddy."

He growled softly, and she scratched his ear. "Yeah, I know. I don't like those nasty things either."

Leaning on her bear, Vex tracked the riders coming in. All around them on the square, horses came to a halt and the Shadewatch helped the travelers dismount. The healer immediately made his way toward the half-elf scout when she slumped on the ground, and one of the messengers dashed forward to help support her. Together they brought her toward the town hall, a proud three-story building that held somewhere between a castle and a large mansion, its stone walls a warm burnt orange, with tall heavy wooden doors and guarded windows.

The scholar slid down his horse and immediately vomited. The bookbinder made his way toward his nemesis, checked to see if he was unhurt, and within moments they were bickering again.

Vex turned around. The dwarves had made their way toward the three ponies the Shadewatch rescued and were frantically examining the animals for wounds or exhaustion before tending to their own injuries. They were both covered in soot and sweat and blood.

A teenage boy with sleep-tousled hair who wore an apron tied around his waist ushered the travelers toward the designated tavern at the far side of the town square. Half a dozen guards converged at the edge of the square to brush off their clothes and weapons. One by one, they began leading their horses away, presumably to a stable of sorts.

Vex's stomach dropped. They were the guards who'd aided their camp. The guards who aided their camp were all accounted for. The other travelers were all accounted for too, and Vax wasn't here.

No, no, no, shit.

She spotted the rider who'd brought her here, who was leading her exhausted horse to a stable, and grabbed her arm. "Wait! Where's Vax?"

The rider turned toward her and fatigue flashed across her face. She brushed Vex's hand off and frowned. "What do you mean?"

Vax was nowhere to be seen on the square, and none of the guards were left behind. She counted them again to make sure.

"Where the fuck is my brother?" Vex demanded, an edge of panic to her voice. She could do nothing to stop it.

The rider stilled. "We brought in everyone, I'm certain of it." Her eyes darted across the square too, counting like Vex had.

"Like fuck you did. Vax is still out there!"

"We brought in everyone . . ." The rider's nostrils flared and she visibly swallowed what she wanted to say. "We brought in everyone we could find."

There were other words there. Vex knew it. But she refused to accept what the alternative options might be.

"Then we have to go back to find him!" Vex snapped. Her throat constricted. She felt sick. "I can't leave him there!"

The rider shook her head. "I'm sorry, Shademaster's orders. The gates are closed and barred, and she's working on putting the barrier up. No one is to leave until tomorrow."

With a determination verging on desperation, Vex reached for the rider's horse. "I'll find him myself if I have to!" He was outside somewhere, surrounded by those ashen dead, without help. Without her. She couldn't even think about it. She couldn't let him be. She needed to get to him.

The rider clamped her hand around Vex's wrist, not hard enough to hurt but immovable regardless. "Not an option. Jorenn is responsible for your safety now, and while you're here, you're responsible for ours. We've risked our lives for you once. *No one* leaves until the barrier is lifted." She softened. "You'll be able to rest in the inn, and we'll ride out first thing. You have my word."

Vex shook her off. "No one is responsible for me. I can take care of myself. I need my brother."

Trinket walked up next to her, sensing her agitation and presumably missing Vax too. He growled softly at the rider, his mouth drawn into a snarl, as if daring the rider to touch his Vex again.

Other guards stopped what they were doing and walked their way. The travelers who were shepherded off toward the inn stilled and looked back and forth between Vex and the rider.

"Make no mistake, we could've easily left you to the mercy of the ash walkers." The rider casually folded her hand over the pommel of her sword. "You don't want to be causing trouble here."

Vex swallowed hard, bile rising up in her throat.

Gods. How often had she and her brother heard those words before? Always with the same dismissive attitude. Other things mattered more than they did. Names. Prejudices. Other people's safety over theirs. They'd always existed at the unwanted edges of other people's worlds, and for once, Vex wished she could be at the center.

She *did* want to cause trouble. She wanted to get to her brother. She felt her panic curl into something hard and untouchable, and she drew herself up like she'd seen her father draw himself up countless times. Shrouded in importance and invulnerability. Someone who couldn't be hurt by what happened around her. "I *demand* a way out of here. And if you can't fucking help me, then find me someone who can. Bring me to the Shademaster if you must."

The rider considered her, and that small, treacherous part of Vex whispered she'd sounded ridiculous. She couldn't pull off those demands any more than she could find her own way out of this town. But Trinket stepped closer and nudged his head under her hand, so she could stare down the rider with a bear at her side. She crawled her fingers into his fur. No one would want to get into an argument with a bear.

Eventually, the rider turned to two of the other guards, who'd lingered nearby, hands on their weapons. Exhaustion colored her voice when she said, "Take her up to Shademaster Derowen. She can decide what to do with her." She turned away while the two guards stepped in and stalked off without another look at Vex, though she muttered something that sounded suspiciously like an invitation to climb over the palisades if she didn't like what was happening here.

She would too, if she had to.

Once the rider continued on toward the stables and the matter seemed resolved, everyone else on the square continued their work, though the other travelers cast curious glances in Vex's direction. Nera frowned deeply.

Vex felt a kernel of worry at the idea of making her case to the leader of town—her track record in those situations was less than stellar—but she balled her trembling hands into fists and kept her thoughts on her brother. She needed to get to him. Now.

The two guards escorted her in uncomfortable silence, while Trinket stayed by her side. They walked the broad street with boarded-up shops on either side, back toward the gates, which were shut and guarded by the Shadewatch. Shouts were echoing back and forth on the palisades, presenting the same structured chaos Vex had seen when she'd entered the town. Archers shot arrows at targets Vex couldn't see.

On top of the palisades, right at the highest point over the wooden gatehouse, stood a slender human woman, her bushy brown hair tied back with a leather band and a tall sword at her side, intensely focused on a distant horizon. She held her left hand in front of her and the air around her hand shimmered where she was casting a spell and raising the barrier that kept the town safe.

She didn't react when Vex and the guards climbed the makeshift parapet, but she tensed and shuddered under the weight of the barrier. The woman shifted slightly and in the pale moonlight Vex saw exactly what was at the center of the still-expanding barrier.

A ring. An intricate silver band with dark cloudy gems and shards of bone.

CHAPTER 11

A tall figure, a half-giant of a man, with broad shoulders and dark eyes, approached them from a covered guard post at the very edge of the parapet. He looked down on the two guards next to Vex, set his warhammer by his side, and folded his broad arms. He had bands of ink crossing his gray skin, peeking out from under his mail shirt, and extending toward both his hands and his face. He wore a leather band around his neck that held a silver pendant with the profile of a dragon etched on it. Unlike most other half-giants she'd seen on her travels, he had short-cropped black hair. "What's this? What do you want?"

"My brother," Vex said. She fought to keep shock and fear from bleeding into her voice. She pushed through her terror. She'd deal with the bloody ring later. "My brother is still out there."

"She's mindful of seeing the Shademaster, Wick," one of the guards said. "Says we missed someone when we brought in the travelers."

Wick shook his head. "You won't be able to get to the Shademaster until the barrier is set."

"I have to get out of here," she said.

She tried to step around him. He shifted and blocked her path.

"You won't be able to, I'm sorry." He turned to the two guards. "Get back to your posts."

Vex took stock of the situation on the palisades. The energy around the battlements was tense, with guards peering out into the night for fear of an attack. Shadows rolled across plains surrounding the town, and the wind rustled around them, blowing clouds of dust and ash down from the hills. It seemed to Vex as though every one of such clouds could hide another group of ash walkers, and the guards certainly reacted that way.

Vex peered at the road that stretched out from the town to see if she saw anything—or anyone—move. The urge to climb over the palisades was dangerously appealing, but the shimmer in the air restrained her. She wasn't sure if she could break the barrier Shademaster Derowen was throwing up—or if she could get past this giant of a man, Wick, who was frowning down at her. He seemed unmovable.

A cry went up on the southeastern corner of the palisades when the clouds overhead shifted and a dozen or so ash walkers became visible in the sudden moonlight.

Nearer to Vex, a young archer sent a useless arrow flying into the night when a bat crested over the palisades and startled him. Despite the tension, the archers around the shooter laughed and ribbed him. As soon as the corpses drew closer to the palisades, they all shifted their focus to the fight once more.

Vex saw the cursed dead down below, and the image of Vax lying facedown on the ground flashed before her eyes. She needed to get out of here, but it looked like the ash walker attacks wouldn't let up.

She reached for her bow, and Wick stopped her again. "No weapons around the Shademaster," he said simply.

"I can't just stand here. I have to do something. So let me help," she hissed, her voice rough with a potent mix of helplessness and determination.

Wick shrugged. He towered over her with head and shoulders, but his smile was kind. "You can help by not distracting her."

"I'm not about to *shoot* her," she insisted.

"Good. I would hate to have to fight you when we just got you to safety," he said reasonably. "The Shademaster is peculiar about her guards when she's creating the barrier, and with all due respect, you're a stranger."

"Fuck, I don't know if you missed it, but my brother is *still out there,*" Vex snapped, raising her voice against this rock of a man who made even Trinket look small. "I want to kill those bastards so I can go out and find him."

Wick raised his finger to his lips, before his shoulders sagged in resignation when a small voice from near the guard post piped up, "Kill those bastards?" A yawn, and then, "Wick? Wa's going on?"

Wick raised his eyebrows at Vex, then turned around to a tiny girl who was curled up inside the guard post, underneath a pile of blankets. She had the same bushy brown hair as Derowen, and it tumbled down around her, framing a round face with large, emerald eyes and a determined expression. Two pointed ears peeked out from under her hair. She held a wooden sword clutched in one hand, cradling it like a doll, and with her other she rubbed at her face. "Are the ash walkers gone?"

Wick walked over and knelt down next to the girl, fluffing up the blankets around her against the chilled night air, and smoothing down her hair with one massive hand. "You shouldn't be awake, little mite. Best bring you home if you are."

The girl glared, though the effect of it was slightly undercut by another yawn. "You promised I could stay here."

"And you promised to hide under the blankets and sleep, didn't you?" He slightly turned to Vex, who was openly staring at the half-giant and the little half-elf girl. "She gets night terrors, and her mother wants to keep her close."

The words were spoken with a gentleness that cut straight through Vex. She'd felt the ground shift beneath her feet at his easy, unguarded affection. She winced, but she nodded.

The little girl followed Wick's line of sight, and she stared at Vex with sleepy resolve. "Why is your brother still out there?" she asked before her mouth dropped open and she pushed a number of the blankets away. "Is that a *bear*?"

Wick immediately piled the blankets on top of her again. "Aswin, you know what we agreed on . . ."

Aswin discarded blankets at the same rate that Wick added them, as if there weren't a siege of shambling dead going on mere yards away, and Vex tried valiantly to gather her thoughts. She could shout at Wick without an inch of regret, but this little girl shouldn't be here. What were they doing keeping her so close to danger?

She cleared her throat, and both Wick and Aswin stopped what they were doing. "Yes, it's a bear. My name is Vex. His name is Trinket and he's my best friend." When she said it, she expected a counter from Vax—something like he thought *he* was her best friend—and her breath caught. She swallowed and continued, with half a glance toward Wick, "He'll come say hi, if you want, but you should really try to sleep."

Wick didn't look thrilled at the prospect, but Aswin nodded enthusiastically, though with a hint of trepidation, and she let Wick pile more blankets on top of the first. She reached out a small hand to Trinket and when the bear ambled forward and sniffed it, she giggled loudly, while a way down the palisades another cry went up.

"Trinket?" Vex said softly. Trinket looked back at her. "Protect her, all right? She needs to sleep."

Wick got to his feet, and Trinket dutifully lay down next to Aswin, who immediately reached out to him and patted his nose.

Vex grabbed her bow again, and she raised her chin when Wick stepped closer. "The Shademaster wants her daughter close, and it looks like you care about that little girl." The words hurt to speak. "I want my brother close. Do not stop me from fighting for the people I care about."

"There's no way for you to get out of town tonight," Wick said. "You know that, right?"

She did know that, because every single person she'd talked to had told her as much. She still refused to believe it. "Then let me at least make myself useful." She needed something to do, she needed to be busy, or else she would lose her mind with worry.

Wick's frown was conflicted. He seemed at war within himself, but eventually he nodded. "Fine. Do what you must, but stay away from the Shademaster. The sooner we fight off these ash walkers, and the sooner I can get Aswin back to her home, the better."

She didn't need another word. She gestured at Trinket to stay with the little girl and ran to where the latest cry had come from, about forty or so yards to the west from the gatehouse. Archers were firing arrows that crested over the battlements and rained upon the ash walkers below. Some of the corpses were hit often enough that it looked like they exploded into clouds of ash, while others flung themselves against the wooden poles, arms outstretched at impossible angles while they tried to crawl their way up, gray flakes and bone dust billowing high like the wind was pushing them higher. One of the creatures pulled itself up, and underneath the layer of soot she saw gaping holes in its arms, where the bones moved and shifted around. Up on the palisades, a guardswoman used a spear to try to fend the dead creature off.

Running, Vex grabbed two arrows from her quiver. She held one between her teeth while she pulled the other one back, aimed, and released. The arrow flew straight through the ash walker, passing through its chest and out on the other side, a trail of gray dust following its path. She sent the second arrow after the first without hesitation.

The archers around her acknowledged her presence only insofar as they stepped aside to give Vex her own space near the battlements. She nodded at them and found a good location, shooting at will as the others did. She let her arrows fly and hoped they'd take away her pain and her worry and the sudden unbearable loneliness.

The walkers were an easy target when they were visible, but in the shadows of the night they were almost impossible to track. The ash provided a layer of protection, concealing them. They fought and withdrew, there and gone again, until another cry went up, and they continued to try to crawl their way up the palisades like spiders, arms and legs akimbo.

If Vex could find her way down to the outside of the palisades now, she knew she would be overpowered before she could draw her bow. So she kept her position up on high, sending arrows toward the creatures until her arms trembled and her quiver was feeling light and the gnawing worry inside her hadn't abated a single bit.

One of the teens who ran messages back and forth between the town and the palisades appeared with a waterskin at her side, and a fresh batch of arrows. She drank deeply and gratefully before returning to shooting.

The night sky brightened around her, like a distant flash of thunder or the sudden flickering of a lamp, and Vex blinked hard, trying to find the source, when one of the archers next to her—a tall human gentleman with a long coat that flapped in the wind, tightly curled brown hair, and sharp eyes—placed a hand on her arm. "Barrier's up," he croaked, nodding in the direction of the Shademaster. "They won't come through now."

The air around the palisades rippled. Vex stared at it. The barrier looked strong enough to keep the ash walkers out. It looked strong enough to keep her in, too.

The creatures that flung themselves at the palisades below stopped trying, caught, it seemed, between the instinct to come closer and the force that stopped them. In their indecision, the ash walkers that remained behind were easily outnumbered, with the archers on the walls picking them off one by one. Finally, the last of them retreated, and a sigh of relief rolled over the palisades.

Vex turned in the direction of the parapet, where Shademaster Derowen lowered her arm and stumbled backward. Wick immediately stepped in to support her, and a few steps behind him Aswin clambered to her feet, tossing blankets left and right, half-stumbling over Trinket, and she shot toward her mother like an arrow of joy. She flung her arms around her and refused to let go.

Vex lowered her bow and placed the arrow back in the all-but-empty quiver at her hip. The exhaustion of the whole cursed night caught up with her, and Aswin's presence rattled her. "I can't believe she brings her daughter here."

The archer shook his head, and something unreadable flashed across his face. "She thinks it's safe, and they wouldn't want to be separated, especially when the ash monsters attack. Town's been breached too many times. But that little girl is a bright spot in this shitty place. Her presence makes everyone fight harder."

Vex tugged at the fletching of the arrow and the feather snapped off the shaft. "So what's the barrier?" she asked. "Does it have something to do with her ring?"

"You noticed that, did you?" The man leaned his well-crafted long-bow against the palisades. He flagged down one of the messengers with waterskins, swirled his mouth with water, and spat it out across the wall. "Helps her keep the ash walkers out and the town safe." He dumped the remaining water over his head. "Stick around here long enough and you'll learn Shademaster Derowen is a hero to all."

Vex shook her head when the man picked up his bow and, whistling a jaunty tune, started making his way down. Yeah, she already knew that. The Shademaster was a hero, and her brother had been hired to steal an heirloom. It just so happened to be the one that kept an entire town safe.

A simple heist? This was already anything but simple. Someone at the Clasp must've been aware of the importance of the ring. If that was the case, why would they want to steal it? What would they gain from denying a town the protection it so clearly needed?

She looked over her shoulder to ask Vax before she realized she couldn't, and she breathed in hard through her teeth when the sight of the empty palisades hit her like one of her own arrows.

At the parapet, Shademaster Derowen hoisted Aswin up on her hip, despite the exhaustion carved on her face, and she exchanged a few words with Wick—and a curiously quirked eyebrow in Trinket's direction—before she made her way in Vex's direction.

Vex kept her shoulders straight, and her broken heartbeat picked up. Something inside her clenched at the approach of the Shademaster who, with her daughter held tightly in her arms, stopped near every archer to inquire about any injuries and thank them for their bravery. If she could just give Vex a way out . . .

When at last she stood in front of Vex, Shademaster Derowen's warm blue-flecked eyes were sympathetic. "Wick tells me you're looking for your brother. I regret that I can't be of aid to you. I have a brother too, and I hope you'll believe me when I tell you I understand your distress. If you'll permit me and in gratitude for your help here tonight—" She tucked Aswin's hair behind her ear in an unconsciously protective gesture. "—let me offer you lodging for the night at the Shade Hall, and tomorrow the Shadewatch and I will ride out with you. If he's wounded or hiding somewhere, we will find him."

"Trinket can stay too," Aswin piped up, peeking out over her mother's shoulder to look at the bear, before she unleashed the full, devastating effect of her emerald eyes on Vex. "*Please,* Vex?"

Vex grew cold. She looked from Aswin to Derowen and back. She glanced at the ring. She needed to find a way out, but she knew it was a fool's hope with those ash walkers still outside. Riding out with the Shademaster first thing in the morning was the best possible course of action right now. The *only* course of action.

All she had to do was stay here for another couple of hours, until the sun rose and they could find their way back to the encampment. But a couple of hours might as well be a lifetime. Every time she closed her eyes she saw Vax lying on the ground, hair splayed out around him, surrounded by the risen dead. Every time she closed her eyes, a different disastrous scenario played out. It made her want to scream.

She needed to find a way out and fuck the consequences.

"Please," Shademaster Derowen repeated. "We'll do what we can do to help you."

At that, Aswin slid out of her mother's arms and bounded over to Vex, grabbing her hand. "The Shadewatch can find your brother. They always find me when I'm hiding."

So Vex did the only thing she could. She nodded. She and Trinket would stay with Shademaster Derowen and Aswin tonight. Without her brother. Without steady ground underneath her feet. With the leader of Jorenn and her half-elven daughter, beloved by everyone.

CHAPTER 12

Nine years ago

The guardswoman had deep-crimson hair that was braided on one side and shaved on the other. She moved with a gracefulness that Vex envied, and she shot with an accuracy that Vex envied even more. She walked around Vex and kicked her feet wider apart. "Ground yourself well. This bow is heavier than the ones you've been using so far, and you need to be able to pull your weight."

The twins had graduated from one tutor to three, to teach them history and languages and mathematics. Iova had been brought in to help them with combat training and specifically with archery. While she seemed hesitant at what to be able to expect from the half-elves, she treated them with a no-nonsense approach that Vex appreciated. It was far easier to handle than the sharp comments of elves who set about reminding them it was their own fault that they were treated as such, because they could never do as well as pure elves, never be as gifted, never be as worthy. To them, half-elves were a stain on the history of Syngorn. To Iova, they were merely inferior in the same way all non-elves were.

Vex breathed out hard. She loosened her shoulders, relaxed her grip around the bow, and brought it up to sight. Breathing in, she pulled the string back to anchor it, and she made sure her elbows were turned just right. Iova had no qualms at letting her bruise herself until she learned, and she saw the disapproving glances of Syldor every time he noticed one of those bruises. And unlike with all the other elves, she couldn't shield herself from his shame. No matter how high she raised her defenses, his disappointment cut straight through.

She could only try to be better. Perhaps if she mastered the longbow . . .

She focused on the target, leaned into her stance, and let the string slip through her fingers, the bow tipping forward in her hand as the arrow sped away. A heartbeat later the arrow buried itself in the target an inch off the side from the tiny red dot that formed its center.

Iova sniffed. "A smaller bow will do."

"No!" Vex's hand snatched another arrow from the quiver and nocked it. "I can do this."

In the year and a half since they'd arrived here, stubborn determination had become how Vex approached all her lessons. The only way her father couldn't find reason to be disappointed was if she proved to him she was as good a student as any of the full-blooded elf children, to learn what they needed to know, to speak Elvish as fluently as anyone raised here. The only way she could force the rest of the city into accepting her and her brother was by showing them they could weather whatever they were dealt. At the very least she knew not giving up meant she didn't have to take their cutting words to heart. Or she could try not to. She very rarely succeeded at that.

Iova looked from the girl to the target and back, before she nodded. "You may try."

So she did. She settled into her stance, brought up her bow, and sent three arrows flying at the target in rapid succession. Only one hit the little red dot, so she did it again. And again. Until she could reliably hit the target with at least one out of every three arrows. Until her arms shook, her hands cramped, and the bow that was nearly her own size trembled in her grasp.

She knew—and Iova knew—that from here on she would continue until she could hit the mark with two out of three arrows, and then until she could hit it with every single one of them. Until she could graduate to other arrows or another bow or a more distant target.

Unlike with all her other lessons, with archery Vex wasn't just aiming for perfection in the hope that that'd be good enough. When she held a bow, it felt like an extension of her arm, a part of her. When she held a bow, it felt like she could take on the world without letting it bend or break her.

Iova reluctantly called it her elven heritage and Vax had scoffed when she'd mentioned that. "This isn't theirs. It's yours. Let no one take that away from you."

He was on the other side of the courtyard now, practicing his blade-work with a teacher of his own. He'd grown taller and lankier, with harder edges than he used to have. An older elf by the name of Tharen-dril, who had told them on several occasions that he only humored Syl-dor's foolish decision to educate them because he owed the ambassador a favor, guided him through his exercises with clear distaste. Of course that level of aversion meant these were the only lessons that Vax paid any attention to, because he'd become nothing if not contrary over the past year and a half. And much like his sister, when it came to blades, he'd found some sort of aptitude of his own. It clearly disturbed Master Thar-endril, but since the man was there because he owed the ambassador a favor, he could not simply walk out. And to his credit, he offered the lessons to the best of his abilities.

Vex pulled the last set of arrows from the target, her hands aching, and walked back to Iova. The guardswoman would expect her to care for the bow and wax limbs and string before she could return to her other duties. She'd also let slip two weeks ago that she felt it was time for the twins to join the other elven children in school, because there was only so much their tutors could teach them.

"If the ambassador wants you properly educated, you should be free to live among those your age," she'd said. "Education isn't merely dry facts but the understanding of where they come from and how to put your knowledge to use. For yourself and those around you."

She'd almost made it sound like a weapon, and when Vex com-mented on that, Iova had shrugged. "Perhaps. It's another tool for sur-vival where you're met with hostility."

Vex handed the arrows back to Iova and bit her lip, not entirely cer-tain how to broach that subject now, when the gate to the courtyard opened and Syldor walked out, followed by another elven woman. She had long cinnamon-brown hair and intelligent eyes. While the robes she wore were not half as decorated as Syldor's, she commanded respect naturally. Both Iova and Tharendril stopped what they were doing and bowed, while two additional guards took up post near the doorway.

"High Warden."

Vex and Vax glanced at each other, uncertain. In familiarizing them-selves with the history of the city, they'd learned of High Warden Tyrelda, the monarch of Syngorn, ruling the city alongside three other Wardens. She was spoken of as a figure of legends; Tyrelda of the bloodline of Yenlara, who founded the city. She was larger than life. The person who, if their father was to be believed, had personally given leave for the twins to stay within the city.

Neither of them had ever expected to meet her, and as she carefully observed them, Vex clasped her hands behind her back and stared at her own shoes, not knowing what else to do. From the corner of her eye, she could see Vax square his scrawny shoulders and stare back at Tyrelda.

"So these are your children." The High Warden spoke with a warm, measured voice. "If I'm not mistaken, they have been with you for well over a year, and yet they have barely been seen in the city."

Vex peeked through her lashes at Syldor, who shifted uncomfortably. "I wished to give them time to adjust to life in Syngorn. They've had a humble upbringing and very little education to speak of. You know, per-haps better than any, the standards to which we hold our young ones."

"What our dear father means is that he is ashamed of us," Vax sup-plied, loud enough for all in the courtyard to hear.

"*Vax'ildan.*" Syldor's voice snapped like a whip. "Don't go causing trouble."

Vax didn't flinch. "Is it not the truth, Father? Is that not what you told us when we arrived here?"

"Is it?" High Warden Tyrelda inquired casually. "Is that why you've kept them away from other elves their age?"

If Syldor seemed chagrined by the turn of the conversation, he hid his displeasure behind a courtier's smile. "It seemed prudent to give them the opportunity to raise their knowledge and skills to a higher level before—" He looked at the two of them and something altogether too much like sadness or grief flitted across his face. "—unleashing them on our young ones and their teachers."

"Well then." The High Warden folded her hands. "Let's see if they have reached the appropriate level of skill. You, girl, take up that bow and show us what you've learned. Let's see if you stand a chance to fit in, as Syldor so adamantly claims."

The focus suddenly on her, Vex balled her hands to fists and tendrils of tension crawled across her shoulders. She allowed herself one pleading look in Iova's direction, but the guard stared straight ahead. "I can try, but—"

"The High Warden does not want you to *try*, daughter. Show us your progress."

With no chance to explain how sore her arms were, or how this was only her first day using the taller longbow, Vex breathed in deeply and retrieved her bow and her set of arrows again. She found her position in the archery lane and tried to find the necessary calm inside her. The stillness that told her she knew what she was doing, that she could master this bow like she had the others. But the weapon didn't feel like an extension of herself. The limbs felt awkward, the string too sharp.

She went through the motions. Feet shoulder wide. Back straight. Feel the air to adjust for any side winds. Sight. Draw. Lock. Release.

The first arrow buried itself in the target. Then the second, and finally the third. All three of them at least a hand width away from the red dot, while one arrow just barely found purchase in the outer edge of the target. It was without question the worst she'd shot in weeks, possibly even months.

The High Warden tilted her head. "I can see why you believe these children are in need of more education, Syldor. I hope the girl's marksmanship isn't an indicator of her other pursuits."

Syldor colored faintly and his nostrils snared. He sneered at Vex. "You call that progress? What a pathetic attempt."

Vex clung to the bow, because she had nowhere to place it, but she wrapped her other arm around her waist. Under her father's dark glare, she felt meaningless, and she wished she could disappear. It would be better than to be here. Anywhere would be better than here.

"Do you believe they will be able to do better?" High Warden Tyrelda asked. "With their heritage . . . Maybe we are demanding too much of them."

Every word they spoke hurt, like they took the fragile, tender parts of her and broke them, one at a time. Her pride in her archery. Her inquisitiveness. Her sense of home.

"It's why I suggest we give them time. Their tutors hold out hope that there is some progress to be made, though perhaps it is a fool's hope. Still, their education here will be easier than amidst the city's young ones, where they will doubtless be outmatched."

Vex had wished for others around her, not half an hour ago, but it was clear now she'd be wrong to want for it. She shook her head. She wouldn't be able to live up to the expectations.

"*No.*" Vax threw his daggers into the stamped ground in front of him and stood in front of his sister, shielding her from the adults. He had half an inch on her, and endless indignation at the people in front of her. "Can't you see she's trying?" he demanded. "She's exhausted herself practicing all afternoon to be as good as you want her to be. Stop treating her like a failure."

The High Warden's eyebrows rose a fraction, but that was the only indication she'd heard Vax's words at all. Instead she'd turned to Syldor, whose pale visage showed his frustration quite clearly. "They do seem to have a certain level of spirit. Perhaps we're looking at it from the wrong perspective. Instead of settling, the challenge might be good for them. Who knows how far they may come. How useful it may be." Her tone left little to the imagination: whatever the ambassador's strategy was, in her eyes it wasn't working. "You will send them to be educated with the other children, Syldor. It's time to stop hiding them away."

"Why do we stay here?" Vex sat cross-legged on the bed, leafing through one of her history books without seeing anything.

Vax flinched at the quiet despair in his sister's voice. They'd asked themselves that question a hundred times. Every time their father scorned them. Every time they failed at one of their tutors' tasks. Every time someone looked at them like they didn't belong, it was harder to believe that they ever could. And the arguments they made—*it'll be good for us, it's a chance for a better life*—became fainter by the day.

The terrifying truth was: so did the alternative. Byroden was a year away and more. It was becoming a whisper in the back of their mind. A soft reminder of smells and sounds and vaguely realized notions. It was the feeling of lying in bed at night with their eyes closed and imagining the outlines of another bedroom around them—one far smaller and cozier, where the floorboards groaned and the shutters creaked and the bedding might be rougher but it was warmer—and not quite remembering the exact details. When he closed his eyes, Vax knew their room had doubled as a seamstress's atelier, which meant that the walls were covered in clothes to be mended and cloth to be cut. At the same time, it terrified him that he couldn't remember the last dress his mother worked on. He didn't know if it had been blue or green, if it had been a job to mend or make. He only knew he should've paid more attention to it.

Home wasn't just a year away, but a thousand miles away, and with every passing day that distance grew.

He placed the knife he was toying with on the windowsill in front of him and slid to the floor. In two steps, he'd crossed the room and climbed on top of the bed behind his sister.

"Well, for one the food is better." He pulled at the leather band that held Vex's braid in place and began to undo it. "And we don't have Padric to grump and shout at us."

She laughed shakily at that. "I would prefer that right now, to be honest."

Vax combed his fingers through her hair, carefully maneuvering around the knots and snags, and bit by bit her shoulders released their tension.

"Once we're off to school, we'll be able to make friends. We can explore the city. We won't just be locked up here," he suggested. He longed to see more of the city and its winding streets and unfamiliar sights. They'd only left the grounds twice, both times in the strict company of their father, and both times had left him with a curiosity so deep it ached. He didn't care for the books their tutors gave them, but he did care for the shadowed alleyways, the exquisitely carved arched passageways, the dancing lights in the trees. He wanted to know and taste the parts of the city that never made it into a history book.

"They'll scorn us like everyone else does."

He reached for a particularly stubborn knot and tried to untangle it. "They can't all be that stubborn and prejudiced," he said, not entirely sure he believed the words himself. "And if so, we'll find others who know better. The other half-elves. The other *visitors* here."

He couldn't control the bite—or the hurt—in his words, and Vex turned to him, her hair slipping from his grasp. She took his hands and squeezed hard. "I don't ever want to feel like I did today again," she said, her words steely and a guardedness in her expression that he'd never seen before.

He squeezed back. "Don't. You don't have to care what they think. You don't ever have to feel that way. We're better than the whole lot of them, Stubby."

She relaxed into that assurance, before her eyes snapped up to his. "*Stubby?*"

He pulled himself up to his full height. "I'm taller than you too, not just older and wiser."

She reached out and punched his shoulder, but she was smiling. Vax guided her in front of him again, so he could go back to combing and braiding her hair like their mother used to. And in the quiet between them, he vowed he wouldn't ever let this city change them.

CHAPTER 13

Everything hurt. Vax felt like he'd been trampled by a horde of stone giants, and the very act of breathing was a struggle. He lay on soft blankets, with something hard underneath, and his back felt like it was on fire. The pillow beneath his head felt lumpy. He coughed, and someone pressed something cold against his forehead. "Good morning, sunshine."

Vax tried to open his eyes, which was harder than he remembered. "Vex?"

"Don't fight it. You needed a fair bit of healing to get you back on your feet."

The voice was unfamiliar. The lilt to the words not like any he'd heard before. Not his sister.

The damp cloth dabbed at his cheeks and his throat, and soft hands pushed a strand of hair out of his face. "Come on now, try to open your eyes. You were so close."

He blinked again. The room around him swam into vision. No, a stone chamber. Rough-hewn stone walls, illuminated by lanterns every couple of feet. Slightly damp air around him, and the smell of dirt. He turned his head and moaned. "Fuck."

"That's what you get for tangling with ash walkers." Amusement made the voice sparkle, and Vax tried to locate where it came from. "You were bleeding out when we found you. That last one nearly tore through you."

The hand with a damp cloth appeared again, and this time, Vax could trace the rest of the speaker, from the long, slender fingers, to the patched-up sleeves of a tunic, to the gentle eyes and the wavy black hair that fell over pointed ears. The half-elf in front of him had rough scars on one side of his face, like multiple claw marks across his brown skin. He looked as young and as world-weary as Vax, in his mid-twenties at most. But his hands were steady, as were his kind ministrations.

"You have to thank Emryn for the fact that you're here with us at all," the half-elf said. "He's the one who saw you fall when they attacked. You looked like you were about to be devoured by the ash yourself, you were such a mess. Emryn got himself nearly torn to pieces as a result. Sencha, our healer, patched you both up as best she could. She may have left you with a few new scars, but you'll wear them well."

"Thanks," Vax croaked, his throat dry and his voice unsteady. The half-elf placed the cloth to the side and helped Vax sit up so he could take a sip of water from a waterskin. His hands were warm on Vax's arms.

"Don't mention it. It's the very least we can do." He smiled wryly. "I'm Thorn."

Vax took another sip of water and tried to speak. "Where's my sister?"

Thorn didn't flinch, though some of the merriment disappeared from his expression. "You were there with your sister?"

Vax nodded.

"You were the only one left behind. All the others were taken in by the Shadewatch. Your sister will be in Jorenn Village by now."

Thorn's words held an edge that Vax couldn't place. He let himself fall back against the lumpy pillow—and immediately hissed when pain arched through his back. He vaguely remembered the glint of moonlight on weapons and insignias. If Vex was inside Jorenn, surrounded by the Shadewatch, she was safe. At least for now. She'd be able to take care of herself there.

"Where are we?" he asked.

Thorn spread his arms wide, like he was touring Vax around a castle full of miracles instead of a chamber with a makeshift cot and a damp glaze along the walls. The coat that he wore over his tunic fell open wide, showing what looked like a snake wrapped around his waist, but when Vax blinked again and focused, it was simply a belt. "You, nameless friend, are in my home."

"Good." Vax closed his eyes for a second, relief overwhelming him.

"That's very good." He wanted to keep talking, he wanted to ask more questions, but with the pillow snugly beneath his head, the healing coursing through him, and Thorn's hand on his shoulders, he promptly fell asleep.

WHEN HE WOKE AGAIN, ANOTHER person sat next to him. For the briefest instant, he thought it was Vex. Then his vision cleared and he realized the other person was a dwarven woman, who was seeing to the bandages around his torso. The lanterns that illuminated her were brighter now, the light as pale as the dawn, and reflected coldly off the gray stones around them.

The dwarven woman had her brown hair dappled with gray tied back under a headscarf, and she worked with quiet efficiency, unwrapping and rewrapping, renewing the poultice across the slash wounds. It smelled vaguely of mint and cinnamon. She placed one wrinkled brown hand over the bandages, and with the other she reached for a small copper hammer on a long braided chain. "All-Hammer protect you." A soft glow emanated from her palms, warming him like the heat of a summer's day. She must be Sencha, the healer Thorn had mentioned.

He followed her movements without saying a word, but when she tied up the last bandage, she didn't seem at all surprised by his being awake.

"Junel is cooking breakfast," she said. "With the healings you've had, you need good sustenance. A bit of moving around can't hurt either. Emryn is sleeping, so I can walk you over."

Vax sat up, and Sencha reached out to him when the world spun around him. "Careful, dear, your body is still recovering. My capabilities are limited, and it will take a while for those slashes to heal properly."

"Ungh," he said eloquently. His sister and he had certainly had their share of trouble doing odd jobs and working for hire these past few years, but those cuts and scrapes were nothing more than what they could handle. They could take care of themselves out in the wild, and once Vex had saved up enough gold to afford it they got into the habit of always carrying herbs and bandages to patch themselves up if things got dire. Usually that was more than enough. But *usually* didn't come with skeletal creatures with sharp claws.

"Thank you," he said.

Sencha patted his hand and gestured at a fresh set of clothes that lay beside him, next to his familiar fur-lined cloak and his daggers. His belt held a few pouches with necessities—travel rations, lockpicks, a small whetstone for his blades. He'd had to leave the rest of his belongings back in the camp. "It's my pleasure. Try to make sure you don't immediately get into another brawl. I know your type, half-elf."

He had an inkling who she might be talking about. "Where's Thorn?" he asked.

She stilled at that, but then she smiled. "That foolish boy went back to your encampment after you mentioned your sister. He wanted to be sure neither we nor the Shadewatch missed anyone."

More flashes from the fight came back to him. Worry too. That edge to Thorn's words. He reached for his clothes. "I should be there too. I have to find her."

Sencha placed a firm hand on his shoulder. "You'll do no such thing. You're in no shape. He'll do what he can. He always does."

Vax waited for the nausea to pass. "Is this something you do regularly? Run in to help strangers fight those ash things?"

Sencha recovered the dirty bandages and swept them all up in a bundle that stood at her feet. The corner of her mouth pulled up in a half smile. "When the occasion calls for it, and the days are free of ash walkers. We're careful with who we bring in here. I'll let Thorn tell you all about that, if he wishes. Foolish boy or no, he calls the shots around here, and I will not betray his trust by telling you more than he wishes to share." She waited for him to get dressed and take the first couple of steps, obviously to make sure she didn't need to catch him if he fell. When he managed to cross the chamber without toppling over, she added, "Especially since you haven't told any of us your name yet."

"Vax," he said softly. "It's Vax."

"Well then, Vax, come and I'll show you where there's food to be had and others to meet. Don't worry about the rest of your clothes. We've saved them for you, but I'm not about to let those wounds get infected again."

She showed him out of the room and through a long stone passageway, where the high ceilings were supported by tall wooden beams. The corridor was lit with similar lamps to the one in his chamber, and shadowed openings led to chambers on either side. Some were used as storage, some used as sleeping areas. Some looked natural, some looked like they were hewn and claimed from the stone itself. Everything around them had a peculiar earthy smell. It was cold and fresh but it also had a metallic aftertaste.

"We're a way underground," Sencha offered, noticing Vax's curiosity.

"A cavern? A system of caves?" he asked. He tried to figure out if he'd seen anything of the sort, any entrance into the hills, while they made their way to Jorenn.

"A mine, actually." Sencha tapped one of the wooden support beams. "Long since abandoned but its structure still holds." She led him around the corner into a wider cave, and from there into another passage.

Vax tried to keep track of the various twists and turns while also trying to stay upright. The walk was harder than he wanted to let on. "Are you miners?"

Sencha looked over her shoulder at him and smiled. "We're many things, dear. But that's up to Thorn to share. For now, we're the ones offering you health and breakfast. You'll have to content yourself with that."

He didn't content himself with it. He also didn't ask more. He held on to his questions and observed the underground world around him, the path that Sencha followed, and the various intersections they passed. Though their years of travel together had brought them to the strangest places, aside from his occasional foray into sewers, Vex and he hadn't spent much time underground, let alone in endless systems of corridors and shafts, and it had nothing of the details he'd grown accustomed to in other places where he needed to find his way. The stone path in front of him was somewhat dusty from use, but still Sencha barely left any footprints. The light sources were evenly spread throughout the various tunnels and chambers, making it hard to gauge distance. It took him altogether too long to realize they'd been walking on a slightly downward slope, spiraling deeper into the mine. By the time he did, his head was spinning and the slashes across his back were aching. Though he was used to dark corners and small spaces, and he'd never been particularly claustrophobic, the mine's innate disorientation left him on edge.

But when the smell of food drifted up toward him, along with the constant rumble of voices, his stomach at least responded with roaring recognition. "Smells good," he admitted, when Sencha laughed quietly.

"Junel knows what they're doing," she said. "If you think my healing is magic, you should try their cooking."

With that, she turned a final corner and led him to a sizable dining-room-slash-kitchen where two long tables were set up, with at least a dozen people at each table. Some were talking and laughing, while others were eating quietly. A number of them showed signs from last night's fight, in bandages and cuts and scrapes. At the far end of one of the tables, a half-orc woman was bent over a book, a pair of glasses clamped around her nose. A battered and tarnished glass sphere drifted above her, glowing with a soft blue light that illuminated her reading. Closer to Vax and Sencha, a trio of young halfling men were huddled together and having an animated conversation in hushed tones. Something to do with a hidden treasure—or perhaps a date. Vax couldn't quite tell. One of them had a bandage wrapped around his head.

When he passed the table, the trio quieted immediately, wide-eyed and with spots of color on their cheeks. As disorienting as the tunnels of the mine was Vax's sudden realization that he was only two, maybe three years older than the halflings. He felt at least twice their age. He tried to remember these hushed and stolen-moment conversations.

Sencha marched past both the tables, toward the far side of the kitchen, where a gnomish individual was cooking breakfast—pancakes and porridge—using magically heated stones instead of fire. Junel dashed back and forth between pans, juggling utensils, and mixing up ingredients, a similar headscarf to the one Sencha wore tied around their hair, and a dusting of flour on their dark skin. They were talking to themself constantly, only holding up for a second when Sencha walked over to them, Vax in tow.

Sencha sat Vax down in an empty seat, planted a kiss on Junel's cheek, and pointed. "He needs to eat. He's recovering from a fight and a healing and the shock to the system of being underground too long."

"I'll be fine," Vax protested.

"You will eat," Junel said, pointing their ladle in Vax's direction, their tone brooking no argument. Soon he found himself surrounded by plates of food. Not merely pancakes, but dried fruit and sweet pastries and various types of meats. If he hadn't held up his hand and cried mercy after Junel set down the first half a dozen plates, he was sure there would've been at least half a dozen more.

Sencha had been right. The food *was* excellent. Simple, and far better than the travel rations they'd gotten in the meager inn in Westruun. It was all the tastier for the company that came with it. Vax wasn't merely surrounded by food, he was surrounded by comfortable conversations and laughter.

It didn't take him long to pinpoint the feeling. Those present here, whether they engaged in conversations or not, all spoke the same language, they saw the same world around them, they shared the same experiences. The arguments sounded like arguments they'd had a hundred times. Across the table, one dwarf's comments were met with groaning from all those around him whenever he so much as opened his mouth. A brown-haired dwarf with a bounce in his step walked in, took the book from the half-orc with a grin, and planted a kiss on her nose before muttering something under his breath.

It'd been like this back home, a lifetime ago.

He was surrounded by a sense of community, and he hadn't felt that in years. All he needed now was Vex by his side.

But when Thorn appeared from another entrance, streaks of ash across his face, blood and mud on his coat, and a cut across his forearm, he was alone. All the conversations paused momentarily, as if everyone collectively inhaled to prepare themselves for what news he would bring.

Sencha immediately rushed over, but he waved her off, and his eyes found those of the half-orc. Anger simmered under his skin. "The package is gone," he said. "Burnt to a crisp. I got rid of a stray walker or two, but the encampment was empty."

The woman grimaced, then got to her feet, taking both the book and her dwarven companion with her, and walked deeper back into the mine. Others who'd finished their meal—or were concerned by Thorn's words—got to their feet and left the room as well.

"Gods, I hate them," Thorn growled. He ran a hand through his hair and took a seat opposite Vax, his movements jagged and abrupt. Thorn's all-consuming anger left nothing of the playful gentleness he'd shown when Vax had woken up midway through the night.

"I'm sorry. I didn't find your sister," he said, before Vax could ask. "She and your fellow travelers have all been taken by the noble Shadewatch, who are either cursed, lucky, or smarter than I give them credit for."

Vax hesitated, because Thorn's words and his tone said two different things. "So my sister's in Jorenn?"

Thorn grabbed one of the knives from the table and turned it around in his hands. "In the care of the great Shademaster Derowen, savior of Jorenn and hero to all."

"You say that like it's a bad thing."

Thorn didn't reply immediately. He twisted the knife around and ran his finger along the blade, then slammed it hard into the table. He looked up to meet Vax's gaze, and underneath his anger was a pain so raw that it took everything Vax had not to flinch away. "The Shademaster may cloak herself in kindness to outsiders, but she controls every single thing that happens in Jorenn. She's a dangerous woman if you cross her or if you happen to fall on her bad side. *My* sister did not live to tell that tale."

CHAPTER 14

The softest of footsteps woke Vex from her sleep. She blinked against the bright sunlight that streamed through the windows, and everything about her felt heavy and tired. By the time they'd returned to the town hall, the Shade Hall, the sky around them had begun to color in dawn and she was asleep on her feet. It must be— Gods, it must be nearing noon. *Shit.* Why had no one come to wake her?

The gentle footfalls came closer, and a tremor of unease ran through her, while the quieter, sleepier part of her insisted it was all right. It could only be her brother. He had to be close, because he could be nowhere else.

But along with the harsh sunlight came the realization that Vax was far away from her. Vex reached quietly for the knife on top of her clothing.

When she felt the comforting weight of the blade in her hand, she turned and pushed the heavy down blankets off her, preparing herself for whatever happened next, and leaped out of the bed.

Aswin walked unperturbed through the room, her hair tied into two braids, and wearing what looked like a child's version of the Shadewatch tunic—a deep carmine with silver triangular shapes that seemed to represent a stylized mountain range—over a gray skirt and stockings. She didn't blink at Vex's knife but only had eyes for Trinket, who'd been given a cot to sleep on next to the window. The bear was sprawled over the cot, his head resting on his paws.

Vex hurriedly dropped the knife on the mattress and reached for a shirt to pull over her nightclothes. She rubbed at her forehead and tried to push her hair back into some semblance of order. "Aswin, what are you doing here?" she asked, her voice still rough.

Aswin stopped an arm's length away from Trinket. "I wanted to come see Trinket," she said, like it was entirely reasonable. "I never had a bear before. Do you think I could have my own bear too?"

Trinket, aware of the attention, opened one eye and adjusted his position slightly so that Aswin had an easier job scratching his chin. Taking it as permission regardless of what Vex might say, the girl leaped forward with glee.

"I think you should ask your mother if you can have your own bear," Vex managed. She reached for the carafe of water that someone had placed on a nightstand and gratefully poured herself a cup. Fresh fruit had also been laid out, but she wanted to wash up before she ate. Her mouth still tasted like ashes. And she needed to get out of here.

"Did you ask your mother too?" Aswin asked, sitting down next to Trinket and pulling up her knees while the bear shamelessly leaned into her.

"I . . . um . . ." Vex blinked, the innocent question cutting straight through her. She gathered the rest of her clothes, which had all been cleaned while she was asleep, even her armor pieces, and tried to locate a bathroom where she could refresh herself and change.

"My mother is gone a lot," Aswin continued, seemingly oblivious to Vex's distress. She spoke with the calm assuredness of a six-year-old girl, who completely understood the world around her. "She always leaves when the ash walkers come. She says she must protect the city and our family. Maybe if I tell her a bear can protect me too, that will convince her."

Vex spied a door off to the side and dashed into it, finding a small bathroom behind it. In the main room, Aswin was chattering happily to Trinket, and Vex freshened up, throwing water on her face and changing into clean clothes. Her satchel with supplies and her bow and arrow were laid out for her, still bearing the marks of the fight. The image of Vax lying on the ground flashed through her again, and she ducked her face into the cold water once more.

When she reappeared, Aswin had taken some of the pieces of fruit off her plate and was feeding them to Trinket. She was completely at ease with the bear, and grinned when Vex walked in. "I think he likes me," she said proudly when Trinket took a slice of apple from her hand.

Vex stared at the fierce little girl for a moment. Despite the fact that she lived in a town frequently besieged by monsters, she seemed not to care at all about the fact that Vex was a stranger.

Vex retrieved her weapons. "Shouldn't you be at your lessons or something?" she asked awkwardly. She wasn't entirely sure what to do with the young girl or how to get to the Shademaster. She wasn't even sure if she wanted to, or if she should leave and find Vax on her own. Her brother was her responsibility, and no one else's.

Aswin sighed dramatically. "I already did my chores and, *also,* I'm hiding from Wick."

"Why?"

"Because I don't like learning my letters. They don't make sense. I'd rather learn what bears eat." She scrunched up her face like she was trying to remember something. "Oh, yes! And there's food for you in the kitchens and Mother says she's ready to ride out with you whenever you are."

"Did she send you here to say that?"

"No." Aswin shrugged. "I overheard her." She took another slice of apple and held it out to Trinket, who was clearly having the time of his life.

Vex slipped on her boots and decided on a course of action. To ride out, to be able to *do* something, would help. And like it or not, she could use the Shadewatch's expertise. "Can you take care of Trinket for a bit while I go talk to your mother, Aswin?" she asked hesitantly.

"I can do that!" The girl nodded so hard, her braids bounced up and down. She paused midway through. "But please don't tell Wick where I am?"

"I won't," Vex promised. It might not be the hospitable thing to do, but she didn't know if she could trust the people around her, and the girl deserved her adventure. She'd been taught the rules of etiquette, and she wholeheartedly despised falling back into that world. "Trinket, take care of her, please?"

Trinket sighed happily and stretched out, and with that taken care of, Vex slipped out of the room. When she'd walked around the town hall the previous night—or rather, earlier that morning—little had been illuminated, and she'd been exhausted. So she wasn't entirely sure how to get to the kitchens or the Shademaster, but she could find her way.

She forced herself to remember which direction they'd come from when the Shademaster showed her to the guest room, and she retraced their steps from there.

The guest rooms were on the third floor of the Shade Hall, in the Shademaster's personal wing, far away from the main entrance and the large rooms and offices that were used for official town business and meetings of the Shadewatch. The rooms and hallways were decorated for comfort, with thick rugs that dampened Vex's footsteps.

She made a mental note of the various entrances and exits, because Vax always insisted on it. On having an escape route at all times.

Soft, muted colors covered the walls around her, rich curtains framed the windows that looked out over Jorenn, and paintings of land-scapes from all across the continent hung on either side of the hallway. Vex glanced at them as she passed. Perhaps under different circum-stances she would've admired the vistas of the Lucidian Coast and of the Frostweald. Right now the only landscape she wanted to see was that of their camp. The same restlessness from the previous night settled inside her.

A door opened to her right, and the half-giant she'd met the previ-ous night walked out, scanning the hallway around him. Wick looked no less imposing in a simple tunic and breeches without a weapon by his side. He still towered over her, and he made the rest of the hallway ap-pear smaller, but when he spotted her he merely smiled. "Good morning, I trust you slept well?"

Vex swallowed a remark about sleeping too long. "Shademaster Derowen promised we could ride out to find my brother," she said with-out preamble. "Can you take me to her?"

"Of course, I'll take you to the Shademaster's office." If Wick was taken aback by her brusque manner, he didn't show it. His gaze drifted away from her, skimming across the tall curtains. "I was looking for Aswin, who is trying to escape her lessons again. You haven't seen her by chance?"

Vex demurred. She didn't care for small talk, and she wouldn't betray Aswin's trust. While the little girl might circumvent her defenses, she knew better than to let others get close.

"Have you eaten?" Wick asked as he walked her down the hallway toward the second floor. When she shook her head, he flagged down a young man in a weaponless carmine tunic, and sent him toward the kitchen to find her a meal.

Vex glanced sideways at Wick. Just the previous night, he hadn't trusted her enough to draw her bow within shooting distance of the Shademaster. Today he treated her like an esteemed guest. "Why?"

He raised an eyebrow. "Because it won't do for you to fall off your horse when you're looking for your brother."

Sure, but that hadn't been her question. Not really. "Why not leave me in the inn with the other travelers? Why care? I'm no one to you."

Wick considered it. He cut an odd figure in the Shade Hall, and she tried to understand his position in the Shademaster's company. He didn't wear the Shadewatch's colors, and his involvement seemed to be more personal, focused on both Derowen's and Aswin's protection before any-thing else. "Because it's the right thing to do. You're in need of help, and we can offer it, much like you offered your assistance up on the palisades last night. We take care of each other here."

She snorted. She didn't believe a word of that. Much like with that bastard back in Westruun, there was a catch. There was always a catch. A cost or a cruelty.

Next to her, Wick narrowed his eyes. "Kindness isn't a luxury, Vex." He pointed her in the direction of another hallway that angled away from the personal wings toward the main building.

She brushed the comment off and continued to mark the rooms and hallways around her. She needed to understand this place. For herself, and for Vax. "Who are you to the Shademaster then?"

He led her down a set of stairs, and she could feel his eyes on her. His curiosity against hers. She didn't know exactly what he was looking for, but apparently he found it, because he answered calmly. "I'm her friend, first and foremost. We traveled and worked and fought together before we settled in Jorenn. She was there for me when my partner died, and I had nowhere to go back to. I was there when she lost her home to the wrong sort of people in Kymal. If it hadn't been for her brother, she might have lost her life too. We were both searching for a new place to call home when we stumbled across this town beset by monsters, look-ing to anyone who might lead them. When she decided to stay here, I decided to stay by her side."

"You protect her?"

He tensed then smiled. "Always." He picked at the band around his neck, and for a second it seemed as though he wanted to say more. He simply settled on, "Jorenn allowed us both to become more than we thought we could be."

Wick reached out to knock on a tall wooden door.

"Ash walkers aside, it seems like a good place," Vex said. Instead of bitingly the words came out soft.

Wick glanced in her direction, and she managed a half shrug. "Aswin. She seems like a good kid, and happy here." It felt like such a pointless observation the moment she said it. Vex knew, rationally, most people didn't care about heritage. They cared about friendship, family, hard coin. But some days, when she felt vulnerable and alone, those years in Syngorn overrode all sense.

He shook his head. "She's the Shademaster's daughter and she's spoiled rotten, but everyone knows she's as kind and brave as any six-year-old can be."

"And they know I will murder anyone who lays so much as a finger on her head," said Shademaster Derowen, from a door opening. She smiled wanly at Vex, and despite the dark circles under her eyes, it looked like she'd been awake for some time. The desk behind her—practical, not beautiful—was covered in various notes, letters, and other pieces of parchment. "My daughter is perfect the way she is. I wouldn't change her for the world."

"Good." Vex managed a smile, though her throat felt too tight and her heart hammered too loudly.

Behind Derowen, someone pushed open the door, and the archer who'd stood by Vex's side the previous night walked out. His damp curls were tucked behind his ears, and underneath a long, flowing coat he wore a rapier instead of a bow. He looked far more rested than the Shademaster, and a thin smile played around his lips. "Where's your sense of hospitality, Dera? Invite her in."

He held out a hand to Vex. "I don't believe we were properly introduced last night. Culwen. A pleasure to meet you."

"My brother," Derowen said, with a slight wince, while Vex introduced herself. In the light of day, she realized his green eyes were as vibrant as Aswin's, though the lines around them were deeper. Culwen held on to Vex's hand, and observed her like he could try to unravel all her secrets. "Nice shooting out there, and under such dreadful circumstances. Derowen could learn from that."

Vex pulled her hand back and managed a polite smile. She wasn't sure how else to respond. "Thank you."

Culwen directed his attention to the half-giant behind Vex, and he grinned viciously. "Wick. Did my niece escape you again?"

Wick—who had taken Vex's questions with good grace—froze, and at the door, leaning against the doorframe, Derowen grimaced. "You're a bad influence on her, brother."

"Someone has to be." Culwen leaned in and pressed a kiss to his sister's cheek despite the fact that she flinched away from him. "Give her my love. Tell her to get into trouble. I'll be back in a couple of days, and I promised her I'd bring a present."

"She'll hold you to that," the Shademaster said, her voice curiously flat.

Culwen tipped an imaginary hat. "I wouldn't want to disappoint her." With a nod in the direction of Vex and Wick, he sauntered out of the hallway.

Vex breathed out hard and tried to pull herself together, but when Wick placed a comforting hand on her shoulder, she flinched.

Derowen watched Culwen walk away before she turned to Vex. She held on to the doorframe, and her ring shimmered in the morning light. She breathed out. "We should go find *your* brother," she said, her voice neutral. "I've sent scouts ahead. Once we find him, perhaps you two can tell me some about where you come from and what brings you here. It's been a long time since I was able to travel, and I miss hearing about the world. You're very welcome to stay with us for as long as you need."

She sent Wick off to assemble the guard and walked back into the office to grab the tall sword she'd worn the previous night, acting with gracious efficiency. Before Vex had time to feel restless, Derowen had organized an escort of a dozen riders, new arrows for Vex, and she'd ordered the food Wick had sent for to be bundled up for Vex to eat while they rode out into the daylight, where the sun had broken through ash and mist.

JORENN LOOKED CALMER BY DAYLIGHT. The shopkeepers who'd boarded up their shops were in the process of opening up doors and windows again. A group of children chased a chicken through the streets. The tension of the previous night made way for everyday ease.

When they passed The Scattered Bar, Nera, the half-elf scout, stood outside the door, deep in conversation with a human man. Her ankle was bandaged up and she leaned against the outer wall. Blotches of pale skin showed her fatigue, but that didn't stop her from arguing.

When she noticed Vex, she held up a hand to stop her and limped forward. "I heard about your brother. I hope you find him."

Vex hesitated, then nodded. She felt a twinge of guilt at the ease with which she'd discarded the scout. She'd fought well, and she'd been nothing but kind. But letting anyone get too close was such an easy way to be hurt. Though no one in this town seemed to care about that.

"Thank you. I appreciate it." She gestured at Nera's leg. "I hope that won't trouble you long."

"I've been in worse situations." The corner of Nera's mouth pulled into a crooked smile and she admitted, "Better ones too. I'll be fine. I'm on my way to Westruun later today. I may travel home afterward. I'll keep an eye out for your twin, just in case."

She held out a hand to Vex, and Vex clasped her forearm. "Safe travels."

"Good hunting."

THE CLOSER THEY CAME TO the spot where Vex had last seen her brother, the harder it was to breathe.

The place where they'd set up camp the night before was ruined. Two horses were half eaten and the rest of their carcasses were left for the birds. The pots and pans they'd used for food were scattered across the campsite, and so were some of their belongings. One of the scholar's notebooks lay crumpled and torn near the upturned cart. Some of the dwarves' tack was ripped apart, bridles broken and brushes thrust aside. A torn-up saddle lay gathering dust and ash. There were stray arrows and footprints everywhere.

It was a miserable memory of an encampment surrounded by gray stalks of shadegrass and grayer hills.

And Vax was nowhere to be seen.

Vex dismounted and walked around the spot where she'd thought she'd seen her brother fall. She combed through the layers of soot, and despite the bright glare of the sun, coldness settled inside her, hard and heavy.

Scouts rode the perimeter, and the guards around her scoured every inch of the place. One of the guards found the chewed-upon corpse of a walker near the remains of the campfire. A once-human woman, whose cursed remains were half devoured by ash, but for bone and some muscle. Her skeletal hands and feet were sharpened to claws, and after the battle, what remained of her was torn apart by the scavengers that roamed the hills. Another guard uncovered a mangled body of a smaller ashen corpse at the edge of the encampment. A third guard picked up the torn up pieces of a half-finished bridle.

Everything else was broken equipment and layers upon layers of gray dust. Whatever had been on the toppled-over cart was long gone. Some of the crates had been smashed to pieces by the impact, but most were simply gone. Carried away.

Something sparkled underneath the gray dust, and Vex dropped to her knees to reach for it, expecting perhaps a coin or some jewelry. Instead her fingers wrapped around a small copper pick, like one used for a zither. Ash collected in the grooves and the edges of the pick, and she dusted it off with her thumb. There was a small horse etched in the copper.

A few feet away, she saw the outlines of a leather bag. She crawled through the dirt and picked it up to feel the familiar wear and tear, the scars along the leather, and the patched-up bits. The world spun around her, and what little breakfast she had clawed its way up. The bag, which her brother had carried with them since their earliest days in Kymal, was empty. She knew what had been in it, and it all seemed so pointless now. Provisions. Rope. Bedrolls for setting up camp. Tinder for starting a fire. Bland things. Supplies they needed, supplies they'd miss, too. Nothing of actual value. Aside from the cloaks they wore and the clothes they'd mended over and over again, aside from the feathers in her hair and their weapons, they hadn't brought anything along from Syngorn. There had been nothing left in Byroden. They carried their homes with each other, and she didn't need this empty bag here.

She needed her brother.

She reached for her necklace and stayed where she was, unable to move. He was hiding somewhere. She would have felt it if something worse had happened to him, she was certain of it. Right?

She balled her fist so tightly around the copper bear, the tiny edges cut into her hands. She felt impossibly cold.

He was out there, somewhere. He had to be.

A hand squeezed her shoulder. "He is," Shademaster Derowen said softly. She'd dismounted and stood next to Vex, compassion in the lines of her face, but worry in her eyes.

Vex hadn't realized she'd spoken out loud, and her stomach dropped at the sight of Derowen. "Did you find anything?" she demanded.

"The scouts found tracks leading away from the camp," Derowen said.

"My brother's?"

"Multiple tracks, actually," the Shademaster replied. "They surmised a handful of people entered the camp after the Shadewatch left, presumably to loot the abandoned supplies. The tracks leading in and the ones leading out don't match up. They can't really make sense of it." She hesitated. "Come, it's best if I show you."

She held out a hand to Vex, who flipped her the copper pick instead before she got to her feet. Derowen caught it with nimble fingers.

"Bandits?" Vex asked.

Derowen led her toward the edge of the encampment, where two women in Shadewatch uniforms were marking the tracks they found. "It's not as simple as that," she admitted. "A group of outlaws, led by a man by the name of Thorn, were a part of our community once. Miners who explored the hills and delved into new mining systems—until they dug too deep." She turned the copper pick this way and that, letting the crudely drawn horse catch the sunlight, and a thoughtful frown crossed her face. "Jorenn Village has always had their share of dangerous creatures that come down the hills. It has monsters. It has horrors. And it has townspeople able and determined enough to keep the town safe, people willing to learn how to protect themselves and their neighbors. But we can't fight what is already dead. The miners disturbed creatures better left untouched, and we all suffered for it."

The Shademaster gestured at the destroyed camp, and Vex grimaced.

"Why would these miners remain here?" Vex asked. She knelt next to one of the guards, and studied the footprints that the woman pointed out to her. Around the campfire, the prints had been too chaotic and trampled to follow, but here at the edge, she could make out what had alerted the scouts. The prints didn't match the boots of the guards, and they overlaid the horses' hoofprints, indicating that people had been here after the Shadewatch evacuated the camp. She followed the ones into the camp and then walked over to compare them with the ones that led out.

"When the Shadewatch tried to break up the miners' endeavors and bring them to justice for the dangers they brought to Jorenn, most of them escaped deeper into the mines," Derowen said. "We've tried to lure them out to no avail. They know the hills better than any one of us. They took up residence in an abandoned mine system not far from here. Claimed to have a right to stay, despite the fact that they endangered our community, and they've been a pest ever since. They know the Shade-watch keeps an eye out in case any of them show themselves above-ground, but they've attacked travelers before. Presumably, they need the supplies."

One of the guards pointed out the tracks leading away from the camp, and Vex traced one of the clearest footprints with a finger.

She clenched her hands into fists. "Do you know where those outlaws are, exactly?"

The Shademaster rubbed at her forehead, and frustration shone through in her voice. "They elude us. If we'd known, we would've raided their camp a long time ago. They're responsible for the destruction of too many homes. They're responsible for too many lost among the Shade-watch as well."

Vex felt tendrils of ice crawl up her spine. She traced the drag marks next to the footprints and followed them, step by step. She noticed every single break in the pattern. The places where the drag marks were inter-spersed by other footprints. The drops of blood. The tracks that indicated that for a while, two people had walked side by side, something heavy between them.

Or someone.

To Vex's left, Derowen held out the pick to a guard, and at her gesture, others began to collect what belongings they could find. She directed one of the guards to a bag of supplies in the corner of the encampment. It was half covered in dust and blood splatters but seemed otherwise untouched.

She followed Vex at a careful distance. "The town controls the active mines now. We've asked the miners loyal to Jorenn to keep an eye out, and the Shadewatch patrols regularly. So far, we haven't had any luck."

The trail led to a rockier patch, where any tracks would be near impossible to follow. But not before the drag marks stopped and a pair of footprints appeared between the two others. Vex immediately recognized the scars and inconsistencies on the soles. She knew Vax slightly favored his right foot. She held her foot next to one of the prints for measure, but she didn't need to see her brother to recognize his presence.

Perhaps the tracks made no sense to the scouts, but they told Vex all she needed to know. There'd been a scuffle here. One of the outlaws had dragged Vax out of the camp, with some assistance of a second person. They'd put him up on his feet here, briefly.

She placed her hand on the prints. The blood spatters she saw around her were bad, but thankfully not so bad as to suggest that he was bleeding to death. He was hurt, though. He needed help.

She followed the traces until she got to the gravelly path that led away from the campsite.

Vax's tracks disappeared as soon as the tracks hit rock. The first set of footprints continued until the ground became too hard, their outline deeper than before. Much deeper. It took Vex a second to realize why.

They'd carried Vax out. Had he seen too much? Did they need a hostage? It didn't matter. There were no good reasons for Vax to be captured, only bad and worse ones.

Where had they gone?

Vex ran her fingers over the splatters of dried blood before she got to her feet. She brushed off her knees. She tried to breathe in. Terror and anger wrapped around her chest and her voice cracked when she said, "They've taken him."

Derowen frowned. "The scouts mentioned there were more tracks here, but—"

"No." Vex shook her head and pointed out what she'd seen, explaining to the Shademaster what it meant. As she did, Derowen's frown deepened and some harsher thought flashed across her face, but she didn't give voice to it, and for that Vex was grateful.

"Those outlaws have taken my brother," Vex said, her voice flat. Now that she knew what had happened, she knew what she must do. "And I will bring him back."

"They're dangerous," Derowen said. She was still staring at the last set of tracks, and her hands clenched by her side. "We don't even know where they are."

"Then I'll find them," Vex said. She couldn't stay here. She couldn't be surrounded by this emptiness, by the fear of losing him, by all their compassionate looks. She walked over to her horse and mounted again. She'd tear down these hills stone by stone if she had to.

Derowen fell into step with her, clearly considering Vex's words. She sighed. "I believe you may have a better shot at this than any of us," she said eventually, though she didn't sound entirely convinced. "But these hills are deadly. Your brother wouldn't want you to endanger yourself, would he?"

Vex patted her bow and arrows and pulled herself up straight. "I can protect myself, and he knows that," she snapped. "If anyone can track them, I can. I need to find my brother, Shademaster, and I won't let anyone hurt him."

Derowen nodded like she'd expected that answer. She gestured for two guards to come closer. "Then allow my riders to stay with you. Nari and Olfa know the area, and they'll be able to tell you what we've found so far. They'll bring you back safely, and if you do find something, you'll need backup. They can alert the Shadewatch. My daughter would never forgive me if I didn't try to help in any way I can."

"I'm better off on my own," Vex said coldly. She grasped for a semipolite way to decline. "I appreciate your assistance and Aswin's care, but they'll only get in the way."

Derowen lifted her chin and pulled her mouth into a thin line. Then she nodded at the guards to mount. "Don't forget your targets are our targets too, Vex. They will join you or they will follow you."

They stared at each other, and Vex saw no compassion in Derowen's eyes. Just ironclad purpose.

"Fine." The fury inside her morphed into determination. Desperation. "If they can keep up."

With that, Vex spurred on her horse to canvas the area around the camp, riding in ever-wider circles to find something, anything. Tracks. Hidden brothers. Something or someone who could tell her that she wasn't alone and wouldn't be alone in this gray corner of the world.

VEX WAS CERTAIN SHE'D BE able to track Vax down, but the hills drained that conviction from her. She started on the other side of the rocky patch and found a trail twice. First, a set of footprints that looked vaguely humanoid. They trailed away from the general direction of the encampment toward the glowing hills where shadegrass made way for green grass. The guards stayed with her, at a distance, and they only spoke if she had questions about their surroundings, the wildlife in the area, and the mines that were long since abandoned.

She followed the footprints for the better part of an hour, until they turned to crawl marks, until she came across a sheltered spot between bushels of heather. Traces of ash covered the evergreen plants, and when she took out her bow and sneaked closer, she found the broken and cut-up corpse that had tried to crawl away, facedown between the flowers.

She stabbed it again for good measure, breathing out hard.

One of the guards spat at the body. "Fucking monsters."

Vex circled the area where the dead walker lay, but the tracks didn't pick up again.

The second trail led in the direction of where the guards told her part of an abandoned mine system was, and it was one of crumbling rocks and flattened shadegrass. She kept on that until the sun crested toward the horizon, and the sky around them turned from the bright blue of day to the pinks and oranges of twilight. The trail gave her nothing more than a torn-up deer, attacked by predators.

She knelt next to it and ran her fingers through its fur, imagining the wounds mending and breath coming back to the broken animal. It didn't, of course. Her hands felt hot and uncomfortable, but there was nothing she could do to fix this pain.

She took a sip of water, rubbed her face, and tried to remember what to do next.

The tracks that had been so clear around the camp seemed to have disappeared.

"No one has ever been able to find them?" she asked hoarsely.

One of the guards—Nari—shook his head. He glanced at the setting sun. "Not yet."

It made sense, too. Being able to hide well was presumably the only thing that kept them alive this close to town. But they had Vax, so it didn't matter. She had to figure out a way to find them.

Vex hightailed back to the encampment. With the rest of the guard gone and the remains cleared out, she could figure out if other tracks led away from the camp. They did, of course, but all in the direction of Jorenn. Horses trampling through ash walkers. Horses carrying guards to retrieve possessions. Her tracks, full of despair. All the other footprints disappeared at the edge of the encampment, like whoever'd walked here knew exactly how to avoid being found.

"We'll do what we can to find your brother for you," Olfa promised. "But we'll have to be back behind the town walls before nightfall."

"He'd want you to be safe," Nari said.

Derowen had said almost exactly the same thing, and Vex cursed. Perhaps they meant well, but it felt as though they were all using her brother against her. None of them even knew Vax. She wouldn't let them hold her back. She *couldn't* let them hold her back.

She balled her fists and focused on the slightest hints of another trail. A set of footprints, leading away from the encampment in the direction of the hills. One person with soft feet. If she closed her eyes and pretended she didn't know better, that she didn't see the footprints were the wrong size and the steps the wrong rhythm, she could imagine *this* was Vax—free from the walkers and free from the outlaws.

With the two guards keeping a respectful—but worried—distance, she kept her focus on the trail and attempted to reconstruct it. The image of a young half-elf, dashing away from the fight. One foot in front of the other. A step to the side, presumably to dart out of the way of an attack. A single footstep that crushed some stalks of shadegrass. The sky darkening around them—around him.

Higher up into the hills, angling away from where the mines were supposed to be. Dusty footsteps across rocky ground. Soot. Disturbed rocks. A half-hidden cairn. A hint of blood?

Vex couldn't tell. She could only follow the tracks.

All she had to do was find him.

It was so hard to breathe.

Then these tracks disappeared too. Everything around was hard stone once more, and no matter where she looked there were no footsteps. No drops of blood. Not even the barest hint of ash. Without prior knowledge of this location, it was impossible to tell which stones—if any— might have been disturbed.

"We really have to go back," Nari insisted, riding up next to Vex. "Shademaster's orders."

Vex felt the words like a gut punch. The hills around them were bright orange and red in the light of the setting sun. And while the vibrant shades cast colorful shadows, she knew she couldn't go on. Not with the safety of the guards on her shoulders, no matter how much she wanted to keep searching.

She could do nothing and she felt so lost.

Purpose and desperation morphed into cold terror again. She fought down the urge to scream in frustration, and instead she pushed out the words through gritted teeth. "We'll go back."

CHAPTER 15

"Keep going."

Sencha walked directly in front of Vax and guided him deeper into the tunnels, where even the light of the magic lamps didn't extend and all they had to go by were torches. Sencha held one of them, illuminating the uneven path in front of them. Others were already farther down.

One of Thorn's followers had raised the alarm when a few guards from Jorenn's Shadewatch stumbled too close to one of the entrances to their underground home. Vax, who'd succumbed to painful exhaustion again after his meal, had been woken up by Sencha invoking the All-Hammer's blessing once more. Her healing magic had helped knit together some of his wounds before she'd forced him down to the lower levels of the mine, along a shaft far steeper than the gentle slope they'd followed to get to the kitchen.

It'd taken him a second to wrap his mind around the situation—and protest. "*No.* If my sister is in Jorenn, she'll be looking for me. I should let them find me." Vex's absence was an ache that settled in his bones and rattled his thoughts. She needed to know to stay away from the Shademaster, and he hated the idea that she might worry about him. And what if the Clasp thought he'd disappeared on them? Would they take their anger out on Vex? He needed to find his way out of here and back to her as soon as possible.

Thorn had passed him by, short swords in both hands, and Vax had found himself on the other side of the man's blades before he'd fully finished protesting.

Thorn shoved Vax against a wall and leaned in close, his eyes flashing. "If they find you here, they'll comb through the mines and find all the rest of us too. We didn't save your life for that. Keep your head down and keep walking."

A handful of other miners passed them by, with weapons by their sides and angry expressions, though whether that was because they'd overheard Vax or were simply emulating Thorn's snarl, Vax couldn't tell.

He swallowed and nodded begrudgingly.

Once Thorn had released Vax, Sencha mercilessly continued dragging him down, past one level, through a long, winding tunnel where the stone walls were sharp enough to cut and where the air around them was becoming colder with every step. It smelled damp and fresh where he'd expected it to be stale, but no part of this underground world made sense to him.

When every trace of light from the upper levels had disappeared and the marching pace slowed somewhat, Vax raised a hand and leaned against the wall. Sencha hovered next to him, vacillating between glancing in the direction in which Thorn had disappeared and the direction that the others followed. She moved her weight from one foot to the other and back again, clearly anxious to keep going. They were surrounded by jagged edges and the darkness was hungry.

"What kind of mine is it, anyway?" Vax asked. He loosened his arms and tried to ignore the pain clawing at his back. The additional healing had helped, but Thorn's anger had torn through that. He needed a moment to catch his breath, and he wanted to know more of this underground maze. If only so he could find his own way back to his sister.

"Ore," Sencha snapped. She placed her hand on his back. Warm comfort spread through his torso and limbs. "You're bleeding again."

"I promise I don't do it on purpose," he muttered.

"I can take a look when we're in the cavern down below," she said, her voice softer now. "Aside from reapplying your bandages and giving you herbs for the pain, I'm afraid I can't do much more for you for today."

Vax hesitated, then continued the walk down. He could hardly demand she'd keep healing him when there were others in need of a healer's touch too. "What kind of ore?" he asked instead, eager to keep talking.

"Silver, primarily."

Vax missed a step and he hissed. He'd take a rooftop chase over this endless winding descent any day. "Did you exhaust it?"

"You better not be thinking about going adventuring, half-elf." Sencha kept a careful eye on his footing. "You don't know what lies beneath and trust me when I say, you don't want to find out. Besides, this mine hasn't been in official operation since the Shadewatch set foot in Jorenn Village. The active silver mines are on the far side of Jorenn Village. They still provide miners approved by the Shadewatch with good work—and the merchants with good income too."

Her voice had taken on an edge of something harder than the kindness she'd showed him so far. Anger, perhaps. Or the same grief he'd seen with Thorn. Whichever the case, she'd told him far more than she'd intended to. "So you weren't approved by the Shadewatch?" he asked softly. He hadn't missed the fact that she'd never really answered his question either.

She pursed her lips and kept walking.

Once they'd twisted and turned through another level, they reached the cavern, and it was immediately clear why Sencha called it that. The last tunnel led beyond the carved-out chambers used for mining and opened up into a large underground cave that was about the size of the clearing where Vex and he had left Trinket when they'd gone into Westruun. It felt like stepping from carefully cultivated craftsmanship into the rawness of nature—and it looked as uncomfortable as anyplace in the wild.

In the cavern, no beams were necessary to support the roof. The floor was filled with stalagmites that protruded from the rock like needles, while stalactites reached down from the rock above. A slender stream pushed between the pillars into a deep pool, and a soft blue glow illuminated the farthest edges of the cavern, where glow worms spread across rock like tiny, stubborn stars. Narrow passages led away from the shared space, and by the time Sencha and Vax made their way down, guards had already been posted at all the passages.

The vast majority of this small community appeared to be here. Thorn's crew numbered perhaps four dozen in all, including the trio of halflings he'd seen in the kitchens, Junel, and at least three younger children, but without Thorn and a handful of others Vax had seen around the kitchen. They weren't here for the first time either. The walls showed how often they'd stayed here. Every inch of bare wall showed intricate black drawings on splashes of bright shades. A beautiful grove silhouetted against a green background, the trees slender and gracious and reaching toward black birds silhouetted against blue. Hearts and stars and names, too. Pictures of homes, built from black paint and memories.

In the center of the cavern, the refugees from the higher levels used the same glass sphere Vax had seen previously to illuminate their work as they were gathering up bags and supplies. Sencha helped him settle down and rebandaged his wounds, but from there all he could do was sit, sharpen his daggers with a whetstone to take his mind off the disquiet of hiding, and stare in wonder up at the glowworms.

THE AFTERNOON HAD—PRESUMABLY—BLED INTO NIGHT when Thorn and the others returned. Junel had seen to it that everyone had eaten and the children were asleep on makeshift cots. Everyone went about their business in the cavern, like they weren't hiding from roaming guards, knitting and sewing, cleaning and sharpening weapons, playing cards or sitting comfortably near one another around a small fire made out of torches. One girl sang a tragic love song that echoed hauntingly against the rocks, until two musicians with instruments took over and filled the cavern with defiantly happier tunes.

Vax had wandered toward the entrance a few times, but every time he tried, one of the miners had casually blocked his path. He'd reluctantly played a few hands of cards with the halfling trio before retreating to a quieter spot near the stream, where he could lean against one of the pillars. His back felt like it'd been shredded, and the idea that someone from Jorenn Village could be near looking for him tore him up too. His sister could take care of herself. He knew that. He hadn't been lying when he'd told her she was the strongest person he knew. Always had been. But Thorn made Jorenn sound like a death trap, and his Clasp-given assignment hardly helped make things safer. He'd walked them right into an impossible situation.

And by the looks of things, they weren't the only ones stuck between a rock and more rocks. This was no simple heist. He'd stumbled into something big enough to make the ring look insignificant.

"If you keep frowning like that, you'll mar that pretty face of yours." Thorn stood over him. His face was pale and his shoulders slumped. His wavy hair fell in tangled streaks around his face. He kept fidgeting with a leather belt that wrapped around his waist like it was too big for him, both ends serpentining down.

Vax craned his neck, to try to get better sense of the man in front of him. "Is this how you live all the time?" he grumbled. "Hidden away and hiding deeper whenever danger is near?"

Thorn growled. "Well, excuse us for saving your life."

Vax ran a hand over his face. "I'm worried about my sister, and I don't appreciate being stuck here."

Thorn plopped down on the ground next to him and leaned his head against the rocks. His scars stood out like raw and tired lines across his face. "I didn't intend to drag you all the way down here either. You can blame the Shadewatch for that."

Vax didn't miss the slight hesitation in Thorn's voice, and with nowhere else to go he tilted his head to face him. "Why did you do it then? Why did you save me and then bring me here? It can't be convenient."

"It isn't," Thorn said, softer. "It's a risk, and I don't play with my people's lives at stake. But I also refuse to walk away when other people are in danger. You got lucky we were there. You had something in your camp we needed."

"What?"

For the longest time, Thorn didn't speak. He picked up small pebbles and tossed them into the stream, watching the water ripple and ease again. "Letters. Evidence."

Vax considered it, mulling over the various options. "Evidence of what the Shadewatch did to your family?"

Another pebble. A soft *plop* when it hit the water. "I don't need evidence for that. I was there. I saw it happen. I *felt* it happen. We all saw our lives destroyed that day."

Inwardly, Vax cringed. "Of the Shademaster's plans, then? She has control of the town and the guard. She's taken control of the mines. So she's using them for what, some kind of evil scheme? Or simply for smuggling? If she controls the silver trade in and around Jorenn, I imagine that's profitable." He'd never met the Shademaster, but based on what Thorn had told him and what Sencha had inadvertently shared, he imagined she was the type of person he could easily dislike.

Thorn stilled. "You pay attention." The words held somewhere between reproachful and begrudgingly impressed. "It's hard to fight a monster beloved by all."

At least it made stealing from the Shadewatch a far nobler pursuit than it had previously seemed. The idea almost concerned Vax. As far as he was aware, the Clasp did nothing for noble purposes.

"We wish to go home too," Thorn admitted. "Hidden away *is* how we live all the time, and it breaks you up, to go without a place where you can rest. To try to form a family from the shattered remains of what is left, while always being surrounded by the ghosts of those you couldn't save."

Vax swallowed and looked away. "I understand."

"Do you, pretty boy?" Thorn tossed one last pebble into the stream and turned to Vax. "Do you know what it's like to lose everything? To worry constantly about the people who depend on you? To think of nothing but to get rid of that cursed Shademaster, because until she's gone, she won't stop killing us and destroying the community we once had?"

Thorn used his words like daggers, Vax realized, and he could only respond in kind. "So how do you propose to slay your monster then? You can't take on an entire fucking town."

"Can't I?" Thorn pushed to his feet. "I'm going to grab a drink. Need anything?"

He was already halfway through the cavern before Vax could mutter, "I do." Despite Thorn's words, it disconcerted him how well he did understand. He understood the longing and the anger in Thorn's voice, and he understood the phantoms that stood among the people in the cavern. The trio of halflings instinctively held a place for a fourth. Sencha sat near the campfire holding Junel's hand, while her other hand clenched and unclenched at her side.

We all saw our lives destroyed that day.

Vax reached to the inside of his cloak, where the ghosts of chalk marks still lingered. If he closed his eyes, he could hear the slight tear of scissors cutting through fabric. If he closed his eyes, the warm smell of freshly washed linen wrapped around him, mingling with the acridity of ash and burnt wood. He knew something about destruction.

If he and his sister had been home when it burned, perhaps they would've clung to its memory too. Some days, he wasn't sure if they would always try to run away from it, or if he was still, constantly, trying to find it.

He certainly wouldn't trust outsiders either.

Thorn weaved through the crowd, stopping briefly for a conversation with the half-orc and her dwarven lover, or to listen to a fiddle and a flute. A few steps farther, he wrapped an arm around a young human woman who'd distanced herself from the others to read a book. She hadn't turned a page since she'd sat down on her own. And Thorn carried the weight of all the ghosts.

Vax waited until Thorn made his way back to him with two mugs of some spiced ale from a kettle that Junel guarded with a large wooden spoon. Thorn held one mug out to him, but when Vax accepted it, he didn't sit down again. Instead he crouched next to the stream and stared. He carried his exhaustion like a thin veneer over the rage that coursed inside him. Or perhaps rage was the veneer over his heartache.

"I'd walk into that fucking town and kill her myself, if that's what it took for the rest of them to live." Thorn clung to his mug and hooked a thumb around his belt. "That's how I want to slay my monster. The two of us, face-to-face. She wouldn't be able to hide behind her guard, and I would pay her back for everything she took from us."

Behind Thorn, several of the people in the cavern cast worried looks in his direction. It was impossible to miss that while Thorn tried to carry the burden, everyone here would do anything to keep one another safe, and his grief permeated all of them.

Vax took a sip from his drink, and it spread like liquid heat through his body, the spices strong and the ale stronger. He wasn't involved in this. He shouldn't be. But this fragile community tugged at him, in ways he didn't fully understand.

"You know there are other options," he said carefully, pulling at the fragments of a plan. "If you're looking for evidence of the Shademaster's schemes, the best place to start is *with* the Shademaster."

"I don't think she'll be open to a nice conversation over tea and biscuits," Thorn scoffed.

"She wouldn't have to know," Vax said. "I assume she has notes. Letters of promise. Correspondence. A place where she keeps such things. It wouldn't be so hard for someone who knows what they're doing to steal in and retrieve what you need."

"And that someone would coincidentally want to steal into town and retrieve his sister as well?"

Vax shrugged. "Do you have a problem with that?" He wouldn't deny that. He needed Vex by his side, and he had other business in Jorenn too.

But that didn't mean the plan—as fragmented as it was—wasn't a great deal better than Thorn's desperation for revenge. Two birds, one stone. Three, if he was lucky and found the ring too. "Unless you have someone else who's good at breaking and entering?"

Thorn drank deeply. "I'm almost curious about your intended pursuits in Jorenn now. Yes, I have a problem with your plan: I would have to be able to trust whomever we sent into town to find their way back here. Or to do what needs to be done if they can't."

"You can trust me."

"I don't think I can," Thorn said, with a genuine hint of regret. "Because from where I'm standing, you've observed us for a day. You may think you owe us, you may even think you understand us, but if we let you go and you're faced with the choice between us and your sister, we don't stand a chance. So no, I don't trust you. I don't trust anyone to do right by us anymore."

Vax didn't have a response to that. There was nothing he could say to convince Thorn, because he wasn't wrong. But he also wasn't right. And he would have to find his way out of here one way or another.

After an uncomfortable silence, Vax fought to change the subject. "Who is Emryn? You mentioned he was the one to find me. I'd like to thank him."

Thorn chugged the rest of his drink in one go. "He would've liked that. Emryn died of his wounds," he said simply. "Shortly before the cursed Shadewatch appeared."

Vax breathed out hard, the words a gut punch. "I'm sorry."

Thorn shook his head. "So if we're all short-fused today, understand that it's not personal. It's hard to lose one of our own when there are so few of us left."

"And all to protect a stranger?" Vax supplied. He set his cup aside and wondered about the ghosts in front of him. He wondered who was holding out a hand to Emryn tonight—and whether any of them would think it was worth it to pull him out of a pile of ash. It was a debt he couldn't repay.

Thorn's eyes sharpened. "Do not go blaming yourself. It isn't like that."

"Could Sencha have used all her healing on him?" Vax shot back. "Would he have been in that position if he hadn't seen me fall in the first place?"

Thorn dropped his cup and moved so fast, Vax had no time to stop him. He dropped down next to him, one knee on the floor, the other locking an arm in place. He had a short sword in his hand before Vax could even think to reach for his daggers, and he angled the blade across Vax's chest. "He chose to help. Do not cheapen that choice with your guilt. We've lost too much already."

Vax raised his chin and met Thorn's rage and heartache. He recognized his loss and the impossibility of the situation. They stared at each other for a fraction of eternity before Thorn sheathed his sword and pushed himself to his feet. He swung around to find the conversations in the cavern had dimmed and most present and still awake had turned to him.

Thorn grabbed Vax's cup from the floor, and held it up high. "To Emryn, bravest of us fools, and all the others we can't forget."

The words echoed through the cavern.

"To Emryn."

"To Emryn, foolish bastard."

On the far end of the room, a dwarf held his own tankard high and added loudly—and before one of the guards near the children shushed him—"To finding our way home."

"To victory!"

"To vengeance," Thorn muttered.

When he glanced back at Vax, there was an unmistakable challenge in his eyes, and then he drank deeply.

Vax reached for Thorn's fallen cup and raised it in a salute of his own. And while the voices picked up around them again, and the music quietly resumed, this was something he understood too. The need to carve out a place—or even a moment—where pain could briefly be forgotten.

CHAPTER 16

Seven years ago

The Tarn Thoroughfare was a place of beauty and wonder, and once he'd found his way there—and a way out of their father's home—nothing could keep Vax away. To walk around the market on the edge of Lake Ywnnlas was to be surrounded by magic. Not the magic of spells and charms or even of people, but the magic of possibility. Here, illuminated by the moons above and the lanterns that gently drifted above the crowds, wearing hooded cloaks to protect them from soft nights and prying eyes, he was like all the other young elves who sneaked into the market. He wasn't the only one who didn't belong here.

He dragged his sister along sometimes. They'd dashed from one vendor to the next, crossing the small canals that led away from the lake, marveling at the stalls and the items on offer, because at the Tarn Thoroughfare, every item held a promise. There were weapons so magnificently made that they had to be made for heroics, and the swords and staffs brought the twins right back to the adventures they'd played at as children. There were potions and tonics reflecting the colors of the floating lanterns above them, offering health and happiness and the most wondrous abilities, allowing one and all to experience what it must be like to fly or speak with animals. Amulets and rings in all sorts of precious metals, with meticulously cut gems that looked like stars clasped in metal.

When Vex came to the market, she loved the glimmer of jewelry, but she could never resist the lure of the bowyer's offerings. Even though she disliked the crowded alleys and the soft elvensong that wound through the streets, she came back every once in a while to stare hungrily at the expensive bows and bracers. At the bundles of arrows and feathers for fletching in a dozen colors. Different shades of gray and brown and white, red too, and even blue. But while Syldor had given them an allowance when they started school, she couldn't even afford the craftswoman's most basic quivers.

Tonight Vax crested past the bowyer's stall without a second glance. Vex had remained at home to study, to prove she could keep up in school, where the teachers were even harsher than their tutors had been. Vax had a different goal. He slipped past two elves who were admiring a mantle of sorts, though they seemed to have far more eyes for each other. He narrowly avoided a collision with a halfling who stamped out of a shop for oils and lanterns with an affronted look on her face. He let the music guide him to a weaver's shop off the main roads, angling away from the lake.

The shop, filled with fine fabrics woven in every color imaginable, was smaller than most around here. It didn't have the shine or sparkle of the popular stalls on the water's edge. It didn't have the mystique of other shops along the canals, with their colorful canopies and odd merchandise. It simply existed, with a storefront that was easy to miss and goods scattered around haphazardly. Drab colors mixed with vibrant ones. Flawed weaves as proudly on display as perfect twills. It was, Vax had come to realize, purposefully bland. The people who didn't know what they were looking for didn't come here. And the people who did didn't care.

Vax didn't care. He only ever came looking for one thing.

He pushed open the door—with some difficulty, because it also purposefully stuck—and Lathra, the owner, gave him a cursory scowl over her glasses before returning to the faintly illuminated small metal springs on her workbench. Despite her being a master weaver, Vax had never actually seen her weave. Instead she always seemed to be tinkering with small clockwork toys.

When he thought about it, he'd never seen her finish one of those to her satisfaction either.

He walked past the rows of cloth and slipped past a long, dark curtain into the back room. Before he'd fully crossed the threshold, a sharp point dug in his side below his ribs. It was immediately followed by a hard breath.

"Gods, Vax. Give me some warning next time."

Vax laughed, some of the tension in his body melting away at the familiar voice. "You enjoy it, don't lie." He reached out and pushed the small dagger away before he turned and faced his assailant.

Cyriel flipped the blade into the air and let it disappear into her sleeve when she caught it. "I don't love nearly stabbing you. I didn't think you'd come tonight."

Cyriel was Lathra's fifteen-year-old apprentice, a lanky girl with brown hair, suntanned skin, and sparkling blue eyes. She was equal parts earnest and lighthearted, her care-for-nothing attitude unusual in this city of splendor. Her presence was turning into a welcome distraction from this shitty place.

"I got into another fight with my dear father," Vax said, trying to shrug and make it seem like nothing. "I needed to make sure he wouldn't catch me sneaking out before I came here."

"Again?" Compassion softened Cyriel's eyes. She sat down and patted the bench next to her. The table in front of her was covered in small piles of gold and silver and assorted curios, and it appeared she had been in the process of filling a few different pouches.

Vax sagged down and leaned against her, staring at the array of riches. "Have you been out yet?"

He could feel Cyriel nod. "Only one round." She gestured at the table. "These are some of yesterday's too. Still counting out the guild's share. With Elvendawn on the horizon, purses are heavier than they usually are."

"Fancy clothes and fancy food?" Vax asked. Syldor had kept the twins away from the midsummer celebration as much as he could, and it had never really appealed to Vax either. A holiday to celebrate the creation of the elves? He refused to entertain the thought.

"Something like that." Cyriel laughed, and Vax leaned in closer. "So do you get more orders too? Or is all of this a front?"

"How dare you." Cyriel shoved him. "We do honest work as well! Some of it, anyway." She slipped an arm around Vax's shoulders. "You want to go out again?"

"Still saving up for that bow," Vax said. This is what they did most nights together. They pulled on nondescript cloaks and mingled in the busiest nooks and crannies of the Tarn Thoroughfare, picking pockets and cutting the occasional purse. It was a dangerous pastime in a city brimming with magic, but Vax had only ever been caught once: the very first time he stomped around the market, when he foolishly tried to lift a few pieces of silver from a girl a little older than he, certain she had been one of the bullies at school. Instead the girl had turned out to be a weaver's apprentice by day and a petty thief by night.

Cyriel had grabbed Vax's wrist, dragged him into a corner, and told him that if he wanted to attempt thievery, he should at least know some tricks of the trade. Over the next night and several nights after, they became the only lessons in this cursed city Vax had ever paid attention to, because Cyriel taught him ways to hide and be invisible, while at the same time being the first person since his sister to *see* him.

To Vax's surprise, Cyriel's apprenticeship had been an essential part of the play. Lathra grumbled at his half-elven heritage, but had looked away when Cyriel had given Vax one of her old, patched-up but comfortable coats lined with half a dozen hidden pockets. Before the two of them had left for the thoroughfare, however, Lathra had pulled Vax aside and blithely told him that while it was good for young people such as the two of them to have profitable hobbies, not to get too close. That Cyriel was meant for better things than one such as him.

"Are you sure? I don't want you to be distracted by whatever nonsense your father tried to tell you." Cyriel casually played with a few strands of Vax's hair.

Vax cringed at the question. "Nothing I believe, I promise. And yes, I'm sure."

"We could also wander. Buy hot cocoa. Find someplace to sit near the water and look at the sprites dancing on the lake," she teased, knowing full well that both of them were too restless by half for a night like that.

Perhaps that was what had pulled them together in the first place. Difference and disquiet. Attraction, too. But the type of attraction that came without attachment. The type of friendship that came without too much trust.

Vax pushed himself to his feet. "I think Lathra would be disappointed if you left it at this."

"Well, we can't have that." Cyriel leaned on the table as she followed suit. She grabbed a pair of wooden crutches and used them to steady herself. The myrtle wood was finely carved, with flowers and leaves and branches circling the crutches from top to bottom. At the very last moment, she also snatched a half-filled coin purse from the table. She reached out for a quick kiss. "Don't think I was lying about that hot cocoa though."

NOT HALF AN HOUR LATER, they were back in the thick of the thoroughfare, where soft music drifted along the floating lanterns and all the conversations were hushed. The elves who'd under normal circumstances looked down their nose at Vax now extended that courtesy to Cyriel. They none-too-subtly turned away from her and whispered behind their hands, while their looks were those of either pity or disgust.

Cyriel attempted to shrug it off, but Vax saw through her masked pain. "They're assholes," he whispered, nudging Cyriel with his shoulder.

Cyriel offered him a faint, knowing smile. "They are."

Her twisted leg wasn't a masquerade. One of the first lessons Cyriel had taught Vax was to recognize what people expected when they saw him. The elves' immediate distrust and dislike over his half-elf status meant Vax had to hide that part of him or remain altogether unseen, because they'd be warier of him. The discomfort and underestimation meant Cyriel could purposefully stumble along the water's edge and never be considered a threat. It gave them different strategies for different situations.

"Watch me," Cyriel whispered, focusing on an older elven gentleman with long gray-and-magenta robes, golden rings on every finger, and a heavy purse hanging from his belt, who was admiring a silver raven figurine in a goldsmith's stall.

Cyriel made her way over to the stall to stand next to the man, and instead let herself topple over. With her crutches outstretched, she collided with the man, the two of them briefly a tangle of robes and arms.

"I'm sorry. I'm so sorry," Cyriel gushed. She tried to heave herself upright, but fumbled, while a young shopkeeper rushed around the stall to help.

"Clumsy, inept—" The gentleman's pale face took on interesting shades of red and hints of purple, but before he could launch into a full tirade, he noticed Cyriel's crutches and clamped his mouth shut. His nostrils flared.

"It was entirely my fault, sir, I'm so sorry." Cyriel reached out to straighten the man's coat, and he instinctually took a step back. "If there's anything I can do . . ."

"Just leave me be," the man snapped. He refused to meet Cyriel's eye or acknowledge the outstretched hand of the shopkeeper, who stood helplessly at a small distance.

"Are you certain? I could make sure your coat is cleaned and seen to. I could—"

"Go!"

All necessary pleasantries out of the way, Cyriel just nodded, the very picture of a shaken teenage elf, and backed into the street. She picked up her pace when she left, as though she was too embarrassed to stay, and dragged Vax into a side alleyway the moment she could.

Vax held up his hands, and from the linings of her coat a laughing Cyriel produced a silver bracelet, two handfuls of gold coins, and a blue gem the size of a fingernail.

"You could've had everything off him with how angry he was," Vax noted. He turned the gem this way and that, letting it catch the lantern-light. His sister would love it.

"Then he would've known for certain it was me. Small gains. He'll likely think he lost something and never think twice about colliding with me." Cyriel grinned and produced a velvet pouch.

Vax poured her winnings into it. "My turn." He pulled his dark-brown hood high over his head, letting the shadows obscure his face. He loosened his shoulders and ignored Cyriel's warm laughter.

"You look like some kind of predator on the prowl when you do that."

He stuck his tongue out. "Hush, you."

"Tell me I'm wrong."

His only response was to flip her off before he dashed away.

Finding the right target was a game. Vax didn't take their petty thievery too seriously, because it was only meant to be fun, not survival. But on nights like tonight, when his father's *good-for-nothing* comments stuck in his head, he needed his own ways to prove his worth and leave his mark on the city. With all its indelible structure, it deserved a little chaos.

Following a winding road that crossed up and over one of the canals, he spotted two elven women walking together, both of them holding steaming cups. They were whispering and laughing, entirely oblivious to the world around them.

Vax scanned the bustling street for the best approach. A group of children ran from stall to stall, all of them whispering reverently. A woman with slate-gray hair and ancient blue eyes tried on a tall hat. A father proudly showed his young son a gleaming shield engraved with symbols along the edge.

Vax's throat constricted. He pulled his attention away and tried to figure out where all the bustle came together. Once he felt certain, he put his head down and angled his approach so he would pass the women by at the same time as the children and as narrowly as possible. He hummed a discordant tune, kept walking, and when the moment came, he reached out and brushed the nearest coat pocket.

His fingers wrapped around a small pouch, and he slipped it into his sleeve before anyone could notice.

Toward the next stall.

And the next.

Those first few moments were crucial. They'd either notice, or—

"Hey!" The voice was loud amidst the song and murmurs. "Stop him!"

Vax tensed. Briefly, he couldn't breathe. He couldn't think. He could just—run, do what Cyriel taught him. Get away from the busy streets as soon as possible. He dashed past the woman with the hat, who yelped loudly, and scattered the children like a flock of birds. He cut corners and zigzagged around other elves. He kept tugging his hood low over his eyes, out of fear that the garment would fall back and make him far too recognizable.

He stumbled through one street and the next. He didn't hear any footsteps rushing behind him, but he wasn't about to chance being safe and letting anyone get the jump on him.

He cut into a narrow alley, jumped up high to find purchase on a wall, and heaved himself up on it and onto the nearest roof.

The light from the floating lanterns didn't extend beyond the rooftops, so the whole world around him fell back in darkness. He paused. Everything was moonlit shadows and starry skies, a spiral-shaped constellation far above him. The different shades of night offered a treacherous path to safety.

But at least he was alone.

Far below, whispered alarms echoed through the street, and with regret he took the pouch from his sleeve. "Don't hold on to anything that can be traced," Cyriel had advised.

He lobbed the pouch over the wall he'd climbed and called himself ten times a fool before he began to make his way over the rooftops, until the quiet of the night sky wrapped around him, his stride lengthened, and his worry fell away. And briefly, it felt like he could fly.

AT THE LAKEFRONT, CYRIEL SAT on a wooden bench, her crutches by her side and two cups of hot cocoa next to her. She didn't look up when Vax plopped down on the bench, but instead kept her eyes on the star sprites dancing on the lake. She took one of the cups and quietly held it out.

Vax's stomach dropped. Was she angry? Disappointed? She'd been correct in her earlier observations. Vax *had* been distracted.

He realized the cocoa Cyriel was holding slushed back and forth, and when he looked up she was laughing silently.

"Gods, Vax, you should've seen their faces. You should've seen *your* face."

Vax snatched the cocoa from her. "*Fine.* You were right. You told me so."

The amusement pummeled the same bruise his father's words left. *Worthless. Good-for-nothing.* He would rather die than believe his father's cruel assessments, but that didn't mean they didn't hurt.

Then Cyriel put her cocoa to the side. She reached out and wrapped her hand around Vax's. With her free hand, she pushed a strand of hair out of his face, the movement so soft and tender it sent chills up his spine. "You got rid of whatever you stole, right?"

Vax nodded, tight-lipped.

"Good. It's not about never getting caught. It's about what you do when you are. You did good." She smirked. "And at least the Verdant Lord's daughter will have a new tale to tell when she comes home."

With that, the last bit of Vax's resistance and pressure melted away, though he fought hard to keep his face passive. "The Verdant Lord as in . . . commander of the city's guard? His daughter?"

Cyriel's grin was as bright as the spirits dancing on the water. "The very same. You know the intention is to *avoid* the guard, right?"

Vax snorted. "Oh, fuck right off."

Cyriel pulled him close and Vax's cup tumbled from his grasp. He could still taste the cocoa on the girl's lips. Nights like these reminded him there were pockets of the city that his father *didn't* control, where the rules weren't made to be followed, where he could survive. At least until he could go home.

CHAPTER 17

People didn't just disappear, but somehow, her brother had managed it. For the past few days, Vex had scoured every inch of the hills and the valleys around Jorenn. She'd asked Trinket to help sniff him out. She'd followed every track and trail she could find—at least twice. And nothing. She might as well have been walking in circles, something she hadn't done since she was a little girl.

Every time the colors around her changed to the bloodred of dusk, she knew she'd lost him for another day.

Every night when she returned to Jorenn, Derowen was there, waiting for her. To ask her how her day went and if she found anything new. To invite her to dinner with her and Aswin, and occasionally Wick. Derowen insisted she keep her room in the Shade Hall, so Vex learned to find her way around. She'd expected a lack of welcome, and instead she was given an abundance of it, and no matter how uncomfortable it was, no matter how much she distrusted it, she could not escape it. When she tried, Aswin would inevitably find her. Or Derowen would check in, to see if she was doing all right. Or Wick would simply wander by. So Vex spent her evenings in the Shademaster's sitting room, reading her books and poring over old maps of the hills to find a route for the following morning.

She knew it was because they'd hoped she'd find something the Shadewatch scouts had missed. But she spent her days aching with loneliness, and at night, they refused to let her be alone.

Earlier, Aswin had tugged at her cloak, eyes wide and brimming.

She'd handed Vex a drawing she'd made while at her lessons with Wick. She'd drawn Vex, hand in hand with Trinket, and another Vex, carrying a sword instead of a bow, hand in hand with a grinning ash walker. Vex wanted to tear the drawing apart, but all she could do was give Aswin a hug as the living nightmare that she fought to keep at bay washed over her once more.

After a handful of days of riding out into the hills with no real clues, Vex realized she was going about her search the wrong way. She returned to the location of the encampment, with Derowen in tow, and stared at the only real tracks she'd found so far. They were marred by time and weather, but she'd be able to retrace them even if no sign of them was left. She took one of Derowen's maps and sketched in the tracks. She added the other set of footprints she'd seen and the direction of the various trails around the campsite and deeper in the hills.

Derowen looked over her shoulder with curiosity. "We know of old mines there, there, and there," she said, pointing. "We've sent in guards before, but all the entrances were caved in."

"Do you know how far down the mines go?" Vex asked. She added notes of the other tracks she found.

"The systems spread out for miles," the Shademaster admitted. She wore a red uniform, her sword by her side, and she unconsciously ran her fingers over the hilt. She didn't suppress the anger in her voice. She'd come without question when Vex told her she might have an idea. "Mining used to be a family business in Jorenn, and knowledge of the mines a closely kept family secret. Those outlaws may be the only ones who know their way around underground, which makes it so hard to fight them and the ash walkers both. We should never have let them escape."

Derowen glanced in the direction of the hills. "We won't make that mistake again, Vex. I believe you can find them. And any member of the Shadewatch worth their salt knows to hunt down any outlaw who shows their face aboveground." When Vex raised an eyebrow, the Shademaster's eyes flashed. "It's a standing order, and I won't apologize for it. They're a threat to my town and to my daughter. I can understand and even forgive many things, but not that. Never that."

Vex nodded. Over these past few days, she'd come to know Derowen as an exacting but fair commander, and as someone who would tear down the hills for her daughter. The anger and worry that fueled Derowen now Vex recognized all too well. And there was only one thing to do about it.

"If they live underground, there have to be ways for them to get to the surface for supplies," she said. "We may not have exact tracks, but we have directions. Traces and mistakes they've made. None of them led anywhere individually, but all of them combined . . ." She took the pencil and extended the lines until they all intersected. It showed an area near where she'd found the last disappearing tracks that angled away from the known mines. "Here. It's the only place that still makes sense."

Derowen considered it for a long moment. "What do you want to do?"

"Scour every inch of this area." Vex raised her chin. While she kept her voice level, her stomach churned. If this didn't work out, she didn't know what else to do. She couldn't even contemplate that. "Follow every cave and every stream. Find out if there's anything you've—anything *we've* missed."

Because if there was one thing Derowen had made clear to Vex over the past few days, it was this: this wasn't only Vex's fight. This was all of Jorenn's. Whether Vex liked it or not, she was part of a community of people fighting for their lives and trying to protect themselves and one another from ash walkers created by greed. So they fought together.

"We've tried combing through the hills before, around the mines' entrances. Perhaps it's time to try again."

The Shademaster relaxed her grip on her hilt. She took in the map and smiled a smile full of sharp edges. "You'll need more guards. Map out the exact area, and I'll assign scouting parties. You're welcome to join or oversee them, whichever you prefer."

Derowen rested a hand on Vex's arm, her ring glimmering in the pale sunlight. "I regret that you came here under hard circumstances, Vex. But your presence is a boon to our town. *Thank you.*"

Vex's shoulder sagged with something akin to relief. This plan was the closest she'd felt to hope since the fight where she'd lost Vax. During these past few days, no one had pointed out to her that the chances slimmed with every passing hour, and she was thankful for that. The reality of time passing was hard to ignore. None of the people they'd met the night the ash walkers attacked remained in town. The dwarves had returned to the Turst Fields, and the bickering duo had apparently found a guide that would bring them into the Grey Valley, despite the potential for further danger. They'd left not long after Shademaster Derowen and Wick visited the inn to talk to the survivors. Only she and Trinket remained.

Vex dreamed of these hills. She could walk them in her sleep, feel the crunch of the shadegrass beneath her feet, hear the whispers of the wind that rushed down the slopes. She kept constantly listening for one voice. She cast her own whispers into the wind and hoped he would hear them. *Come home.*

Still, her search meant she could do something. When Derowen returned to Jorenn, she followed the edges of the area she'd drawn out and mapped them closely, noting every hillside and stream, every rock-slide and path of shadegrass. The smallest details of the nature around her that usually helped her to find her way—the slightest twist of blades of grass, the disturbance of grains of sand, broken and bruised leaves—still mocked her, but for once it didn't make her feel spectacularly useless.

Her determination wavered only slightly when she realized the area she marked was one of several square miles of rough terrain. It would take the guards days to investigate it, and at the edge of day and night, ash walkers prowled in the distance.

Before the sun had fully set, the wind tossed up dust and sand, and it gave the hills an eerie, macabre atmosphere.

"It isn't ash," she snapped at one of the guards by her side, who skittishly avoided the swirls of dust and darkness.

The guard—a middle-aged woman called Beven, with short-cropped blond hair and piercing green eyes—leveled a hard look at her. "I'm glad you're the expert."

She gnashed her teeth, and Beven continued, "I've spent enough time in these hills to see those damned walkers appear seemingly out of nowhere. We follow the Shademaster's orders, but we don't court unreasonable danger."

Vex didn't challenge her, even though she wanted to. She didn't tell her she'd be happy to court any type of danger to get to her brother.

She kept her eyes on the hills around her as though she could stare straight through the rock to what had to lie beneath.

WHEN THE GATES OF JORENN Village came into view again, the guard sighed their relief, while Vex marked down another day. Lost to necessary plans, but lost all the same.

At the gate, Wick towered over a dwarven guard and appeared to be in the midst of a conversation that looked rather unpleasant for the guard—but when Vex rode up to them, Wick held up his hand.

Wick pointed and snapped at the guard once more before he turned to the riders.

He held his hand out to Vex. "May I borrow you?" He grimaced, as if he'd only realized how it must have sounded when the words tumbled out of his mouth. "I have no word from your brother, but I do have something else I'd like to show you."

One of Vex's guards laughed at the poor bastard being scolded, though she immediately sobered when Wick zeroed in on her. "Take care of our guest's horse, please." Though his words were phrased as a request, his tone was rich with command.

"Of course, Wick."

Vex's heart leaped and fell at Wick's words. She let him help her dismount. The guard immediately stepped in to grab her horse's reins, and Trinket walked up to nudge her in the shoulder. She stretched, scratched Trinket's hair, and pulled herself back together.

"What is it?"

"Walk with me? I'd offer you my arm, but I don't think that'd be comfortable for you." He pulled up one shoulder in a half shrug.

"Don't worry about it." She wasn't a lady who needed an arm, she was a sister who needed her brother.

Wick observed her quietly. While she'd gotten used to his presence, he still cut a strange figure here. He was the only half-giant in town, and wherever he went, people stopped to greet him. He wasn't a member of the Shadewatch though all the guards treated him with the same respect they otherwise reserved for Derowen. And while the warhammer he wielded was the same size as Aswin, on those few occasions Vex had observed them sitting around a table for Aswin's lessons, he had at least as much patience as he did strength.

"Derowen told me you marked an area for the guard to investigate," he said eventually, softly, when he guided her toward a long street that ran parallel to the town square and stretched all the way toward the other end of town, with narrow shops scattered on either side between regular houses, with strong wooden façades and colorful awnings that waved like banners in the breeze, cheerful against the drab colors of town. Though most doors were locked for the night, the shopping windows were not boarded up and the lights inside shone boldly. Wick dragged her along with a purpose.

"It's the only thing that still makes sense," she said. She refused to acknowledge that after a long day of riding, her voice sounded thin and tired and far less convincing then when she'd spoken with Derowen.

Trinket nudged her and walked closer, his ambling pace comfortingly close. He smelled of mud and ashes and home.

"It's a good plan," Wick said, all calm reassurance. "Derowen has faith in you, which means I do. And it's not just the two of us either."

She raised an eyebrow. "What does that mean, exactly?"

"You'll see." He smiled, and the boyish mischief tore through her.

He waited for a carriage to pass them by, dusting up the stamped dirt road, then he guided her to a brightly lit building across the road, where the shingle above the door read, in spidery writing, BINDS AND DOLLS. Blue curtains danced in front of the windows, and tiny eyes stared out through the glass. When Vex stepped closer, she realized half a dozen dolls sat on a shelf, their backs toward the shop and curious faces turned toward the street. They were meticulously crafted in all sorts of ways. Some were sewn from colorful swaths of fabric, others built from sticks and pieces of metal. They all had tiny gemstones for eyes. Fragments of ruby and sapphire, an emerald that reminded Vex too much of Aswin.

If Wick hadn't been there, Vex would've turned straight around. But he pushed the door open and stooped to get into the shop. The chimes on the door still pealed when Vex swiftly ducked in behind him, while Trinket stood watch outside.

In the middle of the shop, surrounded by rows upon rows of dolls in all shapes and sizes, all colors, and all states between barely constructed and beautifully polished, sat a young woman with stone-gray skin, darker than Wick's silver gray, and rougher too. She wore a double set of glasses, and though she looked up when the two of them entered, she didn't meet Wick's or Vex's eyes. Instead she stared at her hands and smiled at the half-finished doll in front of her, the newest creature built out of swaths of leather and brightly colored thread.

Beyond the workbench and the doll collection, the dolls slowly made way for books that were neatly stacked on the extended shelves. Small notecards with the same spidery handwriting noted the languages in which the books were written, and they were all structured accordingly.

"Hey, Beryl," Wick said gently. "This is Vex." He continued— hesitatingly—in a guttural language that Vex didn't understand.

Beryl nodded along and replied in the same language, her voice lower and resonant. She glanced at Vex through her eyelashes before nodding toward a book that balanced on the corner of the workbench. A thin volume, its cover mended with the same care shown to the dolls.

Wick picked it up and leafed through. "Beryl makes dolls for collectors and for the children in town, including Aswin. She's also somewhat of a book lover, and so she handles both. When Derowen came in here yesterday to pick up a mended doll for Aswin, she was reminded that you asked her if she had any books about dragons in her study."

Had she? It was probably true. Vex didn't remember. She might have asked. Most evenings she'd spent in a haze of restlessness and discomfort. The books provided her with a sense of focus, and it was the only thing that kept her from clawing at her own skin. She forced herself to think and not to feel, because if she did, she might shatter completely.

Wick held out the book to her. "Beryl found it for you, gathering dust on a bottom shelf."

Vex hesitated. "How much is it?"

"No, no payment," Beryl said. She ducked her head and flapped her fingers when Vex turned to her.

Wick drew Vex's attention back to him. "She wants you to have it. She knows you stood on those palisades besides the Shademaster, and it's her way of saying thanks."

Vex bit her lip. In her periphery, Beryl swayed in her chair, and she smiled gently. Vex wondered what it was that made these people help her without demanding anything in return.

She held the book and pressed it against her chest. She didn't look directly at Beryl. "Thank you."

"WHY?" SHE ASKED WICK WHEN they stood outside. She pushed the book into the pocket of her coat, where it bounced gently against her hip, and for once the idea of a night in Derowen's sitting room appealed to her beyond the opportunity for distraction. For once, the emptiness inside her did not feel wholly overwhelming, and it terrified her.

"Why did she help you?" Wick considered that. "Because she could. Because you helped us and she knows you're *still* helping us, and that goes a long way in Jorenn." He smiled and toyed with the leather band around his neck. "Many think of Jorenn as a harsh place, and it is. We've armed ourselves against the dangers coming down from the hills and up through the mines, and that changes a town. You may find cruelty here. But you'll find kindness too. We take care of one another. We try to make this as fair a town as it can be for all who live here."

He made it sound so simple. She appreciated the words in theory, but she had a hard time believing them. Fairness was for those with the money to buy it. Kindness was reserved for the lucky few, and she'd learned to brace herself for cruelty.

"If nothing else," Wick continued, recognizing her skepticism, "we have a shared foe. Ever since the miners disturbed the ash, we've learned it's far better to fight side by side. Everyone here knows what it's like to lose a loved one. Almost everyone knows what it's like to lose a home. If we don't stand together, what's to stop us from shattering completely?"

With darkness slowly blanketing the city, the streets around them quieted further. But in one of the houses someone picked out a tune on a fiddle. A few doors down, a brusque dwarf shouted out of a window for his daughters to come home for dinner.

"What happened? What were the initial attacks like?" Although she'd been in the midst of their savagery only days ago, it had seemed to her that between the archers and Derowen's barrier, Jorenn had managed to fend them off easily.

Wick rubbed his hand over his face. "Brutal. Jorenn has always suffered from attacks from creatures coming down the hills. When Derowen and I got here, it was no different. We had no way to fend them off, and too few people in Jorenn were trained to fight. I didn't want to stay. Aswin was still a baby, and I was terrified for her safety. Derowen was always the one with vision. She found a corner of the world that she loved and she didn't want to leave it. She saw how Jorenn could become a better place, a *safer* place. And for a while, it was. Until the ash walkers came up from the mines, and nothing could have prepared us for that."

"She didn't have that magical ring of hers?" Vex asked. That cursed piece of jewelry that had brought her and her brother here in the first place. This was no simple heist anymore, if it had ever been. If Vex didn't know the ring's significance, she would've considered stealing it for the pleasure of destroying it, for coming between the two of them.

Wick smiled. "No, not at first. But she had a purpose. She'd started training guard members long before the dead crawled through the streets. She formed the Shadewatch. And when the walkers did come, she helped build the palisades. She gave the people of Jorenn the chance to defend themselves and their loved ones. It wasn't flawless, but it gave hope to people who felt besieged. The ring didn't come until a year later. And even when she did have it, for a while the attacks only increased, like the Umbra Hills themselves were resisting us trying to create a peaceful home here. We had to take control of the mines because the dangers were too many."

"Despite all that, the ash walkers never left?"

"It's made us wonder if the outlaws simply kept on mining. That's also why it matters so much that you are helping us."

Vex mulled it over. Derowen's orders to hunt the outlaws down kept coming back to her, and with every new piece of information she learned they made more sense. It was a matter of survival. If they didn't find a way to stop the outlaws, they'd keep endangering Jorenn. And they would endanger Vax.

"How did Derowen get the ring?" she asked carefully. She'd avoided the subject so far, as focused as she was on finding her brother, but the job still existed in the back of her mind. With every new day lost she couldn't help but wonder what the Clasp thought. She couldn't care less about what they wanted, but perhaps uncovering the information they needed was another way for her to be closer to Vax.

Wick turned them back in the direction of the town square, raising a hand in greeting at a group of dwarves. "Her brother Culwen—you met him on your first day here, and he visits often—he uncovered it. He's a collector of strange and obscure objects. He simply showed up one day after we settled here, and demanded to see his sister. He offered her the ring in return for his own work space tucked away on the third floor of the Shade Hall, now filled to the brim with clutter. Derowen hates it, but no one can deny he occasionally comes up with useful items."

Vex shook her head. *Brothers and their trinkets.*

"Culwen never quite shares where he finds his curiosities. He *procured* the ring on his travels," Wick continued. "He said the stone came from these hills, so it was only right his sister had it. Derowen wasn't fond of it at first, but once she had a chance to study it, once she understood what it did, she realized how much it would add to the protection of the town. Jorenn wouldn't be what it is without that ring."

Vex winced. "So how does it work?"

"I've never used it myself." Something flicked across Wick's face, and his words were begrudging. "The way Derowen explains it, it creates a barrier that holds the dead at bay. Those cursed corpses found their way up and over the palisades before, and it was far more difficult to hold them back. Now only a few get through at best, and we can deal with those." He patted the handle of his warhammer. "Unfortunately we haven't yet found a way to make the roads safer. One day, we will."

"One day." Vex leaned against her bear and scratched his ear. She wanted to pry into the background of the ring, what it did exactly, but there was no way she could do that without raising suspicions, so instead, she let the quiet of the town wash over her.

There was an ease of comfort to Jorenn, in this liminal space between day and night, when the streets were emptying and not filling back up yet, when the last red streaks of the day reflected in the windows and night still held off its definitive cover. In another time and place, she would've heard birdsong now. There was little of that in Jorenn.

But there was joy and defiance, those little corners and cubbies where the townspeople carved sense into the world. Inside one of the houses, a young dwarven woman sang a lewd song that escaped through the open window and echoed through the street. Someone else grumbled at her to shut up, and she laughed loudly. An off-duty guard who passed Wick and Vex rolled his eyes and tipped his hat at both of them. If this was what it was like to live in a city—tearing down your own walls to rebuild them in the structures around you—she could grow used to it. If this is what Vax saw when they spent time in the cities, she understood it.

Wick cleared his throat. "You've asked me so many questions, let me ask you one of mine." His eyes lingered on her, and she shifted uncomfortably, prepared to draw up her defenses again. She was always prepared for that.

Wick scratched his head. "So why dragons?"

Oh.

She tapped against the book in her pocket. She hadn't expected *that* question. She never answered that question. She'd grown adept at skirting around it and many others like it. Where are you from? Why are you traveling? Who's waiting for you back home? Even Aswin's innocent question about her mother she'd managed to avoid, though that was luck as much as skill.

Her brother and she had kept to themselves for the better part of five years. They were fine on their own, and outside of Trinket, they didn't need anyone else. She didn't want to share her pain with anyone else, because it could only be used to hurt her more.

But this ridiculous town did something to her. Wick's solemn confidence gave her hope that some people might be willing to listen. For the first time in a long time, she *wanted* to answer.

She opened her mouth and closed it, and tried again until she found the right words. "Because I also know what it's like to lose a home."

Wick sighed. "I hoped that wasn't the answer. For what it's worth, I'm sorry." He held out his large hand to her and placed it on her shoulder. "You have a home here, now. For as long as you need it."

CHAPTER 18

.

Time passed differently in the cavern. The only way Vax could measure time was by the brightening and dimming of the glass spheres used as magical light sources that were set to emulate the sunlight outside—an old miner's trick, Thorn had called it with a smirk—and by Sencha's continued healings.

Vax's fingers twitched with the need to do *something*. Stand watch. Hide and stealth away. Start a fight. Find his sister. Let the Clasp know he was still toeing the line. Find a way to steal a ring and the miners' homes back.

The miners went about their days as much as possible, setting watches near the surface and carrying pickaxes and shovels deep into the mine, away from the dangerous surface. The mine might not officially be in operation, like Sencha had said, but the miners kept digging. They were obviously used to going without light and air around them, but he became increasingly agitated. He felt useless and conflicted, especially once his back healed. He missed rooftops and endless skies. He missed the rumor and opportunity of cities—even if those chances led to terrible decisions. He missed being able to go unseen, because every move he made in this cavern was observed by someone. And above all things, he missed Vex.

It was a bone-deep restlessness at first. The idea that she should be near or that he should be looking for her. Even at night, someone held a watch near the fire, and Vax didn't have a clue how to find his way out of the mines. As soon as he wandered toward the entrance, someone always followed him. The only thing he could do was to remind himself that Vex could take care of herself, and that she would know to keep her head down and stay away from the Shademaster. He had to remind himself that whatever information he gathered here could only help them, and he would find his way back to her as soon as he was able.

So when two of the trio of halflings disappeared deeper into the mines with Thorn and the third—a brown-haired, flat-nosed gem cutter's apprentice called Felric—invited him for a game of cards after breakfast, he jumped at the opportunity to mine the miners for information.

The game they played wasn't one he'd ever played before, but the rules were easy enough to pick up and Felric was a talkative player. "We all lived outside of Jorenn, near the mines. Silver mines, too. There were troubles, of course, before the Shadewatch. The laws only applied to those who wanted to hold to them, and strange creatures often came down from the hills. We protected each other as best we could. We were all we had. There's a difference, see, between townspeople and miners. Folk in town were terrified of the hills. We know how to live with dangers. There're all sorts of creatures in the deep."

"So what happened?" Vax asked.

Discomfort rolled across Felric's face. "Shadewatch came and kicked us out, didn't they?" He played his hand. "Claimed we endangered the town by digging too deep. Claimed the mines ought to belong to the town, and they should be the ones organizing the mining now. I don't think the townsfolk understood that the silver we found was for the good of all. We kept what we needed and nothing more. Everything else went to Jorenn's council of elders. But the Shadewatch wanted more. Said the town had a right to all and we were outlaws."

Vax hesitated before taking a card from the stack. "Did you? Dig too deep?"

"The Shadewatch claimed we're responsible for the ash walkers." Felric's mouth worked, but he didn't elaborate. He discarded his hand, barely paying attention to what Vax was doing. "That's why they needed to be in charge of the mines."

"Were you?" Vax pressed, feeling the words like claws across his back.

Felric shuffled his cards and looked away. "They destroyed our homes and cut down everyone who resisted." A shadow haunted his expression, and his shoulders twitched. "We barely escaped with our lives."

It wasn't an answer, but it was clear Felric didn't want to continue this line of conversation.

Still. "And the Shademaster . . . she was there?" Vax asked, purposefully playing a terrible hand to keep Felric in the game.

"There?" the halfling scoffed. "She led the first charge. She's the one who ran Anissa—Thorn's sister—through, and Thorn saw it happen." He pressed the spot between his eyes and threw his cards down in front of him. Without another word, he stalked toward the other side of the cavern, where he remained until one of the other halflings came to collect Felric for an assignment in one of the tunnels. Vax didn't miss the fact that they all wore a layer of gray dust and that they didn't seem thrilled by his attention.

He winced. Were they responsible for the ash walkers, and was the smuggling a story they told themselves? Were they still responsible?

Vax glanced around the cavern, at the small community in front of him. With every day that passed, he felt more in over his head. He shuffled the cards before he got up and walked toward the entrance. Immediately one of the elderly dwarves got to his feet too, a frown on his face. Vax might be able to take one—even a few—of them, but the message was clear. They'd stop him from leaving and—accidentally or otherwise—betraying their location. So he turned back and spent the afternoon going through sets of dagger practices, to the delight of the children in the cavern, two of whom stood at a distance and tried to emulate his movements with wooden spoons. Thorn, who wandered in and out of the tunnels, stayed to watch for a few minutes too. Vax noticed the half-elf's presence wherever he went. Thorn's glances were as sharp as his words.

Vax kept going until he tried to twist his daggers and spin around, and instead the world twisted and spun around him. After that, he cautiously sat down next to the tall female half-orc, who had spent the morning in the tunnels and was now once again bent over her book, wearing her glasses. Vax had heard enough to gather that the woman, who went by the name of Tinyn, was Thorn's second-in-command and by far the more levelheaded of the two.

Vax stared at the book. The cover bore no title, and the text was written in a language he didn't recognize.

When he looked up, Tinyn stared back at him suspiciously. "What do you want?"

Vax shrugged and studied his nails. "What was in those messages you lost in the camp?" He'd already tried getting more details from Thorn, but it couldn't hurt to try it again.

Tinyn guffawed. "You're bloody mad if you think I'll answer that." She slapped the book shut, and took Vax in as if she were seeing him for the first time. Her expression was calculating but closed off.

"Fine then." Vax shifted backward. "Did the Shadewatch take them?"

"No, the ashen dead are ferocious readers."

"Where will you go if you get out of here?" Because there had to be another plan than just revenge.

Tinyn looked at Vax as though he spoke a different language, and with something that almost resembled pity. "Simple. We go wherever Thorn does."

She pocketed the book and got to her feet, leaving Vax on his own with a sharp nod. The unspoken message was abundantly clear. They tolerated him. They would take care of him. But he was an outsider, and they didn't trust him. Thorn didn't trust him, and everything always came back to Thorn.

With nothing left to ward it off, Vax's restlessness and loneliness turned into an ache sharper than the wounds across his back. Vex and he had never been separated this long before, never longer than hours. It felt like missing a part of himself, like his heartbeat was only half of what it should be, and he'd been disconnected from the one person who anchored him. If he stayed here any longer, he'd become one of the many with a ghost by his side.

But aside from not knowing his way around, what stopped him from sneaking out once his back felt better was the fact that he *couldn't*. They'd saved his life at the cost of another, and it weighed on him. He owed them a life and a death.

He owed them a better understanding of what had happened. With the miners. With the Shadewatch. With Jorenn.

If he understood, once he got Vex back, he could find his own way toward stealing the proof the miners needed. Between that and the ring, they could settle two debts and be back to their own lives in no time.

Maybe if he kept telling himself that often enough, he'd be able to believe it.

The following night, as the cavern around him grew colder, Vax sagged down on one of the cots, near where Sencha was minding a dwarven woman with a bad leg, and observed the ministrations. The healer was as gentle-but-firm with the woman as she'd been with him, and she didn't make a distinction between him and the miners. Her careful aid consisted primarily of poultices and bandages, in addition to the healing she could manage with the All-Hammer's blessing.

"Does it still help to heal?" he asked when the woman disappeared back into the tunnels. Hers wasn't a recent injury, but seemed to be a permanent one.

Sencha cleaned up her equipment and tucked the necklace with the copper hammer back under her shirt. "It eases her pain some. That's worth it. Especially when no one else gets in trouble and demands my attention." She raised her eyebrows at him, and he grinned back.

She gestured him to turn around and brusquely checked his bandages. It had taken the better part of three days for her to reach a point where she was hesitantly satisfied with his progress. His wounds had closed and didn't open anymore.

"The wounds are doing better," he said. "I barely feel a thing anymore."

"And you wouldn't tell me if they weren't," she replied, running her hands over the newly healed skin.

"Probably not," he admitted.

"Don't play me for a fool. Stubborn boys, all of you."

He had a vague inkling she wasn't just talking about him or Thorn. He hesitated. "I'm sorry about Emryn."

"I am too." Sencha tilted up her chin, and her voice held an edge of warning to it. "I'm sorry I couldn't find a way to take care of both of you. He was a good lad, and he did a good thing, getting you out of that fray."

He clamped his mouth shut. Thorn's insistence that he shouldn't feel guilty still lingered. Perhaps he had no right to feel guilty, but that didn't mean he wouldn't.

Sencha placed a warm hand against his back, and he felt tension ripple underneath her touch. "If you want to be angry at someone, be angry at the walkers that attacked him or the Shademaster who drove us here," she said firmly, taking a step back from him so he could straighten his shirt. "Anything else will only endanger us."

He balled his fists. He had plenty of experience with feeling both anger and guilt at the same time. "What do you mean?"

"What will you do if I tell you that you should feel guilty? Go charging out to try to fix what happened? It will kill us before it kills you." She sat down on one of the cots. Despite her hunched shoulders and her tired eyes, the look she threw him was one of steel and determination. He wondered how often she'd had to tell Thorn the same thing. "You have a sister to go back to, and a life to lead. Keep your focus on that. When we find a way to safely get you out of here—leave. Don't let yourself be distracted by hopeless cases."

Her words threw him. They were hardly hopeless when they were surviving. Everywhere he looked he saw resilience.

"Can you at least tell me about Jorenn? What it was like before the Shadewatch came?"

"Think I'm old enough to know, do you?" she demanded, a teasing note worming its way back into her voice. She pulled a handkerchief from her sleeve and used it to dab her face, and she chuckled when he blushed uncomfortably. She patted the blankets next to her and didn't send him away. "I will tell you what this town once was." Her voice dropped. "Perhaps then you'll understand why it's better to leave."

She didn't speak immediately. She was sitting on the cot and although her face was turned toward him, Vax knew her thoughts were miles and years away.

"Jorenn is a hard place. Always has been. We lived our life surrounded by dangers and disregard. Dangers from the hills and the valleys. Disregard from the rest of the continent. People only ever came this way when they were down on their luck or simply desperate. Foolish adventurers with wandering feet who thought the hills held great riches for them, when for most they only held certain death. But we lived. We found ways to survive, and when we found our way into the mines, both surviving and living became easier."

Vax swallowed hard, the words eerily similar to ones he'd heard a long time ago. A lifetime ago.

"Turns out there was wealth in the mines. Silver ore, like I told you, and pure silver as well. We went from a small community where everyone knew each other—no matter if they lived above- or underground—to what those fools in power considered *thriving*. We were a town full of opportunity, and it attracted all sorts of folk. Outsiders, who wanted us to exhaust the mines, because coin bought influence. Strangers, who didn't understand the way of us, but who forced us to change regardless.

We were a good town, once upon a time. We made our lives between the hills and the valleys, and we needed only the homes of our families, the craft of our own hands, and the songs we sang around the fire. We were happy."

"Until the Shademaster came?"

Sencha shook her head. "She wasn't the first, but she was the first to convince the majority of the people in town to believe in her. Her influence only increased when the ash walker attacks escalated. She promised the townsfolk wealth and safety from danger, and she cut herself a decent profit with the power their trust gave her."

Vax mulled it over. "Did she lie to them?"

"No. She didn't lie to the people who believed in her, not precisely. She kept them safe, at the expense of our lives and our homes."

"Were you responsible for the ash walkers?"

She snorted but didn't seem offended. "Asking the hard questions, are you?" She sighed. "Would it change anything for you if I said we were? That it's a risk we have to take if we want to be able to mine in these hills?"

Vax tensed. If they were responsible for those rotting corpses, it meant they only saved his life from a danger they caused. It meant they were as much responsible for danger and destruction as the Shadewatch were. But did that mean they deserved to be hunted down and killed, like Thorn said happened? "I don't know," he said, honestly. "Are you still mining?"

"Creatures came down from the hills before, and up from the deep as well. It's possible that our miners unleashed them. If we did, the danger was ours. We've always been the ones who died first." It wasn't an answer exactly, and Sencha's words held a note of warning. "Even when the Shademaster found that magic ring of hers, she only ever protected the town. Raised up barriers and warded off the ash walkers from *her* people. She may do right by them, but she needed to get rid of us."

"Her magic ring?" Vax repeated weakly, distracted from the tales of slaughter. He'd worried about asking any of the miners about it directly. When he got out of here, when he managed to steal the bloody thing, he didn't want to be tied to it directly.

"Cloudy thing. Fracture, she calls it."

He faltered but immediately schooled his face into bland curiosity. "She *uses* it?"

"What else is she supposed to do with it?" Sencha scoffed. "It's pretty enough, but Jorenn doesn't have many fancy occasions for dressing up. Though perhaps she wishes to look rich when she meets with her smugglers. That's always an option, I suppose."

Vax stored the information away and met Sencha's frown with a shrug of his own. "I heard rumors about an heirloom. I didn't realize it was magic. Pieces like that usually come with good stories."

She sniffed, but he could see the grief in her eyes. "If it's a happily ever after you're looking for, you won't find one in Jorenn."

A commotion near the entrance caused them both to turn. One of the dwarves who had left after dinner to stand guard at the entrance to the mines returned with a bloody gash over his right eye. "Shadewatch. Four of them," he managed. "They stumbled into one of the tunnels by accident. Thorn and Davok are holding them off."

Sencha had already grabbed for her kit while across the cavern, people reached for their weapons and got to their feet. It looked like a well-structured response, and the sudden array of blades shimmered in the magical glow.

Vax saw his chance. He palmed his blades, and Sencha placed a hand on his arm. "This isn't your fight," she warned.

"I know." It didn't stop him. And this time, no one else did either.

CHAPTER 19

Vax followed the miners, who made their way through the tunnels at an uncomfortable pace. There were half a dozen of them, far more than was likely necessary for the unlucky Shadewatch patrol. They didn't pay attention to him, and that was fine. He needed this. To sate his restlessness and his curiosity, and to get a better sense of the tunnel system around them. To learn more about what was going on here. To find his way out if the opportunity arose.

Thorn and the other dwarf had drawn the guards into the level of the mine where they usually lived and toward the now abandoned kitchen. They ducked across and wove around the tables, doing what they could to keep three of Jorenn's guards occupied. The fourth guard was nowhere to be seen.

The dwarf—Davok—held his arm at an impossible angle and was locked in battle, warhammer against sword, with a guard who towered head and shoulders over him. Thorn had blood spatters across his face, while he kept two others—a human woman wielding a glaive and a halfling man—occupied, darting in and out to lunge at them and taunt them, before dancing out of reach again. Despite being outnumbered, he was grinning dangerously. He relished the fight.

He only faltered when the half dozen miners and Vax ran into the room, tensing at the sudden movement, and he was a second too late to parry the attack from the guard with the glaive. The butt of the weapon slammed against the inside of his knee, and when he went down, the guard followed through with a downswing from the blade.

Thorn shouted, and the miners spread out around the tables, two per guard. Vax did the only thing that made sense. He dropped to the floor so he had a line of sight toward where Thorn lay. The half-elf was bleeding profusely from a cut along his arm.

When Thorn rolled out of the way of another downswing of the glaive's blade, Vax drew his hand back and sent a dagger flying straight toward the guard. It jammed into her calf, and she stumbled.

In that moment of pain and hesitation, Thorn pushed himself up to his knees and ran her through, his sword digging deep into the guard's side. For a brief instant he stood face-to-face with Vax and everything around them ground to a halt.

Then Thorn snarled and twisted his blade. The glaive clattered uselessly to the floor, while Thorn slumped back against the table.

His eyes found Vax, and some of the gentleness of the first night leaked through the cracks in his pain. It made him softer, while the fight around them was quick and brutal.

Then one of the miners stepped between them and reached out a hand to drag Thorn to his feet. Vax crawled out from under the table and retrieved his dagger, wincing at the open, unseeing eyes of the guard and the blood that pooled around her. An unlucky fool in the wrong place at the wrong time. He'd attacked her without thinking twice about it, once Thorn fell.

This wasn't his fight, Sencha had said. But wasn't it? Or had he inadvertently made it his own?

The remaining two members of the Shadewatch were no match for the remaining miners. One encountered the sharp end of a longsword, and the other met the dwarf's warhammer with his face.

Between the guard he and Thorn had attacked, and the two who fell, there were only three guards here. Vax glanced around, and something cold crawled up his spine. "Where is the fourth guard?"

Thorn's eyes scanned the room and he swore loudly. "Did anyone see her? A dwarf with a longsword?"

Denial from the other miners.

Vax shook his head. He cleaned his daggers with his shirt. "She was gone before we got here."

"She'll be long gone. *Fuck*. We can't let her escape." Thorn called out two of the miners' names. "Find that errant guard, and close off the entrance she came through. If there are any horses outside, make sure the tracks lead away from here. Once you're a good distance away, let them go safely."

"We know what to do," one of the miners said, with what she probably meant as a reassuring smile. It looked more like a horrified grimace.

Thorn stared, and she colored and nodded. "Yes, boss."

On the other side of the room, a broad-shouldered young woman cut off a piece of the guard's tunic with her dagger and helped fashion it into a sling for Davok.

"The rest of you: clean up," Thorn ordered, pressing another ripped shirt against his arm. "When you're done, go find Tinyn. She needs to know about the guard who got away. She'll know what to do. Vax, with me."

Vax tried not to stare when miners efficiently and effectively dug through the pockets of the guards, removed any valuables, and bound the bodies together.

"What will happen to them?" he asked Davok as he passed the dwarf.

"Deepest unused mine shaft," Davok replied gruffly. He cradled his arm against his chest despite the sling. "It's the closest thing to a burial we can give them. We can't let anyone out of these tunnels alive."

Vax stilled. "So what do you do with stray travelers you pick up?"

"We try to lure them in and if that doesn't work, we toss 'em in the shaft too. Why, are you worried for your safety?" Thorn answered in Davok's stead. "*Come.*"

He ran out of the kitchen without waiting to see if Vax would follow, and two of the miners fell into step with him.

Without further hesitation, Vax followed.

Thorn's pace was unforgiving, and Vax fought to keep up. With the rush of the fight leaving him, everything reminded him of the fact that he was still healing, and likely Sencha would find a way to scold him as soon as she was done patching up the others. At least without Vex here, that was almost comforting.

Thorn led them through the maze once more, through a tunnel at a steep incline, and with every step they took the air became fresher and felt heavier. Vax pulled his cloak tight around him. He kept his eyes peeled for any markers he saw, and identifying details that would help him retrace his steps. He wondered why Thorn brought him here now. One of his hands snaked toward a dagger, just in case.

Before they reached the surface, the tunnel dipped again, and for the last quarter of a mile they zigzagged. The tunnel branched off into passages that led nowhere, and Thorn followed a twisting passage so narrow that he seemed to disappear into solid stone. Vax followed after him, and he felt sharp edges of protruding rocks dig into his shoulder and back. He pushed through, until the tunnel opened up wider again—and came to a dead end.

In front of him, Thorn placed his hand against the stone and walked straight through. Vax narrowed his eyes and followed, one hand in front of him to reach for the wall that his eyes told him was there, but when he walked closer, he felt nothing. No rock. No barrier of any sort. The faintest breeze. The air felt heavier here than it did down below.

He pushed through. And all of a sudden, he was outside. Underneath an overcast sky at dusk, with hills stretching out as far as the eye could see. It was the type of endlessness that Vax had longed for even as it left him dizzy.

Jorenn Village was nowhere to be seen, though whether that was because they were a long way away or because it'd dipped beneath the glowing of the hills, Vax couldn't tell. With the sun having dipped beneath the horizon and no stars to guide him, he didn't have a clue where they were.

He closed his eyes and breathed deeply. The air tasted of flowers and ash.

Thorn stared out too, the stained shirt still pressed to his arm. Tension arched across his shoulder and back, and he stared up at the clouds like he could fight the sky itself. He screamed his rage and helplessness.

"Are you all right?" Vax asked, though the answer was blatantly obvious.

"No." Thorn didn't meet his gaze, and he laughed without humor. "You know, Tinyn almost had me convinced you were a spy for Derowen, with your curious eyes and your endless questions. It's not the first time we've taken travelers in, and it would be easy enough to hide someone loyal to her in a group small enough to be a target for the ash walkers. But it doesn't matter anymore. None of it does."

Vax flinched at the accusation and the pain. "You saw me fight for your side in there. I didn't let myself get cut up just to sneak in here. You know I wouldn't let myself get separated from my sister."

"Wouldn't that make the story better? Who better to know than she that I'd be sympathetic to it." Thorn's hands wavered, and something in his gaze broke. "She tried so hard to get rid of us, and I don't know how I can stop her anymore."

He looked more dangerous in his grief, and Vax treaded carefully. "Why does she want to get rid of you? She's already got your mines."

"We knew what the mines held," Thorn said immediately, and the words had the cadence of practice. "Every ore and every deposit. Every piece of silver she stole, all the riches she kept to herself. She started stealing from the town the moment the Shadewatch took over the mines, and she must be terrified we could expose her as the monster she is."

Vax took a step forward. "Who would you tell? The people of Jorenn who see her as a hero and who didn't protest when the Shadewatch cleared you out? They think you're the monsters."

"If you're trying to convince me you're on my side, you're doing a piss-poor job," Thorn snapped. Intense fear flicked across his face, until he visibly pushed it away. "Perhaps we are the monsters."

And before Vax could say or do anything, Thorn turned to face him, the weight of the people down below on his shoulders.

"They know where we are now. It'll be hours or days, but they'll find us here and they'll kill us. Leave. Just fucking go. The night isn't safe by any means, but it's better than staying."

It was so tempting. Even though the hills around them were obscured, with only fragments of dusk breaking through the cloud deck above. Even though he didn't have a clue where he was in relation to Jorenn and how to get there. Vex was out there and that ache was a hollowness inside of him.

He took a step forward. This was what he wanted.

All Vax needed to do was find his sister, steal the ring, fulfill his debt, and leave all of this behind.

But.

"No. Not yet." He pushed his fingernails deep into the palms of his hands and steeled himself before he met Thorn's gaze. He felt the weight of his own daggers, flying toward the guards. Of Sencha and Felric's stories. Of Emryn. Of knowing it was only a matter of time before the miners would be attacked by the Shadewatch. "I wouldn't be able to hold my own if any ash walker crossed my path," he told Thorn instead. A half-truth. Or a full lie. He tried to put the rest of it into words. "This isn't right. I couldn't go knowing I'd leave you all in danger."

Thorn's look was completely unreadable, his eyes as cloudy as the sky above. In the end, he simply shrugged and turned away. "Fine, your choice."

"I will need a guide into town when it's safer, though," Vax added.

Thorn simply kept walking.

By NIGHTFALL, VAX WAS CERTAIN he'd made a mistake in not walking out. Or in getting involved in the first place.

The atmosphere in the cavern had changed when they returned. It had gone from comfortably defiant to intense and deadly. Tinyn had taken charge in Thorn's absence, and everyone who could, carried a weapon. Many people milled about like they had before, but they did so purposefully. To prepare themselves for the inevitable. The miners' belongings, which usually lay spread out across the cavern, had been gathered into easy packs that were placed near the entrance and close to the stream and the narrow pathways. No one spoke loudly; everyone whispered. Like they were afraid their voices alone could bring the Shadewatch down upon them.

It was as though everyone held their breaths waiting for the Shadewatch to come bursting in.

Following their return, Thorn didn't say a word to him. He let Sencha patch him up and he spent a bit of time with the dwarves, but he avoided Vax easily.

It wasn't until dinner that Vax realized that Thorn was keeping his distance from most of the group. He skirted around the edges, exchanged a word or two with anyone who asked for his time, but he didn't settle down to eat with them or try to relax around the fire. He kept going back and forth among the cavern, the people who stood watch in double patrols, and the tunnels.

"It's what he does," Tinyn muttered when Vax mentioned it. She had a pair of scimitars by her side and she didn't stay in one place for long either. She'd come out of a quiet but heated discussion with both Sencha and Junel when Vax approached her, and she was scanning the chamber to make sure everyone was where they were meant to be. "He feels responsible."

"He won't rest until he's confident we're safe," Sencha said, with a sigh. "He never considers his own safety."

Twice more that night, Thorn wandered into the cavern, once to grab a drink, once to discuss something with someone and throw a withering look in Vax's direction. When the other miners nervously went to their cots for the night, Thorn was still flitting around. It made Vax wonder if he'd seen the half-elf sleep much at all these last few nights. Even before the Shadewatch had found their way in, he'd seemed to be constantly busy, constantly worrying.

With the others falling asleep around him, Vax skirted around the edges of the cavern and waited for Thorn to reappear. When he did—to discuss something in hushed tones with Tinyn before he pressed a pouch in her hands—Vax followed him. He kept his distance, far enough not to be seen. He was as quiet as he knew how to be, moving silently from shadow to shadow. In doing so, he found a whisper of patience that eased his own restlessness.

Thorn led him deeper into the mines, way past the tunnels they'd traversed and toward another system that was in the process of being expanded. Vax ran his hands along the walls and felt the grooves of pick marks, the harder edges of a different stone underneath. The air around him smelled of dirt.

Vax rounded the next corner and paused, pressing his back against the wall. A few dozen feet away from him, Thorn sat on his coat on the floor, a dull magical light illuminating the pieces of paper in front of him, while he drank from a tankard of ale. He had a pencil next to him and occasionally he took notes, but most of all, he was talking.

". . . lose any more of them," Thorn said, his voice raising the lightest echo around him. He held up his hand to the light, and a green snake wrapped itself around his arm and wrist, slithering and following Thorn attentively, like he was listening. Vax stared at it for a long time before he realized the snake had the exact same color and markings as Thorn's serpentine belt. It was an odd thing, but he couldn't let himself be distracted by it.

"Sencha argues, but they have to leave while they still can. We have no evidence to clear anyone's names, but we have funds . . ." Thorn's voice trailed off and he wrote something down. He looked despondent, sitting there, with only a snake and ale to keep him company. "If we stay and fight, we'll have more raw silver to divide among the groups, and—"

"You're trying to relocate them," Vax said, realizing what the other man was saying. "Was that what those letters were about too? You're trying to gather evidence and funds to give your people a new home, away from the Shadewatch and out of danger."

"*Fuck.*" Thorn snarled and leaped to his feet, swords in his hands, while the snake fell forgotten onto his coat. His eyes blazed, and both of his swords were pointing at Vax's throat. "What the hell do you want?"

Vax raised his hands, showing he was unarmed. He was confident in his skills, but he wasn't sure he could hold his own against Thorn in this state. Even with his arm in bandages, he looked fierce and dangerous. "I've noticed you disappearing into the tunnels a few times before. I was curious."

"Perceptive and determined." Thorn didn't lower his blades. Instead he squeezed them tighter. At his feet, the snake straightened itself, slithered up his leg, and wound around his waist. "We should have left you for the ash to devour."

Vax nudged the tankard of ale toward Thorn with his foot. "You probably should have left me, and I probably should have left you. Since you didn't, and I didn't, tell me what you're trying to do?"

Thorn stared at him, his dark brows furrowed over conflicted eyes. His scars stood out fiercely with how pale and tired he looked. He sagged down against the wall across from Vax, pulled his knees up to his chest, and lay his blades across his knees. "We'll fight, those of us who can. We'll fight here and we'll die here. And if I can kill the Shademaster in the process, it'll be worth it. But Sencha and Junel and the others . . . they deserve to be safe. We'll fight long enough for everyone else to escape and collapse the tunnels behind them, so that it looks like we were the only ones. So that they have no reason to keep looking for others anymore."

"Can't you escape too?"

Thorn didn't answer that question. The flash of rage in his eyes spoke volumes. "I thought with sufficient funds and evidence that we're better than the Shadewatch claims we are, it would be easier to find new work and new homes. Tinyn has been reaching out to other mining communities to see if they can take some or all of us. But they know us as the miners who woke the ash. Without letters of proof, we're dangers to any community. I don't know if the silver we have is enough to pay for a chance to live."

"So you keep mining, despite the dangers?" Vax asked.

"Very perceptive," Thorn said. "Yes. We keep mining. If that disturbs things better left undisturbed, so be it. If it raises corpses that bother a town that abandoned us, then that's not my problem. They know how to take care of themselves."

"And the people like me and my sister? The travelers who get caught in the crossfire?" Twin tendrils of anger and fatigue crawled up his spine.

Something harsh crossed Thorn's face. "My loyalty is to my people, not to anyone else."

Vax waited for Thorn to say more, and eventually the miner's shoulders sagged. "We take in travelers if we can, if it's safe for us to do so. We *are* careful when we mine, because despite what the people outside think, this is our world. Maybe we are the monsters. I can't forget that we're fighting for our lives, Vax. If I let that go, even for a moment, we'll lose. We *are* losing."

Vax sat down too, keeping a careful distance between himself and Thorn's swords. "I offered to find you evidence before. Let me help."

"Why?" Thorn reached for the tankard and drank deep.

"Because I owe you a debt," Vax said. It was the simplest answer at least. He tried for the harder one too. Because of the way Thorn worried about his people and the way they worried about him. Because Sencha and Junel and the others who helped him deserved a home where they could live instead of hide. Because maybe, if the miners were safe and the ash walkers gone, he could steal the Shademaster's ring without worry. He shook his head. "I know what it's like not to have a place in the world, only the people—or person—you care about and nothing more."

Thorn drank deeper still. "A pretty elf like you can't know what it's like not to belong."

Vax leaned his head back against the wall and didn't say anything. He understood Thorn's fierce loyalty to his people—to his family. He understood it. He recognized it. It was part of what made it so hard to turn away.

"As soon as you reunite with your sister, you will forget about us, and rightfully so." Thorn hesitated then pushed the tankard in Vax's direction.

Vax grabbed the tankard, sniffed, then took a swig of what turned out to be a smooth, spicy ale. "I won't forget," he said.

"Sure." Thorn sheathed his swords. He reached for the papers in front of him and haphazardly stacked them on top of one another. His movements were uncontrolled and sharp, and halfway through he grabbed the whole stack and flung it off to the side, loose pages scattering across the stones.

He put the pencil in his pocket and looked up, tired beyond words. "You don't owe me anything. We shouldn't have kept you here." He rubbed his face. "Any debt you may feel you had, you repaid with your daggers."

Vax pushed the tankard toward Thorn again, but the half-elf didn't drink. He stared at his hands. "I don't get involved with any of the travelers we bring in. Sencha patches them up, we escort them out of the mines blindfolded, and send them off into the daylight as soon as possible. We don't let them see the caverns. We don't let strangers come close. *I* don't let strangers come close, because we've all been hurt too often, and I'm responsible for all these people. All of them, Vax." He continued before Vax could say anything, the words tumbling out of him, "But Sencha was busy with Emryn, and you were in pain. I couldn't just let you lie there. It felt so simple. So normal to talk to someone who didn't put his life in my hands. And then I couldn't get you out of my head. I couldn't fucking get you out of my head." The words cracked.

Thorn's jaw worked, like there was more he wanted to say, but he didn't have the words. He pounded his knee with one of his fists. Between the frustration that coursed through him and the questions in his eyes, he had no defenses left. No anger, no challenge.

Just Thorn.

Vax pushed himself to his feet and tentatively crossed to the other side of the tunnel. He sat down next to Thorn and folded a hand over his fist, easing it. "I *won't* forget," he promised. "Let me find the evidence." Once he found his way back to Vex, once he knew she was okay, they could both help.

"I won't leave. I won't stop fighting." Thorn turned his hand, entwining his fingers with Vax's. "You'll have to escape with the others."

"I will come back."

"Whatever." Underneath the layers of exhaustion, Thorn's mouth quirked up. He glanced at Vax. And here, at the edge of disaster, neither moved away.

Vax leaned in closer, his face inches away from Thorn's, and reached out to trace Thorn's jawline. "For the record: this *is* me trying to get you to like me."

Thorn snorted and covered the distance between them. "Gods, you're obnoxious."

CHAPTER 20

Aswin *screamed.*

For a mite of a girl, she had a voice loud enough to startle Vex out of her worries and send Derowen flying to her feet. On the couch, the Shademaster dropped the report she was reading and ran toward her daughter's room. Vex—who'd been sitting near the fireplace, staring into the fire with a familiar map in her mind's eye—let her necklace bounce back against her chest and followed. She had her hand on her knife and Trinket by her side.

Derowen reached for her sword too, before she flung the door open to her daughter's room.

Aswin was on her own. She sat up in bed, her tangled blanket clutched to her chest, and she was sobbing so hard she could barely breathe. Her face was red and puffy from crying, and her hands clenched the blanket so tightly, her bones stood out under her skin.

"They were trying to kill me," she sobbed. "The ash walkers were here and they were trying to kill me and I couldn't hide and they were trying to bite me."

Derowen dropped to her knees next to the bed and gathered her daughter close to her. The comforting presence only caused the girl to sob louder, and she tore at her mother's shirt, whipping herself into a frenzy again.

"They were everywhere. They kept trying to find me and I was so scared."

Derowen patted her hair, soothing her with quiet murmurs, though when she glanced at Vex her face was contorted with pain. "Don't worry, my love, it's only a bad dream, nothing more. You're safe here. They can't ever hurt you, I'll make sure of it."

"I wanted to be brave, Mama," Aswin sobbed. "I don't know how to be brave like you."

Derowen pulled her daughter closer still, and ferocity seeped into her voice. "You are the bravest girl I know, Aswin. You'll be braver than all of us one day."

Vex felt the words squeeze at her chest. She still stood by the door opening, and she couldn't put into words what hurt more: the sound of the little girl sobbing like her heart was breaking, or the endless stream of comforting whispers from Derowen.

When they were younger, Vax would hold her like that when she was terrified, but even so she'd learned not to cry too often. Pretending to be strong was easier when no one saw her tears.

Eventually, the little girl calmed down enough for Derowen to sit up and pull her into her lap, where she held her until the racking sobs turned to quiet hiccups and then to yawns. Once she reached that point, Derowen disentangled herself and carefully laid Aswin back in bed.

Aswin immediately tensed and protested. "No, Mama. No."

Derowen placed a hand against her cheek. "I'll find you a cup of water and a cloth to wash away the tears, but after that you have to sleep."

When she straightened, Aswin whimpered. "Don't leave me alone."

"Vex can stay here until I'm back," Derowen promised, with a quick look at Vex to make sure it was all right.

Vex clenched her hands by her side, but she nodded. Only a monster would say no to a little girl with such heartache. "Maybe Trinket can stay here too." She crossed the room on soft feet and crouched next to Aswin.

Although the girl had dried her tears, her face was still blotched and red. She looked up at Vex with bloodshot eyes and all-overwhelming trust, and then peeked surreptitiously at Trinket, who followed Vex looking for all the world like he didn't spot an opportunity for scratches and cuddles here.

"He helps me when I'm scared too," Vex admitted softly.

The girl frowned. "You were never scared."

"Was too." Vex gently straightened the girl's collar. "I'm scared all the time. Lots of people get scared."

"Not my mother," Aswin said, jutting out her jaw.

Vex nodded. "No, maybe not her." On the other side of the room, Derowen withdrew quietly toward the door and mouthed a simple *all the time.*

"What are you scared of?" Aswin demanded.

"Oh, the ash walkers terrify me," Vex confided, and Aswin smiled wanly. "I'm constantly scared something will happen to my brother too, because he gets in trouble a lot."

"Like how he got himself lost?" Aswin asked. She'd seen Vex ride out every day over the past few days, combing the hills around Jorenn, and always coming back empty-handed.

"Exactly like that."

"Are you scared something will happen to *your* mother too?" Aswin wanted to know. Before Vex could gather her scattered thoughts and answer, she sat up in bed. "Were you scared of *Trinket* when you first saw him? On account of he's a bear?"

Vex gently pushed Aswin back again. "I don't think you can sleep sitting up."

"Well, were you?"

Vex hesitated. She wasn't sure it was an entirely appropriate bedtime story, but for a girl who grew up around these brutal attacks, perhaps it did help to know that she wasn't alone. That everyone was scared sometimes. "Come, settle in, and I'll tell you."

Aswin obediently plopped down on her pillow again, but she propped her head up on her elbow, and she kept her emerald eyes on Vex. She looked at her with such wonder and trust and ease that it squeezed Vex's heart.

"I was scared when I first met Trinket," Vex said, leaning back on her heels, and reaching out to scratch Trinket's ear. Trinket curled up next to her, his chin resting on Aswin's blankets and his soulful eyes focused on the girl. She sniffed and smiled and placed her free hand over his nose.

"I was scared," Vex said, "but it wasn't because of Trinket. He was only a cub, smaller than you are now."

Aswin giggled at that.

"Once upon a time, my brother and I were traveling through the woods. We found a lovely place to stay, and while my brother went into the city for supplies, I stayed behind and I met other travelers, who told me they were passing through on their way to the city too. They came by our camp and they offered to share their food with me." She should have known better. If life in Syngorn had taught her anything, it was to not take kindness at face value, because it inevitably became cruelty.

"I thought they were being nice and helpful, but what I didn't know is that they were actually terrifying monsters in disguise." She lowered her voice and Aswin pulled her blanket up higher, shivering in delight. "So when one of them crouched down by our fire and pretended to prepare a meal, the other walked around me and *grabbed* my arms."

Vex shifted, and Aswin squealed. Trinket immediately pushed his snout closer toward her and nuzzled her hand.

"They took me to their camp, which wasn't all that far from ours, and they locked me in a cage on top of a wagon. And I could see that I wasn't the only one they kept there. They had animals in cages too. They'd captured birds and two young griffins and this good boy over here." She ran her hand over Trinket's head. "That's when I realized that they weren't actually travelers, they just pretended to be. It was as if they'd been hiding a second set of sharp teeth behind their friendly smiles."

In reality, they hadn't looked different at all, but Vex wasn't about to tell Aswin that evil could look so mundane when she already had monsters to worry about. The poachers had been laughing and joking around once they'd captured Vex, and they'd happily eaten the food they'd promised to share. One of them hummed a cheerful tune and tossed an apple onto the wagon that held Vex's cage.

"Were they just as scary as the ash walkers?" Aswin whispered.

Vex considered that. "When I was there, I thought they were the scariest lot I'd ever seen."

"What happened next?"

"I cried," Vex said. "And I tried to escape. I tried to pick the lock, but because I was so frightened my hands were trembling." She hesitated briefly, not wanting to burden the little girl with her despair of being trapped there. Instead, she said: "Then I realized Trinket was trapped in one of the other cages, and he looked so scared. I knew I had to break myself out, and I would have to break him out, too."

Trinket looked at Aswin with his large, brown eyes, and the little girl nodded with equally large eyes. "You had to escape together!"

Vex nodded. It wasn't a complete lie. Trinket *had* been in the cage opposite hers, she just hadn't known he was there. He'd been curled up and hidden, protected by an adult brown bear with scars around her snout and a bloody gash along her ribs. The mother bear's breathing had been labored and thin, her life fading before Vex's eyes.

Vex ran her fingers through Trinket's fur. "I waited until the monsters were asleep, and I told myself I would be brave. I breathed very slowly and I kept my hands as still as I could, until they stopped shaking. And then I tried to pick the lock. And do you know what happened then?" Vex leaned forward with a conspiratorial smile. "Out of nowhere, my brother showed up. He'd come back to our camp and found me missing, so he tracked me down. He helped me get out of the cage, and when the monsters woke up, we fought them together."

"Did you win?" Aswin breathed.

The fight had been wild and chaotic, and she only remembered fragments of it. Her anger. Her despair. She'd woken up in a cold sweat every night for a week after, seeing herself standing in the camp with blood streaks all over her face and clothes, a knife in her hand, and a body at her feet. "Of course we did. Because we'd decided to be brave and we were together, and that was all we needed. If you keep fighting, no matter how scary they are, the monsters can never win."

Aswin yawned and snuggled deeper under the blankets. "And that's when you found Trinket." The words slurred with fatigue.

"We opened up all the cages in the camp and all of the animals had somewhere to go. The birds flew off. The griffins disappeared into the forest around us. Only Trinket remained. So I picked him up and held him close, and I promised to take care of him."

She couldn't have done anything else either. Trinket's mother had been maimed and bloodied, but in her weakened state she'd still tried to keep her cub safe from the cruelty of the poachers. Her wounds had smelled of death and decay, like she'd been left to rot from the inside, and her cries had torn through Vex. So Vex had done the only thing she could. She'd taken a knife and put the bear out of her misery. She couldn't abandon Trinket after that.

"He came with us to the camp and he grew into the biggest, bravest, best bear you ever saw. And the cuddliest one too." Vex leaned against Trinket, and Trinket hummed contently.

Aswin, who was on the verge of sleep again, murmured something incoherent. She petted Trinket's nose and she smiled.

"We lived happily ever after," Vex whispered. And she desperately wanted the words to be true.

"YOU'RE GOOD WITH HER," DEROWEN said softly. "She's quick to make casual friends, but aside from Wick and me, she doesn't let people in. Not even other children her own age. She's seen too much bloodshed here. She's terrified to lose them."

Vex looked away, the gratitude as uncomfortable as the tenuous trust. "I did what I thought was best. And Trinket usually helps. He's far cuddlier than stuffed animals." She would never admit that she regularly needed that same comforting presence. "Besides, she's a good kid. This must be a scary place to grow up in."

Derowen walked around the sitting room to a small wine cabinet, where she poured them both a drink. She held one glass out to Vex and sat on the floor next to the fireplace, in the same spot where Vex had sat earlier. She didn't look at ease there, lines of discomfort creating hard angles along her shoulders. The glow of the dancing flames reflected in her weary eyes. Most days, they worked together in silence, and it seemed sharing did not come easy to either of them. "It's been hard on her. She refuses to stay behind when I have to take to the gates, so she's seen far more than is good for her. I try to shield her from the worst of it, but I can't lie about what the world looks like."

"She knows you're there to protect her. That matters a lot," Vex said quietly. She found a spot on one of the couches, where she could curl up in a corner. It wasn't just the absence of Vax that made her uneasy here, or the fact that she thought she'd spotted tracks today but hadn't heard back yet from the scouts sent to investigate them, but the fact that the people around her kept finding ways to circumnavigate her defenses—or simply acted like they didn't exist.

She hazarded a glance at Derowen's ring and reminded herself: she didn't want their pity or their compassion. She didn't need their understanding either. She appreciated their help, but once she found her way back to Vax, she'd leave this all behind.

Derowen nodded with a sad smile. Over the past few days, she hadn't been able to take a break. The responsibility of the town weighed heavily on her, and every time Vex returned from her days helping the Shade-watch map and scour the countryside, she would find Derowen in another meeting, reading another report, listening to the grievances of townspeople, or being called to pass judgments in matters of safety. Derowen had spent a night patrolling the palisades with Vex when worry leaked through town that dead walkers were wandering around in the vicinity. From the palisades, the guards could see the lumbering gait of the dead along the hills, but none came closer. The night remained on edge but thankfully quiet, aside from the lingering echo of the horns.

The Shademaster looked exhausted, and even the glow of the fireplace couldn't mask how wan her face was and how her worried frown was becoming a permanent fixture. In those few days Vex had seen her work, she never let her responsibility sour to malice. She didn't allow her exhaustion to become carelessness.

Eventually, Derowen leaned closer to the fire, close enough that it might burn. "I hope that one day, she'll understand I do what I do to ensure that she won't have to. I want to make Jorenn safer so that she won't have to be scared. I want to be sure we prosper so that she won't have to worry. I want to teach her how to fend for herself without the risk of surrendering her power. How to be strong enough so that she doesn't have to be frightened of losing. She's all I have, and there's no one else who could take care of her but me either."

"Her father?" Vex asked, despite herself.

"A merchant. A charmer, and I was a fool. He told me beautiful stories about his lavish home and the future we would have together, before he disappeared into the night. He knows she exists, but he has no right to call himself her father."

Vex stared into the fire. The comfortable heat didn't seem to extend to her spot on the couch. With Trinket still by Aswin's side, she hugged her legs closer, and all she said was, "She's lucky to have you."

Derowen pushed away from the fire and glanced over in the direction of Aswin's room. "I'm lucky to have her."

The words made Vex's chest constrict, but she smiled and she forced her voice to sound steady. "Please remember that when she asks you for a bear as a pet."

Derowen groaned. "I'm excited for the many conversations we're going to have on that subject. I've already asked Wick to keep his eyes open. I'm hoping we'll be able to distract her with a stray kitten."

"Easier upkeep," Vex acknowledged.

"Terrible on the curtains, though."

They sat in an easy silence for a while. Derowen eyed the stack of reports on her desk and purposefully turned away, while Vex slowly disentangled her knotted limbs. The treacherous voice inside of her told her to not trust anyone, told her to run and get out. It warned her that the company and trust Derowen offered her could never last, and she'd only get hurt again.

But when the silence lengthened, and the comfort of the room extended around them, one question slipped through. It had been weighing heavily on Vex for days. "Why did you help me? Before you knew that I could try to help find the miners?"

Because while she understood they had a common goal now, what Derowen had done for her those first days went far beyond simple hospitality or helping because her daughter asked. Vex had offered to take her belongings to the inn and search from there, but Derowen had wanted nothing of it. "It's not like you have the time to spare to take in a stray. You could've sent me on my way without another thought."

Derowen scratched her neck, and she took a sip of her wine. "Whoever made you feel like you don't deserve to be paid attention to was horribly unjust," she said. "I helped because I would want someone to help me, were I in your situation. Because I have people that are more important to me than my own life, and I would not know what to do without them."

"Your brother?" Vex asked. The Shademaster had alluded to that the first night, on the palisades, but what she'd said in public and what Vex had witnessed in private were two different things. The conversation between the Shademaster and her brother had seemed less than pleasant.

Something harsh flashed across Derowen's face, though she visibly, immediately, pushed it away. For a brief moment she looked more vulnerable than Vex had seen her in all their days together. "My daughter, first and foremost. Wick, though neither of us would freely admit that." The corner of her mouth inched up in a wry grin. "Others, perhaps, once upon another time. I understood your pain. I also felt responsible for your encampment getting attacked so close to our city."

Vex pulled at her necklace again and shook her head. "You weren't responsible for it," she said.

"Then let's say I recognized your worries," Derowen said. She unconsciously ran her thumb over the band of her ring. "And your strength."

Vex raised an inquiring eyebrow, and the Shademaster laughed. She got up to refill her glass, and when she turned back to her, any trace of vulnerability was gone. "This is a difficult place to live in, Vex. I wasn't lying when I told you I sometimes desire news from far-off places, because a part of me still longs for the road. But if I've learned anything in the years that I've spent here in Jorenn, it's that we can only stand against the dangers that come from the hills when we stand side by side. We form a stronger, more resilient community when we help our neighbors. I hope you know you are welcome here too." Her gaze drifted to the stack of letters that still lay on her desk, and she sighed. "Though I should find a way to ensure that hospitality doesn't come with endless record keeping."

"If your daughter is ever to follow in your footsteps, I'm sure she'll appreciate that."

Derowen shook her head sharply. "Aswin will be free to do whatever she wants."

Before Vex could ask what she meant by that or needle Derowen for more information, a sharp rapping at the door echoed through the room, and Wick peeked in. He wore a heavy coat, like he'd just come from outside, and his gray skin was pale. "Our last scout just returned from the hills," he said breathlessly.

Vex immediately got to her feet. "And?"

"Your plan worked," he said. "She found the entrance to the mines, and she barely escaped with her life. She can lead us back there. We can march on their hideout."

CHAPTER 21

Three days passed following the incident with the guards, and while Shadewatch presence in the area increased every day, they hadn't marched on the mines yet. Instead they spread out across the hillside in a clear attempt to block every possible exit.

Three days passed, and every miner inside the cavern knew it was only a matter of time until they attacked. Restlessness battled with determination. Vax was as agitated and impatient as the rest of them, especially once Sencha judged his back to have healed adequately. If not for the guards outside, he would have tried to sneak out the hidden exit Thorn had shown him. But with the Shadewatch roaming the hills, there was no saying what they'd do if they saw him come from the mines. He wasn't about to risk a stray arrow or crossing an overzealous guard. He couldn't be responsible for another compromised passage. Even so, every hour that passed between now and the inevitable was an hour too long.

The only distraction came from the people around him. With Thorn's tacit approval, the group of miners expanded to fold Vax in for what little time they had left. Vax managed to gather as much information as he possibly could: on the Shademaster and her ring, on the layout of Jorenn and what Vex might face on the outside, and on their plans for the oncoming battle.

During the day, he joined the miners in their weapons practice.

Thorn told Vax about the songs the miners would sing while working, their voices echoing for miles, accompanied by rhythmic knocking. He hummed one with a playful melody, and others in the cavern immediately picked it up. "Ash walkers aren't the only creatures that hunger below the surface," he sang softly, while Vax remembered Sencha's words that they were always the ones who died first. "We've learned to respect and give thanks to the ones that let us work in peace and plenty."

Later, Thorn told him about the belt—after making proper introductions between Vax and the snake. It was a present from his master, he said, when he was still an apprentice who longed to see the world. "To keep me company in mines so deep the light won't reach."

"Grim," Vax muttered.

Thorn shook his head. "Townsfolk like you have no appreciation for our work."

On the third night, after one of the guards had reported Shadewatch scouting out the entrance to the caves, Thorn sat Vax down and mapped out the way from Jorenn to what would be the survivors' hideout—even though Tinyn scolded him for it. Thorn's second-in-command still didn't trust Vax and wouldn't trust Vax, and Vax couldn't fault her for that.

But Thorn made Vax repeat the route back to him over and over, until he was certain Vax would know how to get to the hidden drifts and tunnels. "After all," he said when they sat alone near the stream, the glow of the glass orb fading to a dimmer light, "you promised to come back."

The words took an effort, and Vax didn't immediately respond. He still felt tense and restless. He stared at his fragmented reflection in the gently flowing water. His hair rippled around him. His eyes were indefinite. "I did."

"So you should know where to find the survivors," Thorn said, trying valiantly to make it sound like it was no big deal—and failing equally heroically. His distorted, rippling reflection made his eyes look darker, like shards of iron that didn't move with the stream itself, and his determination anchored them.

After a moment, he lay down and stared up at the glowworms above them, like a pale imitation of a sky full of stars.

Vax leaned back on his elbows. "As soon as I've found my sister and know she's okay, I'll find a way to get you your evidence."

Thorn kept his eyes on the ceiling. "As soon as I know my people are safe, I'll fight until I can't fight anymore."

And in the end, it was as simple as that. It was the determination and loyalty that Vax admired and that drew him to Thorn that kept them both at arm's length too.

ON THE MORNING OF THE fourth day, Thorn woke Vax before the light turned to dawn and dumped Vax's old clothes and patched-up cloak on top of him. He was pale and his eyes were expressionless. "They're here."

"This is it?" Vax asked, changing into his old outfit. The shirt and cloak had been cleaned, but the smell of ash seemed to persist. As did the bloodstains across the back of the cloak.

"This is it," Thorn said, his words flat. The gentleness he'd shown Vax over the past few days had disappeared under his mask of responsibility and purpose.

On the other side of the cavern, Felric strapped on a crossbow and a quiver full of bolts. He tipped his head when he realized Thorn was staring. The other two halflings carried swords and brave smiles. The dwarven woman with the bad leg, the one whose pain Sencha eased when she didn't need healing spells for others, juggled a heavy steel warhammer. Junel wrapped a tablecloth around their knives.

Everywhere Vax looked, miners were preparing their weapons and gathering their belongings, while others were getting ready to leave. Junel had gathered the children who'd imitated Vax's weapons practice, and they all looked somber and scared. The oldest miners carried the littlest ones, and two teenage girls had heavy bags with supplies and memories slung over their shoulders.

Two young dwarves grabbed picks and hammers and ran past them all, deeper into the mines.

Vax slid into his boots and pulled the cloak on over the musty shirt. Relief and anticipation coursed through him. He'd find his way out of here today. "What will happen to you?" he asked.

"We'll fight," Thorn said simply. "*I'll* fight and if I'm lucky, I'll take the Shademaster down with me."

Vax pressed his lips together. He'd tried to convince Thorn that instead of fighting, the miners could *all* flee, deeper into the tunnels and caverns, out of the Shadewatch's reach. But Thorn had made up his mind.

"The Shademaster doesn't know how many we are, and that's our luck. That's our *chance*."

Thorn straightened. "This is what we decided on together. No one here fights because I ordered them to. They fight because they chose to. If I could think of a way to keep them all safe, I would. I won't deny them the chance to make a difference. We fight, so that the others may live. If we flee, the guards will keep coming after us, and that puts everyone at risk." It was a plan of desperation, made to steal time not victory away from the enemy.

On some level Vax understood Thorn couldn't escape either. He'd keep searching for vengeance if he didn't find some semblance of justice. It was an inevitable collision course.

"Get out with the others when we give the sign, Vax," Thorn said, not for the first time. "Once the Shadewatch is distracted by the fight, make your way to Jorenn and your sister, and if you can find proof for the survivors, that would mean the world. But don't get in too deep. It's hard to find the surface when you do."

Vax drew in a sharp breath, ready to tell Thorn that he knew what he was doing, that he'd fast-talked his way out of plenty of tight spots before—though never quite as dashingly as his sister—when he stopped. To Thorn, he and his sister were still regular travelers, on their way to Jorenn Village running errands or looking for work, like so many others before them. Thorn wondered, but he hadn't outright asked, and Vax hadn't volunteered the information.

So instead, he simply held out an arm and waited for Thorn to grasp it. "I'll find something useful. I promise."

Thorn clasped his arm, and nodded. Without another word, he turned and walked to the center of the cavern.

And the mood changed, with the snap of a finger. A wave of fear rolled through the cavern, so palpable everyone felt it.

Thorn climbed on top of one of the tables. His voice carried, steady and brooking no argument. "The Shadewatch made their move. They're on their way to the mines, and they outnumber us three to one. We can't all fight. We won't all fight. I won't put the children or the families at risk. Not again." His words were met with stony determination. "We've discussed our escape plans. Those who will stay and fight come with me. The rest will follow Junel. You know what to do."

No one present looked happy about the plans, but no one hesitated either. The miners who would stay and fight fell in around Thorn, and the others made their way over to Junel. They clasped hands, held on to each other, whispered goodbyes, and Vax kept his distance, unable to take in the scenes in front of him and unable to look away.

If he had to choose between his sister's life and his own, he'd choose Vex in a heartbeat, but he could not imagine being torn apart like this.

"We all knew it would come to this, especially when no one else wanted to take us in. This is the best chance we have. *We* are the best chance *they* have." Tinyn wandered up next to Vax, and she stared him down with deep, steady eyes. "I will come back to haunt you if anything happens to the survivors or if you endanger them."

"I would never," Vax said steadily.

Tinyn considered the words, then she shrugged. "Thorn trusts you. I don't have to."

"Understood."

Without another word, Tinyn reached for her scimitars and her eyes found her dwarven partner Faril, who lined up with those sneaking out of the cavern. The space between them was emptying—except for Sencha, who lingered near the cots with her bag full of medical supplies—but the unspoken words between Tinyn and Faril could fill the whole chamber.

At that point, a loud clanging began to echo through the tunnels. Metal on metal. Swords on shields. And the pounding of footsteps.

Junel called for the survivors to follow them into passages that led deeper into the hills, away from the Shadewatch waiting above. Sencha would be the last to escape, collapsing the tunnel behind those who would stay and fight.

Tinyn led the first group of miners up toward the surface, with a deep sigh, a squaring of her shoulders, and a determined frown.

And Vax hesitated.

On the other side of the cavern, at the head of the second group of warriors, Thorn called out to him. His eyes sparkled dangerously. "When you get back to the rest of the civilized world, anywhere but Westruun, tell the most outrageous stories about us," he called out. "What we do here should live on."

His words were met with cheers and laughter.

"Westruun isn't civilized enough for you?" Vax wanted to know. He reached for his daggers and stole another glance in Junel's direction. There too, groups were making their way out of the cavern.

"Wouldn't know, never been. But the Shademaster deals with the Westruun Clasp. They're her intermediary between the mines and the market. So I'd prefer it if they didn't find out about us. I have too many powerful enemies already." Thorn grinned. All the tension he'd carried with him had fallen away when he picked up his weapons. All his gentleness was gone. All that was left was the fight ahead.

With a final nod, Thorn walked toward Felric and out of the cavern, oblivious to the fact that his words still echoed around Vax.

The Shademaster deals with the Westruun Clasp.

It clashed directly against another comment, from longer—half a lifetime—ago.

Much like gold, information must be earned.

"Fuck!" The cavern emptied around them. The last of the miners who hoped to escape turned around to stare at him, and Vax snarled, a thousand questions swirling around him. He should follow. He should get out of here, find Vex, and let what would happen in the fight happen. He owed Thorn and the others nothing more than to try to aid them. He could find answers on his own, with his sister by his side.

But if the Clasp assignment had been a trap all along, he needed to know what they were getting into. He didn't need a powerful enemy either.

If he believed the miners, this plan, to stay and fight or to escape, was a choice between certain death and certain survival. But it wasn't. It couldn't be. It had to be a choice between likely death and possible escape.

Thorn had warned him not to get in too deep, but that warning had come far too late. He already was, and long before he got here.

Vax palmed two of his daggers, and ran into the tunnel toward the fight.

VAX FOLLOWED THE PATH UP to the higher levels, miners in front of him and tension all around them. He expected chaos. He'd fought before. He'd been trained to fight. He'd been at the center of some painful misunderstandings in various towns' seedy underbellies. Nothing could have prepared him for this.

Everywhere Vax looked, he saw red uniforms and miners covered in the soot and dirt of the mines. The dust on the ground swirled around his feet, like the ash had in the encampment. He clung to his daggers and pushed through.

He made it to the main level, where the kitchen had once held the sounds of laughter and now held the sounds of dying. In the room where Vax had recovered from his wounds, five Shadewatch were facing off against two miners—and the miners were losing. Everywhere people were fighting. Tinyn was locked up in a battle with three guards at the same time, and while her rage was potent, so were their weapons.

Three groups of a dozen miners each had left the cavern, and at least half a dozen of them lay dead in the tunnels already, while the Shadewatch guards streamed into the tunnels, shoulder-to-shoulder. The sound of metal on metal filled the space, of swords hitting shields and blades glancing off armor. Grunts and shouts and screams of pain.

They fell. One by one, the miners fell.

Vax felt cold. He reached for a dagger and sent it flying without allowing himself time to aim. It buried itself in one of the guards' shoulders, but it didn't stop the man from swinging down his sword and cleaving into the young dwarf in front of him. Death was loud and messy.

One of the other miners—a young halfling woman—managed to stab a long, slender blade into the side of the guardswoman in front of Vax, sneaking underneath her breastplate. She gargled and blood streaked from the corners of her mouth. She looked at the miner with such rage before her eyes broke.

Vax swung around to stand with his back to the halfling, and he parried a guard who slashed a sword in his general direction. He followed through with an easy swipe of his dagger, but it barely drove through the man's armor. And behind him there were three more to take his place.

He glanced around to locate Thorn. The other man was nowhere to be seen.

He ducked out of the way of another blade and hooked his foot around a guard's so the man went crashing to the ground. Even over the din of battle, Vax heard the sickening crunch of bone breaking.

It wasn't like when the guards had found their way in. That fight had been quick and brutal and though it was bloody, it was survival. This was slaughter. And the Shadewatch kept bleeding into the tunnels, with endless blades and merciless cruelty.

Felric darted past him, his crossbow loaded. He twisted and shot a bolt at the guard who took a swing at him, but before he could straighten and dart deeper into the mine, to find a safe vantage point, a tall woman in Shadewatch colors slammed her quarterstaff into his knee and sent him tumbling to the ground. Another guard followed through with an ax.

Vax shouted. The butt of a polearm crashed into his side, and he doubled over. He brought his dagger up out of reflex more than strategy, and stars danced in front of him when the blade of a spear glanced off his weapon. By the time he straightened and could bring himself to attack, Felric was bleeding out on the floor. He mumbled something and tried to bring his hands up to his throat, but the fight bled out of him too.

In the chaos that followed, multiple things happened at the same time.

The dust around them kicked up and one of the guards called out a warning. "Ash walkers!"—as a trio of lumbering, cadaverous creatures crawled their way up from the deepest tunnels. One of the tallest cornered the guard and used its claws to cut deep into his chest.

At the same time, the Shadewatch kept filtering in, with a group of guards forming a tight formation around a pale human woman, who held a broadsword like it was a rapier. She had her brown hair tied back in a thick braid, and she shouted commands. "Break in two! Beven's squad, keep an eye on those bloody corpses! Do not engage unless you must! Olfa's squad, continue your assignment! We have to clear these mines."

Two guards—presumably the people she'd named—responded with a crisp, "Yes, Shademaster." They followed her orders with some of their own, and a handful of guards pushed deeper into the mines while others strengthened the protective forms around the brown-haired woman.

Vax expected Shademaster Derowen to be a monster, based on the stories Thorn and Sencha had told. He thought he'd see the bloodlust in her eyes. He didn't. She wasn't. She focused on something far beyond them both, and he saw the dark circles underneath her eyes. The way she clung to the hilt of her sword with her gloved hands folded over each other. Her carmine overcoat showed the wear and tear of many hours of weapons practice, but her sword and armor were bloodied, and she and the Shadewatch gave no quarter. Two of the guards in the Shademaster's retinue ran their swords through a miner without hesitation, like she was simply in the wrong place at the wrong time.

Vax pushed himself into the shadows that hugged the walls when he stilled.

Coming up behind the Shademaster was a figure he knew all too well. He saw the tip of a bow point out over the Shademaster's shoulder before he saw anything else. An arrow flew out into the fray, and Vex stepped out from behind her. She had her cloak pulled tight around her, and her eyes scanned the area. Looking. Searching.

Vax didn't think. He stepped forward, oblivious to the fight around him. Oblivious to the Shademaster's guards who immediately tensed. When their eyes met, everything that had mattered so much only minutes ago disappeared to the background.

He took another step forward. "Stubby?"

And right at that point, another face became clear in the blur around him—and Thorn sprinted toward the Shademaster.

CHAPTER 22

"Vax!"

Her brother appeared in front of her and disappeared as easily again, dashing out of the way of the Shadewatch, roughly pulling another figure with him. The guards filtered out around her to deal with the combination of ash walkers and outlaws, and the low light in the mines lent an air of chaos to the fight. Vex clung to her bow and tried to find Vax again.

Derowen placed a hand on her shoulder. She scanned the surrounding area too, her eyes sharp and concerned. "Your brother is here?"

"He's here," Vex repeated, nearly choking on the potent mixture of relief and worry. She'd seen him. He had to be close, but why had he ducked out of the way again?

Derowen looked at her intently. "Go find him."

Vex pushed through the guards that encircled both her and the Shademaster, and dove deeper into the mines, where the fight around them was as desperate as the fight against the dead had been that first night. The guards who'd gone in with the Shademaster all knew that the last time a patrol found its way into these mines, three of their own were killed and only one managed to make her way out. They had all clashed with the dead, and they knew the dangers these outlaws posed to Jorenn.

And they all fought like it.

Vex knew she'd underestimated their dedication, but when she pushed deeper into the tunnels, past chambers with old picks and hammers on the walls that showed the outlaws had made their home here, past flecks of old blood on the ground that only enraged the guards more, she was grateful to have them at her back. If they could find their way through this tangle of tunnels, it wouldn't just be about her and Vax. Perhaps they could leave Jorenn a safer place than they'd found it, where little girls didn't have constant night terrors.

She saw a lanky figure dash through a cloud of dust and ash, and she followed in the same direction.

"Vax!"

The tunnels were everything and nothing like she expected.

Storm clouds had raged above them when they left for the mines, Derowen at the head of the Shadewatch, and Vex and Trinket not far behind. They'd been soaked through within minutes of leaving the town. Underneath the darkened sky, their vision had been obscured by a heavy sheet of rain that stretched from the hills into the valley, casting the world around them in shades of dark blue and gray, but it had still been brighter outside than in here. All the more so when lightning coursed through the sky, and loud cracks of thunder underscored the rumbling of the guards' voices. Attacking the mines was all they'd talked about, all they'd known over the past few days, and the closer they'd come, the harder it had been to stop imagining the unknown dangers ahead, especially when those dangers involved Vax.

Now that Vex was here, all she could hear were the sounds and screams of battle. The dizzying, toxic combination of one side's inescapable death and the other side's imminent victory. They'd entered the mines with as many guards as the town could spare, leaving only the bare minimum on the palisades and in the Shade Hall. And they pushed through relentlessly; where one fell, the next immediately took their place. But their enemies hadn't been as many and as ferocious as she anticipated.

The chambers she passed looked simple and homey, with rickety chairs and tables and sleeping cots. Cabinets that held dried herbs and rabbit skins. Wooden swords and a deflated leather ball in a corner, covered under a layer of dust. Shadows and chalk drawings on one of the walls.

Vex leaped out of the way when a female half-orc and two guards tumbled into one of the smaller tunnels that arched away from the main cave, a tangle of limbs and weapons. She recognized one of the guards as Nari, the scout who rode out with her. A third guard lay lifeless on the ground in the chamber behind them, and the half-orc was bloodied and limping, but she fought ruthlessly with two scimitars. Still, she was no match for the guard. When she spun an attack in the direction of a broad-shouldered dwarven woman, the guardswoman ducked underneath. Her sword sliced through the muscles of the outlaw's lower leg and she dropped to a knee.

Following up on the guard's attack, Nari took his sword and jammed it into the half-orc's neck, just above her clavicle.

When Nari stumbled away from the half-orc, one of the woman's scimitars was lodged in his rib cage, pointing up toward the heart.

Vex gagged, and farther down the tunnels Beven's voice rang out above the fray. "The ash walkers are everywhere. We have to retreat!"

"Vax!" Vex tried again, her voice rough. She pushed forward past the bodies of outlaws and the bodies of guards, while the Shadewatch around her began to pull back, until Derowen's voice rang through the mines. "Keep pushing through!"

The crush of bodies around her was suffocating, and the same nightmarish questions ran through her mind over and over again. What if Vax fell in the fight before she could get to him? What if he'd fallen to the ash creatures? What if she was too late?

Vax.

With the dust of the tunnels and the fight swirling around them, she found him again, a handful of steps away from her at the narrowing of a secondary tunnel. He wore the same dirty and torn clothes as when she'd last seen him, like no time had passed at all. But there was blood on the cloak, and on his dagger. There was blood on his face, and he looked at the people around her like they were the enemy. His eyes landed on her, and for the first time since the initial ash walker attack tore them apart, the world felt *right* again. "Stubby." She didn't know one word could be so full of pain and relief.

He didn't walk toward her. Instead he held on to the tunic of another half-elven man, with dark hair tumbling around his scarred face and pure, unabating rage in every line of his body. He tried to shake himself loose. "Get out of my way, Vax."

"No."

"Vax." She took a step forward, hesitantly.

Behind her, she heard the heavy footfalls of the Shadewatch and the voice of Derowen, barking orders. The fight in the tunnels had quieted. Fewer people cried out. The last remaining outlaws were bound and taken in the guard's custody. Blades didn't cross many blades anymore, though she did hear the dull thud of blade against bone from deeper below.

An arrow zoomed past her head and missed the half-elf by inches. Voices sounded all around her. "It's him. It's Thorn." "He set more of the ash walkers loose." "He's responsible for all of this."

"I want him alive." Derowen's words were loud and clear, echoing around Vex and her brother and the third half-elf. Thorn, leader of the outlaws. "He needs to be brought to justice."

Vex hissed. "Vax, what are you doing?"

Vax shook his head. His jaw worked, and he glanced over Vex's shoulder at the oncoming guard. He seemed completely at a loss. "I'm sorry."

Then he stepped in front of the other half-elf, shielding him, and pushed him deeper into the mines. "This is not what revenge looks like," he said, his voice barely loud enough to carry to Vex. "Look around you, there is nothing left. Take it and run and live to fight another day. Anissa wouldn't want you to throw your life away, and neither would Sencha and Junel."

Thorn snarled. He stumbled and would have turned back, but Vax blocked his path. "They need you. And I need you to trust me."

Vex stared, unable to quite comprehend what she was seeing. During all these days when she tried to stop herself from fretting, she'd worried they'd be too late. That he'd been hurt or killed in the first fight—or by these mine dwellers. She'd worried that they'd imprisoned him. She'd worried that he'd antagonize them and put himself in harm's way.

Not this.

She'd expected to find her brother anywhere but on the other side of this fight.

"What are you doing?" she hissed. "He's a criminal."

Vax took a deep breath. He didn't turn to look at her. She didn't need to see his face to know how conflicted he was. It was clear in the tense lines of his shoulders, the trembling of his hands. When he spoke, his voice was laced with a peculiar sadness. "He saved my life, Vex'ahlia. His people got me out when those dead things attacked, and they patched me up."

"But . . ."

Behind him, the other half-elf still lingered, and Vax kept blocking the path.

Behind her, the Shadewatch had noticed the standoff. Their shouts echoed around them. She felt the weight of every single one of their stares.

"I need you to trust me too," he said quietly. "They only hide out in the mines because the Shademaster destroyed their homes."

She was stunned into silence. She couldn't wrap her mind around her brother's words, and her ears were ringing. Despite the questions between them and the fight around them, Vex did the only thing she could do. She crossed the few steps that separated them, and flung her arms around him. In that space between heartbeats, the world stopped, the fighting quieted, and they were all that mattered.

"Of course I trust you, you idiot." She buried her face into his shoulder and breathed in the familiar scent of blade polish and midnight. She held him as tightly as she could, terrified he'd somehow disappear again if she let go.

Vax clung to her with the same ferocity, his presence strong and steady and *there*.

Behind Vax, Thorn stared at them. She heard the footsteps of the Shadewatch running toward them, and she saw the hatred in his eyes. While Vax held her, he could slip past and she wouldn't stop him. But lines of grief crossed his face, and he shuddered. With the twins between him and the Shadewatch, he turned on his heels and ran into the shadows of the tunnel.

"Stop him! Get out of the way!"

One of the guards dashed past her, and Vex pulled apart from Vax, grabbing his sleeve in an attempt to pull him aside. Instead he squared his shoulders and reached for her hand. He kept his stance, the second guard nearly crashing into him and plummeting to the floor. He shook his head. "He deserves a fair chance."

"He's responsible for all of this!" she shot back.

"He isn't," Vax said, looking at a spot behind her.

She twisted and saw Derowen stare at them, hands folded over each other, and her face twisted with anger. In an instant, Vex felt her relief drop away and worry crash into her, and anger overrode her confusion.

She reared and punched Vax in the shoulder. Hard.

Vax arched back and rubbed his shoulder. "Vex . . ."

"You shit," Vex seethed. It was such a relief to be mad. "I've been looking for you for fucking *days* and you run away from me for one of those miners? Do you have any idea how fucking worried I was?" She threw her hands into the air, and would have turned around, when Vax grabbed her and pulled her into another tight hug.

"I've missed you too."

Vex stomped lightly on his foot, but she stopped struggling, letting him hold her. He still effectively blocked the tunnel, and she could hear the Shadewatch draw closer.

"I need him to get out of the way, Vex." The Shademaster, her voice low and furious.

Vax took a step back and spoke low enough so only Vex could hear. "I can't. They'll kill him. Look around you. The Shademaster is *dangerous*. This wasn't a fair fight, it was a fucking massacre."

She breathed out hard, and she matched his quiet tone. "It was the only way for the Shadewatch to fight back. These people are responsible for the ash walker attacks, Vax. I'm grateful that they took care of you, but they're a danger to everyone around them."

"If that's what she told you, she hasn't told you the whole story," he whispered, glancing over her shoulder again. She felt someone step closer. Shademaster Derowen cleared her throat.

Vex tensed. They could figure this out. Later. Outside. *Together.* "Please, Vax."

"This wasn't how I envisioned us meeting, Vax," Derowen said loudly. "I will have the guard remove you if you don't step aside."

"They have to protect their homes, brother. She fights for the future of her daughter."

Behind Vax, the two guards who'd made their way past were facing off against a trio of fading dead, their skeletal forms covered in soot and ash. The tallest of the creatures had its claws into one of the guards, while a smaller one—his posture and gait like those of a halfling—tore into the woman with his sharp teeth. The other guard, a bulky human man, swung with his sword to try to carve her free.

Other crumbling corpses pushed their way out of the tunnel, coming from the direction in which Thorn had disappeared.

Vax kept his eyes on his sister, like he was searching for something. Then he nodded. He moved aside and immediately, guards slammed past them. Vex grabbed hold of him and dragged him out of the way, while the remaining guards filtered into the tunnel in search of the leader of the outlaws.

Vax watched them run past, and his shoulders dropped. He glanced in the direction of the Shademaster once more. "Appearances can be deceiving, Vex'ahlia."

CHAPTER 23

Six years ago

Appearances could be deceiving in Syngorn, but when it came to Vax's innocent smile, Vex knew exactly what it meant. Trouble for both of them.

"Are you certain we should be here?" she asked, not for the first time.

Vax dragged her toward the lake. "Live a little, Stubby."

If it were up to Vex, she would've used the day off to study. She had to review historical texts, Elvish conjugations, and a tome on Syngornian culture and etiquette. That last one seemed specifically designed to make her feel inferior. In the two years or so since Syldor had sent the twins to school, the teachers kept coming up with different reasons why they were not up to par. Which was to say, in her case they were different reasons. In the case of her brother it was simply that he didn't care and had stopped trying.

And now he'd convinced her to spend the day out in the city, taking full advantage of the fact that their father had business elsewhere. It was tempting, yes, but she could also keep studying. She could go through her archery routine once more, to polish her technique and eliminate all the flaws and the mistakes she made. Even if she could never learn how to live up to the grace and poise of her fellow students, she could try.

"What better way to learn about Syngornian culture than to spend time in it?" Vax asked slyly.

She groaned. "Ugh, you're the worst."

"You know you love me."

Vex rolled her eyes, but she followed, because he insisted and they didn't spend enough time together. At Syldor's suggestion, their teachers had decided to split them up, and when she spent her nights studying, he sneaked out to spend time in the city too. Sometimes, he didn't come back until near morning, looking no worse for wear, but presumably sleeping through all his classes. He told her he looked for his education elsewhere. She just missed him.

So she was here, and although the sky was overcast and the weather was colder than it had been on the day that they arrived here, Lake Ywnnlas was as crowded as ever. At least two dozen boats were coasting across the surface that she could see, all of them decorated in colorful shades. In one of the closest boats, three children were blowing bubbles while their mother made dancing lights appear inside them. Farther away, two girls were sharing what appeared to be a romantic lunch with candlelight and cake.

"What are we doing here, Vax?" Vex asked quietly. "The lake is beautiful enough, but can't you see them all staring at us?"

On the lake, in the closest boats, a few elves did. On the lakefront too, a girl their own age leaned against a sea-green boat with gently painted storm-blue patterns, a pair of crutches by her side. She had her arms crossed, and her eyes followed their every step with intense curiosity.

"They can all drown," Vax said cheerfully. He stalked off in the direction of the girl. "We're going for a boat ride."

"Vax? Wait." She rushed after him, suddenly concerned. She'd eyed the boats before, hesitantly. She would happily spend whole days in the forest and—before—on the marshland, come rain, shine, or storm. She'd walked the meditative Reverie Walks and marveled at how ancient and powerful a place it was. She didn't mind—and in fact she loved and respected—the forces of nature. But the gentle rocking of the boats made her feel slightly queasy and nauseated.

And the girl with the smiling eyes looked like she was as much trouble as her brother. When Vax approached her, they exchanged a few words while Vex was out of earshot. Or perhaps it was more accurate to say that the sudden rushing sound in her ears drowned out everything else, and she couldn't stop glancing at the mirror-smooth lake.

"I'm really not sure this is a good idea," she said, to no one in particular, as the girl's grin widened.

"It's not so bad once you get used to it." She didn't seem to be perturbed by their half-elven status and, far more intriguingly, appeared to be a friend—or at least some kind of acquaintance—of her brother's.

She raised an eyebrow at Vax. "Want to introduce us?"

Hints of color appeared on his cheeks. "This is Cy—Cyriel. She helped secure the boat."

She bit back the *oh, really*, and instead nodded at the elf. "A pleasure."

Cyriel bowed at her, gallantly, but looked at Vax. "As pretty as you *and* manners? Why does anyone give you the time of day?"

Vax glared, and Vex laughed in spite of herself. "I like her. Why didn't you introduce us before?"

"For this exact reason. Thank you for the boat, Cyriel. Please go." Vax started pushing the girl away and Cyriel grabbed her crutches and fled out of his reach. "Everything's as you requested. You know where to find me once you get back."

"Thank you. *Go.*"

"You know where to find her, don't you? So is that where—or should I say who—you're off to during those late nights?" Vex stored the knowledge away for future reference and smiled when Vax's color deepened. She couldn't remember the last time she'd teased her brother like this. She couldn't remember the last time she'd had cause. "And here I thought you weren't trying to fit in."

"I'm not," Vax grumbled. He rolled up the sleeves of his shirt and pushed the boat toward the water.

Vex shuddered when it breached the surface and rocked gently back and forth. If her brother had arranged it for them, she would climb in, but perhaps next time they could go on a comfortable wyvern hunt or a gentle stroll around an active volcano.

With his feet in the water, Vax held on to the boat and reached out a hand to her. "Come on, climb in."

She took a deep breath and shoved away her discomfort. She pulled herself up on the edge of the boat instead, ignoring the outstretched hand. The boat rocked precariously, and she swallowed hard.

"Are you turning *green*?" Vax demanded, incredulously.

"I'm fine," she snapped. "Get into the boat, brother, before your scrawny arms can't hold it anymore."

He leaped with a grace she hadn't seen before. These last few years, he'd been so lanky and uncoordinated compared with all the elves around them, but it seemed like he was coming into his own. The grace suited him, but the jump so violently rocked the boat that for a long moment she considered leaping out of it again.

Vax whispered the boat's command word to set it floating farther onto the lake, and the waters around them calmed. The rocking motion became a gentle rolling, and Cyriel's words proved to have a core of truth in them. It did become easier. Even so, Vex felt out of sorts. She leaned back and clung to the sides fiercely, letting the soft breeze ground her.

She forced the worry out of her voice. "So, Cyriel . . ."

". . . is just someone I hang out with."

She raised an eyebrow. "Are you sure? Because that looked very friendly to me."

"I'm sure." Vax's words held a hint of warning. He didn't tear his gaze away from the lake, navigating the boat with calm nudges and spoken command words. They didn't go all the way to the center of the vast expanse of water, but stayed just within sight of the shore. Around them, the sun made the surface look like liquid crystal. It was painfully bright and painfully beautiful.

She nudged him with her foot. "I just wanted to tell you I'm happy for you. I want you to be happy here."

He faced her then, and his frown made him look older than his years. "I'm not. I won't be. But wherever I'm with you, I'm home and that's what matters." He tilted his head slightly. "Still, I won't deny this place has saving graces. And she's one of them."

"What are the others?" she wondered.

He didn't immediately respond. He navigated the boat to a specific spot with minute precision and commanded it to stop. The water here was so calm, the boat barely moved, and Vex relaxed her grasp on the edges.

"This." He pointed at the city around them, and she forced herself to watch.

Objectively, Syngorn was a majestic place to be. From their spot on the water, a colorful horizon spread out around them. The peaceful lake seemed like a gentle extension of the sky overhead, while mountains and trees encircled the city. The Emerald Citadel towered high over all the other buildings, and the sunlight lent the whole city a gentle green glow. In the far distance, she spied the labyrinth of trees and rocks that formed the Reverie Walks, and somewhere near the Memory Ward would be their school. She could see the beautifully designed bridges around the lake and crossing the various canals, and if she squinted she could imagine the dancing lights around the tall red trees. As a bonus, if she kept her eyes on the horizon, it helped her stomach settle faster—and she didn't have to consider the passengers of the other boats, and what they might think of the two of them.

"I wanted you to see it," Vax said softly, with determination, "not because I think it's home or because I think we could belong here, but because I want you to remember that there's beauty in this world and you deserve to see it. Besides, our father's heritage isn't *all* prejudice and arrogance. It's creation, too."

Something inside her loosened at those words, and she pulled her knees up to her chest to keep herself from unraveling.

"There's also this," Vax said softly. He reached behind him and pulled out a long, linen-wrapped item that she'd completely missed when she climbed in—or he'd had it hidden well.

"What's that?"

"Take a look." He held it out to her, and despite her better judgment she took it without a second thought.

The moment her fingers wrapped around the gift, she stilled. When she unwrapped the linen and the deep-brown staff peeked out, she gasped.

Briefly, Vex forgot she was on the water.

She pushed the remainder of the linen away, and she could only stare.

The hazelwood longbow was the best the bowyer had on offer. She knew it well, because she'd spent countless nights admiring and lusting over the bow. It was the right size for her, it had the perfect draw weight, and now that she held it, it fitted in her hand as though it had been made for her. Vex almost laughed at her younger self who'd thought any bow could be an extension of her, because once she wrapped her fingers around this bow, she knew what a lie that had been. No other bow could ever match it.

"Vax . . ." She didn't know what to say.

He smiled a crooked smile, obviously pleased with himself. "I saw how much you wanted this, so I saved up."

She raised an eyebrow at that, while her hands kept stroking the staff. "How? No, wait, I don't want to know." They got the same allowance, and even if he hadn't spent a copper piece of it in three years, that still wouldn't be enough to cover the cost of this bow. And beyond Cyriel, she still didn't know exactly what he did when he went out at night. He came back more confident than she'd seen him in a long time. If this was a part of that, she couldn't refuse. She never wanted to let go of the bow.

"But why?" she asked, after another long moment.

Vax rolled the discarded linen into a messy ball and tossed it straight at her face. "You deserve a bow that lets you be the best archer you can be. I see how the teachers look at you when they don't think we notice. You're good, Vex'ahlia. I don't care what they try to tell you, you're as good as any full elf that ever passed through this city."

She grimaced at that. "They only tell me all the things I need to improve before they can consider me passable." *Before I matter,* she didn't say. She cradled the bow close.

Vax breathed out hard. "So listen to me. You know I wouldn't lie to you, not about something as important as this. You're the best archer I know, and they know it too."

Vex still had her hand clenched around the bow's grip, and she felt her hands tremble. She turned her face toward the afternoon sun, toward the direction where their home had once been.

"Saving graces, right?" she asked, with a hint of wonder. This bow was one, without question. One she didn't know she deserved or should accept, but she did so regardless.

"I want you to be happy as well, Stubby."

She wanted that too. For both of them. She imagined, briefly, what it would look like, but she didn't linger on it. Because even if she could dream, it wouldn't change reality. This, right here, right now, this was all that mattered. With her brother and the most gorgeous of bows, in a boat, in a majestic city.

Today was *good.*

"I'm home wherever I'm with you too, Scrawny." Vax had the dignity to look affronted at that, and she laughed at that. In the middle of the lake, she laughed without reservation. Home together. Always and no matter what happened.

CHAPTER 24

The storm rolled over the town, and the sheet of rain had turned the road into a blanket of mud. Vax kept his eyes on the frontier town in front of him, and the way it gradually grew larger as they neared it. The wooden palisades around the town were tall and proud, flanking the entrance and burrowing into the hillside, so the town itself was protected on all sides. Archers stood atop the palisades on either side of the gate, looking half drowned and miserable even with the cover of guardhouses. Next to the road stood two members of the Shadewatch, taking careful note of everyone who passed them by. They straightened when they saw the first group of guards make their way back from the hills.

His heartbeat picked up, anticipation wrapping itself around him. The sky brightened, with streaks of early-morning sunlight pushing through the clouds, but Vax's mood didn't.

He rode with his horse tethered to Vex's, and his sister looked at him with so many questions in her eyes.

Thorn had disappeared. By the time the Shadewatch made its way deeper into the hills, all that had been left were the corpses that had crawled their way up from the deepest shafts. The guards had fought, with Vex and a handful of others providing assistance. At the same time, they'd been very careful to keep Vax out of the way. He'd been allowed to keep his weapons. He'd even been returned his thrown dagger. But he hadn't missed their looks of disgust—or pity, when directed at Vex.

The fight continued for the better part of the day, from the initial attack on the miners to the struggle with the ash walkers. Derowen had said nothing else to him than that they would talk once back in Jorenn, before she sent scouts deeper into the mines, in the hope of finding Thorn.

Eventually, day made way for dusk, and every single one of the scouts came back empty-handed. None mentioned any trace of the miners who'd escaped with Sencha and Junel either, and Vax breathed a little easier.

Later that night, when the Shadewatch had set up camp in the hills, with bright fires and double guard shifts to ward off any remaining ash walkers, his sister and he sat around a campfire, and everything felt like it was the way it should be. The two of them, together against the world.

He'd run out of the cavern with the insistent knowledge that he could fix more problems than he caused, but the fight and the storm had washed away that confidence. He should never have brought them here. He should have found another way to deal with the Clasp. One sword hanging over him would have been better than the tangle of weapons he'd run straight into.

Gods, what a fucking mess. He understood all too well that Vex had questions, because he did too. He wanted to know about Derowen's involvement with the Clasp. He wanted to know about the origin of the ash walkers and the miners' culpability. The stories Sencha and Felric had skirted around. Thorn hadn't lied about the Shadewatch hunting them down and slaughtering them, but what if the Shademaster had spoken the truth too? What had she done to earn his sister's admiration, when neither of them trusted easily and she least of all?

He'd been too exhausted to figure it out. They were both too exhausted for the conversations they needed to have. So they'd sat together, leaning against each other, and he stared out at the bodies that had been brought out of the mines. A handful of fighters had been captured, but most everyone who'd followed Thorn into the fray had been killed.

"Who were they?" Vex asked, following his gaze.

"Tinyn. Felric. Whit. Lenda." He named the other two halflings. The other miners he'd seen enter and fall. He couldn't name all of them. They'd managed to hide safely for months, if not years, and still all of that could break in hours. "Yours?"

"Olfa. Nari. Beven." Vex named almost a dozen guards. She swallowed past the hoarseness in her voice and stared out into the distance. "They all helped me try to find you."

"Too many of them," he said.

"Far too many," she agreed.

THE FOLLOWING MORNING, THE SHADEMASTER rode at the head of the column, and when she reached the gates, she halted to speak with the guards. From farther down the line, Vax couldn't make out what was said, but he recognized the mixture of elation and grief that passed through the guards. A battle won, and lives lost.

Derowen turned and nodded at the first group of guards, who rode in ahead of the others and fanned out beyond the gate. No doubt to spread word of the fallen, to reassure everyone the guards on foot were still making their way home, and to prepare the healers for the wounded on the carts behind them.

Once they passed through, Derowen and her closest commanders followed, and so on. By the time Vax and Vex approached the gates, the guards didn't give him a second glance, talking excitedly among themselves. One guard punched the other in the shoulder. "Does that mean we're safe now?"

The other guard grinned. "You heard the Shademaster, she'll protect us."

"With the miners out of the way, we can wipe out the other dangers in the mountains," the first guard said, full of resolve.

Before Vax could hear what the other guard had to say to that, they'd passed them both. And without further ado, Vax was in Jorenn Village.

The dusty, muddy streets around him were empty, with only those who couldn't avoid it venturing out into the rain. Inside the shops and homes, warm light glowed, as everyone who could hid in their bubbles of comfort. Two women with closed baskets ran across the street to get from one house to another. Outside one of the larger houses, a young dwarven boy sat playing in a puddle of water, while a dog twice his size stood watch.

It didn't look like the hard place Sencha had made it out to be. It looked like any other place where people lived: complicated, dirty, and full of details he was curious about.

He wondered if the miners' houses had looked like this.

He also wondered how many of these homes would be emptier tonight for the lives lost in the tunnels—or the lives lost to attacks by the ashen corpses.

He must have made a sound or let some of the questions bleed through in his expression, because Vex looked at him. They'd done that a few times during the ride—glance at each other to make sure the other one was still there.

"Where do we go from here?" he asked.

"The Shade Hall, first," Vex said. "Derowen wants to talk to you, and after they helped me try to find you, I think you should."

"Is it an invitation or an order?" he wanted to know.

She rolled her eyes. "Don't be an ass. It isn't like that. Derowen has been good to me. She wants to understand why you took away their best chance to capture the leader of the outlaws that have plagued them for years. Give her a chance, please?"

"She took care of you," he said simply. Because despite everything he'd heard from Thorn, that was true too, and he owed her for that.

Vex didn't react to that. "Trinket is going to be so happy to see you. He would never admit it, but he missed you."

"Aw, I missed him too," he replied. He smirked. "And his farts to keep me warm at night."

"You shit." She reached out to slap him, and he ducked out of her reach.

"Will you show me around the Shade Hall too?" he asked after a moment, noncommittally. Having a legitimate reason to be inside the town hall would make breaking into the Shademaster's office so much easier. He had all the more reason to do so now. Not just to find evidence for Thorn and the survivors, or to get the ring he needed to find, but because he needed to know the truth. Derowen was someone his sister cared about, and he refused to see Vex hurt. Not if he could do anything to stop it.

Vex glanced around her. Something like concern flashed across her face, but he knew she'd tell him about it in private. And she nodded. "I'll introduce you to Wick and Aswin. Give you a tour of the place."

She nudged him like she was aware of the tangle of thoughts inside his head. "But promise me no rash actions."

"I promise I'll consider all my actions carefully," he said.

She raised an eyebrow. "That's hardly reassuring."

"When have my rash actions ever gotten us into trouble?"

"Would you like an itemized list?"

"Hey!" He drew breath to argue, when a smile teased at her lips and this felt right too. Despite the days between them, and the ashen divide.

Some of the tension melted from Vex's shoulders. "It'll be better once you see this place. And if you don't want to stay in the Shade Hall," Vex continued, "there are other options around Jorenn." She pointed to the square that spread out before them, right in the middle of town.

On the far side stood an orange-brown-brick building with guards on either side of the tall wooden doors. Another pair of guards lingered on the roof, half protected by the overhang. Closer by was a simpler building, with wooden planks across its façade, and a shingle that read THE SCATTERED BAR. The doors were closed and the shutters were too, but soft voices and music drifted out from the inside and Vax could smell the spicy warmth of a fireplace.

"This is where the Shadewatch brings in the travelers they rescue from the ash walkers—all the corpses stalking these hills," Vex commented. "It's a chaotic place, so I think you'd like it. Wick told me that the innkeeper earns a fair bit of coin providing lodging for stranded folk, but the man is so terribly bad he spends it on all the wrong things. The chairs miss legs and the tables wobble, but the silverware is beautifully wrought and he has nearly a dozen tapestries on the walls."

She rambled, and Vax wasn't about to stop her.

"There's a bar hidden behind a bookcase at the hill's edge of town too, but it's only old dwarves drinking away their sorrows, and there's a dodgy chapel attic with far too many fairy lights strewn about it up near the miners' gate that holds a tavern of sorts. No good drinks, and a whole lot of apprentices trying out potions and pipes and dancing to the tune of a fiddle and a song. I walked through to make sure you weren't there." Something soft and gentle flitted across Vex's face.

"You've tried them all?" Vax asked.

She shrugged. "I couldn't discount the fact that your questionable tastes would've led you there."

"If I'd found a way out of the mines, I would have come to find you," he said.

She stared out at the Shade Hall and swallowed. "Why didn't you?"

"I couldn't leave," he said. "I couldn't find my own way out and I . . . I promise I'll tell you everything. Not right here and not right now."

They rode up to the steps in front of the Shade Hall, where Vex dismounted first and then waited for him. She still had soot and blood from the mines all over her cloak and clothes, and she ran her fingers along the necklace she wore.

But they shared a look that told him, louder than words, it would be better now that they were together again.

THE ONLY WAY TO UNDERSTAND Jorenn Village was to uncover its secrets, hidden away behind cracked stones, in deep mines, and in the stories the Shadewatch told. By the time Vex had led Vax up to Shademaster Derowen's office, he had a decent understanding of the Shade Hall. It was a maze not of tunnels but of bright and colorful hallways. Despite the storm clouds outside, it was light and warm here. He noted every door and every window, every lock and every opportunity. He'd mapped the path they'd took from the Shade Hall's entrance, and he had a rough idea of the best escape route.

"Give her a chance," Vex hissed, when she knocked on the door.

"No rash actions," he muttered. Diplomacy had always been her forte far more than it was his.

Inside, Derowen was busy unbuckling the leather breastplate she'd worn. Pieces of armor already lay on a stack next to her desk, and her brown hair fell in tangles around her face, like she'd run her hands through her hair once too often. She'd peeled off her gloves and the overcoat in Shadewatch colors. "Come in."

She dropped the breastplate on top of the rest of the stack when they walked in, and she straightened. She dismissed the apprentice in front of her, who picked up the pieces of armor and dashed out of the room, staring wide-eyed at Vax.

The Shademaster folded her arms. "I've heard so much about you, it's like I know you already." The words held a hint of venom.

Vex cleared her throat and stepped up to the desk. "This is my brother, Vax'ildan. Vax, this is Shademaster Derowen, commander of the Shadewatch and the person who's helped me look for you since you disappeared."

There was a soft warning to her voice, so subtle he knew anyone but him would have missed it.

Vax met the Shademaster's gaze. From up close, she didn't look like a monster either. She looked tired and frustrated, but that didn't make her monstrous. "Thank you for taking such good care of my sister."

"I believe we got off on the wrong foot. From what I understand, you spent days amidst the outlaws, and it's only understandable that you've grown some attachment to them." Derowen gestured to a table with chairs set up on the far side of her office. "Can we try to understand each other?"

"I'd like that," Vax replied absently. He glanced at her outstretched hand and stared at the ring that flashed in the light of day. The bloody ring that started this entire mess in the first place. Desired by the Clasp. The bane of the ash creatures. Essential to the fight between the miners and the town. It was at the center of everything.

Next to him, Vex's features tightened. A promise in her eyes. *Later*.

Not before he made his way through the maze of a conversation in front of him.

"You've been in the mines all that time?" Derowen asked as she moved to the table. She played with the ring on her finger, seemingly unconsciously. "How did that happen?"

"I didn't choose to end up there," Vax said carefully. He sat down next to Vex. "I fell to one of those walkers that tore through our camp. I couldn't tell you the details. All I remember is being in the midst of a fight, a searing pain across my back, and stumbling face-forward into a pile of ashes. When I came to again, I was quite a distance away from the camp. A group of miners took me in to bring me back to health. The same miners your men killed."

Next to him, Vex tensed, and something harsh flashed across the Shademaster's face. She pushed it away with a casual smile. "If that's the case, you were lucky to escape with your life twice. These miners—these outlaws—have long since been a threat to our community. They are responsible for introducing the ash walkers to our town with their carelessness, and it's my duty to protect the people who've entrusted their lives to me."

"The miners I met tended the wounds on my back and fed me," he countered. "They didn't say much, but they did well by me when they had no reason to. I would hesitate to call them dangerous."

Derowen narrowed her eyes, taking him in. "You're right. My experience with these men is vastly different from yours, and I'm certain they acted compassionately toward you. I shouldn't expect you to judge them so harshly. It speaks well of you that you would think of them so kindly, especially considering they were ultimately responsible for your pain." She had a lilt to her voice, a discomfort that he couldn't entirely place, and he recognized the challenge in her words. "I regret your actions were to the detriment of our mission. I can't fault you for trying to help. Knowing your sister, I should've expected nothing less."

To any outsider, their conversation might appear innocent. Sharp, perhaps, but innocuous. But Vax felt increasingly torn between her words and the various stories he'd heard tell about her.

He felt Vex's eyes drill holes into his back.

Vax kept his voice level and even. "I couldn't stand by and see them hurt. No more. Your guard was very thorough in their duty to protect the town."

The corner of her mouth tipped up. "Not just their town, but their livelihoods. Their families. There is no one among us who hasn't lost something or someone to outlaws or ash walkers. We were all different people before they brought danger to our homes."

He nodded. "I believe that." And he did. It was the itch of the last few days. Of the ash walkers *in* the mines, and the dwarven boys who'd run into the tunnels prior to the fight. Of the honest relief on the guards' faces. What if Derowen's comments and observations *were* genuine? What if the miners were the monsters all along? He'd believed Thorn— but he trusted Vex.

"The man you helped escape is their leader. The most dangerous of them all. Surely you must know that," the Shademaster said, and it was more of a statement than a question. When he nodded, she sighed, and she got up to pour them all a drink.

The second she'd turned her back to them, Vex punched him hard in the arm. She'd gone pale and tense at his side.

"What are you *doing*?"

"Getting to know her," he whispered back.

The Shademaster returned with two cups of wine in one hand, and a third in the other. She held the drinks out to them. "I am curious, Vax'ildan, when you stayed with these outlaws, where in the mines were you? How many of them were there? We'll have to decide on our next steps. We cannot let this man Thorn go without facing justice, and it would be helpful if you shared your information with us. Is there anything of use you could tell me and the Shadewatch? Did they introduce themselves? What did they tell you about their plans? What did they tell you about Jorenn Village?"

The questions were rational, reasonable. But the cautious part of him was certain he could hear the unspoken question: what had they told him about her? It was the question of someone who'd been running a con for far too long.

He scratched his head, like he had to give it considerable thought. The conversation itself took on a cadence, like one of the endless dances he'd been taught at school. Once upon a time . . . "Well, those first few days, I drifted in and out of consciousness. They told me little more than that I had to try to keep drinking and that they'd patched up the slash marks on my back." He shifted, like he was still in pain.

The Shademaster's eyes softened and she showed genuine concern. "I'm so sorry. We should get those wounds seen to. We couldn't have it if they got infected so shortly after Vex found you."

"Thank you." He didn't know what was truth anymore. "As for the other days, I'm afraid I won't be able to tell you much of use. We were in the tunnels you found. There were maybe two, three dozen of them? They mentioned they were in an underground system, but I wouldn't be able to tell you where it was if I tried. Apparently I wasn't the first to spend a night there after an ash walker attack, and they've learned to blindfold their guests." The only thing he could do was hedge his bets. He'd laced his lies with as much truth as he possibly could. "And you're free to ask my sister. I'm far more comfortable in cities. The rocks just looked like rocks to me."

"Of course. Although the circumstances of our meeting were not ideal, please know I'm not interrogating you," Derowen said. "Anything you may remember could be of use to us. Any stories about Jorenn? Surely you must have had some conversations?"

"We talked about sisters," he said. He cast a smile in Vex's direction, whose stony expression did not budge. "I know Thorn was their leader, but I really only ever spoke to him as a brother. About family and how important it is to take care of your loved ones. I'm afraid that's not particularly helpful to your cause."

It was a risk that paid off when something sharp flashed over Derowen's face once more. A crack in her mask. Her fingers tightened around her cup, causing the ring to sparkle in the light streaming in from the windows.

The ring was an intricate piece of work. The silver filigree was finely made, while the gems were storm clouds made tangible.

When Derowen noticed Vax staring, she turned the ring around her finger so the stones were on the side of her palm, protected from prying eyes.

Vax shook his head. "It's a thing of beauty, and it reminded me: we also talked about mining and silver and what a profitable trade it can be. I don't know the first thing about any of that, of course, but I listened carefully. Is that ring from around here, Shademaster? It's beautiful."

This time, it took longer for the ice in Derowen's expression to melt. She smiled thinly. "It was a gift, actually. Since you mentioned siblings before: my brother gave me this ring, many years ago."

"Is it an heirloom?" he pressed. He felt Vex's annoyance radiate off her in waves, and hadn't there been a table between them and the Shademaster, his shin would've been bruised and battered by now.

The Shademaster didn't blink. "It's a treasured family possession."

Right at that moment, someone knocked on the door, and before Derowen could bid them enter, a tiny whirlwind burst into the office, brown hair flying around her face, and her dark-blue dress tangled around her legs. She crossed the room without so much as glancing at Vex and Vax, and crashed into the Shademaster. "Mama, you're back! You're safe! I knew you'd be okay!"

A second later, a far bigger and furrier whirlwind crashed into Vax. With two large paws on top of his sternum, he struggled to breathe. Trinket didn't care and he happily licked Vax's face.

"Gross," Vex muttered.

Vax threw his arms around the bear's neck and pulled him closer, grateful for the relief. "Trinket's just happy to see me."

She shook her head. He angled his head so he could press his cheek against Trinket's fur while simultaneously looking at her. "He was with the little girl?"

"Aswin likes him, and he can't come with me into town."

They'd left Trinket in clearings and even caves before, when taking a bear into cities and towns would draw too much attention or be dangerous for them. But Vex had never left Trinket in someone else's care. She found him a place where he could fend for himself or where Vax or she could mind him. Those were the only options. But now there was a little girl.

He raised an eyebrow. She raised one in return.

Trinket slumped back, pulling his weight off Vax and plopping his head down on the table between the twins, looking at the two of them with big, droopy eyes.

On the other side, Derowen untangled herself from Aswin's fierce grasp. "This is Vex's brother, Vax," she said, nodding at Vax. "You should say hello."

Aswin barely turned. "Hello."

Derowen frowned. "You can do better than that, little miss."

Vax bit back a smile when Aswin's shoulders slumped and she rolled her head back, like she'd already done her lessons and it was outrageous of anyone to demand more. Still, she straightened her skirt and she turned to Vax with a look of absolute disinterest. "Nice to meet you."

Once that was over with, she turned back to her mother and pulled on her sleeve. "Mama, you're boring me and Vex and Other Vex too. Can we go play with Trinket?"

Derowen ran a hand over the girl's hair. "Not yet, darling. I still have more work to do and guards to visit. If Wick says you're done with your lessons, you can go play for a while." She winced. "And Uncle Culwen is coming tomorrow. Remember he promised to bring you back a present last time he was here?"

"I remember. I love it when he brings me presents. I wonder what it is! Do you think it's my very own bear?" Aswin brightened and she skipped around the room to the chants of "A present! A present!"

Trinket yawned and followed the girl's movements wearily.

Derowen watched her go with a soft smile. Then she got to her feet. "I do have work left to do. I need to visit with the wounded, but I'm sure we'll talk later." Her smile warmed when she nodded at Vex, and tightened when Vax rose too. She stared at him. "Aswin is why I do what I do, Vax'ildan. That little girl is my everything."

"I understand that," he said, and he did.

"I think we understand each other quite well," she replied. "So keep that in mind while you enjoy our hospitality."

CHAPTER 25

"What. The. Fuck. Were. You. Thinking?" Vex punctuated every word with a punch against his arm.

"Ouch." Vax darted out of the way and kept a careful distance between them. He rubbed his arm. "All I did was ask her a couple of questions. Is that a crime?"

"It wasn't just about the questions! You might as well have told her you don't trust her and she should consider you an enemy!" Vex snapped, her eyes flashing. "You helped that outlaw get away. You all but accused her guard of murder and what—smuggling? Thank goodness Aswin showed up when she did or you would've ended up in a fucking cell. You never gave her a chance."

The tension—and the lingering concerns—of the conversation still coursed through him, and his discomfort immediately spiked again. "Like she didn't give any of the miners a chance? It was a bloodbath, Vex. You saw it."

Vex bit her lip. "I saw her fight against the people who endangered her home and her community.

"They saved my life," he snapped.

"And she saved *mine*." She rubbed at her temples. "You weren't here, Vax. You haven't seen her fight for the people of Jorenn. Everyone I've spoken to says the same thing. She works hard to ensure everyone in town prospers, and Jorenn is better now than it was when she came here. Besides, she helped me when I had no one else."

Vax flinched. "I know that. I'm just trying to understand too. The miners told such different stories."

"Like what?" she demanded.

He shrugged helplessly. "Stories where she is a villain and a murderer."

They'd gone to Vex's room in the guest wing after one of the healers from the Shadewatch—a gray-haired human man who communicated in grunts and disgusted frowns—had checked Vax's scars and considered their healing well beyond needing anything more, and Vex had dragged him here, to the room she'd been given, where her clothes were carefully stashed away in the cabinets and her bow and gear was spread out across the dressing table, and where Trinket had been given his own sleeping mat right near the window. A marked-up book lay on the bed, half under the pillow, an arrow tab peeking out as page marker.

Vax had recoiled at the room at first, and how thoroughly Vex had made it her own, whether she intended to or not. It didn't look like a room where she simply stayed the night. This place looked lived-in. It even smelled of her bow wax . . . and bear.

Vex sat down hard on the bed, reaching for the book before it tumbled to the floor. She leafed through it and gathered her thoughts. "You know what her ring does, don't you?"

"I know," Vax admitted. "Sen—one of the miners told me she uses it to ward off attacks from the ash walkers. I know she does good with it, but that doesn't make her a good person."

Vex's face fell and she picked at the corners of the book. "You'd keep their names from me too?"

"I don't know what to make of this, Vex'ahlia." He leaned against the dressing table, well out of hitting distance and still disoriented, and scratched his neck. "You're at ease here. I don't want to hurt you and I don't want to come between you and the Shademaster. Not if they've taken such care of you, and you care for them."

She didn't speak for what felt like an eternity. She kept staring at the open book on her lap, and she folded over the corners of pages with her nails. It took him too long to see the silent tears that were falling onto the pages.

He sighed. "Vex . . ."

She snapped the book shut and flung it across the bed. When she looked up at him, she had spots of red anger on her cheeks. "I care about *you*, you fuck. What do you think I've been doing since you disappeared? I spent days running around those fucking hills. I followed every trail I could find. I spent evenings scouring the darkest corners of this town. You were my every waking thought, but I needed to be able to *breathe* too. The only reason I feel at ease here, the only reason I can sleep here without losing my mind, is that Derowen promised to help me in any way she could and she never once looked away or stopped trusting me. Aswin plays with Trinket because it makes it easier to believe not everything in this godsforsaken corner of the world is horrid. So yes, I care about them. But if you think there's anything more important to me than the two of us, you can go back to those bloody mines, for all I care." She snarled. "Go back to your ash walkers and your outlaws, Vax, because you've already picked their side."

The words cut deeply, and he snapped. "And you haven't? I have a right to care about them too! They lost their homes and their families. They're not the villains here, and if you'd spent any time with them, you would see that too."

"They are a danger to the entire town. They're not as innocent as you think they are." Vex shook her head. "Don't let your judgment be clouded by a pretty face waiting to betray you, brother."

"Then don't let *your* judgment be clouded by your desperate desire to be accepted," he lashed out—and immediately regretted it.

She crumbled. "Fuck you. I'm not some kind of heartless monster."

With that, she grabbed her cloak from the back of a chair and stormed past him, right out of the room. The door swung on its hinges in her wake before it settled back into the frame with a quiet snick, and the silence somehow hit harder than if she'd slammed it.

Vax sagged to the ground, his back against the dressing table, and he cradled his head in his arms. This was not how anything was supposed to go.

He didn't have to put on an act to look lost, because he felt lost. The world was unsteady underneath his feet and his heart hammered the wrong rhythm. Part of him wished he could take one of the paintings on the walls of the Shade Hall, one of the endless vistas, and disappear inside it. Maybe that would be easier.

When they left Syngorn, and again when they left Byroden, he'd made himself a promise: that nothing would ever come between him and his sister. And now something had. *He* had. He'd lost her again, and this time it was his own foolish fault. He'd chased her away, and he understood why she ran.

These last few days had formed an invisible force between them. He wanted her to understand his side of the story. He assumed she would, because they *always* understood each other. Even when everything felt impossible. Even when they didn't *agree* with each other. They could fight and figure it out, because they knew that when it came down to it, they'd always have the other's back. And for the first time, he wasn't sure about that. He felt cut loose. He didn't know how to breathe without her.

He could only do the next best thing. When Vex returned, he would explain what the miners had told him. Why he did what he did. The truth. The smuggling. The ash walkers. The history of the mines. No exceptions. No details glossed over. Everything, no matter if it hurt, and he'd find proof to back it up. The evidence that he'd promised Thorn, to show his sister the world he'd come to know.

And if that didn't work, he'd steal that bloody ring and they'd run away from here. Because no promise mattered more than Vex's safety. There was nothing more important than the two of them.

He targeted a narrow meeting room adjacent to the Shademaster's office. The guards who patrolled the hallway glared at him but let him wander. He claimed a place near the windows where he could keep an eye on her door while also pretending to be lost in thought, staring out at the town as it stretched out before him.

Jorenn Village existed in shades of brown. It'd been a small community once, Sencha told him, and from this high up, it was easy to see. The buildings around the Shade Hall were weathered and determined, the wooden frames caked with dust and the walls scarred with time and perhaps the occasional attack by the dead. The streets that circled the town's center were younger, the houses like young saplings sprouting up between old trees. Vibrant and hopeful.

He wondered what the miners' homes had looked like before the Shademaster destroyed them.

The guards who moved around in the hallway didn't come closer to him. Vax knew well enough that if he kept his patience, eventually he'd fade from their awareness altogether. All he had to do was stand here and wait, and he had experience with waiting. Waiting was just part of his work. Learning how to pick pockets had been more waiting than action. The life of a thief hinged on waiting for the right opportunity to strike and not letting himself get distracted by anything else. But today waiting meant being alone with his thoughts, and he hated it.

He forced himself, regardless. As time passed around him, the sky outside changed from its sickly yellows to brighter blues. The patrolling guards no longer dropped their voices when they passed him by. A servant walked in to clean the room and startled when she realized he was there. The half-giant Wick, on his way to carry a message to the Shademaster, did immediately notice him, but didn't say a word. Though he had no reason to trust Vax and most likely didn't, he showed no true concern either. He simply shook his head and walked away.

When Wick knocked on Derowen's door to remind her of a meeting with her captains in half an hour, Vax knew he'd made the right decision in staying here.

He casually changed positions to be invisible from the hallway, pushing himself between the folds of dusty green curtains, and he distracted himself by picking the lock on the window, pushing it open ever so slightly.

Half an hour passed and the Shademaster didn't leave her office. Another fifteen minutes passed, and Wick returned to knock on the door, with an amused sigh when she opened the door and cursed. "You forgot again, didn't you?"

"Definitely not."

"Liar."

"Bully."

"At your service."

Vax listened while the Shademaster's footsteps retreated into her office and back out again. The door closed and the lock clicked, and Vax wondered if Wick used that time to stare into this room. To ponder what he'd been doing here or if he and Vex had made up yet. He knew better than to peek around the curtains to check.

Eventually, both of them walked toward the main part of the Shade Hall, and Vax counted to a hundred to make sure the coast was clear, and neither of them returned to pick up a forgotten coat or piece of paper. He edged along the wall of the room and checked to see the hallway was abandoned before dashing over to the office door. He had his lockpicks out before he reached it.

He crouched in front of the door, and when he inserted the picks into the lock, something inside him calmed. Nothing in this town made sense, but this he understood. The feel of the tumblers beneath his fingertips. The slight pressure that would be enough to turn the doorknob. The knowledge that this was something he was good at, and something he enjoyed.

His breathing slowed. He listened for any sound, any change in the hallway around him, and he carefully applied pressure with a wrench, feeling around in the lock with a crooked pick. Locks like the one the Shademaster used were simple and straightforward, and it was exactly what he needed right now. No one had ever been able to take this away from him.

When the door had fallen shut behind Vex, it had been quiet. When Vax opened the Shademaster's door, he was equally quiet.

He allowed himself one last peek at the still-empty hallway before he slipped into the office and pushed the door closed behind him. He turned the lock from the inside.

Shademaster Derowen's office was left in a state of chaos. The embers in the fireplace smoldered, filling the room with a comfortable warmth. On the desk stood half a cup of tea and an untouched lunch of bread, cheese, and salted meat. The cook had placed a small branch of late-summer berries by the meal, but even that had apparently not interested the Shademaster.

Vax crossed the room and studied the tall windows behind the desk. He pushed one of them open further, and made a mental note of the ledge on the other side of the street behind the Shade Hall, to give himself an emergency exit should he need it.

With that secured, he ran his hands over the desk. The papers on top didn't interest him, not right now. Someone so careful and structured as Derowen would not leave evidence of her smuggling operations in plain sight.

The desk was beautifully made, of rich redwood and silver ornaments. It had large drawers on either side, all of which Vax opened, to check for hidden compartments. A single tier of smaller drawers, with storage for pens and inks, was built on the surface of the desk, its main purpose practical rather than providing privacy for the writer. The only exception to the low row of drawers was the frame that was built in the center of it. Carved into a wooden panel, the details uncanny, was the likeness of the Shademaster's daughter.

She fights to protect the future of her daughter, Vex had told him. It seemed this was her way to be constantly reminded of that purpose.

Vax opened all of the smaller drawers as well. He picked the locks of the ones that were locked, and found nothing of interest inside. The files on the desk and in the open drawers were all what he would expect from a guard commander who ran a city. Reports about the Shadewatch's latest recruits. A whole stack of complaints from the people in town, and another folder with complaints from the people out of town. A list of dates that marked the ash walkers' attacks, though there did not seem to be any reason to it. It's not like they only attacked by the light of two full moons, or when the stars were in a certain alignment. They attacked whenever they wanted, and the casualty numbers sobered Vax. The attacks were deadly.

The papers inside the locked drawers were nothing out of the ordinary either. Personal notes. Drawings that her daughter had made. Letters from her brother, about the towns he'd visited, the knickknacks he'd found, and the presents he'd bought for his favorite niece.

The desk held nothing at all that convinced him she was the monster Thorn had made her out to be. If this was the Shademaster Vex had got to know over these past few days—one who listened carefully to complaints and who kept even the least impressive of her daughter's scrawlings—he understood why she didn't believe him. *He* wouldn't have believed himself.

The door rattled. Vax slammed the smallest drawer next to the panel shut and was halfway through the window when a small voice echoed on the other side. "Mama?"

Vax stilled.

"Mama? Are you there?"

He glanced at the door, and in the little light that shone underneath it, he could see the shadows of two tiny feet, pacing in front of the office. The determined loneliness of the gesture tugged at him.

"You'd promised we'd go look at Beryl's dolls," Aswin said quietly. "I don't want to go riding again. I want to be with you."

Vax's gaze ran over the desk and he breathed out hard when he saw the small drawer he thought he put back still stuck out. He pulled himself back into the room, and edged back toward the desk.

He pushed at the drawer again, but it wouldn't give.

He pulled it out entirely, and found a narrow groove along the bottom edge of the drawer, so instead of returning it to its position, he stuck a finger inside the empty hole and felt for anything that might match the groove.

Against the back panel of the cabinet, he felt a small lever of sorts.

He pushed it.

Something near the center panel clicked.

Nothing happened.

He made to push the drawer back, determined to come back to figure out the entrapments of the desk at a time when he hadn't spent the better part of an hour inside and when there wasn't someone demanding attention on the other side of the wall. Then he paused. Maybe . . .

He reached for the small drawer on the other side of the portrait.

When he pulled it out, it had the same narrow groove along the edge—and the same lever inside.

He pushed it. Another click. Again, nothing.

Both levers shifted back into place.

With a sarcastic prayer to whomever was watching and didn't mind guiding a stray thief, he activated both levers at once, and this time, the click was immediately followed by a soft whirring.

Outside the door, Aswin sighed. "Fine. Okay."

Inside the office, the panel with her portrait on it rolled gently out of the way, revealing a compartment that held a leather-bound notebook. Vax's hands stilled. His heartbeat pounded in his ears. He carefully dug it out and skimmed through the pages. While it was written in a shorthand he didn't understand yet, the purposes of the book were quite clear. It was a ledger. And he'd bet anything that this was a ledger Derowen didn't want anyone to know existed, because it would prove everything Thorn had told him was true.

He flicked to the last page and paused. He grew cold.

Without giving himself time to reconsider, he slid the notebook into his pocket, pushed the panel back in place, and returned the two drawers as well. When they both snapped in place, the panel tried to move back out of its own accord, but Aswin's likeness already stared back at him.

Sad girls and offices. It had never been a good combination before, and it wasn't now. He couldn't keep his unspoken promise to Vex immediately; he had to keep his promise to Thorn first. Once Vex saw the list, she'd understand.

She had to.

And they would both have to get out of there.

While outside of the office, Aswin padded back to her own rooms, inside Vax gave the desk a once-over to make sure nothing was out of place. He patted the pocket with the ledger, and he jumped out of the window.

CHAPTER 26

Six years ago

The master of history's office was a flamboyant and chaotic place, and *some* part of Vax knew this was both irresponsible and ridiculous. He also knew neither of those things would stop him. He could lie to himself and say he wasn't entirely sure what brought him to be in this situation, but he knew exactly what it was. He'd been dared by some of the boys to find a map of the Gladepools, and the only master who might have a copy was the master of history, so Vax had sneaked in here during their lunch break. He'd paid one of the boys—a shy elf called Siren—to stand on watch for him, and while none of the full-blooded elves actually liked him, he gambled on the fact that they wanted to see this dare through. Because that was the only way to ensure that there would be another. And another.

While Vex was studying as hard as she could, he was becoming quite proficient in taking unnecessary risks. They were good distractions. They made the long days more bearable.

He tiptoed around the desk, careful to stay away from the windows, and shuffled through the papers on top of it. Alongside countless books, the shelves on the walls all contained colorful keepsakes from far-off cities and distant places, like pieces of research into strange cultures. A miniature skysail. A bracelet with three eyes woven into silver filigree. A necklace with fragments of a golden amulet attached to it. A doll made from fine threads and fabrics sat on the topmost shelf, where it stared down at him and constantly made him feel watched.

There were no maps visible anywhere. Vax knelt in front of the desk and counted three locked drawers and two locked doors. He took a set of crudely crafted lockpicks out of his pocket. It was an old set that Cyriel had given to him for Winter's Crest, but she never held her promise to teach him how to use them. Her work began to take up more of her time, and so did one of the goldsmith's apprentices. When he showed up at the weaver's shop two nights ago, Lathra had refused to tell him where Cyriel was. So Vax had taught himself how to use the picks, and while they still occasionally ran together, most nights, like last night, he visited the thoroughfare on his own. It was easier that way. The distraction and the company were still very welcome, but in this hated city he could only—truly—rely on his sister.

Vax took out the wrench from his lockpicks and settled next to the first drawer.

There was a fair chance, of course, that the master's desk was warded with magic as well, but that was yet another risk he'd have to take. To prove to the other boys that he and his sister had a home. That they hadn't simply been found along the side of the road somewhere, and that they'd every right to be here instead of being shipped off to some distant city or other.

They'd spent five years in this place, and still the narrow-minded comments kept coming. Aside from Cyriel and Tharyn, whom they saw on duty on occasion, no one had made an effort to get to know them. No one had warmed to them. Five years, and they were still as insistent on looking down their noses at the twins as they had been on that first day. No matter how hard Vex worked. No matter how wise and cultured the elves claimed to be.

Vax drew a deep breath, braced himself for some form of magical retribution, and inserted the wrench into the lock.

And that's when the door to the study was flung open.

"I TRULY BELIEVED THAT WITH the right guidance, you might become something more than what you were destined to be," Syldor said. For the past fifteen minutes, he'd been pacing around the twins, his usually pale visage red and his usually measured voice on the verge of cracking. "You might have been able to reach higher than the low life that you were destined for. It appears that all good intentions aside, I was a fool."

Vax kept his eyes locked on the painting hanging on the far wall of the office, and willed his face emotionless. For the masters to send him home under guard instead of punishing him at school seemed unnecessarily cruel, but he didn't understand why his sister needed to be here too. She'd been pulled from class despite having done nothing wrong.

On the contrary, she did everything *right*. She didn't deserve this.

"I tried to do my best by you," Syldor continued, his voice a notch softer. "I hired the very best tutors in town for you. I let you stay here and learn in peace, away from the cruelty of others your age, for as long as possible. I provided you with clothes you might never have dreamed of wearing had you stayed in that village. The finest martial training in Syngorn. I even overlooked some of your"—his eyes found Vax's—"transgressions, believing it might be educational for you to explore the city on your own time, in your own way.

"Was that not enough?" The volume rose again, and a vein near Syldor's temple throbbed. He was fighting a losing battle between embarrassment and anger on the one hand, and his normally cold and distant demeanor on the other. "Do you know the shame you bring to my name when you are found breaking into your masters' offices like a common thief? Can you imagine my having to explain to the Dreamweavers why my ill-born son not only carried lockpicks but apparently knew how to use them?"

Vax opened his mouth to reply, his own temper rising. Syldor hushed him with a gesture. "I am not done yet."

He picked up a piece of paper with neat handwriting on it. He read it over, and the paper trembled in his grasp. "I have here a letter from the Verdant Lord, detailing a number of incidents in the thoroughfare of late, where merchants and customers alike tell of a cloaked figure behaving quite suspiciously around them. A number of incidents where later they were found to be missing coin or jewelry. Can you explain that to me?"

Vex fidgeted nervously. Vax's heart sank at the report, but he squared his jaw. "I don't know. Perhaps you should ask them what happened. It sounds like they were careless."

"Insolent boy!" Syldor slammed the report on the table. "Do you not think the Verdant Guard has means of investigating such claims beyond the mundane? Did you not consider there are eyes on you the entire time? Do you think me so ignorant that I wouldn't notice you buy expensive gifts for your sister?"

He gestured to the corner behind them, where the hazelwood longbow that Vex normally kept in their room leaned against the wall. Neither of them had realized it was there when they'd been marched in by the guards.

Vax grew cold inside. "I didn't think you'd noticed us at all, *Father*."

Syldor didn't respond to his comment. He turned on Vex instead. "And you, did you know about this? Have you been covering for your brother all this time? I thought you were smarter than that. I thought you might in time be able to convince the masters of your intelligence and usefulness. If you cannot see the difference between what is good and proper and what is wrong, then perhaps I was mistaken."

Vex flinched, the words hitting her like punches, but she didn't dignify the accusations with a response, so Syldor continued, "Perhaps I thought too highly of you."

"She didn't have anything to do with it, so lay off her," Vax snapped. He took a step forward and placed himself between his sister and their father.

Syldor snarled and got to his feet. He leaned forward on his desk and spoke solely to Vax. "Do not press your luck, or I'll . . ."

When he didn't finish that sentence, Vax sniffed. "You'll do what, Father? Make life miserable for us? I can't imagine what that would look like."

His bitterness was obvious, and Syldor's shoulders hunched. He paced back and forth through the room and aggressively rubbed at his face. "Gods, this was folly. This is what I get for trying to do good by you. I should've let wiser voices prevail. You could've been sent to one of the outposts to be educated, like other—" He stopped abruptly once more.

And like before, Vax pushed. "Like other *what*?"

Syldor tilted his chin and didn't flinch when he looked at him. "Like other undesired children."

The words packed a punch, but it was nothing compared with what Vax felt when he heard the soft catch in Vex's breathing. The pure, unadulterated rage that filtered through him left him nearly breathless too, and it took everything he had not to pick up one of the paperweights and hurl it across the room. "You could've left us at home, where we belonged!"

"You were wasted there."

"We were *happy*." Vax glanced at his sister, and his heart sank at the tears in her eyes. He kept shielding her as he rounded on his father. "If you want to lay into me, have at it. She has nothing to do with this. Give her the bow back, and let her go."

"This bow?" Syldor took Vex's prize bow and turned it around in his hands. "No, I don't think so. This is a piece of art, and better than you deserve."

With that, he placed his hands on the ends of the bow and brought them down hard, pushing against the grain. The supple wood gave, at first, used to the strain of shooting and cared for gently by Vex. But it couldn't withstand Syldor's abuse, and with a soft cry, the wood snapped.

And Vax felt something break inside of him too.

VEX FELT EMPTY. THEY'D BEEN sent back to their room, and the only thing she knew how to do was sit on her bed and stare at the wall. She'd tried to count the wooden paneling. She'd wrapped a strand of hair around her finger and twisted it, only to forget what she was doing halfway through. Somewhere deep inside, she knew that she should rage or cry or hurt, but she couldn't. She felt empty.

Vax paced through the room, all hard lines and anger and tension. He would wear a hole in the floor like this, and it wouldn't help anyone.

She made a sound in the back of her throat, and he immediately focused on her. His face fell. He crossed the room, and sat down next to her. "I'm so sorry, Vex'ahlia."

She swallowed hard before she found her voice. "It's not your fault." The words stuck in her throat, and she knew she sounded rough and broken.

"If I hadn't taken that ridiculous dare, if I hadn't sneaked out all those times, none of this would've happened."

She didn't point out the obvious. If he hadn't, she'd never have had the bow in the first place. Though right now, she didn't know if that was better or worse. She couldn't even be mad it had been a dare that set this chain of events in motion. It was always going to be something like that. It had been inevitable. "He hates us, doesn't he?"

If she could hate him too, that would be so much easier.

In her periphery, Vax darkened, and his anger cut through her. They'd spent years here. They'd both grown into their own, taller, stronger, and arguably wiser, but when her brother hurt, he looked just like that ten-year-old boy who'd first arrived here, wide-eyed and angry and lost. "I don't ever want him to hurt you again."

"I'm all right. I'll be fine," she said, though she didn't feel it.

He wrapped an arm around her shoulders and pulled her against him, and she could feel the tension course through him. "Don't lie to me."

"I'm not," she protested, then hesitated. "Well, maybe a little."

"You're not all right, but you will be fine." He said it like a promise, like a threat, and with so much intensity that the only thing she could do was nod. And he held her, as a shield against the void. "This place doesn't deserve you. It doesn't deserve either one of us, and I never wanted it to change us. I refuse to let it break us."

She clenched her fists, desperately reaching for a place of solid ground. "So what do we do? We go back to school like nothing happened? And we pretend that we're okay?"

"Unless you want to leave," he said softly, "we do exactly that. We hold our heads high. We keep going. Or we get out of here and go home. We leave and never look back."

It had been so long, she fought to remember what home looked like.

Another thought struck her. Something jaded and colder. She angled away from her brother so she could look at him. "Vax . . . do you think your friend . . . do you think Cyriel is a part of it? Father said you were being watched."

He flinched like she'd punched him, but his answer came immediately and full of cold determination. "No. There are countless others who could've seen me. She isn't one of them, I'm sure."

She wanted to be so sure too. Sure that she could find a way back to attempting to belong here. Sure that she would stop feeling like it wasn't just her bow but a part of her that was broken. Sure that some elves did care. She didn't want to feel loyal to a city that gave her nothing, and still she did.

She wrapped the stray strand of hair around her fingers again. This time, her brother reached out and plucked it out of her grasp. He held a shadow in his eyes, but smiled at her. "Let me."

He unwound her hair, and it unwound something inside her. With slender fingers, he combed through her hair and his own breathing eased too, like he needed this as much as she did. And she remembered: this was what home felt like.

"Wait." He climbed off her bed and jostled the mattress, almost making her smile. He crossed to his own side of the room and took something out of his coat, hiding it up a sleeve, away from her prying eyes.

She leaned forward. "What is it?"

"No peeking."

He sat down beside her and went back to his braiding, working in comfortable silence. He worked slowly, untangling her hair and braiding it ever so carefully. As time passed, she felt her shoulders loosen and her clenched hands settle. The slight pull of the braids helped her ground herself.

Vax tugged at the braid, and she felt something scrape gently against her skin.

"There," he said. "Take a look."

She pushed herself off the bed, feeling ever so slightly dizzy, and made her way to the gold-framed mirror on the wall above the dressing table. The dressing table itself was covered in all sorts of odds and ends, including trinkets Vax carried in after long nights out. A handful of coppers. A carved wooden flower. A small pouch that at one point had held a dark-blue dust, though aside from a few stains on the linings, it was empty now. A knife. A whetting stone. Wax for her bowstrings. A handful of books that she used for her studies.

She moved in front of the mirror, and when she looked at herself, she gasped. She was pale and tired, and she felt like she might break. But her hair was braided back carefully, and behind her ear, Vax had braided in a pair of vibrant blue feathers.

She reached out to touch them gently. They were perfect highlights in her dark-brown hair. They matched her cloak. They matched the trimmings of many of her dresses.

"I got them for you as fletching," Vax admitted. "But I like this better."

"They're beautiful."

"*You're* beautiful," he corrected.

"Saving graces?" she asked, remembering what he said that day on the lake.

He shook his head. "Byroden pride. A reminder that Elaina's children are not to be trifled with."

She gave him a firm nod, her fists clenched. And she cried.

CHAPTER 27

Vex waved the guard away when he offered to call for backup. She definitely didn't need the Shadewatch with her today. She needed her bear by her side, and her absolute mess of a brother too. She'd cooled down by the time she returned from her rain-soaked walk through Jorenn yesterday, and while his words still cut, she knew she could and would always forgive him anything. If they didn't see eye-to-eye on this, they'd find a way to meet each other in the middle. She needed to have him close.

But he'd been distant and distracted when she'd found him in the sitting room. He hadn't been able to look at her, his thoughts apparently a thousand miles away.

He hadn't been the only one out of sorts. Aswin had been moping around and she clung to Derowen, far more frightened than she had been before the fight. When the Shademaster had asked her what was wrong, Aswin had looked at her with large, serious eyes and told her, "The ash walkers will come again."

So everyone tiptoed around the girl, and Vex decided to let the argument with her brother rest for a night.

Today, immediately after breakfast, he'd told her he'd go for a walk. He had dark circles under his eyes, and he needed to clear his head. So she did what any reasonable sister would do: she gave him enough of a head start to convince him he was alone, and then she followed him. She wasn't going to lose sight of him again.

He had walked, at first. Around the town square and the random shops, his feet kicking up dust now that the rain was a distant memory. His shoulders slumped, and he didn't return any of the curious greetings thrown his way.

It was easier to follow him there, skipping from corner to alley, letting the carriages and travelers on the road function as a shield. He looked over his shoulder once or twice, but she was certain he didn't see her. If he had, he wouldn't have kept walking.

He wandered toward the miners' gate, on the north side of town, and slowed down, glancing at the windows of the various buildings, though there was little to see. The miners who lived in this part of town spent long days in the silver mines, leaving before sunrise and not returning until nightfall. She'd seen them pass through the gate—which was nothing more than two poles on either side of a mountain path—once when she ran around in circles in the hills. Dozens of miners, with tools and work songs and the pallid complexion of dwarves and humans who didn't see enough sunlight.

She didn't have a clue what Vax wanted here. This part of Jorenn was abandoned. Even that ridiculous tavern in the defunct chapel attic wouldn't open until much closer to midnight.

All of a sudden Vax turned around and paced back toward the main gate of Jorenn, and Vex ducked around the corner, pressing herself against the wall and holding her breath, but not before she got a glimpse of the frown on his face and of his exhausted eyes.

When he confidently made his way out of town, despite the curious and suspicious glances of the Shadewatch, Vex's anger returned with the fires of hell. She wanted to scream. Instead she gathered her bear from Aswin's care and followed.

Trinket harrumphed when she dragged him back out into the hills, and she leaned down to scratch his head. "I know, buddy. Blame Vax."

At least she knew which set of tracks to follow, so it was easier to keep up with her brother. She channeled her rage toward survival. She kept him at the edge of her line of sight, nothing more than a small shadow in the distance. It was riskier than allowing him the safety of being completely invisible, but she couldn't bear the thought of letting him out of her sight again.

Now that the storm had passed, the pale late morning sun cast the hills into muted browns and bland grays. She could still see the ghosts of the tracks she'd followed before, and the scarce green was covered in mud mixed with ash. Perhaps her unease hadn't only been the absence of her brother; perhaps it had been the dead grass and the scars that cut across the landscape. Nothing here was quite as it should be.

Vax led her past a shallow stream that had flooded in the downpour. He stood next to it for a while, as if trying to figure out where to go next. She could tell him the options. The mountain path that had once led deeper into the Umbra Hills was now a dead end as a result of a rockslide. The grasslands that would inevitably lead back to the main route—the Blackvalley Path where they were ambushed. Or another rocky passage that ambled past a half-hidden cairn she thought was one of the outlaws' landmarks. This was nowhere near where they'd found the entrance to the mines. When she had investigated it, she'd lost the better part of a day following the slopes and inclines. She'd slid down an uneven path and nearly broke her leg.

Of course, it was the exact direction Vax chose. He headed directly for the cairn, and his footing became more confident, more sure of where he was going. His shoulders loosened, and she'd very nearly lost sight of him twice when his stride lengthened.

"What have you gotten yourself into, brother?" she muttered.

Trinket responded with a soft grunt.

She knew where he was going. Or at the very least, she had a decent idea. And the thought of it, the thought of him not trusting her enough to tell her, cut through her like one of his daggers. They could disagree with each other. They could fight. They had and would again. But she didn't know how they could come back from not trusting each other, when it had always been the two of them against the world.

He slipped out of her line of sight again, and she picked up her pace, keeping a firm eye on the tracks and burying the hurt inside of her as deep as she could.

She followed the tracks for the better part of half an hour, and the longer he stayed invisible, the more apprehensive she became. She could see his footprints. She just couldn't see Vax. She wasn't used to losing him in the wilds, even these weird hills. She was the better tracker of the two of them.

The tracks led her across a rocky path, where she could only keep up because of the shift in rocks and dirt underneath. Because she knew he had to have come this way. When she reached a collection of large boulders, the topmost rock with a cracked line that made it look split in two and pushed back together again, even those minuscule traces disappeared.

Her heart sank, and Trinket made a worried, mournful sound.

"He has to be here somewhere," she said firmly to her bear. "He can't actually have disappeared."

She crouched down next to the boulders and ran her hand across the last of the markings—the toes of a footprint and broken blades of shade-grass. If she hadn't known to look for them, she'd never have found the tracks. And while she crouched, she could see other subtle tracks too. The random clumps of grass that sprouted up amidst the rocks all showed signs of traffic. The small pebbles that were stamped into the dusty ground underneath.

If she hadn't known Vax had passed through this place, the traces would've been small enough not to alert her or any hunter. But they were so obvious now. Others aside from Vax had walked the same path he had. And it was as if they'd walked straight into the boulder.

She stilled.

Perhaps they *had*.

She pushed herself back to her feet and motioned for Trinket to stay back. She reached for her bow, so she could have it drawn in an instant, and took a step toward the boulder. Then another. Hesitant, torn between the knowledge that she'd find solid rock beneath her fingers, and the hope that the stone might hold some explanation of why she hadn't been able to find her brother before.

One step closer.

Her hand pushed straight through the border, like it wasn't even there.

Before she could wrap her mind around it, something sharp dug into her side, below her ribs. "Not one step farther," a young voice warned her.

She pulled back from the boulder and slowly raised her hands. She turned until her assailant dug the blade deeper. From the corner of her eye, she could make out a slender girl in a black cloak wielding an impressive glaive. She was in her teens, and the polearm was taller than she was.

"Tell your bear to calm down too, or we put an arrow into him." Another voice, from above her.

She craned her neck and saw the silhouette of an older halfling man with a longbow, an arrow locked on Trinket. Cold rage coursed through her, and her hands trembled, but she cleared her throat.

"Stay there, buddy."

Trinket growled to let her know that while he understood, he wasn't happy about it.

She wasn't either, but she had to find a way to distract the halfling archer before she could attack. She wouldn't risk any harm coming to Trinket.

"What do you want?" she demanded, speaking in unison with the girl wielding the glaive.

The blade pressed harder. "You first."

"Sightseeing," she snapped. She couldn't reach for her bow without attracting attention, but she might be able to get to the knife in her belt. "Looking for a good place for a picnic. Can you recommend any decent rocks? Nice view of the valley, maybe?"

She squinted at the boulders, where the halfling archer was busy dividing his attention between her and Trinket, his hand wavering slightly. She'd have to pick the right moment.

She edged away from the glaive.

"Cute," the girl snarled. "Now give us your real—"

Vex didn't wait for the rest of the sentence. She jammed her heel into the rocky ground underneath, sending pebbles and dirt flying toward the girl. They wouldn't harm her, not beyond getting stuck in her boot, but they didn't need to. Vex gambled on a distraction.

She angled away from the glaive's blade, and in the same motion reached for the knife in her belt. Instead of trying to get away from the girl, she grabbed the glaive's pole and used it to pull her off balance. By the time the girl recovered, Vex had already crossed the distance between them, and she kept her own blade at her assailant's throat. She made sure to keep the girl between herself and the archer, who'd swung his bow toward them but still kept an eye on Trinket.

"Your turn to answer," she hissed.

Right at that moment, a familiar half-elf stepped straight through the boulder she'd been investigating. He had his black hair bound behind his head, and rough scars across one side of his face. A new cut ran along his jawline, and he carried the weight of grief in his eyes. He wore a long coat that came down to his knees, full of pockets and mended tears. He folded his arms and looked exhausted when she glowered at him. "I do believe this is what they call an impasse."

She recognized him as the man her brother had stepped in front of when the Shadewatch raided the mine. Thorn, the leader of the outlaws, and the man Derowen wanted to bring to justice.

She kept her knife at the girl's throat, despite the wave of disorientation at seeing the half-elf manifest in front of her, when another figure stepped out too. Vax shrugged helplessly. "Drop the blade, Vex."

"What the *fuck*, Vax?"

"My people will stand down too," Thorn promised. "Though you and your guard ensured there are fair few left of them."

She felt the tightening of her throat. "Yours first."

Thorn tilted his head slightly, as if measuring her up, but he nodded. With a single gesture from Thorn, the halfling relaxed his bow, and the girl dropped her glaive to the ground. Vex felt her tremble, though whether it was fear or anger she couldn't tell.

Vax nodded at her, to tell her she could drop the knife too, and perhaps she wasn't quite so ready to forgive and forget as she thought, because hot anger coursed through her. She pulled the knife back and sheathed it. The look she shot her brother was sharp enough to cut.

"You must forgive us the welcome," Thorn said, harsh edges to his voice. "We don't often entertain guests here." He looked between her and Vax, and then at the hills around them. "But while you're here, let's have this conversation inside. We'll be comfortable there, and I'm sure you understand we don't want to draw attention to ourselves."

She didn't feel like being comfortable anywhere quite yet, but she twisted to call Trinket over, and with her bear by her side she nodded. "Let's."

If Thorn had any opinions about the bear, he didn't show them, he simply nodded. "This way."

She glowered when he turned and walked into the solid stone again, while Vax remained where he was. He had one foot inside what must be a cave, and from her vantage point it looked like it was sticking in a rock.

He reached out a hand to her. "Come on, Stubby. I'll show you."

The only thing that would outweigh her trepidation was her irritation. She ignored the outstretched hand and walked through the rock where Thorn had disappeared. She'd expected it to feel cold or different somehow. She'd expected some kind of resistance, but inside all she could see was the daylight being swallowed by a long passage that barely led along the surface before it dove deeper underground. Thorn was already making his way into the maw of darkness.

Behind her, Trinket moaned, and she popped her head back out. "Come here, Trinket. It's okay. Just follow me."

Vax cleared his throat. "Do you want him to wait outside? It's safe there."

"No." She didn't look away from Trinket, who slowly walked closer, hesitation evident in every step. "I'm not letting either of you out of my sight."

Trinket paused in front of the boulder with a questioning grunt, and Vex placed her hand on his nose. She smiled. "Just follow me," she repeated, and, one awkward step in front of the other, Trinket walked through the illusionary rock.

Vax followed immediately behind the bear. He'd curled his fingers around Trinket's fur, and they were briefly connected through the bear. Then he pulled his hand back and pushed it inside his cloak.

"I'm sorry?" he tried.

"For what?" she asked. "For not trusting me yesterday? Or for not trusting me today?"

The words hit like blows. "I do trust you. I trust you with my life. I trust you with my heart. I'd made up my mind to tell you everything yesterday, until I realized these weren't my secrets to share, and I needed to figure out what to do."

"So you decided to just abandon me again?" She only realized that was what she was angry about when the words left her mouth. The mere concept was an emptiness inside of her.

Vax recoiled. "*No. Never.* I wanted to make sure you didn't get caught up in this."

"I'm already caught up in it!"

"I know you are, but I needed you to be able to deny *my* actions, for your own safety. I needed Thorn to know what I found. I owed him that." He pointed out the path in front of her, and it was so easy to fall into the old rhythm of walking together.

"Why?" she asked. "You've already saved his life once. What can he tell you that I can't? Why is he the one to make the decisions?"

They meandered farther down into the tunnels of an extensive mining system. Some of the tunnels were naturally created, others carved or expanded from what was already there. It had to be connected to the mine where they fought, but outside of the fight, she'd never seen anything like it in such detail, and it pulled her in and made her want to explore.

"Because he's not the only one who's left here," Vax said. "They took care of me and I have a responsibility to them. Especially now."

She narrowed her eyes. "What does that mean?"

He leveled a look at her. "The Clasp is tied up in all of this."

She stopped and Trinket nearly collided with her. "The Clasp," she repeated. "The it's-just-a-simple-fucking-heist Clasp? That Clasp?"

"Information is as valuable as gold," Vax muttered.

"What?"

"Something my contact told me. It's definitely as valuable as silver around these parts, and much harder to come by." He indicated they should keep walking. "That fucking Clasp. Derowen deals with them. And I don't know what the fuck to do about it or what that means for us or why they'd want to endanger their own operation in the first place. I do know we have to get to the heart of this. Thorn is the only one who may have the answers we need, and this is the evidence *he* needs." He continued, "He takes care of everyone here, everyone who's been hurt by the Shadewatch. Everyone who's left. All they have is a small hideout. He's been fighting to find them a home for so long, and now he's lost everything. Again." There was something else underneath the tension in his voice, something softer, and Vex considered it. She listened not merely to what he said, but how he said it.

They turned another corner to a more brightly lit hallway. A gateway led to a dark, damp chamber with sleeping cots set up along the walls, and a single lantern for light. When Vax glanced inside with a peculiar sort of curiosity, she realized her pretty-face jab at least hadn't been far off the mark.

She nearly laughed. "Really, brother?" She shook her head and would have slapped him if he had been closer. "I've been worried sick about you, and you spent your time here dallying with this new friend of yours?"

Vax swung back to her. "It isn't like that," he protested.

"Of course it fucking isn't. Go ahead, tell me I'm wrong."

Of course it wasn't. Fuck, she couldn't even blame him for it. Sometimes the easiest way to deal with heartbreak was to find someone who didn't mind the pieces. She had before too. But she'd never let the pieces cut her brother.

Inside the room, Thorn sat down at one of the cots. He had a leather-bound notebook in front of him. He raised an inquiring eyebrow and slowly looked Vax up and down, before turning to Vex.

"I lied about the comfort," he said, gesturing around him. "This is what we have now."

"I've heard stories about you." She crossed her arms, declining to sit. She needed to keep standing to keep her balance.

Thorn sighed and tipped up his chin. The slightest shift in demeanor, and he went from casually friendly to closed off. "Ah, I see it's like that."

"Even if I hadn't, your guards threatened my bear," she said. It was a shitty comment, she knew that, but it was absolutely what she was going to be angry about.

Trinket growled, as if to put force to her words.

"They were protecting their own," Thorn said. "You can hardly blame them after the last couple of days. And from what I could see, you were handling that situation quite well."

She hadn't. She knew how to handle a blade because once upon a time she'd had the finest fucking teachers in Syngorn, but in a direct fight she would've been overpowered. Still, Thorn didn't need to know that.

"Vex." Vax rubbed his hand over his face. He reached for the notebook and held it up. "This is the truth. I stole into the Shademaster's office yesterday. I found evidence of her smuggling. Getting the miners out of the mines was never just about the ash walkers. These are notes of all her transactions with buyers in Westruun and in the Turst Fields. With every shipment of silver that comes out of Jorenn's mines, at least a quarter disappears before it makes the official records. She's been stealing the town's reserves."

She snatched the notebook from his hand and leafed through it. All the notes were in shorthand, but Vax had included loose pages with chaotic scribbles and attempts at breaking the code. Lines that included transactions of raw silver. Some gems and craftwork. Destinations, too. Westruun. Turst Fields. Traders in Drynna and Kymal, and lists of agreements to deliver new shipments of silver. The coin she made in gold.

She kept reading to find new names of new contacts. Dates for deliveries. Places Vax hadn't been able to translate yet. Names that were all still in code.

Vex looked up. "You figured all of this out on your own?"

"I didn't sleep much last night. I was hoping Thorn might be able to help. He deserved a chance to see it, at least." He managed a hint of a smile. "Or maybe I should've asked you. You were always better at our studies than I was."

She ran her finger over one particular line of transactions. "Westruun?" Vax had managed to translate both the place name and a word starting with *C*. "The fucking Clasp. Fucking pieces of shit."

"There's more," Vax said. "Turn to the last page."

She didn't want to. She did. The last page was a list of names, nearly two dozen of them. They were written in a messy scrawl, and next to at least half of them, in the neat handwriting that Vex recognized as Derowen's, was the same word repeated over and over again.

Eliminated.

She felt her anger drain away for something colder. A void inside her. The betrayal of the people she'd come to trust despite all her best efforts.

Thorn got to his feet and when she nodded her permission, he leaned in and pointed out the second name on the list. *Anissa.* She'd heard it before.

"That's my sister," he said, and something in his voice caught. His finger trailed lower, to where his own name still stood unmarked.

Vax's explanation was barely audible. "This is a list of the people she's killed to get her hands on the mines. All the people who stood in her way. She is dangerous, Vex. She's deadly."

Vex felt faint. "No, it can't be."

"Thorn saw her run through his sister with that tall sword of hers, and he recognized some of the other names as miners who were killed. Others were part of the town's guard and council before Derowen took over. You saw how the Shadewatch fought here. They came in to kill everyone but Thorn. That isn't about justice, it's about cruelty and revenge."

"She knows you're a danger to her community."

"She knows we're a danger to her trade," Thorn countered flatly. "Most of us only want to get out of here and settle somewhere else, so why should the Shadewatch hunt us down? Even if we could escape, everyone she's ever dealt with knows that we're the miners who woke the ash walkers. No mining community will take us."

"She wouldn't have made a list, Vex." That was her brother. "If it had just been about outlaws, she wouldn't have made a list."

Derowen was always the one with vision, Wick had told her.

The words wrapped around her chest like vines, tighter and tighter until she struggled to breathe. And Thorn, being the annoying gentleman bastard that he was, caught her arm and guided her to a chair before the world tipped out from under her.

CHAPTER 28

"That doesn't mean your hands are clean in all this either." Vex tried to gather her strangled thoughts, and the mines around her felt cramped and oppressive.

"They're not," Thorn said simply. "Would you not fight to protect your brother?" He got to his feet and wove the long end of his belt through his fingers absentmindedly. He was restless but he kept his eyes on her. He answered her questions without hesitation. "I only do the same thing."

She shook her head. She would but—

"She made Jorenn safer. You can't deny that."

Trinket came up to her, and nudged her with his snout, quietly reminding her of his presence.

"I *don't* deny that," Thorn said. "She fought the cursed dead that were our responsibility. She dealt with other dangers in the hills. She made Jorenn Village a safer and a better place. But only for some of us."

"You were responsible for the ash walkers," she said, remembering what the Shademaster had told her the very first day they went out to look for her brother.

"Yes." The simple admission took her breath away.

"The notebook is one side of the truth," Vax said, coming to stand next to Vex. "Only one side. We deserve to know what happened with the ash too."

"Do you?" Thorn ran his hand through his hair. He looked so tired, like he hadn't slept since the fight.

Vax stared him down. "Yes. I put my life on the line for you—"

"You didn't have to do that," Thorn interrupted.

"And my sister was taken in by the Shademaster and the town," Vax continued, brooking no argument.

Thorn stared at Vex, like he was trying to see straight through her. "Fine." He sat down hard. "I don't know what Derowen told you exactly, but I expect most of it is the truth. It makes the lies easier to believe. If you want to know all of it, here it is. We lived in Jorenn long before Derowen came. All of us miners and our families before us. We kept to ourselves, mostly, but we were part of the community in all the ways that mattered. We fought side-by-side with our neighbors when dangers came down from the hills. We danced and drank together during holidays. We shared meager meals when trade or harvest was lean.

"At the same time, we lived a different life than most people aboveground. Mining wasn't just a business for us, it was who we were. The mines were our home. They were the stories we told and the songs we sang. Every one of us here grew up knowing every drift and every tunnel around Jorenn, and while mining wasn't always profitable by any means, the mines provided for us. For every fragment of the mine we exhausted, we found places where we could expand and dig deeper. We opened up veins that were easily exhausted, sure, but we also found pockets of silver dust and the occasional nuggets. There was a balance to life underground.

"Until one day, my sister led a group of miners to expand the tunnels. The shaft they were carving collapsed into an older tunnel. She might have fallen to her death, but instead she plunged into the remnant of a long-forgotten drift, where she stumbled upon a large deposit of silver ore. Veins that led deeper than any of us had ever ventured. Tinyn was"—his voice cracked—"Tinyn was by her side. She was Anissa's best friend. I was still an apprentice then. The way the two of them talked about it when they came back, it was like they found a hidden treasure. They said there was silver enough to draw new miners to town and to ensure we had work for years. It almost seemed too good to be true."

"And it was?" Vax prompted when Thorn put his head down in his hands and remained quiet.

"There are slightly over two dozen of us left. Of all the people who worked those mines," he said, his voice rough. "*Yes,* it was too good to be true. But for a year or so, it was just good. We thought we'd just had a lucky break, and with so many riches at our fingertips we had no reason to push deeper. We simply mined and Jorenn expanded around us. We gave part of our profits to the council, and what we did was good for all. When the town grew, the guard grew, and it helped us find safety. We lived in harmony, even when Derowen came and took over command of the guard. She made us stronger too."

Thorn glanced up at Vax, as if daring him to say anything. Vax kept his mouth shut.

"My sister, with her nose for ore and veins, became our leader. She'd always understood the mines better than any of us did. She negotiated with the council. She kept them apprised of new deposits. And while they were both outsiders in their own way in Jorenn, she formed a tenuous friendship with Derowen." He smirked. "Anissa used to say, they bonded over having brothers who were too clever for their own good."

"I understand that," Vex muttered. Vax sniffed.

"It was a good time, and we should have been content with what we had. But Anissa—and with her many others—was convinced there was more to the tunnel she'd accidentally uncovered. She wanted to push farther. She was convinced the tunnel was part of an older, perhaps even ancient, mining system. She wanted to know where the entrance to that place might be, and who was mining here long before us. She was also convinced there were more riches to be made. Instead, all she found was death.

"She dug. So far below the surface, even our magical means had trouble dispersing the darkness. She carried lanterns down into tunnels that had not seen light in centuries and found that the walls around her glinted with pure, raw silver, far richer than the ore we commonly found. Nuggets large enough to promise us all a stable future. And not just silver: gems the color of thunderstorms, rarer and richer than anything we'd ever seen, simply embedded inside the veins. Everything was covered in layers of dust—or so we thought when she brought us down there—and ancient. A long-forgotten drift. So we set to work digging it up. We shouldn't have, in hindsight, but how could we know?" Thorn rubbed his neck, and he stared past them. "We ventured deeper still. We found more than silver and gems. Bones. Skulls. Tunnels, all of them blocked, and once we opened them up we found countless skeletons inside—like a mass miners' grave—and enough silver to last us a lifetime."

"Did you excavate it?"

Thorn raised his chin. "Of course. We were arrogant fools, and while all the moldering corpses creeped us out, and we told each other stories late at night about curses and waking the dead, we had no reason to think them dangerous. We thought only of the opportunities those riches could buy us, and the town at large. So we recovered the largest silver nuggets and set to work extracting the ore. We carved out the gems too, and we thought we did the right thing. But once we took those gems and opened up the veins, it was as though we disturbed something deep inside the tunnels. The dead began to wake. The very thing we had scoffed at actually came to pass. Rising up out of the blankets of ash they lay in, all those corpses came to life, and fell upon us."

Before either of them could say anything, he continued. "They were cursed. All of them. And we opened up the way out for them. We fought. Over half a dozen of us were slaughtered before we knew to run, and the ones that died—they came after us too. By the time we knew what we'd done, it was too late to stop the ash walker attacks, because the dead simply kept clawing their way up to the surface. We tried to block the tunnels. We tried to put the gems back in their destroyed settings. But nothing helped. For the better part of a year, crumbling corpses tore through Jorenn at night. Too often we'd wake to people screaming. Too many others fell when trying to ward them off, only to be claimed by the ash themselves." He sighed. "You saw the destruction of our mines. We saw the near destruction of a town. Things only improved for the people of Jorenn when Derowen found that ring of hers. Whatever those gems were that we excavated, she had similar stones in her ring, and the ashen dead reacted to their presence. The ring helped her chase them off, somehow. But there was nothing left for us there. She realized she could use Fracture to control the mines and the silver inside so she took them. By force and greed. She took everything from us."

He cleared his throat and tapped the cover of the notebook. "Those mines were as much part of us as we were of them. I didn't need these notes to convince me of what I already knew, but now we might be able to convince others. We may be able to find a new home. Because we fled. We followed our underground paths. We took these abandoned tunnels as our own, but who did we harm? The bats? The glowworms? The mines you found us in were almost exhausted, and we needed a safe place, because she kept hunting us down."

Vex swallowed as her perspective subtly shifted. Still, "The fight in the tunnels. There were ash walkers all over them that day."

Thorn didn't reply, lost in the long-gone disaster that had brought them all here. When he eventually turned to her, his eyes were dark and unflinching. "We were not responsible for any attacks after the Shade-watch chased us from our homes. We kept mining, because we needed the funds, but we were careful to stay away from the drifts that went too deep. We all knew too well the cost of Anissa's greed. But once the Shadewatch found their way to our hideout, I knew we would be over-powered. I didn't want to go without putting up a fight."

Next to her Vax flinched.

"You woke more of those cursed corpses, on purpose?" It made her feel ill.

Thorn walked over to her and plucked the notebook from her. He stuffed it into his coat pocket before offering her a hand. "May I show you what's left of our community? It may help to put things into per-spective."

It wasn't an answer, and if perspective meant heartbreak, she didn't want it. She got to her feet regardless. She shared a look with Vax, who fell into step with her, and his shoulder bumped against hers. She stiff-ened before she leaned into it, while Trinket quietly trod behind them.

"I'm sorry," he said again. "I know you care about them. And I'm sorry for not telling you everything immediately."

"Shut up, you idiot," she grumbled. "You've apologized enough."

Vax guided her to a tunnel that sloped gradually downward. "So what do we do now?"

"Whatever we do, we do it together," she said resolutely. "No more sneaking off alone. We figure out a way out of this mess, or if it becomes too dangerous—"

"We'll walk away," Vax said. It was the promise they'd made each other when they left Westruun.

She glanced down the tunnel, where Thorn walked a distance in front of them, his hands stuffed into his pockets, looking like he didn't have a care in the world. He couldn't have sold the act better if he'd whistled a dainty tune while he walked.

She dropped her voice. "Even if that means leaving the ring where it is. I won't leave this town without any defenses against the dead. It's not worth it." She glanced at her brother when she said that, and perhaps it was the low light and the shadows that reflected off the walls, but his eyes darkened. The muscles along his jaw ticked.

They made their way through another tunnel, turned another corner, and the passages around them narrowed over slippery and unhewn slopes. The dim quiet of the halls was replaced by a soft murmur of voices that grew louder the closer they came. The passages weren't carved out here—though she did see a few markings to show miners had made the hallways wider—but were uneven and raw. And suddenly, the walls opened up, like arms spread wide.

Vex gasped. Bright light illuminated a ledge in front of her, while beyond it, the cave fell into a deep and dark void. Mage light caused an intricate interplay of shadows along the ledge, and the luminescence around the cave's edges was exquisite. The ledge itself formed a plateau barely large enough for the people it held. Half a dozen children and twice as many teens. Older miners as well, all huddled together and protecting themselves from the deep.

But despite their crowded accommodations, despite the fact that every person here had dark circles under their eyes and grief in their gaze, they found a way to live. In the nearest corner, an elderly human man used a piece of chalk to write letters on a flat section of wall, so the children sitting in front of him could copy them down on their slates. One of them turned when they walked in, and they pointed and gawked at Trinket, eyes wide. In another corner, a group of young dwarves and humans were practicing using hammers and pickaxes as weapons. They were laughing uproariously, a sharp counterpoint to the drawn faces of the people around them. Near the end of the plateau, a middle-aged dwarven woman bent over a teenage girl with bandages around her arms. She whistled a tune that echoed off the farthest walls. A gnomish individual was in the process of slicing up dried fish, their eyes darting over the group like they were counting those present, again and again, and again. Vex tried to wrap her mind around it all. She'd never seen any of these people, but it felt like she understood this place without ever having been here before.

"Welcome to our humble abode." Thorn stood near the entrance with fierce protectiveness etched in his features. "It's humbler than our last stay, and we can't offer you sunlight here. I hope you understand who we are."

Vex felt the pressure of too many eyes on her, but she also saw the looks of recognition and relief when the people around her spotted her brother. A dwarven man sat against the wall, staring at a book without ever turning the pages. On a chain around his neck, he wore a pair of glasses that were far too big for him, and he kept running a finger along the metal frame. He looked up when they entered, and nodded once at Vax.

The dwarven healer, meanwhile, glared ferociously when Vax smiled in her direction before she turned around and stalked away to the other side of the ledge.

In spite of herself, Vex snorted. Her brother did have that effect on people.

Vax rolled his eyes, like he knew what she was thinking, and dashed off to talk to the woman. When he reached her, she punched him and wrapped her arms around him, causing Vax to tense before he leaned into it.

"Sencha is not fond of patients who do not know how to rest," Thorn explained. "And she'll never admit it, but she was worried about your brother. She carries the weight of all those we've lost like a stone around her neck."

Gods. She didn't want to know all of this. She didn't want to see the relief and the welcome, the pain and the determination. She didn't want to know that, despite everything, these were not the people she'd been led to believe when she'd helped set the guard on their path. She didn't want the void of betrayal to grow bigger.

She followed Thorn onto the ledge.

"How long will you stay here?" she asked through gritted teeth.

Thorn tilted his head, and she saw a flash of helpless anger in his eyes. "As long as it takes for the guards to stop searching for me or for all of us to find a way out. We've been on the run for the better part of two years. We know how to make the best of a bad situation. We spent some time up in the hills as well, but Faril is scared of ghosts, so we couldn't stay." When he spoke those words, he crouched down next to the dwarf with the glasses and squeezed his shoulder. "I know it's hard, my friend, but I need your help."

Faril reluctantly closed the book. "What do you want?" His voice was as flat as the plateau on which they were standing.

Thorn dug Derowen's notebook out of his pocket and placed it in front of him. "Take a look at this. It might be helpful."

Faril leafed through, and his eyes grew larger with every new page and set of notes. His mouth set in a tight line, and his pain made way for anger. He set to work with a determination that was mesmerizing.

"He has an eye for code, and he needs the distraction," Thorn murmured in her ear, and he steered her to another side of the ledge. "And this way, perhaps, Junel might get him to eat today."

When they were out of earshot, he added, "Faril would steal into town on his own to free those of us who were captured, and frankly I don't blame him."

"You're making grand prison break plans too?" she asked.

He didn't answer.

Over the next half an hour, Thorn guided her past the many members of his community. Junel, the cook who made every meal tasty, even ones prepared from dried tack and limited supplies. Sencha, the healer who saved Vax's life and was in the midst of telling him how she'd haunt him for all eternity if he put all her good work to nothing by getting himself killed for no good reason at all.

When Vax spotted Vex and Thorn making their way in his direction, he leaned over and gave Sencha a kiss on the cheek mid-sentence, before he dashed out of her reach and joined the two of them.

"Breaking hearts left and right, brother?" Vex teased.

He grinned self-consciously.

By the time Thorn guided her to a safe place to sit, Vax had been called over by Faril to answer questions about the notebook, and Vex's head was spinning with all the new faces and names and fragments of information. She sat down at the edge, her legs dangling over the void. Trinket had found a place to lie down too, and yawned. She pulled her hair out of her braid and retied it. "I understand where you're coming from," she told Thorn. "That doesn't mean I agree with you, or that I like you. But I understand."

The cave did provide perspective. And perspective did mean heartbreak.

Thorn nodded, but he didn't say anything.

"I'm going to sit here, for a little bit," she said, pulling up her knees to her chest and staring out into the distance.

IT FELT AS THOUGH THE cavern stared back at her. Eventually, she got to her feet and wandered around the ledge. The small community of survivors noticed her but made no attempt to stop her. The elderly man continued his lessons. Vax, Thorn, and Faril sat huddled around the notebook. She felt her brother's eyes on her, and waved at him to continue.

Instead she found a spot near a young dwarven man who sat cleaning his warhammer. The weapon was propped up across his knees, and with one hand he used a piece of cloth to oil the hammerhead, while the other arm was tied against his chest in a sling. When Vex approached, the weapon slipped out of his grasp and clattered to the floor.

She picked it up and held it out to him. "Need a hand?"

He wiggled the fingers of his bandaged arm and immediately blanched. "Shit. Fuck. No, I'm good." His voice was gruff, and his eyes tired. "Thank you."

"Mind if I join you then?" She gestured at a spot next to him.

He shrugged and resumed his work. "Be my guest."

Taking out her bow, she sat down. When she grabbed a small jar of wax from her pouch, he nodded at her. "Nice pointy thing. Bit too light for my tastes, but it'll do."

She raised an eyebrow. "You prefer to get up close and personal?"

A faint blush crawled across his face, and he scratched his head. "Just saying, far better to smash someone's brain in."

Vex winked, and he immediately blushed harder. He held out his good hand. "Davok."

She clasped it. "Vex."

He glanced in her brother's direction. "So is it just the two of you, or are there even more?"

"Just the two of us," she said, and he breathed an exaggerated sigh of relief. They chatted for a bit, before they fell into a comfortable silence. And Vex couldn't help but wonder what Wick would make of this. She'd remembered his words about Jorenn. *Everyone here knows what it's like to lose a loved one. Almost everyone knows what it's like to lose a home. If we don't stand together, what's to stop us from shattering completely?* This place was no different. And that's exactly what made it so hard.

When the lights that illuminated the cavern had dimmed to an afternoon glow, Davok took his leave to stand guard in the tunnels, and Vex returned to the ledge, where a handful of children were pointing and gawking at Trinket from a safe distance.

Vax appeared next to her with a plate full of freshly baked bread and dried pieces of fish. The smell of Junel's baking had permeated the entire cavern, and Vex's stomach growled. She didn't know how the gnomish cook had managed it, but she'd watched from a distance as they had magically heated two stones and used those to bake flatbread with flour from a crate and water from a pail that two girls carried in from another tunnel.

Vax scratched at Trinket's ear and offered the bear his own plate of dried fish. "The first chance I had to get away was right after the Shade-watch escaped the tunnels. Thorn knew they would be attacked, and I couldn't leave them to that."

Vex placed the bread on the ground next to her. "I understand that."

Vax tore at his bread and ate it with purpose. He stared into the cavernous deep below, and the luminescence from the glowworms re-flected in his eyes. "The notebook buys them their freedom. If we leave it here, it's the evidence they need to convince other mining communities they aren't a threat."

"Aren't they?" Vex shook her head. "Fuck. It's the same evidence that will destroy Derowen, and with her, the town." She picked up a piece of bread and chewed without tasting. "If we take the notebook, the miners will have no defenses. And if we steal the ring, the town will have no defenses. I don't want to choose between them, Vax. I don't want us to choose differently."

"Still?" he asked.

She looked at the children who were giggling and nudging each other while pointing at her bear. "There's a little girl who needs her mother. There are others in Jorenn who should not suffer for what Derowen did. And none of them should have nightmares about mon-sters in the dark."

The silence that wrapped itself around them was made imperfect by the rhythmic tapping of the hilt of a dagger against stone. Then an arrow, against a cup. Vex swirled around in time to see Faril put the notebook away and start to sing. It was just his voice at first, lower than she would have expected, with all the pain he carried with him. Sencha joined in next, her voice rich and uneven. It cracked at the edge, but it was the perfect counter for Faril. Then Junel. Some of the younger miners. Even-tually even Thorn joined in. The children who didn't sing took over the rhythm, and Vex felt her heart beat in tandem.

It was a simple song, about a miner lost in the deep with no way to come home. It was a song of heartache and longing and the shadows beneath the surface. And while the song echoed around them, briefly, it was as though the ledge was twice as crowded. Like each and every one of them sang the song to someone they missed.

When it quieted down, carefully, the voices around them softened to a murmur.

And that's how they heard the rumbling that came from deeper in the cavern. It bounced across the walls, echoing like it came from everywhere around them. Until the sound grew sharper, like a pair of footsteps, tumbling over each other.

The teenage girl with the glaive ran in, her face streaked with sweat. "The Shadewatch," she panted. "They're back."

CHAPTER 29

When the Shadewatch had first attacked, fear had rolled through the cavern as thick as mud, and Vax had thought he'd felt the worst of it. But this was despair, and despair was worse. What was left of this small community—that he'd once thought was cast in rock—seemed to shatter. Theirs was a never-ending fight. Or rather, it was a fight that could only ever end one way.

Vax reached for his daggers. Next to him, his sister scrambled to her feet. Trinket swallowed the last bite of fish, but his ears pricked up and his eyes were wary.

On the ledge, elders picked up the youngest children. Everyone who could reached for their weapons. In the center of it all, Thorn flexed his shoulders, light glinting off his swords. He looked at the small community of survivors—the two-dozen-and-some people who were left—before he walked over toward Sencha.

Vax looked at Vex. "I don't know if this counts as choosing, but . . ."

"We have to find a way to help? Intervene? Something? I know." She closed her eyes briefly, and he wondered what she must be feeling. These were the people who'd been kind to her. They'd both come to understand kindness in so many different ways.

She breathed out hard. "*Fuck.*"

"I can go. You can—" He choked on the next words because his sister pushed her forearm against his throat and silenced him.

"The next time you suggest separating, I will use you for fucking target practice, brother."

He threw her a grin that was too bright for these hard surroundings. "You'd have to catch me first."

"Do not tempt me." Vex turned to Trinket and embraced him hard, hiding her face in his fur before she pulled herself up. "Let's do this. Stay close, buddy, the tunnels will be dangerous."

Trinket grunted, looking between the two of them with eyes that understood too much. He nudged Vex, as if to tell them both that he'd be fine.

Vax reached for Vex's hand and brushed it before he turned toward the miners. They'd all gotten to their feet, and Thorn seemed to be arguing with every single one of them. He stood in front of Sencha and Faril, and he held on to the notebook Vax had brought in. His face was set in a stubborn frown, and one hand clenched and unclenched by his side. He swayed back and forth. When Sencha stopped talking to him, her words not loud enough to carry but her gestures sharp and angry, he moved from one foot to the other and shook his head. "No. I've made my decision. It's enough."

He turned on his heels and intersected with Vax and Vex near the entrances to the tunnels. "The Shadewatch must have followed you. According to Crispin, they're already inside. They'll comb the tunnels like they did before, and they kill everyone who gets in their way."

"I didn't lead them here," Vex said steadily. "I wouldn't. If I had known . . ."

"Neither of us," Vax added. "You know that."

"I know. It doesn't matter. They can't keep fighting." Thorn motioned in the direction of the rest of the group, where a teenage boy had wrapped his arms around the girl with the glaive, and Sencha still stared daggers at Thorn. No one had put their weapons away, but they were arguing among themselves.

"They've lost too much. They're all grieving. And the longer that I'm here, the more I'm putting them at risk. They don't deserve that." Thorn looked past Vax at the depths below and something cracked in his expression, exposing a wound as bottomless as the cave. It hadn't had a chance to scar, unlike the others. "Derowen won't stop looking for me. She hasn't stopped looking for me. And this needs to end."

"What are you saying?" Vax asked.

"You need to leave." Thorn looked over his shoulder to Faril, who stood next to Sencha, both of them trembling with rage. Catching Thorn's gaze, the dwarf made his way to him. Thorn shook his head. "This is my fight, and I should never have made it anyone else's. They deserve to be safe, and you deserve to be safe too." He grabbed Vax by the arm and squeezed painfully hard. "You've helped us in more ways than you can even begin to understand. Get out before anyone sees you. Derowen may be loyal when it comes to her friends, but she's lethal when it comes to her enemies, and you've defied her once already."

Next to Vax, Vex grimaced. "No true friendship is built on false promises."

Thorn managed a nod, and Vax knew he hadn't seen the way his sister's hands trembled, or the sadness that flashed across her face. He believed her, and he was right to. But he didn't realize the cost to Vex. She was good at making it look like her pain didn't matter.

When Faril reached them, Thorn pushed the notebook into Vax's hands. "Get yourselves to safety. Get *this* to safety before the Shade-watch can find it. Faril will show you the path out of here. It's narrow, so your bear may struggle, but it will lead you out before the Shade-watch comes."

Vax wrapped his fingers around the notebook. "What will you do?"

"I'll walk out and surrender. They have no fight with any of the others here; they are no threat to Jorenn. It's me the Shademaster wants. It's me she'll get."

"She'll kill you," Vex said bluntly.

Thorn shrugged. "Not immediately. She wants me alive, and perhaps she'll make the mistake of meeting me face-to-face when they've captured me." He hooked his fingers around his serpentine belt, and his smile was a smile of knives.

I'd walk into town and kill her myself, if that's what it took for the rest of them to live. That's how I want to slay my monster. The two of us, face-to-face. She wouldn't be able to hide behind her guard, and I would pay her back for everything she took from us. Vax remembered exactly what Thorn had told him that night.

"It's not right," Faril argued, his hands running over the too-large glasses once more. "Every one of us would fight to the death for you."

"Tinyn already has," Thorn snapped, and the words brought another crack in his façade. Faril flinched like he'd been slapped, and Thorn sighed. "Fuck. I'm sorry. This is why there are no other options. It's done. No more."

"And the others?" Vex asked.

"The tunnels are narrow. Single file. A way for a runner to call for help or a messenger to escape. This place was never meant for all of us. We'll take our chances here," Faril said, the words a challenge.

Thorn unhooked his two swords. He leaned them both against his shoulders, and the blades reflected elements of him. The silver ring in his left ear. The scars across his face. The tense lines along his jaw. And his desperate determination. "So take *your* chance and go. Get out."

Thorn leaned in and stole a kiss, and Vax's fingers dug into his shirt, feeling ragged wounds and scars underneath—a moment of comfort in this place where comfort was no longer to be found.

"Go." Thorn let him go and harshly pushed him toward the other side of the plateau, far from the ledge that held the survivors, past the tunnel that would lead him to the Shadewatch.

When he passed them, every single survivor stood to watch him. He didn't look back, not once.

Faril's jaw worked when he watched Thorn leave, then he pushed past the twins and stamped toward a new passage in this endless maze of tunnels, chambers, and dangers that lurked below.

They made it to a jagged scar in the wall, where Faril muttered something under his breath. He made a throwing motion with his hand, like he was scattering crumbs, and sparks of pale-blue light spread out from him and clung to the outline of the cave. "Just keep walking," he said. "The only way is up."

Vex stepped in first—and all hell broke loose behind them.

HALF A DOZEN SHADEWATCH BURST out of the main tunnel and onto the plateau, weapons raised and shields held high. Two of the guards dragged a bloodied and struggling Thorn with them, and wrestled him to the ground. "Shademaster wants him alive!" another guard warned, but that didn't seem to stop the first two from roughly pulling Thorn's arms back until one of them snapped.

The tallest guard—a human man with an impressive red beard, a mace in one hand, and Thorn's swords in the other—barked orders at the other miners. "Drop your weapons and surrender! If you resist we'll drag you out by force!"

The guards continued to bind Thorn like he would disappear if they let up. Thorn didn't struggle. He turned his head toward the other miners—who all stood to face the inevitable, clinging to swords and kitchen knives and picks—and nodded.

The guard shouted something else, but Vax couldn't make out what. The words didn't register.

One by one, the miners let go of their weapons—until only Junel still held on to their knives. Despite the impossible situation, the gnome clung to them, their knuckles pale from their death grip. Until the Shadewatch shouted again and, with a desperate snarl, they flung the knives into the hollow deep.

Thorn slumped to the ground. Faril keened. Vex reached out to grab Vax's arm, and it was the only thing preventing him from running back in.

"We can't help," Vex whispered, and she held on tightly. "We can't."

"I need you to run." The dwarf's attention shifted to Vax. "Run and don't look back, do you understand?"

Vax's jaw clenched. "Faril . . ."

"No." Faril's nostrils flared, and he could feel the raw power radiate from him. "This was our fight long before you came here. If you want to do right by us, by him, by Tinyn and everyone we've lost, then take that notebook and get out of here. Now."

It was the most he'd heard Faril speak in all his days with the miners, and the dwarf's musical voice was rough with sharp edges. Like broken glass, or broken hearts. Faril's fingers dug into Vax's skin, and he didn't let go until Vax slumped. "I will."

"Go."

Behind them, the Shadewatch were talking vigorously and pointing in Faril's direction. One of them whistled and shouted something to the man in charge before he began to walk over. Vax saw the recognition in their posture, even though Vex tried to push herself back into the darkness of the passage. Trinket grunted and followed. Vax looked at his sister and she looked back at him, and as one they moved.

"*Run!*" Faril snapped his fingers, extinguishing the lights around them, before stepping between the twins and the Shadewatch.

It wasn't enough. It wasn't meant to be enough. But it didn't matter. They ran.

CHAPTER 30

Five years ago

Vax had dreamed about leaving a hundred times. So often, it felt surreal to pack his bags and finally go through with it. He snatched his daggers from the windowsill and saw the world darken outside. Half a city away from here, the Tarn Thoroughfare would come to life. The floating lanterns would light up and elvensong would wind across the canals underneath the moonlit sky. Cyriel would be there, somewhere. He wondered if she still kept an eye out for him. Vax had managed to sneak out a handful of times since Syldor had broken Vex's bow, but it hadn't been the same. Whatever might have existed between them before—a sense of comfort, a distraction from this shitty place—it was gone. That night had changed something in him.

It's why Vax knew they had to leave, before this cursed city would take more from them, after it had already taken so much. If they didn't, it would inevitably leave them with nothing. Perhaps they should've left after the bow incident, but getting into another fight with their father—this time over a worthless piece of jewelry—had been the final straw. Perhaps they should never have come here at all.

"Do we have everything we need?" Vex asked, staring at her own small bag. They'd both only packed the essentials. Their room held all the memories of years of living here. Beyond their clothes and their weapons, there was very little they wanted to keep. There was little they wanted to remember.

Vax shrugged. "Your bow and arrows, my blades, and each other."

"We also have a bit of coin for anything we could need on the road." Vex patted the pouch on her belt, and its contents jangled faintly. Everything she'd saved up, perhaps in the faint wish she could afford a replacement bow. She had a simple one now, of course. Still of elven make and of high quality, but it was nothing like her hazelwood weapon. "I wish we could get a horse or two, but I don't know how practical that would be. Or if they'd simply let us leave. Besides, we can find our own way too, I'm sure."

Vex put on a brave façade, but she kept picking at her money pouch, betraying her nerves. The idea of leaving had become bigger than both of them, over time. The world outside had become bigger than both of them too.

Vax reached out and squeezed her shoulder. "Stubby, we'll be fine. We'll pass by the kitchen on our way out, grab some food, and once we're out of here, we know where we're going."

"You make it sound so easy," she said, as if she wasn't entirely convinced by that. "We're hundreds of miles away from home."

Vax took the dark-brown cloak he'd worn at the thoroughfare countless times and clasped it around his shoulders. While it hadn't offered perfect protection against prying eyes, it was comfortable and should protect him well enough from the elements. Next, he took her cloak from the wall too. The bright, vibrant-blue fabric didn't show the wear and tear of long nights of training and determination. It was well cared for, soft, and—he assumed—just as practical as his. "The hardest part was deciding to leave. We've done that. Now all we have to do is walk."

No one in the city stopped them. They might have, if they'd seen the twins sneak out of Syldor's home. Now the two of them were simply half-elves, going for a late-night stroll among the endless houses, towering trees, and temples. In the encroaching darkness, the lights circling the tree branches shone ever brighter, and the warm glow from inside the houses radiated out to the streets. With the relative quiet around them, Syngorn looked so peaceful. It looked happy.

Vex shook her head. If they raised any eyebrows of the people they passed, she didn't notice. She purposefully didn't look.

When they got closer to the high jade walls that protected the city, however, the gravity of what they were about to do hit her. Once they crossed that barrier, she was convinced they wouldn't be allowed back. They'd have run out their welcome, and she doubted the High Warden would extend it again. And the world outside had been *outside* for years. What if they couldn't find their way back? What would be waiting for them there? They weren't happy here, but would the vast endlessness be that much better?

Vax caught her eye, and the corner of his mouth curled up. "Time to put an end to our visit, right?"

It didn't surprise her that he read her mind—or was thinking along the same lines—but it was comforting nonetheless. He was right. Bow, blades, and each other. She nodded. "Let's go."

The heavy gates, with their deep-blue sigils, were closed and guarded for the night, but when they approached, none of the guards reacted. The watchers on the walls kept their focus on the forest beyond them, worried about what might approach the city, not who chose to leave it.

While Vax walked up to one of the watchers on this side of the wall, Vex turned around to look at the city one last time. She wouldn't miss it, she *refused* to miss it, but if she closed her eyes and let the night breeze wash over her, she felt an ache of homesickness. With her eyes closed, she could still see the sunlight sparkle on the lake and illuminate the graceful and majestic buildings. She could walk the steps of the Reverie Walks in her dreams and imagined the leaves changing colors. On days when Syldor wasn't home, she'd stood in his office to stare at the charcoal portraits on his shelves, and she'd wondered if they were relatives of his, if they were part of her family too. She would miss what Syngorn could have been—had things been different.

Behind her, the gate swung open and the slight creak of the hinges felt disproportionately loud to her. The forest beyond it was all midnight green and shadows, made so much darker in contrast with the bright city around them, and the attentiveness of the watchers increased tenfold with this temporary break in the city's defenses. Vax walked her way and grabbed her hand.

"Come on, Vex'ahlia." He squeezed. "We're going."

And they did. Step by step. Through the gate, hand in hand, with the eyes of half a dozen watchers on them, all of them with their own questions and observations.

One step in front of the other. Not yet sixteen and unafraid.

Until the gate shut behind them—and they were outside.

Vax breathed out hard. "I wasn't sure they'd let us keep walking."

"I wasn't sure *we* would keep walking," Vex admitted. "Do you think Syldor will come after us, once he notices we're really gone? Presumably one of the guards will run to him right now."

Vax's hand clenched in hers. His head twitched, like he wanted to look back over his shoulder. He didn't. "I think he'll make a fuss for appearance's sake, but he'll secretly be relieved. He can go back to living a life of comfort and recognition now."

"I don't *want* him to stop us," Vex said with determination. He probably wouldn't either. But a small voice inside of her reminded her that despite everything, she wanted him to *try*.

She took that useless feeling and buried it deep.

And they kept on walking. With their backs to the city and the endless green and red and yellow trees in front of them, all of them seemed to arc away from Syngorn too, as though they were caught in the same struggle of reference and escape. Vex trailed her fingers through the greenery and snagged on a small purple flower. As the petals fell into the underbrush, it released a honeylike fragrance.

"Careful with that, it's probably poisonous," Vax muttered, his voice strained.

Vex nudged him with her shoulder. "Not everything in the wild is."

"Not everything-everything. Just mostly everything?"

"Some animals are venomous. Some flowers sting." But everything out here, uninhibited by the affairs and determinations of elves, was beautiful.

"Great," Vax muttered.

They followed the path and tensed at every snapping branch, certain the Verdant Guard would ride out to drag them back again. At one point, a loud rustling caused them both to grab their weapons, but it was nothing more than a bird taking flight from a low-hanging branch in one of the trees. They kept walking farther away from the grand, beautiful city of elves. And no one tried to follow or stop them.

When they were far enough away from the city that the towering walls were only distant jade shadows, the Stormcrest Mountains dark peaks that loomed over them, Vax sat heavily on the forest floor and Vex knelt down next to him. She reached out to grab his hands and felt them tremble. Or maybe *her* hands were trembling.

Or perhaps, both.

Around them, the forest began to come alive and prepare itself for nightfall. Here, there were no floating lanterns to illuminate the path. No star sprites that danced across the leaves, and no fairy lights woven through the tree branches. Instead they were surrounded by the whispering and chattering of the forest. The wind rustled through the leaves, the nights were beginning to grow colder, and some small woodland creature dashed through the undergrowth. In the far distance, a wolf howled, and somewhat closer by an owl hooted.

When Vex made to rise, Vax tightened his grasp. So they sat in silence while the woods came to life around them and the night sky shifted overhead. Both moons rose high, and the stars seemed endless. Eventually, their hands stopped trembling. Vex loosened her shoulders but she didn't let go.

Instead she closed her eyes and reached out her awareness to the nocturnal forest. She listened to the animals and the birds, like she had as a young girl with an eye for broken twigs and barely visible markings, and she felt her perspective shift. Maybe this was the right choice after all. From here on, everything would be better.

For the first time in years, she breathed. She opened her eyes and looked at her brother, asking the question they both knew the answer to. "Where do we go now?"

"We go home," Vax said.

CHAPTER 31

They had nowhere to go.

They followed the narrow passageway as it went on forever, with the echoes of the fight behind them, the rumbling of falling stone, and dark emptiness ahead.

They walked for the better part of an hour. Longer. The air they breathed tasted of mud and cold stone. The passageways were pitch dark, and undulated through the hills. They passed intersections, twice. A place where the main path forked into two and then, farther down, into three. They both scanned for tracks and found hardly anything, and all they could do was keep walking. Vex let her instincts guide the way. She wasn't sure why, but she understood the logic of these underground passages, like she understood following the hidden trails of a forest or of the hills around them. She was certain she could figure out the best way out of these caves.

At an intersection, she didn't hesitate to choose the narrower of two paths.

The steeper tunnel at another intersection.

She wasn't sure how long it would take to escape this maze, but she kept walking.

A turn left, instead of right.

Another left, and then a right.

The stone around them brightened. The world gradually grew from nothing to shades of darkest gray, then even that became lighter. When the first glimmers of true sunlight reflected on the walls around them, her shoulders dropped and relief coursed through her. Vax stopped and breathed in deeply. Then he reached out and slammed a fist into the wall. "*Fuck.*"

She immediately reached forward and grabbed his arm, to prevent him from breaking his hand on the rock. His shout echoed through the passages behind them. Louder. Quieter. Distant.

Trinket growled low at the sound and crawled closer to her. She scratched his snout but kept her eyes on her brother. Every part of him was wound so tense, she could've used him as a bowstring.

Slowly, he got his breathing back under control. "I don't know what exactly it is we're doing most days. I don't know exactly what we're look-ing for. But I thought maybe I'd found it—maybe I'd found part of it—inside those mines."

She bit her lip. "Are we looking for anything?"

He smiled sadly. "I *can't* walk away from this, Vex'ahlia." After a second, he added a quieter, "And maybe I don't want to."

Vex shook her head and pulled him toward the exit. "I know that, you idiot."

She knew what he meant too. She would have expected no less, be-cause he had always been the more sentimental of the two of them.

Vex knew they only needed each other. Her brother was all the home and all the family she'd ever want, and he had been since the moment they started traveling together. She didn't have to let anyone else come too close. She wouldn't. It was far safer not to be too vulnerable. If they spent the rest of their lives traveling around together, that would be all she needed and that would be enough.

Even so, these last few days, they both got a taste of different lives. Wick had helped her when she wouldn't let him. Aswin had wormed her way past her defenses. The people in Jorenn could've sent her on her way with a map and some provisions, which would've been the sensible thing to do—aside maybe from ignoring her completely and simply saying, *Oops, we lost your brother? Our bad, good luck.* But they hadn't. They'd in-vited her in like it had been the only reasonable option, like it hadn't been hard to carve out a space for her. A space where someone besides her brother cared that she found her way back safely, even if she didn't find what she was looking for.

It was a taste of a life that may not be in the cards for them, but she couldn't turn her back on the people who had helped her. Just like her brother couldn't.

She didn't want to walk away either.

THE AIR AROUND THEM NOTICEABLY changed. It was thin and heavy, and they pushed through the last quarter mile of the tunnel as it morphed into a pass, with light filtering in from above. Until it at last opened up to a small shadegrass meadow on the side of a hill, between a cliff drop on one side, and a thin stream that ran down to the valley.

What daylight still lingered around them retreated quickly, and the hills that loomed in front of them were painted in dusk colors of reds and purples and oranges. There were no tracks of guards or others here, and Vex was certain she wouldn't miss them. She only found a handful of animal tracks, and in a different time when the hills weren't covered in ash and dead plants, this might have been a perfect place for a goatherd.

Now, it was empty. The mine they escaped had been exhausted. And Jorenn Village loomed on the northwestern horizon.

She found a place in the grass and sagged down. Vax sat next to her and picked at a blade of grass, tearing it into tiny little pieces with his nails. Trinket lay down, eyes still on guard, while the sky around them darkened and the winds picked up, letting the ash dance across the grass.

She lazily kicked his foot to the side.

He pushed hers in return. "You are all the home and family I'll ever need. But I don't know where we belong, Vex. And I do miss that. If we do what we do just to survive, then that's fine by me. Maybe there is no way to change it. But . . ." His voice trailed off. He shrugged helplessly.

She frowned and asked, "If you had the chance to do what Thorn wants to do—find a way to reclaim a home—would you do it? Would you want to go back to Byroden?"

"I want to go back to the home we left when we were ten. I don't want to go back to a place full of ghosts and memories of things I should have done different." He ran his hand through the brittle stalks of shadegrass, and it left a dusting of gray on his fingers, like all of it was grime and if they scrubbed hard enough, it would show the green underneath.

He brushed his hands on the cloak that had been like new a week ago and now looked like it had been dragged through hell and back, with rips and blood spatters everywhere. She ran a finger over one of the holes and the loose threads that peeked out, and when she snapped off one of the threads, the wind picked it up and blew it away.

"It seems like everything we could do only creates more trouble."

"So we either walk away from this or fix it, and I believe we decided we're not going anywhere yet." Vex straightened, as if she could stare down the very hills themselves and wrest control back from what was happening inside the mines. "So which problem do we want to solve? Aiding the survivors, keeping the town safe, or protecting ourselves?"

"All of them," Vax said without hesitation. Some of the restlessness inside him stilled at the thought of a plan. Or creating a plan, at least.

"They're not all our fights."

"But they all matter."

She nodded. "So we need to find a solution that fits them all, one way or another."

"Bows and blades?" The corner of his mouth pulled up.

"Yes, the two of us, against a whole town." She smiled as well. When Trinket grumbled, she reached out to him and scratched his chin. "The three of us. Against a whole town. And mines full of ash walkers. And a criminal organization. We'll be *fine*."

CHAPTER 32

The sky around them darkened further and the first blues of night streaked across the sky. The ground grew colder and the shadows starker. They needed to get up and get to safety, but not without deciding on their next steps. So Vex started a small fire before she grabbed the notebook out of her tunic and wiped at one of the bloodstains. She leafed through the pages and the loose inserts, thumbing one of the names. "If the ring isn't the key, then the notebook is. It has to be. Everything that happens here is connected."

Vax paced around her, his hands in his pockets, and the weight of the world on his shoulders. "We could use it as leverage," he suggested, staring down at Jorenn, where the first lanterns were being lit against the night. It made the town look like a beacon in the darkness. And it would be. They wouldn't stay away. "Go to Derowen and tell her we'll release the information unless she releases the miners and hands over the ring to us."

"She'll add us to that list of names before she'll let either of those things happen," Vex said with determination. "It will leave Jorenn too vulnerable. And I don't want to fight her."

"So one of us goes in, and the other one—"

She smacked him with the notebook. "Remember what I said? I'm not letting you out of my sight again. Besides, she watched me search for you for a week. She knows we're each other's weakest point."

He rubbed his arm, recalling the spireling's words in Westruun with a stab of guilt. She was more right than she knew. "What do you sug-gest?"

"Let me talk to her about the miners," Vex said. "If I can convince her that they won't be a threat to Jorenn anymore, that they just want to leave, it's the best option for all. She's not an unreasonable woman, Vax."

Maybe she wasn't, but she was still a murderer. Vax didn't fool him-self. If he hadn't allowed Thorn to escape, he would've been dead days ago. And if Thorn hadn't stepped in front of them, they would be prison-ers now too.

Vex's mouth twitched. "I would like to hear her side of the story. Maybe, instead of threatening her, we can offer to trade the notebook for her promise that she lets the survivors go in peace."

Gods, how he wanted to be able to do that. To fulfill his promise to Thorn that they'd help. "That still leaves the bloody ring. And she doesn't deal well with anyone knowing about her side ventures."

She grumbled.

Vax crawled over and sat behind Vex. With practiced fingers, he took her braid out and ran his fingers through her hair, careful not to snag the feathers tucked behind her ear. Vex kept staring at the notebook, but her shoulders relaxed, and Vax worked on combing the tangles from her hair. With every pass he made running his fingers through his sister's hair, some of her tension slipped away.

Some of his own tension dissipated as well.

Vex turned to him, the movement pulling her hair out of his hands. "We don't have the full story," she said intently. "You told me back in Jorenn that what I'd heard was only half the story, and Thorn's was the other half. But we're still missing one side."

He cursed. "The Clasp."

"Exactly." She tapped her fingers on the pages restlessly.

Vax winced. "If you want to tell me *I told you so*, you'd be right to."

"I want to tell you that we should never have come here." She shook her head. "And even that would be a lie."

Illuminated by the faint glow of the campfire, the wind picked up ash that covered the hills around them and sent it dancing through the air. The swirling clouds reminded Vax of the encampment before it got attacked, before they fell headfirst into the chaos around them. It left him uneasy. Even if there were no shadows in sight here. No darkness deep enough to hide their enemies. The drifts didn't turn into figures— just clouds. It felt like a warning regardless.

Vex ran her fingers over the list of names again. "There *has* to be a reason they gave you this assignment. Especially if she works for them. What if we figure out who she works with on the side of the Clasp? Perhaps you'll recognize names." She scratched letters on a scrap of paper. "Do you suppose it's a test? A way to figure out if you can be loyal?"

"No. There are easier ways to test my loyalty than to send us both on a wild-goose chase to a town in the middle of nowhere." He closed his eyes. Unbidden, the image of Lyre, the thief, changing into his sister, rose before him. He swallowed hard and reached for Vex's shoulder, to remind himself she was right there in front of him.

She hissed.

He loosened his grip. "Sorry, I—"

"No, this name. I recognize this name." Vex pulled free. Her hair fell in loose strands over her shoulder. She pointed at one of the lines in the notebook, at the *C* word under the Westruun column. "It doesn't say *Clasp,* like everyone assumed, it says *Culwen.* Derowen's brother. I met him the night of the ash walker attack when we were separated, and he's supposed to come back to Jorenn soon. Aswin said so yesterday too, remember? Uncle Culwen promised her a present."

Vax breathed in sharply. "That's not the only time I heard that name." He stared at the page she held up to him, and at the shapes of the coded letters. The name sounded so familiar.

Then it hit him. "*Fuck.*"

A conversation between Spireling Gideor and the halfling near the tavern door.

"Is Culwen back from his assignment?"

"I think it means both." He pulled the notebook from his sister's hands and checked the code against the cypher. The Shademaster had made a few changes for the coded names, but Vex was right. "Derowen's brother is her Clasp contact."

"Are you sure?"

"I heard the name when I was there. It might be a coincidence but I don't think so." Spireling Gideor had been very careful about what he'd shared with Vax, and he didn't seem like the type to *accidentally* let slip details about members. Information, after all, was as valuable as gold.

Vex got to her feet and fixed her eyes on Jorenn while she ran her fingers through her hair and pulled it into a loose braid. She tied it together with a leather band. "They hardly seem to like each other though . . . I can't imagine the two of them running a smuggling operation together."

Vax shrugged. "Can't you? If she thinks it's a way to keep her and her daughter safe? If we'd stayed in Syngorn and become the prim and proper children our father wanted us to be, perhaps we would've thought stealing was too big a risk too. It's an easier choice if the alternative is hunger."

"She's secure here. She has everything." Vex straightened the feathers behind her ear. "She has a home, money, a name. What more could she need?"

If she had a taste for smuggling now, it wasn't about need, but about want, Vax thought. "I'm not justifying what she did. Before I knew she'd helped you, I was ready to hate her on sight. I'm only saying sometimes people are complicated. Perhaps this is her way to secure her daughter's future."

"At the expense of how many?" Vex shook her head. "Brothers and their trinkets," she muttered.

"What?"

"Something that crossed my mind when Wick—" She closed her eyes, and he could almost see her running through conversations, adding up all the details. "When he told me how Culwen found Fracture. He was the one to give it to Derowen."

Her words were like individual elements of a trap, all falling into place and snapping together, and he still had no idea how to dismantle it. "So we have a Shademaster who deals with the Clasp, through a brother who is a member of the Clasp, and the one thing to keep her safe is a ring the Clasp now wants us to steal," he summed up. *"Why?"*

Vex rounded on him, and she stabbed him in the chest with a finger. "I fucking told you so."

He narrowed his eyes. "Feel better?"

"No!" She threw her hands into the air. Her voice rolled over the hills. "Culwen promised to come back to Jorenn. Derowen told Aswin he was supposed to arrive today—if he isn't back already. If anyone can give you the answers you seek, it's him."

"What do you want me to say to him, Vex'ahlia? *So the criminal organization you're a member of wants me to steal from your sister, any tips?* I don't think that'll go over well."

"Perhaps *he's* willing to make a trade. Help and safety for the notebook. Something of equal value, so the Clasp will be satisfied."

Vax shook his head. "I don't think that's how the Clasp works." And if push came to shove, he'd choose his sister's safety over that of this deadly, treacherous town in a heartbeat. She'd be angry at him, but at least she'd be alive.

She placed a finger on her lips and looked pensive, worried. She took the notebook and leafed through it. Once. Twice. "If the Clasp wants that ring and didn't send Culwen for it, there's got to be a reason. They don't trust him? They want to send a message? They're not actually involved in the smuggling? Because from what I can tell, this notebook never mentions the Clasp in Westruun; it only ever mentions him. It may be that he's doing to the Clasp what she's doing to the town and that's why they're perfectly willing to endanger the operation."

"If that's the case, he'll have a good reason to help us," Vax said, following Vex's line of thinking. It opened up a world of possibilities. It would be a dangerous game, but: "That's an awful lot of conjecture."

"Can you think of another explanation?" Vex asked quietly.

He couldn't. At least, nothing that didn't put Culwen at odds with the Clasp—or with Spireling Gideor.

"This is why I was always the better student, brother." Vex nudged him, and her eyes reflected the rising darkness around them. "If they both have a stake in making sure this notebook doesn't fall into the wrong hands, we have a better bargaining position before they can match up their stories. Find their weak spots and press down on them."

"The last time I did that, you shouted at me," Vax teased.

"A conversation isn't the same as standing underneath a spider the size of my bear," she snapped back.

"It is when you're walking into the monster's nest too," he said simply. "Are you certain about this, Vex'ahlia?"

"I am if you're certain that Jorenn's Culwen is also the Clasp's Culwen."

He ran the conversation over in his mind. The throwaway comment. The spireling's threats and the hungry gleam in his eyes. "I am."

"Then I am too."

Vax nodded. He slid out of his cloak and laid it out on the ground. He placed the notebook in the center of it then folded the fabric around it. Gently, so as not to tear the pages. Tightly, to protect it from the elements.

"What are you doing?"

"If we talk to them, we can't have the notebook with us. Nothing would prevent them from simply killing us unless they think the notebook is out of their reach. So I thought I'd hide it here. If we mark it, you'll be able to find it again, won't you?"

She made a strangled sound. "Do you know how much that cloak cost?"

He stared at her. "I'm planning to hide it under a few rocks, not send it off to battle."

She sighed in frustration, but looked for rocks to build a hiding place and a marker to remind them where to find the notebook. With night rolling down from the hills around them, they had to work fast.

When she had her back turned to him, she spoke up again, hesitantly. "If we have to get to them before they get their stories straight, we should talk to them both separately . . ."

He hesitated, midway through knotting the edges of his cloak together. He paused and waited.

She drew breath to speak, but the words didn't come. Then she did it again. A whole range of conflicting emotions flashed over her face before she buried her head in her hands and groaned.

Vax walked over to his sister and crouched in front of her. "Vex?"

She peeked up at him, doubt in her eyes. "I know I said I wouldn't let you out of my sight again, but . . ."

Vax realized what she wasn't saying, and his stomach dropped. "Derowen won't trust me after everything that's happened, and I will have an easier time convincing Culwen I know the Clasp." He wondered how well that would go over without a brand, but he bit back the words. This was no time to doubt anymore. He'd have to bluff his way through.

"Exactly." She made a small circle of stones and gathered enough to stack them on top of the notebook as well. "I can't think of a better option."

He knew it wasn't fair to her, but it had been so much easier when he was the only one running into danger. "I don't like it, Vex. We thought we'd lost each other once. I don't want to send you in there alone."

At this, she turned. "I don't want you to go in alone either. But it's better if Derowen doesn't see you. She trusts me."

"They saw us in the mines. She won't trust you."

"I can get her to trust me again," Vex said with conviction. "I know what matters to her. I can appeal to her kinder side, because I know she has it. But it's better if you find a way to talk to Culwen without her knowing you're back in town. Let the two of them convince each other."

He gazed at the beacon of a town down below. "No."

She crouched a few feet away from the circle, at the edge where meadow met steep incline, and placed a trio of stones in the subtle shape of an arrow. "I wasn't asking for your permission, brother."

"Vex . . ." He tied up the bundle like he could tie all his worries and concerns into it.

She rocked to her feet. Some of her anger from the last couple of days slipped into her voice, and determination steeled her. "This is the best chance we have. I want us to be able to do this together and to decide on this together, instead of trying to make decisions for each other."

"I just want to keep you safe."

"And I need you to trust me."

"I *do* trust you!" He got to his feet too, and placed the notebook in the center of the circle, before he haphazardly covered it with stones.

Vex walked over to him, gently took the stones from his hands, and rearranged the structure so it covered the cloak and the notebook completely and would stand against the weather. She reached out and pushed a strand of hair behind his ears. "We survived a week. We can manage for another day." She smiled through her worries, and he could see through her strength and her fears before she put the walls around her back in place. "Don't you see, you fuck, I don't have to choose between them. I choose you. That's the only real choice I've ever had."

SHE CROUCHED DOWN AND DREW in the sand amidst the shadegrass. Long lines and small stars, lit by flickering campfire. "This is what the Shade Hall looks like from the inside. You've only had a day to walk around; I've had a week. Wick mentioned that Culwen has a work space in the Shade Hall, somewhere on the third floor. Shademaster Derowen's personal quarters are here"—she made a small mark on her makeshift map—"and these are the rooms above her own office. If I were to guess, that's where her brother will stay."

Vax committed all of it to memory, overlaying the parts of Shade Hall he'd already seen. "What if he isn't there?"

"He will be," she said with such determination that it teased a smile from him. "I won't leave this bloody place without a solution."

She talked him through as many of the nooks and crannies as possible, while the ash around them picked up and danced higher until Trinket suddenly scrambled to his feet and growled. Vax leaped up, daggers in hand, while Vex had an arrow on the string of her bow before either of them fully realized what was happening.

From out of the tunnel the twins had used to escape, crumbling gray corpses crawled into the night. Their glowing eyes were embers in the darkness, their hunger sharp and deadly. As if on cue, the wind picked up around them and gray dust danced off their stretched and rotting hides.

"*Vax*," Vex hissed.

"Fuck." He pushed closer to her, his blades at the ready for the moment the creatures would attack.

Another walker appeared, ashen skin and pieces of fabric clinging to protruding bones. While some of the other ash walkers looked fresher, their gray features still recognizably dwarfish or human, this one looked weathered and old. Vex loosed an arrow with the soft *twang* of her bowstring, and the arrow sped through its rib cage, flying haplessly off the side of the cliff.

"Do you think Thorn . . ." Vex didn't finish the sentence.

Vax shook his head. "He said he woke the walkers because he knew the Shadewatch was coming. He would have no reason to do so now, and no time either. He thought they were safe here." He added, "And I believe him when he said they've been careful."

Trinket slammed into the next corpse that crawled out. His claws raked along the creature's shoulder blade, and the impact created a cloud of dust—but the lumbering creature didn't falter.

In fact, none of the walkers paid attention to the bear or to the twins.

Instead they crawled out and kept their focus on Jorenn down below, like they were drawn to its lights.

Trinket backed away until he stood against Vex, and Vax pressed closer too. Back-to-back with his sister, ready for whatever happened next.

They circled, and he could feel her rapid breathing. His own heartbeat was probably as erratic as the scenes around them.

The ashen corpse of what looked like a slender human crouched near the ground and pushed at the rocks, its limbs angled in unsettling directions. It skittered past them.

He pulled his daggers closer. "Why aren't they attacking us?"

Vex turned and shot at the crawling creature, but while the arrow stuck in its chest, it didn't pause. It twisted and pulled its limbs closer, and kept moving.

One by one, the ash creatures made their way down on the far side of the cliff, and while some moved graciously, others all but tumbled down, like dolls falling down a flight of stairs. Still they continued their way.

"Like moths to a flame," Vex muttered beside Vax.

"They are." Vax sneaked closer to one of the corpses and steeled himself. The ashen figure came up to his chest and moved with heavy, focused steps. Its eye sockets smoldered and one of its arms was nothing more than a sharpened, fragmented bone. Vax reached out and poked at the creature with a dagger.

"Vax!" Vex hissed. "What are you doing?"

The rotten corpse turned to face him, its eye sockets empty and burning. Ash flowed around the figure, like a long mane of hair, and for a moment Vax was certain it was going to attack. It pulled back an arm—

And let it fall limp by its side, turning back to Jorenn instead.

Vax turned to his sister. He frowned. "Stubborn creatures, aren't they?" And as far as he knew, there was nothing here to disturb them.

"I guess we follow their lead?" Vex asked. She stamped out the campfire and used her foot to wipe away the markings of the map so that only her way signs were left.

Neither one of them could tear their gaze away from the corpses in front of them. Three more appeared and followed the path of the first, fixated on the bright beacon that was Jorenn Village. Gusts of wind picked up rock and bone from the ground, and it danced around them.

Until it finally died down. While the walkers continued their march, no others appeared. The small meadow around them quieted.

Vax and Vex traded confused looks. The only real choice they had was to find their way down as well—back to the town with the answers.

CHAPTER 33

Five years ago

The Gladepools looked smaller than they remembered. Of course they knew the whole area was vast and full of many hidden spots they'd never seen. It was a vibrant place, filled with the chatter of birds and woodland creatures, and everywhere around them an endless landscape of different greens. They'd even spotted a hunting party in Syngornian gear once, and immediately turned around to make their way deeper into the marshlands.

But the lakes and ponds near their home had always seemed endless too. And the closer they got to them, the more they realized they weren't. The pond where they used to go hunting was not a tenth the size of Lake Ywnnlas. They would walk around it easily now, when before it had been a full day's trek. The tree stumps and crawling roots had seemed gargantuan, like they had been part of a primeval place where tree branches had reached all the way up toward the stars, and their branches could encompass whole lakes and houses. Now they were no different from the trees and greenery in Syngorn. And they were entirely different all the same.

With every step they took, memories came flooding back to her. This was the same pond where she and Feena had once gone fishing. Feena was two years older than the twins, and she'd only wanted to talk about the boys in the village, while Vex had just wanted to go fish.

This was the clearing where they'd celebrated Duncan's birthday, when his fathers had used the bakery to bake every type of pastry imaginable. They ate until their stomachs hurt, played hide-and-seek until Tym got stuck in a hollowed-out tree and had to be rescued by a few of the hunters of Byroden. That night, they'd slept under the summer sky and they'd counted all the stars they could find, making up constellations as they went along. If she tried, perhaps she could still find the Hayloft and Three Dogs Playing. And of course the best constellation of all: Mistress Fara, where a scattering of stars looked just like the healer did when she glowered at her patients.

Vex bit her lip and wondered if any of her old friends would recognize them now. If they still lived in Byroden, or if some of them had fallen prey to the curse of wandering feet. She could tell them now: the rest of the world didn't beat a place to call home.

She spotted a gathering of gnarly tree roots digging through the earth like fingers, and nudged her brother. "Do you think anyone ever found that boggle?"

One corner of Vax's mouth curled up in a crooked grin. "If they did, someone better have stories to tell. We spent days tracking the cursed thing."

She shrugged, her expression carefully neutral. "Perhaps it didn't exist at all. Perhaps you misheard Old Wenric when he muttered about it."

"I did not—" Vax started to respond, and then immediately snapped his mouth shut. A sense of wonder crossed his face, in the recognition that so much had changed and yet so much hadn't. This close to Byroden, they were no longer Syldor's unwanted children. They weren't those teenage half-elves dressed in the fineries of Syngorn, with the city's habits and culture drilled into them but always looking out of place. They were the seamstress's twins, who'd escaped their mother's notice and who had spent the afternoon—or the past several years—finding their way in the wild. They had to be home by nightfall, in time for dinner.

Without saying a word of it out loud, they both picked up their pace, creating new tracks where the old ones had once been, their footsteps covering long-forgotten and long-overgrown prints.

Their hearts felt lighter, and their steps were lighter too. Weeks had passed and years had passed. When they'd started their trek here, the hundreds of miles had felt like an insurmountable challenge. And not because of the distance either: Vex had been terrified they wouldn't be able to find their way home because it was no longer theirs to find.

She'd been wrong about that. She knew that now. She remembered every branch and every bit of bog like it had been seared into her mind. And she would never forget it again.

She reached for her brother's hand, and pulled him toward the edge of the woods.

THEY WALKED OUT BETWEEN THE TREES, a few hundred yards away from the village, and for a brief, heartaching moment, everything looked exactly as they remembered it. The farms at the edge of town. The familiar shadow of the mill that ground their grain stood proudly against the late-afternoon sky. The shrine near the cemetery. Byroden's Bliss, raggedier than ever. The mining facilities on the far side of Byroden, near the strange and spooky chasm. It looked so like what Vax remembered that it hurt.

And then he saw the ruined buildings. He didn't immediately know how to interpret the large scars and burns on the sides of the structures that still stood, barely any of them left unscathed. They looked like crawling shadows or twisted decorations. But when the twins stepped closer, other details became visible. The houses and farms and stores that were once proud homes, family heirlooms that were passed on alongside necklaces and legends, were gone. Rubble was all that was left of them.

Vex spotted the ruins not a heartbeat after Vax, and he heard how her breath caught. Her voice cracked. "What happened?"

"I . . ." He didn't have an answer to that. Whatever they saw in front of them, it wasn't real. It had to be an illusion. It *couldn't* be real.

He'd thought about leaving Syngorn a hundred times, and every time he'd imagined how the escape would go, how this trek back would go, and especially, what their homecoming would look like, one thing had always remained the same: the house where they lived would still be there. It would still smell of fabric and chalk and the candles their mother burned to be able to sew late at night. And she would be there, in the door opening, waiting for them.

He was running before he fully realized he was running, and Vex was right by his side. His head spun and his chest constricted and the closer they got to town, the more distant the dream seemed.

Because Tym's barn, where the children of town used to play during chilly winter days, was flattened. The mill that stood so proudly was surrounded with heavy wooden beams to keep the roof from collapsing. The only part left of Byroden's Bliss was the original façade, though a new, temporary structure had been erected around it. The courtyard where they had once danced had been mostly cleared of rubble and stones and turned into another grave site. And beyond that . . .

Beyond that there was nothing. No homes. No buildings. No farmlands. Nothing but scorched earth.

A void where their home used to be.

"No," Vex whispered. "No, no, no, no."

Ash where fabric and chalk and memories used to be.

There was nothing left.

The world turned and twisted and Vax's vision swam. Next to him, Vex retched. Vax doubled over, his hands on his knees. He tried desperately to breathe. No matter how hard he tried, he couldn't. He wanted to reach out to his sister—to *cling* to her—but the moment he tried, a hand clamped around his arm.

"Halt! Who goes there?"

Vax reacted without thinking. He brought his arm up to slap the hand away, while in the same fluid motion reaching for one of his daggers. He was going to be sick, he was probably going to be knifed himself, but what did it matter? *There was nothing left.*

He blindly stabbed at the figure trying to hold him, to create a space between them. His body remembered the endless drills, even while his mind was screaming with grief.

The blade of the dagger met with steel and a gruff exclamation of surprise, as his assailant blocked and jumped to the side. "Hey! What's wrong with you? Don't—" The other figure closed his eyes abruptly. Something clattered to the ground. The same steady grasp wrapped around the wrist of the hand in which Vax held his dagger, pulling his arm down. "*Vax?*"

Vax stilled, tense against the iron grip, and the tall halfling in front of him laughed without mirth. "I'll let you go if you stop trying to stab me."

He looked to be about sixteen or seventeen. Taller than most halflings, his shoulders had filled out and his arms looked like those of a blacksmith, not a baker. A long, wide scar led from his hairline to his jaw, clouding one eye and pulling the corner of his mouth up in a grimace.

"Duncan?" Vax swayed, and the halfling still held on to him.

"Been a while, hasn't it?" Duncan glanced over to Vex, who'd straightened and pushed her hair out of her face, staring at the halfling with bloodshot eyes. "Good to see you too, Vex."

"You . . ." Vex didn't know what he'd wanted to say. Everything inside him was in an uproar. He could only stare at his childhood friend.

Duncan gently let go of his wrist and waited for Vax to put the dagger away. He picked up the sword that lay by his feet and sheathed it with a nonchalance as if he'd always had a weapon in his hand. "I try to tell those few passersby we have that I tangled with the dragon himself, but the truth is it was nothing quite so heroic. I got stuck when the bakery collapsed. But I do what I can. We all take turns protecting our home."

Vex's voice was painfully bland when she repeated, "The dragon?"

"Big, red, scaly wyrm." He blanched when neither of the twins responded. "You didn't know? I thought Old Wenric sent word to that fancy city of yours."

"Duncan." Vax fought to keep his voice even. Instead it sounded pointed and cold, because it was the only way to protect himself from this pain. "What the fuck happened here?"

Duncan winced. He gestured helplessly at the town around him, but those few others who walked the streets kept their eyes on the road. A young halfling girl, no older than six, held the hand of an older half-elf woman. They both wore dark flowers braided around their arms, and the girl skipped. A human farmhand, a handful of years older than the twins, used a cane to propel himself forward. He missed the lower half of one leg.

"Duncan, please," Vex said softly.

Duncan sighed. "Come then, we'll have a drink and I'll tell you about the day the dragon came. It's not a story I want to tell out in the open, because it's not one most of us want to hear. I'll ask Iselle to take the rest of my watch."

"Even when it's still daylight?" Vax asked.

Duncan set his jaw, and he looked older and sadder than his years when he answered, "Turns out, daylight doesn't stop dragons." He turned his face westward for an instant, a habit he probably wasn't even aware of. And Vax imagined what it must have felt like to be here, to see this vision of death bear down on them, his fiery breath burning everything to ash, for the air around them to be filled with nothing but smoke and screams.

He didn't want to ask the question he knew he had to ask. He reached out to his sister and gathered her close, and he could feel her trembling uncontrollably. "Before you tell us anything else," he started softly, "what about Elaina? What about our mother?"

Duncan's eyes flicked westward again, and his shoulders dropped. "I'm sorry."

VAX ROSE BEFORE THE SUN did, his head and heart aching. His sister still lay curled up inside the blankets in the loft near the smithy, where Duncan worked. She'd cried herself to sleep, and her face was blotched. She twisted and turned, sobbing in her sleep. He couldn't blame her. The story Duncan had told, of a large red dragon that tore through the countryside, had been harrowing. Not one of them had seen the danger coming, and no one had escaped unscathed. Houses had been destroyed. An entire harvest burned. Everyone had lost someone. Duncan's fathers were gone. Mistress Fara. Feena. Even that old grumpy farmer Padric, who'd died standing in front of his farm, holding up a pitchfork against a dragon.

The ones who were left tried to rebuild as best they could, but they found it was hard to rebuild on the same ground that held loved ones.

Vax knelt next to Vex and ran his hands through her hair until she calmed. They could stay and help—Duncan had made that much clear. They were still of Byroden and they were welcome here. But Vax knew they weren't and they wouldn't stay. The pain was too much, too all-encompassing. It was everywhere they turned.

And everywhere he turned was the reminder that if he had been there, he could've done something. Could've tried something. He would've made sure their mother hadn't died alone.

He bent down and pressed a kiss to his sister's hair and sneaked out of the loft, careful not to jostle the ladder. In the soft light of predawn, he crossed through the village to the new cemetery where all the casualties of the dragon attack had been buried. The graves were marked only with small wooden plaques. A few stone slabs still remained to remind him of the courtyard that once was, but they were cracked, and small green plants pushed through. A small wreath braided from grass was placed on top of one of the stones.

Some of the graves were decorated too, with flowers and small tokens. Vax walked amidst the familiar names until he found the wooden plaque with Elaina's name on it. She was placed next to Mistress Fara, and he smiled at that. He couldn't remember the two of them ever not getting into an argument.

Vax sat down next to his mother's name and dug his fingers into the solid earth. "I'm sorry." He'd so longed to tell her they'd come home. They'd come back to stay and be happy. But the words wouldn't come. No other words, either. There was only coldness and grief and regret.

He sat until the sunrise colored the sky and turned the blues around him into soft oranges and reds. He sat until another shadow crossed his, and Vex knelt down on the ground next to him. She wrapped his cloak around his shoulders and curled up next to him, her warmth spreading through him. "I keep waiting for her to walk up and tell us we're late for dinner or something."

"Me too."

"I just want to see her smile at us. I thought we had all the time in the world," she said. "I thought we could always go home."

He nodded.

"The people of Byroden rarely ever leave their town." She looked from grave to grave and took a deep shuddering breath. "Where do we go now?"

"I'll go wherever you go, Stubby," he said. There was an unspoken promise in his words: they only had each other now, and he wouldn't let anything happen to her.

She bit her lip and nodded. "Then we'll keep going," she said. "We'll keep walking. Away from here."

He let her drag him to his feet, and when he saw her determination, he knew there was an unspoken promise in her words too: to keep walking until they could leave this place—this pain—behind. Even if it took them until the ends of the world and beyond.

CHAPTER 34

Out of sight from Jorenn, Vex embraced her brother and held him tight, before she and Trinket went one way and he went another. She couldn't believe they'd actually talked each other into this. Every step she took, the same refrain bounced through her head. A dangerous plan. A terrible plan. It was the best they had. So Vax would circle Jorenn and find his way in through the miners' gate or over the palisades if he had to. Of the two of them, he was better equipped to do so.

Meanwhile, she and Trinket would circle until they reached the main road and then would simply follow the Blackvalley Path into town. Which had seemed like the easier option of the two, until a trail of corpses made its way down the hills and the trek to town felt like a dash to stay ahead of night itself.

She wasn't the only one either.

When the ground around them stretched and flattened into the valley that held Jorenn, and she and Trinket reached the edge of the town's scattered light, the relative quiet of night was broken by the sound of weapons clashing and people shouting.

She nodded at Trinket and picked up her tired feet to find another group of travelers in trouble, within sight of the town's palisades. Like their encampment, this group of travelers had been ambushed by the dead coming from all sides, while at the same time other ash walkers—

perhaps the pack she and her brother had seen higher up in the hills—were flinging themselves against the palisades and lending an air of chaos to the fight.

Two walkers tore into a horse, which bucked and threw its rider, only for a third to immediately rip into the traveler. Trinket bit at one of the dead creatures, and this time he managed to snap through bone.

Like the first night, the Shadewatch rode out to help, with three riders picking up travelers by foot, and a handful of others bearing down on a large cart that was in the middle of the fray. On top of the cart stood a tall human gentleman with tightly curled brown hair and a long coat that flapped in the wind. Culwen wore a rapier at his side and held the well-crafted longbow he'd had with him the first night, heavier than the one Vex used. He shot his arrows with ease, despite his unstable footing and the dim light from the town, and she recognized his determination.

At least the Shademaster's brother would arrive in town today.

He glanced at her and nodded once.

Vex slung her bow from her shoulders and shot a tall, scrambling corpse on the outskirts of the fight before she joined the fray. It was a twisted reminder of the first time she'd been in this position, once more surrounded by ash creatures and guards. This time, however, it wasn't a simple matter of a camp overrun. Even the act of standing side by side with the Shadewatch tore at her, and a small part of her couldn't make up its mind between the relief of familiar faces and the memory of what she'd seen in the mines. But she knew this was the only way to get back into town without suspicion.

Without more suspicion than she could handle, in any case.

Next to her, Trinket roared and clawed at one of the walkers that came too close. The Shadewatch attempted to help the fallen rider, but the guards had to fight their way through the undead horde to come closer.

Vex sent an arrow straight into the cheek of a lumbering ash walker as it slashed toward a guard—a young dwarf with two slender axes. The young man rolled out of the way of the walker's grasp, hacked into its knees, and kept running toward the traveler.

The fight around them was deadly. The Shadewatch riders who didn't bring travelers into the town fought themselves closer to the cart, to be able to flank it. Vex followed their lead.

Up on the palisades, archers covered the fight as well, and above the gate, like that first night, stood Derowen. Vex peeked at her, then kept her head down and fought. She fired arrow after arrow, falling in the same rhythm as Culwen on top of the cart. Some arrows stuck into their horrible targets. Others cut straight through them.

It helped to find her focus. She marked one of the creatures as it skittered closer, its gait uneven, like every step caused bones to break and re-form. It looked like it had just crawled out of the mines, with its coat still whole and only a little dusty. The ash walker's eyes shone bright. She sent an arrow flying, and it drilled into the dead figure's rib cage simultaneously with another arrow. She glanced up at the cart, where Culwen kept firing with purpose, though his focus was on his sister on the walls.

Vex lost herself in the fight, until the cart began to roll forward. The Shadewatch kept pace with it. And when she blinked and looked around, the battle had shifted, with over a dozen walkers lying smashed to pieces on trampled ground and still others being driven back. The wretched horde continued to move crookedly toward the gates and the cart, but the guards around the cart had opened up an escape route. Some of the cursed creatures fell back, after that, like predators who found themselves outmatched by prey, even though others still flung themselves at the walls.

It nagged at Vex, as so many things did in this strange corner of the Umbra Hills, and she had no time to observe the behavior of the walkers any longer.

She reached for Trinket to make sure he was by her side and jogged alongside the cart, sharing a look of relief with Culwen, who sat down but held his bow by his side.

He grinned.

※

This time, upon entering Jorenn's gates, Vex didn't wait for anyone to bring her to the town square. She turned immediately away from the hustle and bustle of getting the travelers to safety and ran for the nearest ladder that would bring her up the palisades.

Derowen stood above the gate, her arms wide and a look of concentration on her face. Wick flanked her, his hands on his warhammer. She didn't think Aswin would be far behind.

Her heart leaped at the sight, and immediately tumbled again. It hurt, the pain of betrayal, and she didn't know how to make it better. She simply found a spot between two guards, who both looked at her with confusion and more than a bit of suspicion, and planted her feet on the wooden planks. She raised her bow, found a target, and let an arrow fly.

She'd shot all of three arrows before the buzz of voices around her died down. She heard the silence and she knew what it meant, but she took an arrow from her quiver and sent it toward one of the ash creatures regardless. The projectile cut across its shoulder harmlessly.

She was reaching for a fifth arrow when a broad hand fell onto her shoulder and stopped her. She lowered her bow and turned to Wick, who towered over her and looked as immovable as he had that very first night. A frown marred his face, and his grip was none too gentle.

She'd come to know his gentleness and his sense of humor, but this was his loyalty to Derowen on full display. He protected her. He would always protect her. And right now, Vex was a threat.

"What are you doing here, Vex?" he asked quietly.

She realized that the guards who'd flanked her had each taken half a dozen steps back, focusing on the world outside the palisades like there was nothing else to see. The way they stared out into the night sky, they would've brought down bats that came too close.

Honestly, she couldn't blame them.

Vex drew in an unsteady breath. "I'm fighting, Wick. You've seen me do it before."

He wasn't amused, and his grip around her shoulder tightened. "We've heard reports from the mines. We know you were there with your brother. We know the miners protected you, and I don't know what to make of that."

"I was there," she said. She wouldn't deny that, because there would be no sense to it if they already knew. If Vax managed to steal his way in to confront Culwen, she had to get this right. If she wanted to get to Derowen, she had to go through Wick. She knew which story to tell. "We fought, when you released Vax to me. He didn't understand what was happening. He formed a bond with some of the miners, and I couldn't make him see sense. So when he sneaked out, I followed him. I wanted to understand. I couldn't lose him again."

Wick didn't answer, so she continued, "I didn't think he knew where the rest of the miners were hiding. I didn't think he'd lie to me. All I wanted was to get my brother back, you know that."

"I thought I knew," Wick replied. His grip didn't relent. "Now I'm not so certain anymore. You could've asked for help, and any members of the Shadewatch would have come with you. Instead you left on your own, and from the reports of the guard, the miners trusted you."

"They trusted Vax," she snapped back. "Do you think if I cared about the outlaws at all, I would help you find the mines in the first place? Why would I do that?"

Wick frowned, and she wondered how much he knew. If he was a part of Derowen's schemes too. She couldn't believe that. She refused to believe it.

"I'm here alone, in case you haven't noticed." Something of her fear shone through, and she let it. Let Wick make of it what he wanted. It was a terrible way to bargain if she gave him too much information too fast.

He didn't falter. He didn't relax. But his gaze softened. The corners of his mouth pulled down, and it tugged at her unexpectedly. She really didn't want him to be a part of the schemes.

"Where is he now?" Wick asked.

She shrugged. "I don't know. Probably still in the hills somewhere." Though if they timed it right, he should be finding his way close to the miners' gate soon. While the attack made her way into town more complicated, it would provide a wonderful distraction for him.

Vex casually glanced over to Derowen, who was still focused on the barrier, her face pale and her arms wavering. Her brother stood by her side, talking quietly. Vex clenched her jaw. The attack would provide an excellent distraction for *anyone* who wanted to get into town unobserved.

She pushed away the thought of the ashen dead clambering toward Jorenn and faced Wick. First things first, before her belief in this town shattered completely. She thought of Aswin, and Beryl, and the archers on whose side she'd fought.

"I wanted to come back here. I wanted to come home here. Why else would I be here if I didn't care about Jorenn?" She took hold of Wick's hand and carefully wrested her shoulder free, rolling her arms in the process. She gave him as much truth as she could. "They took my brother from me, while Derowen and Aswin took me in. If you believe nothing else, at least believe that. I wouldn't have come back here if I didn't care about them, Wick."

Wick took a step back and gave her space. He folded his arms cautiously. "I'm still trying to understand that, too."

She felt him relent and pushed harder. "You told me everyone here knows what it's like to lose a home. You gave me one for a few days." She raised her head and locked eyes with Wick. "I know I can't stay here either. I'll travel on in the morning, if you want me to. I just want to talk to her. If nothing else, allow me to thank her for her help and say my goodbyes to Aswin. Let Trinket do so, too."

Trinket looked up at Wick with his big, soulful eyes, and he tilted his head slightly, like he was the star performer of a traveling acting troupe. Despite herself, Vex bit back a smile. She and Vax were either a terrible influence on her bear, or an amazing one. She voted for amazing.

"I'm not a threat to the Shademaster. You can hold my weapons if you must. You can stay with us in the room. I'll do whatever it takes to convince you that I'm not a threat. Just let me talk to her." She swung her bow back over her shoulder and let her hands fall to her sides. She'd played all her cards. She had no other option than to wait for Wick's decision.

In front of them, the barrier shimmered into place, with the same flash of light that promised the people of Jorenn another safe night from the shadows that haunted them. She felt relief ripple over the palisades like it had the first night, and though she didn't take her eyes off Wick, she was certain she felt Derowen turn to her and observe them both.

She knew she'd find another way in to talk to the Shademaster if she had to, but she still found herself holding her breath. She wanted this to be the best solution. She wanted Wick to trust her.

She wanted to be welcome.

"Wick, please."

After a silence that felt like it stretched on forever, where his large figure towered over her and his gaze saw straight through her, the archers around them glared at her only to immediately turn away again, and she grew all too aware of her pounding heartbeat, Wick nodded. "One conversation. What happens next is up to Derowen."

And two conflicting emotions surged through Vex at the same time. Regret. Relief. It was the first step of the plan, set in motion. Now it was up to her brother to figure out the next part.

CHAPTER 35

V ax noticed two things when he approached Jorenn from the hills. First, even several hours after the attack, the town remained entirely focused on the main gate, leaving the northeastern side open to anyone who might wander down this mountain path, as though walkers couldn't—or wouldn't—find their way here. Two members of the Shadewatch, who patrolled the path toward the mine, kept their guard down, yawning and whispering worries between each other. They were young and well meaning, but completely oblivious to the world around them. They were lucky too; they'd be easy marks for any thief, if that had been his purpose tonight.

He circled the town and kept his eyes open for an easy way to slip past the palisades and into Jorenn. While the hills offered the town decent natural protection, embracing it with tall boulders and steep cliffs, the landscape was not so insurmountable that he couldn't climb the ridges and edge past the back of buildings.

A whisper of movement a few hundred feet in front of him gave him pause. With the fingers of one hand clinging to a rocky ledge and the other hand pressed up against the back wall of a chapel, he froze. Another hint of movement, and this time he could make out the contour of a figure. A girl, perhaps, or a young woman, dashing along the rocks parallel to the mountain path. Judging by her nimble feet, Vax was certain she was trained in the finer arts of stealth and thievery. A Clasp member?

Or simply a local petty thief? A part of Derowen's scheme? Or just another poor fool, trying to get by?

She carried a small bag over her shoulder, and she passed by the two guards without them being any the wiser. When she slipped by the one closest to her, she brazenly slit his purse and deposited it in her sleeve. In the soft glow of the guards' lanterns, the girl's clothes appeared torn and oft mended, while dirt streaked her face and her eyes shone.

She dashed in Vax's direction just as his grasp on the rocks began to slip.

Vax pressed his back against the stone, and she froze, as attuned to any hint of movement as he was. Her eyes glinted in the moonlight, and when she spotted him, she grinned, flipped him off, and let herself slide down the rocks, disappearing from view. He shook his head. Suspicion pushed at the back of his thoughts. With so much at stake, even the most mundane interactions seemed to hide sinister secrets. Vax took a deep breath and pushed aside his wariness. He needed to focus on the task at hand.

Vax curled his fingers around the jagged pieces of rock. The northeastern side of town was also entirely open to anyone who might wander down this mountain path, who did not wish to be noticed.

Vax let himself fall, but only far enough that he didn't accidentally set any rocks tumbling. He followed the path she'd unwittingly laid out—in the opposite direction. When the guards turned away from the gate, he put his head down and darted from shadow to shadow, from the side of the path to the start of it—

And into Jorenn.

The town made more sense under the cover of night, as all towns did. Under the light of the moons, they all existed in shades of midnight gray and blue and all the streets and buildings were like the tumblers of a lock. All he had to do was figure out which path to follow to unlock the secrets before him.

He knew the way from the miners' gate to the Shade Hall. He'd walked the streets earlier today—had it only been today? It felt like a lifetime ago—to clear his head and understand where Thorn was coming from. He backtracked and made certain to stay away from the square, where the silence of a town asleep rolled through the air.

The excitement of the nightly attack had long since passed, and morning did not hold off for undead sieges.

Vax followed the dusty streets and circled the square until he got to the back of the Shade Hall, where a long road wound along the old buildings he'd seen through the window. He'd given this part—the exact right approach—ample thought during his wait in the hills.

Finding irregular ways to leave the Shade Hall had been easy. It'd only involved leaping out of a window. Finding a way in unnoticed, however, was trickier. He couldn't saunter in for fear of messing up his sister's story. He couldn't let her be seen with him at all. He didn't have the time to scout out the place for any weaknesses.

So he did what he did best: gamble. He found what looked to be the most ramshackle of buildings and used the unevenness as purchase to scramble higher along the wall and onto the roof. He climbed to the highest point, which put him at eye level with the second floor where Derowen's office was—and the room where he'd waited. It was hard to tell from this distance, but he was certain the window was still partially ajar, and that was all he needed.

He needed to get in.

He needed to keep his sister safe.

He needed a way to fix this mess.

If this was what Spireling Gideor had in mind when he'd told Vax it would only be a simple heist, then he might get his wish after all. Vax started at the farthest edge of the roof, used every inch of available space to run and gain momentum—and he leaped.

He fell. He saw the wall of the building rush to meet him and grabbed the window ledge with his fingertips as he slammed into the wall, all breath rushing out of him. His shoulders and hips ached with the impact, and he fought to keep his grip. He clung to the rough stone and crawled up, digging the toes of his boots against the wall. He managed to push himself up one step. Another. He cautiously let go of the ledge with one hand and before he lost his balance, he wrapped his fingers around the windowsill.

The window itself barely opened up past it. He pulled himself up farther and dug his fingernails into the soft wooden frame. He pulled. His arms trembled and he kept kicking up against the wall, scrambling for purchase and slipping down again. If anyone walked by and looked up, he would be in deep trouble. But if there was one lesson he'd learned on the rooftops of Syngorn, it was this: very few people ever looked up. Staying above other people's line of sight was the easiest way to be invisible.

The night remained quiet, and the window edged open. Inch by painstaking inch. It slipped out of his grasp once and he nearly fell back. His hands started to sweat and he kept having to adjust his grip.

It swung wide, but close enough overhead that he felt his hair move. With the last remaining effort, Vax placed his feet as high as he could, gripped the frame as tight as he could, and hurled himself upward. His shoulder scraped along the frame and his foot tangled with the curtains, but he made his way through and landed silently in a dark and apparently sleeping Shade Hall.

He pulled the window nearly shut, leaving enough of a crack that he could easily push it open again if need be. He straightened the curtains and waited. Waited to see if he'd alerted any guards. Waited to listen to the sounds around him.

The hallway that had been busy during the day was empty now. Presumably, the doors were closed, the Shademaster was secure, and the guards were asleep. So he slipped out and, with quiet feet in these loud halls, made his way to the third floor.

Soft light burned from the Shademaster's personal wing, and guards patrolled on a regular basis, but the floor above her office was empty. A long, practically decorated hallway with rows of closed doors on either side. Nothing here was lit, and no light shone from underneath any of the doors either. The deep slumber of darkness made stealing in easier.

Vax passed the doors with names or other signifiers on them. One door held a brass plate that marked it the quartermaster's office. Another belonged to the sergeant at arms. Another plate simply read RECORDS.

Of the doors that were unmarked, three were unlocked and led to dusty rooms that held nothing more than tables and chairs, and in one case: boxes full of Shadewatch uniforms.

Three other offices remained and Vax set to work finding his way in, until he'd opened all the doors and only one of the offices was filled with a chaos of curiosities and clutter that reminded him rather of Spireling Gideor's office back in Westruun. Gemstones of all colors. Weapons of all sorts. A sizable collection of figurines. The start of a letter, in a very familiar handwriting. A scratchy but neat scrawl. Vax had seen it before as a list of names, of people to be eliminated.

This had to be the right office.

He closed the door with a quiet snick behind him, and made himself comfortable sorting through all the clutter. Books and notebooks, though none of them as interesting as the notebook he'd found in Derowen's office. Whetstones, oil, and cleaning cloths for blades. A child's drawing of a horse with seven legs. Coins of all sorts and makes. Nothing that implied a connection to Westruun or the Clasp.

It was a risk, staying here. Until Vax spoke to Culwen, there was no way to ensure that he was the Clasp member Gideor had mentioned. It could simply be another person with the same name. And even if all the other details added up, he might not visit his office today—or at all.

There were a million ways in which their plan could fail. But it was his best chance to speak to the Shademaster's brother privately, while Vex reasoned with Derowen herself. And a chance was just what they needed.

THE SOFT PINK LIGHT OF dawn blinked into the room. Vax opened his eyes and stretched, careful not to make a sound. He didn't know how much time had passed, though the pale light indicated it was early. He'd found a sheltered space amidst a stack of boxes, out of immediate eyeline from the door, and he held his daggers in his lap. The Shade Hall and Jorenn Village woke up around him, and he picked at some of the tack and dried fruit, waiting. Thinking.

Vex and he had started running when they left Syngorn, and they hadn't stopped until now. If this didn't work they'd run again. She might not want to. *He* didn't want to, but he would always place his sister's welfare above anything else. Every other choice he made fell second to that.

Sunlight continued to filter into the room, and dust motes danced in its beams. Vax shifted his position and picked up a dagger, right when the handle of the door turned.

He changed to a low crouch, letting the clutter in front of him shield him, and held his breath.

The handle rattled again, and the door opened slowly, cautiously. A broad-shouldered man with wet curls and a scowl entered the room, one gloved hand on the hilt of a rapier. The elusive Shademaster's brother and probable Clasp member. The man he'd only heard about through rumor and stories. He looked like Derowen. He shared her hair color and her frown. He carried himself with the same cautious arrogance.

The moment Culwen pushed the door shut behind him, Vax came up from his hiding place, his daggers out.

"Good morning. We should have a conversation."

Culwen had his rapier out as soon as Vax moved, but instead of charging, he took a step back. "I thought someone had toyed with the lock. A burglar with manners. How quaint." He took Vax in, and his scowl turned into a sly grin. His guard was up, but his gaze was calculating. "Ah, you must be the prodigal brother."

"I must be," Vax acknowledged. He walked closer, blocking the door and Culwen's escape route, though it didn't look like the man planned to make a run for it.

The ease with which Culwen held his weapon belied his mocking amusement. "Tell me then, what should we have a conversation about? I admit, I usually don't talk business before I've had breakfast, and I rarely do so on the other end of a weapon"—he glanced at Vax's daggers—"or two. But it's clear you went through a lot of effort to ambush me here. I can't say I'm not intrigued."

"The Clasp sent me," Vax said. He managed to keep his voice even.

"Did they now?" Culwen turned and walked to the desk. He sat down and leaned back, putting his dusty boots up on the desktop. The carelessness, the fact that he didn't seem to care at all that Vax held two weapons ready to throw, rankled, but at the same time Vax couldn't deny he admired the man's gall.

Culwen pulled the collar of his tunic down far enough to show Vax the edges of his brand, confirming at least *that* theory. There was an edge to his voice. A warning. "I'm sure you have some way to prove your claim?"

Vax didn't. And he knew that once he couldn't identify himself, Culwen was far less likely to listen to him. Already the conversation was as impossible to control as the ash walkers up in the hills—and as intangible too. If his meeting with Shademaster Derowen had been an unpleasant sparring match of words, this was like the fight in the mines: full of sharp edges and dangers that lurked beneath the surface.

The only way not to fall too deep was to keep pushing forward. "Do you know *why* the Clasp sent me here?"

Culwen didn't let himself be drawn out. He merely raised an eyebrow. He took a cloth and a small bottle of oil from a desk drawer and with casual focus he polished the blade of his rapier. "I wouldn't know. I don't concern myself with other members' assignments, and I certainly don't concern myself with . . . *aspiring* members." He made the words sound like something dirty. "You should know the Clasp isn't fond of people throwing their name around."

Vax scoffed. In for a copper, in for a magic ring. "They asked me to steal the Shademaster's ring. Fracture. It made no sense to me, when I heard the rumors that are buzzing around town and in the mines."

Culwen stopped polishing his rapier. He carefully folded the piece of cloth and placed it on the desk. "Rumors, eh?"

"That Shademaster Derowen's dealing with the Clasp herself. Everyone here knows that." He put it on a bit thick, but the way the man's eyes widened slightly and his hand flexed at his side, subtle tells that he bought the bluff, told him he hit a mark.

"Right. Who did you say it was who gave you that assignment?" Culwen asked. He put the bottle of oil away. He removed his gloves slowly, with that same air of nonchalance, as though they were discussing a favorite bar in another town, or the latest fashion from Emon.

Vax walked through the room, careful not to turn his back to Culwen, and he peeked out between the curtains in front of the tall window to give himself a chance to think. The town square was full of Shadewatch, bringing in the survivors from the mines in pairs. Other guards rode out to presumably go back into the hills to weed out any last survivors. Even the children were bound, and Thorn was nowhere to be seen. The sight opened up a void inside him.

Vex had to be successful. And so did he. If they were wrong, if the Clasp did know and set him the assignment regardless, giving up the spireling's name would be a direct route to finding himself on the receiving end of that tongue staff and its witchery and Vex in the hands of whoever wanted her.

He ran his thumb over the hilt of one of his daggers and he did the same thing he had the night before. He leaped. "Spireling Gideor."

"Ah, of course. He's always been a fan of more circumspect confrontation." Culwen didn't sound shocked by the information.

Vax looked him up and down—

And froze.

Culwen wore the same signet ring on his finger as the one Vax had seen on Gideor's. A broad silver band, with the Clasp's symbols engraved into it. He turned it around and around, pensively. His rapier lay in his lap, and he slipped a parrying dagger with a triple blade from a sheath at his hip.

He stared straight at Vax.

"My esteemed colleague has been worried about my power for some time now. Ever since Kymal. I do believe he thinks it's a threat to him." *Spireling* Culwen smiled thinly. "He's right, of course, but this is such an inelegant way of trying to solve the debate between the two of us."

"I don't particularly care about this debate between the two of you." Vax pushed the words out and he fought to keep his shock from showing. He remembered the way the Clasp's tavern had stilled when Spireling Gideor walked in. The mixture of reverence and fear on too many faces. If Culwen was as powerful as him, Vax had picked a formidable enemy—or ally. He tightened his fingers around the hilts of his daggers. He took a step back toward the door. "But he threatened my sister, and I couldn't let that happen."

"I do understand that," Culwen said softly. He took up the rapier. "But you see my problem is, *I* don't particularly care about your woes."

"But you care about your business, don't you?" Vax took another step back toward the door and while he rushed to keep talking, he managed to keep his voice steady. "You see, once I realized you're a Clasp member too, my assignment only made sense to me when I realized the Clasp—or Spireling Gideor, specifically—wanted the ring not despite the Shademaster's agreement, but because they weren't actually a part of it. *You* were. And I have no intention of getting in the way of that, but every intention of protecting my sister. So I want to propose a trade."

Culwen got to his feet and faced Vax. If he'd seemed confident with a rapier before, the casually lethal way he held the parrying dagger in his off hand displayed a level of skill that could only be honed by blood and resolve. He shrugged. "Seems to me you broke into my office, and there's nothing that stops me from protecting myself and running you through. How's that for a trade? It'll make *my* day brighter."

While every fiber in his body screamed at him to protect himself, Vax kept his daggers pointed down. He met Culwen's gaze, lifted his chin, and smirked. "You can do that, but I have proof of what you and the Shademaster are doing. Should anything happen to me—or to my sister—I can assure you that proof will make its way to Spireling Gideor, and I can only imagine that it will make your debate quite a bit more complicated."

Culwen regarded Vax, trying to gauge if the threat was a bluff or something to be worried about. "Perhaps it would, or perhaps getting rid of an early-morning know-it-all would make me feel better, and I'll figure out what to do with that blasted dwarf myself." He hesitated. His nostrils flared. "What kind of proof?"

"Your sister's notebook. With a long list of transactions, contacts, and payments. Even the names of the people you decided to eliminate. It's quite a work of art. And I imagine if one were to lay it next to a calendar of recent ash walker attacks, there might be some similarities that the people of Jorenn Village would find incredibly interesting, too." The last was pure conjecture. A theory based on an escaping thief and a town whose northern defenses were far too easy to breach. On handwriting and coincidences. Vax grew cold when Culwen gnashed his teeth and didn't deny it.

"What would you want in return?" the spireling asked. Any trace of nonchalance had made way for ice-cold fury.

"From your sister? The release of the prisoners from the mines. From you?" Vax saw the opportunities open up before him. The idea that they might pull this off after all. "I want to get out of my Clasp contract. It's something that should be within your reach, if you're as powerful as you claim."

Culwen narrowed his eyes. "The Clasp isn't in the habit of breaking contracts."

Vax shrugged. "I don't think it's in the habit of letting members—even spirelings—skim off the profits either." When Culwen drew breath to protest, he pressed on. "I don't care about your business with Spireling Gideor or your business here in Jorenn any more than you care about my problems. I'm looking for a solution that benefits us both. It might be complicated, but it's a fair deal. It wouldn't break your cover or your trade. You can continue on as spireling and smuggler and whatever else it is that you desire. I'm sure you can even find someone to continue your debate with Spireling Gideor for you." He didn't believe for a second that that debate wouldn't result in someone's death sooner or later, but that was a Clasp problem. They played by their rules, now he'd play by his. "Like I said, my sister will make her own deal with yours, so we'll see what your business is worth to her as well. Or if you can convince her to see reason. We simply want to find the best solution for all."

Culwen considered it. He kept his eyes on Vax, and the only outward sign of his anger lay in how tightly his left hand wrapped around the hilt of the rapier. His fingers were skin and bones and rage. "And what's to stop you from betraying me to Gideor after all? He'd pay you handsomely for it."

Vax sighed and used his forearm to push stray strands of hair out of his face. Vex would disagree with what he was about to say, but, "Strange though it may sound to you, I'm not in it for the money. I'm in it to keep my sister safe. Once I'm out of my contract, I will keep on traveling and I'd be satisfied if our paths never cross again."

"If that's the case, you're an even greater fool than Gideor is. That's not how the world works, half-elf. If you do not have the guts to make the hard choices, it will eat you whole." Culwen shook his head in disgust, but he folded the triple blades of his dagger together and sheathed the weapon. He used his rapier to point at Vax. "You play a dangerous game, and I can only hope our paths *do* cross again after this."

Rage and revulsion rippled over Culwen's face, and it took him a long time to speak the next words. "I'll need a few days to get my affairs in order and find a way to work around my oh-so-esteemed colleague. By the sounds of it, I will also need to have a . . . . conversation with my failure of a sister. Meet me here at sundown three days from now, and I'll make sure you get what you asked for."

"There's a tavern in the attic of an abandoned chapel near the miners' gate," Vax countered. "We'll meet there, tonight."

Culwen started to laugh, cold and sharp. The sound cut through Vax like knives. For all that they might ally themselves for a shared cause, Vax knew he'd made an enemy here, and the knowledge settled like ash inside him. It'd been one of the upsides of always traveling on. They never stayed anywhere long enough to find comfort, but they also never stayed anywhere long enough to find real trouble. Angry shopkeepers. Broken contracts. Occasional broken hearts. Nothing beyond that.

But if he were to venture a guess, and based on Culwen's hope that their paths would cross again, the spireling's grudges were as deadly as his blades.

Still, that would be a problem for another time, after he'd escaped the Clasp's grasp. When Vex and he would be far, far away from here. For now, all he had to do was see this negotiation through to its impossible solution.

They were close. So close.

"Tonight," Vax pressed.

"I'll see you in the chapel," Culwen acknowledged, sheathing his rapier with a thud. "And what a *pleasure* doing business with you."

CHAPTER 36

"I gave you hospitality. I trusted you with my daughter. And you betrayed me." Shademaster Derowen looked at Vex like she was a stranger, and it cut straight through her.

Vex had spent what remained of the night in the room that still held some of her belongings, and had woken to find her weapons and her bags taken from her. Only her clothes, boots, and finely carved bracers were left. When she'd been summoned to the Shademaster's office and two guards who'd been posted outside her room fell into step with her, Trinket lumbering behind them all, she knew she'd gone from guest to threat, and nothing she could say would change that. Especially when Derowen met her in full Shadewatch regalia, her uniform crisp and her sword by her side. She looked nothing at all like the woman who'd smiled at Vex and told her they'd look for her brother. She hooked her thumbs around her belt, sent the guards to join the search for any remaining outlaws, and forgot whatever kindness there had been between them. All that was left was a chasm of betrayal.

Vex pulled herself upright. "You *used* me," she challenged. "I trusted you. I defended you when my brother told me stories that you were dangerous. And you lied to me."

"What do you want, Vex?" the Shademaster asked flatly.

"I want to hear your side of the story." Vex set her jaw. She plucked at the bracers around her forearms to keep her hands from trembling. "I know you're better than this. I just want to understand."

At this, hurt flashed over Derowen's face. "Understand what? Why I sent another group of Shadewatch into the mines? Why I wanted to find these outlaws in the first place? I'm sorry if it felt like I used you, but you managed to do what none of my scouts could. I needed to keep Jorenn safe, and I couldn't let the opportunity to do so pass me by. You've heard my side of the story, Vex. You may not believe me, but I never lied to you."

"The miners—" Vex started.

Derowen cut in. "Endangered our community. They may have given you and your brother some kind of dramatic sob story, but they were criminals. They *are* criminals. And they always will be. I only ever protected my people. I thought you understood that."

She wanted to believe it. How she wanted to believe it. That all Derowen had ever done was for the good of her daughter, Wick, and the people around her. That it had only ever been about the town's safety. That a place like this, where people took care of one another without asking for anything in return, gave gifts without strings attached, could truly exist.

She'd found the book on dragons Beryl had given her on the nightstand in her room, like nothing had changed while she'd been away. She'd leafed through it, past the notes she made, and she'd wondered if she should give it back to the craftswoman. She'd pocketed it instead.

"I know the miners were responsible for the ash walkers. I don't deny that."

"Then what is your problem?" Derowen demanded. She ran her hand across her face and sighed. "I was up most of the night to fight off those bloody creatures and my daughter's nightmares, so make your point."

"My point is your trade with silver merchants in Turst Fields. In Drynna. In Kymal. Does protecting your people involve stealing from them too then?" Vex asked quietly. "Was it ever about making Jorenn better? Or was it only about lining your own pockets?"

Derowen didn't blink, but her eyes skimmed over to the office door, and she walked around her desk. She rummaged through the drawers and reached deeply inside the desk. Vex heard the sound of a small compartment clicking open, followed by a hissed curse from Derowen. "You have some nerve to come here and accuse *me* of stealing."

"Why did you do it?" Vex asked. The words felt heavy in her throat. "The people here, they trust you. They look up to you."

"And I have given them everything," Derowen countered. Her voice held an edge to it that Vex hadn't heard before. "What I've taken in return is *nothing*. Nothing more than what I need to ensure the safety and security of my family. A future for Aswin. Would you deny me that?"

If that had been all—silver and security and nothing more—it may have been nothing. But it had been a matter of lives. "There were children in those mines," she said. "No older than her."

"Don't you *dare* make me the monster, Vex," Derowen snarled. Rage flashed across her face.

"I came here to offer you a deal," Vex said softly. "The notebook for the freedom of the survivors and the ones you captured in the mines. Let them leave Jorenn and the Umbra Hills in peace, and we'll make sure you get the notebook back."

Derowen's hand twitched by her side. Her rage made way for something colder. Something harder. Like an animal in distress, she became far more dangerous than she was before. "I saved you. What's to stop me from trading your life for the notebook? I'm sure your brother wouldn't want to see any harm come to you."

"If you harm me or my brother, the notebook finds its way directly to the Clasp in Westruun. I imagine *they* would not be amused to find out what you and *your* brother have been doing," Vex countered, fighting to sound casual. She'd liked this woman once. She'd admired her.

"Ah, so you just happened upon a random bystander in these abandoned hills to carry out your threat?" Fury dripped from Derowen's voice like flames. "We're far away from the rest of the world here, Vex. No one cares about what happens in Jorenn."

Vex raised an eyebrow. She'd prepared for that question. "There was a scout who was a part of our camp that first night. Nera. You must have met her. She knows her way around these hills."

She held Derowen's gaze and clung to the implication that Nera had been more than an accidental traveler to them. Derowen had seen the two of them talk outside of the inn. One survivor to another. One traveler to another. She only needed it to be convincing enough to be threatening, the risk too big to call her bluff.

The Shademaster considered it, then slammed the drawers of her desk shut. Whatever mask of kindness she'd worn had shattered, and Vex wasn't sure she'd ever be able to mend the pieces.

"Look out of the window, Vex. Tell me what you see," Derowen said coldly.

Vex did. She walked over to the window and stared out over the square, where the Shadewatch were bringing in the miners they'd captured. Two at a time, they were led to one of the quartermasters, who marked down their names before separating the children and the adults. The children were escorted by Wick into The Scattered Bar, with guards posted outside to watch them. The adults were escorted to the town jail. "The survivors."

"The last of them. There are many people in town who would see them hang for what they did to us before I ever laid hands on those mines, but believe me when I say we do try to make this town better than it was. I know they're not all responsible. The children are innocent and will be cared for. They'll find loving homes here if they have no families to go back to. The outlaws who didn't fight back will have their chance to face justice. No matter what else you might think of me, I don't condone unnecessary cruelty."

Perhaps Derowen genuinely believed in what she did. Perhaps it was easy to be merciful when she'd already killed most of the outlaws. Vex didn't know and she didn't want to know. Not anymore. "You can't take children from their families," she said. "My offer stands. Their freedom— *all of them*—for your proof. They're innocent."

"Not all of them. No deal. Not on those terms." Harsh lines spread across Derowen's face, and they tugged at something deeper, something far more primitive. Hurt for hurt. *Fear.* "I will make you another one. Come, walk with me."

Without waiting to see if Vex followed her, she stalked out of the office and down the hallway. She waved away two of the guards who snapped to when she passed, and led Vex down to the foyer on the first floor, which spread out from the large guarded doors to the great hall and several hallways that split off into the working quarters of the Shadewatch. It was chaotic here, with one of the Shadewatch's quartermasters handing out maps to select guards. Maps Vex had helped to prepare. They weren't done scouring the mines yet, and it made her feel sick.

Derowen nodded at the guards they passed, traded smiles and friendly words with them, or soothing hand gestures at the ones who recognized Vex. And that made Vex feel worse.

She made her way past a large set of doors that Vex had learned led to the great hall, where the commanders of the Shadewatch met and where, presumably, Jorenn Village's council of elders had once gathered, and into a darker hallway. Past another set of doors, and away from the murmur of the guards, to a smaller door off to the side. An antechamber.

Derowen took a key from her pocket and opened the door to let Vex and Trinket in. The room was sparsely decorated. The table that, judging by the dents in the faded crimson rug, had once stood in the center of the room had been pushed to the side. The chairs that went with it were stacked on top of one another and pushed out of the way too, creating an inadvertent barricade in front of one of the tall windows, where sunlight and a shallow breath of fresh air filtered in through the cracks. What remained in the center of the room was the rug, and—shackled to one of rings in the wall that under normal circumstances held torches or lanterns—the crumpled body of a male half-elf with tangled and matted hair, and torn-up clothes.

Thorn had a large gash over one eye, and no one had thought to clean the blood that had matted his hair and trailed down his face. A deep cut below his right clavicle had been bandaged with what looked to be a torn-up shirt that did little to stop the bleeding, but did stop him from making a mess. His nose looked broken and his right arm hung limp at his side, while some of his fingers were swollen and bent into impossible positions.

Derowen positioned herself in front of him. She kept her gaze firmly on Vex. "I'll give you the others. I will keep him."

Vex stared at Thorn without comprehension. She stared at the Shademaster without comprehension. "What did you do to him?"

Thorn stirred at the sound of her voice, but she didn't want him to wake. Whatever oblivion he was in was surely better than this place.

"Nothing he didn't do to my Shadewatch a dozen times over, I assure you," Derowen said. She nudged him with her foot, and he groaned. "You may think of him as some kind of noble martyr, but few in Jorenn would agree with you, and certainly not the families of the people he has killed."

"I didn't think *anything* of him," Vex snapped, shock rushing through her system. "I didn't even care about him. I cared about you." Now . . . she shook her head. "I thought you were a hero. What would the families of the people *you* have killed think?"

Derowen shook her head. "They probably understand that sometimes in life, you have to make hard sacrifices to protect a town or a family. I do what I do to give my daughter a better future, and with her all the children in Jorenn. Do you think they had any perspective, before I came here? This town, overrun by the dead pouring out of these hills and with no sense of how to take care of themselves? I taught them everything I know about survival, and once again when these miners endangered everyone with their greed." She stared past Vex into some unknown distance. "Yes, my brother saw an opportunity when I had access to the mines. No one had to know. The mines provide enough for all."

Vex narrowed her eyes. Wick had told her Culwen had simply shown up here with the ring, one day. "That's why he gave you the ring."

Derowen focused on Vex again. "You spent enough time here to see what a beautiful thing it is when a community comes together. Wouldn't you want that? I know judgment and how badly it hurts. Do you not long to shed yourself from it and find a place where you're wanted? I would protect Aswin from the ash walkers, from the outlaws, even from Culwen, if I had to."

Vex's breath caught. "Do you? Have to protect her from your own brother?" She tried to add up what she'd heard. What she'd seen. There seemed to be no love lost between the siblings, but from what she'd observed, Aswin was fond of her uncle.

The Shademaster met her gaze calmly. "I would kill for her." She nudged Thorn again, the toes of her boot pushing hard against his wounded side. He blinked and whimpered, and it made him look small and vulnerable. "What's weeding out a few unhealthy elements to make a town like this prosper? I will leave this town better than I found it, and he can't say the same thing."

"Vex . . ." Thorn's voice was barely recognizable. He tried to straighten. "Are they safe? Are they alive?"

She wanted to go to him, but Derowen held her back. The Shademaster regarded the bound and bloodied miner with a curious look of pity. "So that's the deal I propose."

Vex blinked against the sudden pivot.

"I will agree to your trade, it's fair enough. I'll call off the guards and let the survivors travel freely out of here. Their safety for my notebook. But not him. Not Thorn."

Those last two words carried so much weight. "What happens to him?"

"Oh, Vex." Derowen shook her head. "He does not make it out of his town alive."

"*Why?* Because he's on your list? Or is it your brother's list? Do you merely follow his directions?"

Derowen sighed but didn't deny it. "He knows too much, and that makes him a threat to us. Not to Jorenn, but to my brother and me. It makes him a threat to Aswin."

Vex stared down at Thorn. He'd been willing to risk his life for his people once before. He looked like he was on the verge of death. If Vax came through with his side of the bargain, it would be the best solution they could hope for. For all of them.

She bit her lip.

"Do it," Thorn croaked, a voice like gravel and filled with pain. "Keep them safe."

Vax would hate her. She knew he would. He'd be right, too.

She would hate herself if she went through with this. "He won't be any trouble to you," she tried. "He'll disappear with the others and you and your brother can go on with your business without any interference from anyone. You can protect Aswin's future and no one will have to be hurt again."

As she spoke the words, she realized how untrue they were. She realized how untrue Derowen's utopic words had been. Someone would be hurt again, and if not Thorn than the next person who accidentally found themselves in the Shademaster's way. Or Aswin, if she ever found out what her mother did.

It wasn't about the notebook. It wasn't even just about the ring anymore. She couldn't let that happen.

"You remind me of her," Derowen said. "You really do. I hope that one day, my daughter grows into a young woman who is as brave as you are. But I hope she'll be able to recognize a losing battle before she jumps right into it."

"She's already brave," Vex said. "I hope that when she grows up, she'll be better than me. I hope she'll be better than you. I hope she understands right from wrong, and sees the difference between necessary choices and cruel choices."

She locked eyes with Thorn, and he shook his head, though it was barely perceptible. With his unbroken hand, he cradled his wounded arm to his chest, and he attempted to push himself up. "Not your fight," he managed, slurring his words.

She smiled at him. He was wrong. It hadn't been, perhaps, but it was now. She claimed it as such. And she wouldn't stand by and let him be used as a sacrifice. "No." She stepped around Thorn, so she'd draw Derowen's attention away from him. She gestured at the windows, at the town outside. "I want all of them to be safe."

She hesitated then added, "And if you think that's too steep a price, talk it through with your brother. He knows about the notebook. I'm sure he doesn't want the Clasp to learn about his business."

Derowen sucked in a harsh breath, and genuine fear sparked in her eyes. Her mouth twisted. "Culwen knows? You *told* him?"

"He knows." Vex crossed her arms. "So it's your choice. Your notebook and all it entails—your business, your position in this town, even your family—or your vengeance. You can't have both."

"Do you know what you've done?" Something violent and hard crossed Derowen's face. A despair so sharp it caused Vex to step back. Suddenly, she was aware that they were teetering on the edge. And if the Shademaster fell, she'd take everyone around her with her.

"You don't see it, do you?" Derowen slid her hand to the hilt of her sword, and she held the weapon with the same unflinching determination that Vex had come to admire even as, underneath her armor, the cracks became visible. "If he knows, it doesn't matter what I do. He trusted me to keep him safe too, and if I can't . . ."

A pleading note crept into her voice, and calculation furrowed her brow. "But the notebook isn't the ace you think it is. Don't you see? I uncovered information that someone close to me had taken to smuggling and stealing from the hardworking people of Jorenn. Not wanting to risk alerting the thief, I took note of everything that happened, as quietly and meticulously as I could. The notebook details what I found. And while I regret that I couldn't stop this heinous act, the people of Jorenn will understand that I have and always will keep them safe." She swallowed hard. "Don't you understand? Words on paper are merely words, Vex. It's how you tell the story that counts."

With one fluid movement, before Vex could even reach for the bow she didn't carry, Derowen unsheathed her sword and the blade sparkled in the early sunlight before she brought it down into Thorn's stomach. "I can't let him endanger that."

Thorn gargled and coughed, and clawed desperately at the blade. Blood gushed from the wound. It was a cruel wound. A dirty wound. The type of wound that any good hunter would avoid, because it would take Thorn a long time to die. His weak struggles were full of pain and despair.

Vex took a step in his direction, and Derowen withdrew her sword, with a soft groan from Thorn and a trail of blood. "Not another step closer."

At the exact same moment, a soft voice echoed through the room. "Mama? I don't want to do my lessons."

One of the doors to the hallway opened, and a small, brave girl with big emerald eyes padded in.

CHAPTER 37

Everything around her fell apart.

Derowen dropped her sword and moved to stand in front of Thorn, while Vex doubled over like she'd been punched. Aswin scanned the room without a hint of worry and saw Vex before she saw Thorn. She squealed. "Vex, I didn't know you were back! Can I play with Trinket, please? Uncle Culwen is outside, but he wasn't paying attention to me either. No one is, and I don't want to do endless lessons. They're *boring*."

Wordlessly, Vex nodded at Trinket, who lumbered up to the little girl. She immediately ran over and buried her face into his fur, but when she looked up again, her eyes grew impossibly wider.

"Mama, is that man sick?" She pointed at Thorn. She kept one hand curled in Trinket's fur, and there was a hint of trepidation to her question.

Derowen had blanched to the point of turning green, and she took another tentative step toward Aswin. Her voice wavered, and she wasn't able to pull the mask of kind and helpful Shademaster back in place. She turned her ring around her finger unconsciously. "He is, darling. He is sick, and we are trying to find the best way to help him. But you shouldn't be here. You should be with Wick and learn your lessons like the big girl I know you are." She brushed her hand on her tunic, and Vex wondered how obvious the blood was on the red fabric. If that was why they'd decided on that color.

While the Shademaster carefully walked toward her daughter, Vex took a step toward Thorn, whose coughing had turned into a wet wheezing sound, as if trying to breathe only sucked his lungs full of blood. A trickle of red ran down from the corner of his mouth, and he still clutched at the emptiness around him. His eyes followed her. She saw him drift in and out of a haze of pain.

With her foot, she pushed the Shademaster's sword in his direction. Even if it wouldn't be of any help to him, she'd rather it was out of Derowen's reach too. She wished she had a way to help Thorn. All she could do was protect him.

When Derowen took another step toward her daughter, Vex positioned herself between the Shademaster and the dying miner, and she cleared her throat. "Trinket, will you bring Aswin back to Wick for her lessons?" The words tore through her. She'd much rather have Trinket close by. She didn't want to be alone. But she also couldn't bear the thought of Aswin's curiosity meeting Thorn's pain. Aswin had already seen too much pain and bloodshed here. She didn't deserve to see more. "He can stay with you for a little bit, if you like."

Aswin's face brightened. "I'd like that. Is that okay, Mama?"

Derowen threw a genuinely grateful look in Vex's direction, but it disintegrated to an intense look of fear when she realized Vex's position. She breathed out hard. "Of course it is, darling."

Trinket hesitated, and she nodded her encouragement. Let him take Aswin out of this room and hold her safe. She trusted no one more to protect her, because he knew how to be a refuge to scared girls. "I'll come find you both as soon as we're done talking," she promised.

In her periphery, Derowen nodded too. "We'll take care of the sick man, Aswin, but it's time for you to go back to Wick."

"I will." Aswin looked as if she wanted to walk toward Derowen. Then she hesitated and thought the better of it. She scrunched up her nose and kept one hand curled in Trinket's fur as they both turned to walk out of the room.

As soon as the bear and the little girl pushed out the door and it fell closed behind them, Vex crouched down and snatched up the sword. It was too heavy for her, and it had been a long time since her father had had her train with blades, but she felt better holding a weapon. She was done letting anyone hurt her. "No deal, Shademaster," she said softly. "I want him too."

Derowen stared intently at the ring around her finger. She turned it around, and the stones seemed to glimmer in the light, and after a moment, she laughed incredulously. "You really don't understand, do you? I would thank you for what you did for my daughter, but—"

"I only did it for her. Not for you." Vex held the sword loosely. "I don't want to fight you, Derowen. I didn't even want to choose between the two of you. Not after what you've done for me. But I will if I have to."

Derowen sighed. Then she reached down to her boots and when she rose, she held poniards in both hands. "I don't want to fight you either, but neither of us got to make that choice, did we? You do everything because of your brother—and I do everything because of mine."

"No," Vex whispered. She steadied her voice. "I *chose* to be here."

At her feet, Thorn coughed. His breathing was impossibly labored. He sounded like a drowning man, gasping for air. He sounded like death, and it rattled her. She raised her sword to a guard position. "And I would do anything *for* Vax."

"Then stand and fight." Without another word, without a hint of regret or hesitation, Derowen attacked. She fought with the same determination that she used in every other part of life, and whatever masks she wore, whatever kindness she cloaked herself with, it all fell away when she fought.

She had one singular purpose: to win, and it cut as sharp as any blade.

Vex brought up the sword to protect herself. It felt heavy and awkward in her hands. She missed the grace of her bow.

She was able to block a strike, but immediately the Shademaster pivoted and used the poniard in her other hand to take a stab at Vex. The point of the weapon tugged at her sleeve and tore through the fabric. It just missed the skin as Vex jumped away.

This was exactly what she'd had feared when she'd come to the entrance of the mines. She couldn't survive in a swordfight. They were locked in an exquisite but deadly dance, where every step could spell either victory or disaster, and Derowen had the lead.

But while Derowen was determined and strong, Vex was quicker. When the Shademaster parried a strike and followed through with a measured thrust upward, Vex arched backward to avoid it. She used the momentum to swipe at Derowen's feet with her boot, very nearly knocking the Shademaster and herself off balance.

When she stumbled, Vex leaned in low and cut at her. Her weapon caught on part of Derowen's uniform, digging into her side. The Shademaster lashed out in retaliation, and one of her poniards cut deep into Vex's left forearm, slashing into one of the bracers.

Vex tried to use her few half-remembered guard positions, which were meant for lighter swords. Her arms ached, her muscles unused to the short burst of movement. Derowen fell into an aggressive pattern of offense, a rhythm of thrust and lunge, slash and sidestep.

Vex felt the sweat pour down her face, and her arm ached, making it hard to cling to the blade. "It doesn't have to be like this," she tried once, breathlessly.

"It does." Derowen used one of her poniards to slash at Vex in a downward arc, and when Vex blocked it a second too late, she took the other, stepped in, and stabbed.

Vex felt the blade cut through her clothes as she let herself fall back at the last moment. Holding on to the sword with her right hand, she scrambled farther backward. She wouldn't be able to keep this up.

"What was it you told me?" Vex threw at her. "That you wanted to teach Aswin how to be strong enough so that she doesn't have to be frightened of losing?"

Derowen flinched at the impact of the words, but instead of surrendering, she pulled her pain closer and used it as another weapon, and in that moment her kindness and despair came together. Two sides of the same coin. "I've already lost so much. I won't lose her too."

She swiped at Vex's legs. Vex pushed herself up to her feet and circled the Shademaster, ready to block the next attack. She was a second too late when it came. Once more, Vex felt the tip of it cut through fabric and skin, and across her ribs. This poniard dug, and she cursed. The edges of her vision swam. She forgot about Thorn. She forgot about the notebook, about the ring. Everything fell away but the two of them, their blades, and the life and breath of the fight itself.

It became harder and harder to hold up the sword.

Until the sound of a horn wound its way through the Shade Hall. Raised voices. Feet stamping. Shouts. Screams. Derowen threw a furtive glance over her shoulder, and Vex lunged. With one hard strike, she sent one of the poniards tumbling to the ground, and the balance of the fight shifted. Vex stepped closer to kick the weapon far out of the Shademaster's reach.

Derowen stabbed at her, but the poniards didn't have the same reach as the sword. Vex slashed at the Shademaster's shoulder and cut deep. Blood pooled in the wound and coated the red tunic.

Derowen's hand trembled, the blade falling in and out of guard. So Vex turned to attack her from that side once more. Again. To find a way to disarm her. To find a way to—she didn't know how they'd get out of here.

Right then, the sound of horns echoed through the Shade Hall a second time, followed by voices. "We're under attack!" The shouts came from outside the room. "Ash walkers! We need the Shademaster!"

This time, both women swirled around to the sound. Vex used the opportunity to take a few steps back so she could lower the sword. Her arm ached, and the cut to her ribs was bleeding.

"It's impossible," Derowen breathed. She backed away too, her gaze first on the door and then on her ring. "I didn't . . ."

Vex glanced across the room for an escape route, and grew cold.

The chairs and table in front of the window quaked and wisps of ash blew in through the cracks, like tendrils that reached into the room to grab them. Outside, the horns sounded again and the voices became louder and more frantic.

Out of nowhere, ashen hands clawed at the windows and gaunt, decaying faces pressed in. One of the corpses ferally slammed an exposed elbow against the glass, and the cracks widened. A second joined it, and another one. The glass shattered and hands and arms reached through, pushing chairs away.

Fuck, they had to get out of here. Right now.

She looked back toward the door where Derowen had been and found the room in front of her empty.

Vex froze. She heard footsteps creak behind her, but she was too late. The sword dropped too low, and Derowen took full advantage of her distraction, grabbing her arm and pulling her off balance while at the same time lunging at her side.

Vex twisted, but not far enough. Derowen stabbed deeply. Her blade cut through skin and sinew, above her hip, and Vex felt it tear into her. Her vision swam. Her leg gave way from under her.

She dropped to one knee and the sharp stab of pain that arced through her was the only thing that kept her grounded. She tightened her grip on the sword and slashed at Derowen's leg, slicing straight through the calf muscle.

She brought up an arm to push away the downward lunge of the poniard, and it skidded off the leather bracers. Somehow, Derowen managed to keep standing, and Vex rolled out of the way, desperately trying to find cover.

All she saw was blood and ashes. Skeletal hands pushed the windows open. Tendrils of ash solidified around them. The sun's glow danced through the motes, and it gave the talons and faces an eerie glow.

The walkers pushed through and skittered closer. They seemed to congregate on the Shademaster, circling her, circling them both.

Vex tried to crawl away from the dead when Derowen stepped closer, her blades at the ready. She knew she had seconds left, if that. And she waited for the regret. The all-overwhelming realization that they should have left when they had the chance, that they never should have come back.

It didn't come. She knew they'd done the right thing. She'd chosen the right fight. The only thing she regretted was that her brother wasn't here. That after they'd lost each other and found each other again, after all her hopeful promises and better plans, after the distances they'd walked together and the miles she thought were still to come, he'd wait for her and she wouldn't come.

The voices outside grew louder, and the door slammed open. A shocked voice boomed through the room. "Derowen, call them off."

Vex turned her head and saw Culwen stride into the room, outrage marring his features. He'd changed into a more comfortable outfit, though he still wore his gloves. He frowned at her, and she saw the flash of recognition. The tightening of his jaw.

"Of course." Culwen shook his head. "I'll deal with you and your brother later."

She gasped around the pain, and tried unsuccessfully to push herself up to her feet.

"What are you doing here?" Derowen demanded, and for the first time since she'd faced off against Vex, pure fear coursed through her voice. "I have this under control. I promise!"

"I don't think you do." Behind Culwen, a flash of red indicated the Shadewatch outside. With the heel of his foot, Culwen pushed the door closed, though it didn't shut completely. Someone put a hand between the door and the frame. "There are ash walkers *inside* Jorenn, Dera. And this one and her brother *know*. You swore to me you'd be careful. You promised me you would take our arrangement seriously, for the benefit of our whole family. I thought you were better than such carelessness. It seems you've disappointed me once again."

Vex crawled to the side of the room and watched Culwen step closer. Derowen shifted her poniards to one hand and used the other to cover the ring. "I know what I'm doing, Culwen." Derowen's voice took on a hint of panic, of old threats and old arguments never quite forgotten. She shrank in the face of him. "Trust me, I'll handle it."

The dead and decaying crawled closer, like a protective barrier around her.

The barrier. Vex's heart skipped a beat and fresh pain coursed through her when she added up everything she knew. The cursed corpses, reacting to the gems. The ash walkers with their singular purpose. The increased attacks after Derowen got the ring. *Call them off.* "These things . . . Whatever they are . . . You're not using the ring to fend them off, but you're *summoning* them somehow?"

They *should* have stolen the fucking thing.

Culwen's eyes flashed when he looked from his sister to Vex and back. The tight set around his jaw hardened, and he pulled his rapier. "I thought I could trust you, Dera. I thought I'd finally found a good investment, after saving your life turned out to be such a poor one." He laughed and it was cold and bitter. "After everything I've done for you, after the enemies I made to keep you safe, and everything I've built for you and Aswin. How could you have been so careless?"

"Don't you *dare* talk about my daughter." Derowen disengaged and stepped back. She clung to her blade, but her hands trembled.

Before Vex could bring up her sword to protect herself, Culwen bore down upon them both, rapier in one hand, dagger in the other. She wouldn't close her eyes. She would meet him head-on. But her breath caught and her heart skipped when he lunged—and cut straight through Derowen's defenses. "You're a failure even now."

The Shademaster cried out in pain. She dropped her guard and raised an arm to protect her face. "Culwen!"

"It's as I promised you, sister. You owed me a life. Now, I would have happily taken hers in payment, but I think this works out better for all. Your daughter needs someone to set her a proper example."

He stepped in again and ran the rapier straight through her.

The shock that coursed through Vex gave her enough strength to push herself to her feet and remain standing. She swayed and staggered out of the way, around the ashen shadows that were starting to circle her. It felt as though they were sucking the light out of the room—or perhaps that was her own vision narrowing. She used the sword to keep herself upright.

"Vex!"

A guard slipped through the open door behind Culwen, and her eyes widened. There, in a bright red Shadewatch tunic and with his daggers out, stood her brother. He took the situation in—her wound, Thorn, the fight between Derowen and Culwen—and the color drained from his face. He held the door open with his foot and gestured to her.

"Go! Find help!"

She didn't hesitate. Still clinging to the Shademaster's sword, one hand pressed against the cut to her side, she dashed past him into a chaotic hallway where Shadewatch were tangling with another unrelenting wave of the dead. She stumbled and pushed herself forward. And for the second time in as many days—

She ran.

CHAPTER 38

When Culwen had stormed out of the room, Vax leaned against the wall long enough for his heartbeat to settle and to get his breathing under control—then he followed. He sneaked back into the hallway and retraced his steps to the room with the Shadewatch uniforms. He hadn't planned to stay in the Shade Hall. His and Vex's plan had been to leave as soon as possible and to reconvene in the chapel attic.

But something about Culwen's words didn't sit right with Vax. While he trusted his sister's plan, he also knew she'd been right about one thing: it was wrong for them to be separated. He didn't want to leave this building without her. So he slipped into the room and freed a Shadewatch uniform from the crates. He found a tunic that was only slightly too big and could fit over his own shirt. A pair of carmine pants that he knew he had to change into if he didn't want to be unmasked with a simple glance.

He couldn't do anything about his face, and he didn't know if the Shadewatch employed any half-elves, but he hoped to make his way through the hall fast enough that no one would have time to observe him in detail.

When he left the third floor, Culwen was nowhere to be seen. He descended the stairs carefully, keeping his head down and his ears perked up. While the second floor was still relatively quiet, when he came down toward the first floor, it was a hive of activity. Guards walked in and out, discussing the outlaws they'd captured, and wondering how many others were still hiding out in the hills. He heard anger and relief and glee from a younger guard, who demanded to know what kind of justice the Shademaster would mete out. An older guard cuffed him around the head for that.

Culwen stood in the middle of the foyer, oblivious to the happenings around him. He was deep in conversation with a bald man who held on to a torn-up man. He shook his head, as if to say he didn't know the answer to Culwen's questions, and Culwen impatiently stepped closer. It caused the people around him to quiet and cast him curious glances.

In the midst of his conversation, a little girl tugged at Culwen's coat, waited for a moment until it was clear he wouldn't pay attention to her, and then wandered away. Aswin tilted her head and beelined for the double doors that gave passage to the great hall, listened, and then wandered to the next door. Two more, before she walked into a hallway that led to the side of the great hall. Near the fifth door, her face brightened and she pushed in.

Vax crossed to the other side of the railing and tried to make out what was being said. All he could hear was Derowen's name and something about a private conversation. He glanced out toward the square, wondering briefly if the Shadewatch garb would be enough to sneak to wherever they held the survivors.

A dwarven guard in a red uniform ran past him, taking the stairs down two at a time. She barely spared him a glance. "Don't stand around there! Hurry up!"

He picked up his pace, but paused again when the doors that Aswin had disappeared into opened up and she walked out with a very familiar bear by her side. She held one hand in Trinket's fur and chattered at him constantly, and in the hallway that had been filled with angry voices and cautious silence, all eyes were on her.

One of the guards muttered something, and another elbowed him and told him off. A blond-haired human girl who stood at the doorway gave a thumbs-up in Aswin's direction and called, "Love your new familiar, little princess."

When Aswin grinned, a guard who seemed to be working as a right-hand man to the quartermaster suggested, "Wick's on the prowl, As. Be careful of the north wing."

She stuck her tongue out at him. "He'll never find me."

Trinket huffed, and Vax knew the bear had different ideas, but Aswin's proclamation was met by shouts and jeering, and he suddenly, viscerally, knew why his sister loved this place.

In the chaos, Culwen tried to disentangle himself from his discussion with the guard, but the man—with an impressive gray beard to go with his bald head—grabbed his arm and continued their conversation.

While Trinket and Aswin padded away to another corner of the building, Vax took the last few steps to the first floor and walked through the gathered guards. He made sure to keep his distance from the Shademaster's brother and his head down, and as soon as he got closer to the door that Aswin had appeared out of, he pushed his back to the wall and hugged the shadows. He couldn't walk in without blowing his cover, but he wasn't sure if staying close was enough.

He'd cast another glance in Culwen's direction when someone outside the Shade Hall *screamed*.

Two guards came charging back inside, out of breath and with their blades in hand. "We're under attack!" the tallest, a dwarf with dark braids and weathered dark skin, called out. "Ash walkers! We need the Shademaster!"

Vax pushed himself deeper into the darkest corner of the chamber and watched the room around him descend into chaos. A wave of dread coursed through all those present and slammed them off balance. Other shouts and screams came from outside.

All the guards who were present reached for their weapons and made their way to their posts inside and outside the building, streaming around one another like ants in an anthill. The bald guard let go of Culwen's arm and ran over to a tall horn that was placed in front of a tall, somewhat dusty window; he sounded a near deafening blast. Before he'd even finished the last note, tendrils of ash were crawling through the open door and along the edges of the windows. Someone shouted a warning. Someone else called for the Shademaster again.

Cold fear slithered along his spine. These gusts of soot were like the shadows they'd seen in the hills, but they'd been surrounded by miles of nothing but wind and night. They didn't fit here. And if it meant there were walkers on the loose during the day too, that only made them all the more dangerous.

He palmed two of his daggers. Before he could cross the hallway to the room where Vex was, Culwen passed him by, a calculating look on his face. They were a few feet apart at best, but the man didn't notice him.

He had his hand on his rapier, and he checked to make sure he wasn't being followed before he slammed the door open. In a flash, Vax could make out his sister and the Shademaster, locked in a fight.

When Vex stumbled, Vax felt panic cut through him, and he leaped forward.

Before Culwen walked in and pushed the door closed, Vax caught it so he could follow. *"Vex!"*

Inside was pure chaos. Culwen descended on Derowen, while Vex staggered away from them both. Across the room, Thorn lay twitching in a pool of his own blood. Ash rolled across the walls and the floor, while a handful of walkers flocked around the Shademaster.

For a brief moment, Vax thought Culwen aimed to target the dead—then Culwen ran his rapier straight through Derowen's chest and Vax knew exactly what he'd meant when he said he wanted to get his affairs in order.

Before the spireling could shift his attention to Vex, Vax called out to her again. He held the door open and gestured to Vex to get away from Culwen. To get out of here. They couldn't handle this on their own.

If Vex trusted that this town could be better than it was, he trusted her.

"Go! Find help!"

DEROWEN STARED AT HER BROTHER in bewildered pain, and she clawed at the blade in her chest. He pulled it out and stabbed again, an inch or so lower.

"Why?" she croaked.

"Because you've damn near ruined us," he replied. He grabbed her by her uniform and pulled her closer, the rapier still between them. "I made enemies, when I bargained for your life in Kymal, and you ran away from me. I tracked you down and found you that bloody ring. All I demanded in return for saving your life and your little project of a town was loyalty. How could you have been so careless, Dera?"

"I didn't ruin us. You did. I protected us from you." She coughed and it racked through her. Her eyes glazed over as she turned her face in Vax's direction. "I protected Aswin from you."

Vax inched closer. Despite everything, he believed Derowen. He believed the pain of betrayal in her expression, the fear that coursed through her, and her insistence that she'd done everything for her daughter.

Culwen leaned in closer. "I will protect her now."

The light in Derowen's eyes broke.

Vax balanced the dagger in his hand, aimed, and sent it flying across the room. It skimmed one of the ashen corpses that was pushing through to get to Derowen, and buried itself deep into Culwen's shoulder. With a snarl, Culwen let go of Derowen. His sister slumped to the floor and the spireling reached out behind his head and coldly pulled the dagger out.

Vex wasn't the only one who could call for help. Still at the door, Vax pushed it open with his foot and, not looking behind him, shouted, "He's killing the Shademaster!"

The dagger came flying back toward him, and he ducked out of the way at the last second, reaching out a hand to keep his balance. He felt the blade cut toward him, and without considering the absurdity of the act he closed his fingers and plucked it out of the air. It was luck, more than anything, combined with deep cuts along the soft tissue of his fingers and in the palm of his hand.

He held the dagger and savored the look of fury on Culwen's face. "I changed my mind. I refuse to do business anymore." Vax flipped the blade over.

Confused voices and footsteps sounded behind him, two people lay dying in the room in front of him, and hungry dead were climbing in through the windows. This casual heist had cost far too much. He didn't wait for the door to open. He ran toward Culwen and brought his daggers up. And he fought.

It wasn't pretty. It wasn't how he usually fought. It wasn't how he'd been trained to fight. It was a fight for survival. He fought, because he was tired of everything breaking.

He held a dagger in each hand, and used every skill he had to stay alive. He closed in to stab at Culwen, and at the very last moment dashed away from the spireling's roving blades. He lunged at him and disengaged. His daggers tore through the fabric of Culwen's sleeve and the muscle and sinew of his forearm, and his parrying dagger cut into Vax's leg.

"Oath breaker," Culwen snarled.

Vax ducked to avoid another cut. He scoffed. "And you're a smuggler, a murderer, and a far worse brother than me. Not to mention, a fucking hypocrite. Now shut up and fight."

They both lashed out at each other, got too close, and backed away again. It wasn't a fight that followed rules, but one that hungered for death. When Vax stepped in to strike Culwen again, aiming his dagger for the soft spot above his clavicle, Culwen caught the weapon with his parrying blade, trapping it between the triple prongs. He twisted the dagger out of Vax's hand, sending it scattering across the floor. He immediately followed through with a shallow slash along his jaw.

Their blades were not the only ones that were ravenous.

The dead came closer. Ash walkers circled around Vax and snapped at him, their broken teeth glinting in the sunlight. For every corpse he slammed out of the way, another one pushed closer again. Sharp, bony fingers carved into his side, and ashen tendrils reached out and circled his throat. He felt like he was choking. He was breathing in ashes and no air, and for a moment he lost sight of Culwen.

The spireling turned away from him, and he dropped to his knees next to his sister's body, which lay unmoving under a thin blanket of gray dust, walkers closing in around them. Without hesitation, without apparent regret, Culwen sank his dagger into Derowen's chest a third time, like he wanted to be absolutely certain she wouldn't rise again. Ash immediately curled into the dagger wound, while Culwen reached for his sister's hand and frantically tried to pull the ring from her finger.

Vax steeled himself and pushed through. He leaped toward the spireling. He hit the floor and kept rolling, pushing himself back up on his knees. He came to a stop between the Shademaster's body and Thorn, who lay struggling and bleeding out, and he let his dagger fly.

The blade carved its path through the air and hit true. It tore a deep cut along the side of Culwen's neck. Culwen let Derowen's hand fall as he reached for the wound. Blood immediately coated his fingers and he groaned, while Vax reached for the last remaining blade in his boot.

The door swung open, and Culwen raised a bloody finger to point at Vax. "Stop him," he croaked. "He's killing the Shademaster!"

Vax felt the world slow down around him. He glanced around to see guards filter into the room, all of them showing the wear and tear of battle, and looks of anger and revulsion upon recognizing him. Or recognizing who they thought he was. Walkers prowled around him, their bones crackling, their claws scraping across the tiles. One of them still had patches of hair that fell in dead streaks in front of its gleaming eyes. They slashed at Vax.

He turned back to Culwen, who had turned away from the guards in the doorway and now used the cover that provided to slowly pull his dagger out of Derowen's body again. In a moment of absolute clarity, Vax knew that no one would stop Culwen from throwing the blade at him, and the spireling could have the weapon loose before he could pull his own. The corpses would tear away at him, and no one would stop them either.

None of the guards would believe him if he told them their beloved Shademaster was stealing from them with the help of her brother. She'd been a hero to all, and she'd done right by so many. He was an interloper who fought against them, and to everyone who entered the room it would look like her brother had valiantly tried to stop him from murdering her.

He heard the weapons being drawn. He saw the victorious leer on Culwen's face. He felt the onslaught of the dead.

He saw no way out.

Something cold and sleek slithered past his knee, and when he looked down, he found the green snake that kept Thorn company on his broody days. The snake curled up to Vax's knee and looked straight at Culwen, his tongue flicking in and out, and his serpentine body twisting and turning.

In a flash, Vax snapped into action. He kept his eyes on Culwen's hands as he withdrew his parrying dagger. With one hand, he curled his fingers around the hilt of his third dagger, and with the other he reached out to the snake.

He offered a silent apology to the belt-turned-animal, took a deep breath, and tossed the snake into Culwen's face.

The spireling reacted instinctively, raising both his hands to pull the slithering and hissing animal away from him, and in that second's distraction Vax retrieved the dagger from his boot, aimed, and threw.

The blade cut straight and deep into Culwen's throat, and blood streamed over the man's shirt. He dropped the snake and toppled over, groping desperately at his throat.

It was all Vax could focus on, while heavy footsteps and angry shouts closed in around him. Culwen's eyes dimmed, and his fingers slackened. Ash curled around him, reaching up from Derowen's corpse to cover and devour her brother too.

Vax lunged at both of them—and at the snake that had fallen between them. While the snake, affronted, slithered back to Vax and circled his arm before any guards could step on him, Vax swiped his fingers over Derowen's hand. Culwen had already loosened her ring enough that it easily disappeared into his sleeve.

He grabbed hold of his dagger and wildly lashed out at the walkers around him, as one tore into his leg, and another lurched toward his chest. He crawled backward, away from the dead. Away from the Shademaster. Away from the approaching guards.

"I didn't attack the Shademaster," he called out, before he breathed in a gust of ashes and started to cough. The cuts and bruises of the fight were catching up with him, and he felt the room spin. The loud footsteps of the guards echoed around him, and there were shouts of horror from new guards filtering in.

"It was her brother," Vax tried again. "He attacked first. I tried to stop him." He wanted to risk a glimpse at Thorn, to find out if he'd sent the snake. To find out if—

One of the walkers leaped on top of him, its decaying face pushed up close to him and a rotting tongue lolling out from between its teeth.

Vax shoved the creature off. His serpentine companion hissed angrily at it. But before either of them could do anything more, the guards circled around them and descended on the walkers and on Vax.

CHAPTER 39

The Shade Hall outside was chaos and despair. The whole town around her was crumbling, and everything hurt. Her chest throbbed and her heart ached and Vex still held on to a sword that was too heavy for her. The sea of corpses had found their way in here too, with sharp claws and predatory hunger. Vex felt the waves of fear roll off the guards who'd stayed to fight, the sound of battle clamoring all around her. She also saw their looks of shock and disgust when she passed them, but she could do nothing about those.

They'd helped her find Vax. She thought she'd helped them. She'd thought they'd cared, once.

Vax's voice still echoed in her ears. *Get help.* Culwen's snarl. *I'll deal with you and your brother later.*

She bore down on the quartermaster, who stood firm in the middle of the foyer, where he'd discarded the maps in favor of a mace. She stepped up to him like the weapon didn't register—because it barely did—and faced him. "Where's Wick? And where's Aswin?"

He narrowed his eyes at her, and anger flashed within them. Splotches of red appeared on his pale cheeks. Briefly, she thought he'd attack her, so she stepped closer until they were toe-to-toe and gave him her anger instead. "Where is Wick?" she repeated, the words slow and threatening.

He scanned the foyer for help from any of the other guards, who were all caught up in their own battles. She felt him tense and relent. "Outside," he snapped. "Wick is leading the fight in the square. Aswin is in her room, with your bear."

She grunted when a flare of pain coursed through her. "Good." She swayed and pressed a hand to her side. "Fuck."

She reached for the quartermaster's tunic and pulled him closer, in part to keep herself on her feet, too. "My brother and your Shademaster are in the antechamber down the hall. The Shademaster's brother is attacking them. They need help. You have to help them."

As if on cue, a shout echoed through the hallway. Vax's voice, but she couldn't make out the words over the clattering of swords and fearful voices. She just recognized the tone and the anguish that tore through her.

Confusion bled into the man's face, and he stared down at the sword Vex was carrying. He tensed when he recognized it. "How—"

"Help them," she half-shouted, half-begged. "Help my brother. Until I can get Wick."

With that, she let him go, and they both stumbled. She didn't stay to watch if he would help. She still wasn't sure he was on her side. She ducked out of his reach, swore at the stab of pain, and dodged past the remaining guards and ash walkers.

Vex reached for the tall door, and when she pushed it open, bright sunlight filtered in. Outside, the situation was worse. At least two dozen Shadewatch were fighting a legion of ashen dead.

It wasn't merely guards fighting either. Across the square, in The Scattered Bar, the innkeeper and his son leaned out of a second-floor window, shooting arrows at the creatures, while the miners' children threw plates and cups at them. The people in surrounding houses and buildings were doing the same thing—finding higher ground and using whatever projectiles they had to attack the creatures. Be it arrows, darts, earthenware, or in one case: buckets of waste. On top of one of the buildings at the southern edge of the square, Vex spotted a familiar gray-skinned young woman. She held a doll in one hand, and with the other she shot what appeared to be bolts of fiery light at the attackers.

Wick was in the thick of the battle. He swung his warhammer like it weighed nothing more than a stick, and the weapon *crunched* when it collided with one of the skeletal creatures.

Vex held the Shademaster's sword, mourning the fact that she didn't have her bow and arrows near, and joined the fray. She couldn't stop to think about the cause of the fight. She couldn't worry about her brother. She had to make her way to Wick as soon as possible.

She bit through the pain and slashed away at the corpses in her path. There wasn't a method or a strategy to it. She just kept the blade moving so she wouldn't drop it. The sword glanced off bone and long-dead flesh. It got stuck inside a slender walker's rib cage. A guard stepped in and cut into the creature with an ax while Vex twisted away. A third walker appeared where the first had fallen, and it slammed into the guard. It looked like a teenage girl, covered in dust, with the strength of the hills at her back.

Vex raised the sword and slammed it into the corpse's spine.

A step closer to Wick. The ash that exploded from the creatures reached for her, long tendrils crawling along her shoulder and neck. The taste of it in her mouth. She pushed herself past it. She felt breathless. A guard stepped back to dodge an attack when bony hands, the fingers sharp and bloody, slashed open his side.

Vex had to dodge out of the way when he fell toward her, still clinging to his ax. She felt the world twist and turn underneath her and nearly toppled over.

Directly in front of her now, two dwarves in Shadewatch uniforms were engaged with another trio of walkers, both guards fighting to reach the other. As she angled past them, one of the guards stumbled and fell, and two of the cursed walkers were immediately upon him, tearing into him, while the second guard screamed his fury and horror.

Wick was so close. He towered over all those present, and she called out to him. "Wick!"

He started, but didn't turn. His warhammer slammed into another ash walker, tearing through its shoulders and leaving behind a trail of ashes.

"Wick!"

Vex's shout was met with a growl that drowned out all the sounds around the square, and she swung around, recognizing it instantly. A large brown bear galloped out of the Shade Hall and roared at two cursed dwarvish creatures coming toward her, with hungry eyes and ferocious snarls. He stood on his hind legs and slammed them away before he tried to grab the shirt of the small girl in front of him.

Everything around Vex stopped. Her heart skipped a beat, and she nearly dropped the sword.

Because Aswin stood outside too. She had Vex's bag swung over one shoulder, dragging it through the dirt, and her quiver over the other. She held on to a bow that was a foot taller than she was and she fumbled with her arrow, while Trinket tried to pull her back before another ash walker could attack.

"Wick!" Vex screamed. *"Aswin!"*

She ran. Away from the half-giant and toward the little girl and her bear. Vex felt the heads around her turn, heard others pick up her call, but all she could see was the ashen figure that bore down on Aswin as the girl shrugged herself out of her coat and out of Trinket's grasp. She dropped the bow and instead held the arrow like a sword in front of her, and Vex knew it would do absolutely nothing for her.

She desperately lengthened her stride.

The decaying figure, its face a contortion of ash and bones, reached out a hand, ready to strike, and Vex knew she wouldn't be able to get her sword up between them in time, so she did the only thing she could do. She jumped and skidded to a halt between Aswin and the dead figure, shielding the girl with her body and taking the brunt of the attack herself. She felt the sharp claws of the creature rake across her shoulders and arms. At the same time, she had to dodge out of the way to keep Aswin from accidentally stabbing her with the arrow.

"Trinket!" She let go of the sword and picked up Aswin in one fluid motion, still keeping the ash walker behind her. She felt her arms tremble, her vision narrow, and blood trickle down her back. Aswin stared at her, wild-eyed.

"What are you *doing* here?" Vex demanded.

Aswin jutted her chin out. "I wanted to be brave like you, so I went to find your weapons. I wanted to do like you said. If you keep fighting, no matter how scary they are, the monsters can never win. And I don't want them to win."

Fuck it. She unceremoniously lifted the girl onto Trinket's back, all the while bracing herself for another attack. She kept her eyes on her bear. She was going to be sick. "Take her inside. Go!" Trinket grunted.

Vex turned to Aswin. "Your mother will be so proud of you, but next time, she'll have to find you weapons that fit, all right?"

Aswin's bottom lip trembled. She nodded. She curled up atop the bear, her knees to her chest. She pulled her bag and her quiver over her shoulders and handed them to Vex with small, determined hands. "I just wanted to help."

"I know." Vex found herself swallowing past a sudden lump in her throat. "Right now, the best way to help is to stay inside."

Aswin frowned but before she could argue, another voice spoke up. "Kela and Yorn will stay with her and *not* let her out of their sight."

Vex turned to find Wick standing over the shattered skeleton of an ash walker, gesturing at two dwarven guards to accompany Trinket and Aswin. Wick had hooked his warhammer on his belt, and he held Derowen's sword in his hand. He looked at Vex, his eyes impossibly deep and full of hurt.

She scooped her bow off the ground and hissed when the deep slashes across her arms and shoulders reminded her of their presence, when the cut to her side blossomed with pain. It felt right to have her bow in her hands again, but her balance shifted and tilted.

"Careful." Wick reached out to steady her, and when his hand clamped around her upper arm, she felt a warm glow spread through her. She flinched away before she leaned into it. His touch lessened the agony but not the anguish.

He kept holding on to her and showed her the sword. His hand was shaking. "Care to explain this?"

She thought of all the lies she'd told him—or at the very least implied—just the night before and winced. Jorenn had looked so different then. Now, everything she needed to say tumbled right out of her. "Derowen's in danger. She's using the ring to summon the walkers. We need your help. Do you trust me?"

Wick looked to Trinket, running toward the Shade Hall with Aswin on his back, and a whole range of emotions coursed through him. Relief. Anger. Anguish. He shook his head in confusion. "I probably shouldn't, but yes. Where is she?"

The words warmed her beyond reason. They made her feel better than the healing had—and infinitely worse at the same time. "Antechamber off the main hall. She was fighting with her brother when I ran out." She began to make her way there and immediately had to pick up the pace when Wick darted past. He took the steps to the great doors two at a time, and she followed breathlessly.

"Culwen? *Why?*" He swung around and looked at Vex, and all color drained from his face.

The sword slipped out of his fingers, and when he tried to catch it, he cut himself on the edge instead. "No."

He tightened his grip around the blade and shook his head. *"No."* And he was off in the direction Vex indicated, pushing past guards and shadows, past the great hall and the men who called out to him. He slammed one of the skeletal walkers out of the way with such force, its bones scattered.

"Wick, wait!"

The door to the antechamber was open, and guards ran in and out. Vex's blood grew cold when she approached, when she heard only soft murmurs inside.

Wick burst in, and immediately skidded to a halt, Vex three steps behind him. Her breath caught. The sounds from the fight were muted here. The oppressive silence inside was far worse.

The guard who'd called out to Wick caught up a second too late. He was a young man, with strands of red hair clinging to his face. He was deadly pale. "Wick, the Shademaster, she's—Derowen is dead."

VEX FELT LIKE SHE WAS rooted in place. In the center of the room, on the bloodstained carpet and flanked by guards on either side, lay two bodies. Cloaks had been draped over them both, but their faces remained uncovered. Derowen looked peaceful in death, more so than she had in the last hour that Vex had spent with her. Lines of strength and determination still contoured her face, while Culwen's expression was twisted in shock and anger.

"No!" Wick stumbled and dropped to his knees beside Derowen. He let her sword fall to the ground. He reached for the pendant around his neck and placed his other hand on her chest. Vex couldn't look away from him. She could hear him mutter something, over and over again. She couldn't make out the words, but he sounded increasingly desperate. Wick balled his fist. He pounded Derowen's chest. But the Shademaster remained calm and still in death.

Wick *keened*. His shoulders twisted inward and he turned to Vex. "Why? What happened?"

Vex took a step back, away from him and the ferocity of his grief. "I didn't do this." She shook her head. She scrambled for an explanation, but none would come. She could only stare in horror too.

They'd come here to find a solution. When she'd run out of the room, she'd left Derowen and Culwen to fight, but she hadn't given it more thought. She hadn't considered this outcome. For all that they'd found themselves on opposite sides of an argument, Derowen was supposed to still be here. To be proud of Aswin. To protect the town from the ash walkers that were flooding it. And where was—

"My sister didn't do anything." Vex's heart leaped at the familiar voice. Vax stood in the far corner of the room, his wrists bound tightly together. He had cuts and bruises across his face and neck. His daggers were taken from him, and a serpentine belt curled around his arm. "Culwen killed the Shademaster. He coerced her into stealing from Jorenn's mines. And I killed Culwen."

On top of the table behind him lay a third body, though Thorn wasn't covered with a cloak, and despite being pale as death, the ghost of a peaceful smile on his face, his chest still rose and fell. Clouds of ashes rolled over the floor underneath him and around Vax's feet, but it was less threatening here than it had been in the foyer and especially outside. The broken remains of moldering corpses lay all about the room. Vax's gaze skimmed over the guards, over the quartermaster who stood watching him from a distance and finally settled back on Wick. "He's dying too." He nodded toward Thorn, and tremors of fury racked his body. "Your guard refuses to let healers come close to him."

"He's one of the outlaws," a young female guard protested. "He woke the ash walkers, Wick. He brought them here."

Wick turned to the guard, who immediately snapped her mouth shut, though the half-giant man seemed to have barely registered the words. He stared at Vax and then tore his gaze back to Vex.

"*Why?*" Wick asked again, and his voice was like rocks breaking, like glass shattering. He'd picked up Derowen's sword again and held it so tightly blood ran down his arm. He didn't even seem to notice how deep the blade cut.

Vax sighed. His Shadewatch uniform was torn up and bloody. "She wanted to secure her daughter's future. And Culwen held that girl over her head as a threat."

Wick opened his mouth and closed it again. A desperate rage consumed him, and his gaze shifted from Derowen's body to that of her brother. He got to his feet and walked over to him. With a guttural roar, he plunged her sword into Culwen's chest. He gestured to the guard.

"Get his body out of here. Now. Find the miner a healer, and untie the half-elf. Head to the town square if you can."

Wick didn't stop to see if his words were obeyed. He raked his fingers through his hair, leaving bloodstains across his face, and he knelt by Derowen's side. He held her hand and squeezed it tight. "Oh, Dera. Aswin needs you. Jorenn needs you. You should have come to me. Why didn't you come to me? What do we do now?"

The same question echoed in Vex's ears. There was only one answer she could think of.

Call them off.

She needed her brother.

Across the room, Vax's eyes met hers, and she rushed over to him. She snarled at the guards who got in her way, and she slid the bag Aswin had returned to her off her shoulder. She dug around until she felt the blunt edges of the vials and the jar of salve she'd bought back in Westruun and she grabbed it. The antivenin would be useless. The herbal salve wouldn't do much in the way of aiding Thorn either, but perhaps it would help stem the bleeding. It would give him time. Maybe. She placed it next to Vax, grabbed her belt knife, and began to cut through the rope around his wrists. Her hands trembled.

"Are you okay? Do you need a healer too? The town is being overrun, we have to find a way to—"

"Vex . . ." Vax's shoulders had slumped when Wick had called for a healer, and now relief broke through on his face. He opened up his hands. Halfway through cutting rope, Vex stopped. She stared.

On her brother's palm, something sparkled. Between his bound hands, he held an intricate silver band with dark cloudy gems and shards of bone. Blood speckled the familiar stone.

That cursed piece of jewelry that brought them here in the first place. Vex breathed out hard. "You stole it?"

"I recovered it," he said.

She reached for it but didn't pick it up. It wasn't just the ring Vax held in his hands. It was so much more. It was the start of this disaster. The cause of this fucking mess. The solution they hadn't even dared to hope for. It meant safety for the two of them. "A simple heist. That fucking piece of shit."

The ring meant safety for the town too.

"Definitely not my style." Vax turned the silver band around between his fingers, before he looked at her intently. "What does it do, Vex? It will get rid of the ash walkers?"

"*Yes.*" Vex pushed the last pieces of rope away. She held Vax's wrist, clung to him, and glanced over her shoulder at the entrance to the room, to the guards who were running out to join the fight once more. "I thought it was just about raising a barrier. Here. In the mines. But the dead react to the ring. Or those stormy gems," she said. Some of her own hurt and confusion bled through. She swallowed hard. "Derowen found a way to control the ash walkers. She summoned them when we fought. That's why they attacked today."

Vax stilled. "*She* summoned them?"

Vex gestured at the remains of the walkers around them. At the dead and the wounded. She knew he'd put the pieces together. "They were as focused on her as the ones we saw in the hills last night were on Jorenn."

"Fuck." He blanched. "I thought they used the distraction from the attacks to sneak out. I even told Culwen that it was such a good cover for their smuggling. And the miners . . ." He curled his fingers around the ring and squeezed so tightly his knuckles went bone white. "All that time, the two of them let Thorn and the others think *they* were the only monsters."

Vax hesitated. He glanced over his shoulder at Thorn, and she could see his thoughts churn. See him weigh every element and every decision. "You believe there's something worth fighting for in this cursed town?"

"There is." There was. Despite everything, there was.

"And you've seen Derowen use the ring? Create that barrier?"

She nodded.

"Then I think you need to figure out how to use the bloody thing," he said. "Use it to send those fucking corpses away again."

"Are you sure?" Vex lowered her voice as relief coursed though her. "Vax, this is what we came here for. If we used the ring to help get rid of the walkers, I don't see how we can get it back—"

"Screw the Clasp." Vax's whisper was fierce and determined. "There's a little girl who won't have her mother. Let's at least try to protect her home." Vax pushed the ring into her hands, and Vex slipped the jar of salve in his, and they held on to each other. "Someone here should do something good for a change, Vex. Show them what you're capable of. We'll figure out today's problems today. The rest is for tomorrow."

CHAPTER 40

A *little girl who won't have a mother.*

Derowen looked so much kinder in death, but tension ticked along Wick's jaw. The shouts and screams of battle were everywhere. Vex couldn't tell if he'd heard every word or he had been lost in thought while he softly combed Derowen's hair around her face, but when she walked closer, he immediately got to his feet and turned to her. "Dera did this." A flat statement. A question he couldn't ask.

"We fought. That's how all of this started. We fought and Aswin walked in, and she was upset. She called the walkers." Vex tried to find the right words. "For what it's worth, I don't think she meant to do this. Not today."

"But other days?" he asked.

She couldn't deny that. She could only be relieved that he didn't know, and that relief hurt too. "She did what her brother told her to do."

"May I see the ring?" Wick sounded defeated and worn.

When she placed it in his palm, he curled his hand into a fist around it. He closed his eyes and when he opened them again, something inside his gaze had shattered. He didn't meet Vex's look of concern but instead snapped his fingers, and when the remaining guards turned to him, he cleared his throat. "Double the guard near Aswin's room, immediately. I won't have her accidentally wander in here or out to the town square again." He pointed at Thorn and Vax. "And aid them. Whatever they need."

He held out the ring to Vex once more. "I don't know if I can make this right. I don't even know if I can make it better. But I can try. Will you let me help you?"

She shook her head. She needed to give him the chance. "You should be the one to use it. I don't know if I can."

"I'd rather not even touch it," Wick admitted with a wince.

Vex looked at him, and for a moment it felt like she saw every side of him. The anger and defensiveness when she'd appeared on the palisades. The gentleness when he walked around town. And his utter loss now. He still towered over her, but he looked so much smaller.

She grabbed the ring and gestured toward the square. "How then? We need to put an end to this fight."

"We can't push through the palisades, but there's another option. Follow me."

She expected him to go back to the square. Instead he led her deeper into the Shade Hall, with all its bright colors. The carmine-and-silver drapes that ran along the staircase seemed to mock them as they climbed the stairs to the second floor. The paintings that hung in the hallways taunted them when Wick led Vex to a meeting room that overlooked the square, the ash walkers, the guards, the carnage. Despite the Shademaster's death, the fight hadn't lessened. The guards and townspeople who were wounded and dying were still wounded and dying, and the dead tore into their adversaries. There was so much needless bloodshed.

"The fight in the mines was cruel," Vex said. "And so is this. Cruel and pointless."

"Jorenn looked like this when we arrived here," Wick admitted. "And when the first ash walkers came, they wouldn't be stopped by palisades or guards. There'd be fighting in the streets too. We tried to make it better. I truly believed we did."

Wick shuddered. He pushed open a double set of doors that led to a narrow balcony. From here, Vex could see everyone fight, from guard to doll maker. From broken ash walkers to desperate survivors.

"When you came, the people you hunted and killed still had a home here," she said quietly, remembering Thorn's words.

Wick shrank at that. He nodded at the silver ring she rolled between her fingers. "I never asked questions about that bloody ring when Culwen first showed up with it. Derowen asked me not to, because she thought it would offend her brother. Just like she told me not to rise to his shitty comments, and I did my best to protect her from his ire. She told me he always came to her aid, and that was what mattered. Besides, she knew what the magic did, so why fuss about it?" He stared out at the town. "I didn't. I should have, and I didn't. I trusted her when she told me it was meant to protect us. I failed her when I promised to protect her— even if it meant protecting her from herself. I failed them too." He nodded at the battle below.

Vex didn't say anything to that, because there was nothing to say. She couldn't absolve him from his pain or his guilt. "We will help now," she said, empathetically.

She placed the ring on her palm. It was strange to look at it. A simple piece of jewelry, woven into the very fabric of the town itself, and with it the fates of too many people. A simple piece of jewelry with stones that had once been part of a curse or part of fractured wards that kept ashen creatures at bay. A casual heist. It had never been anything of the sort. "What do I do with this? I don't think it protects, but it does control."

"How fitting then that Culwen was the one to bring it here," Wick said. Something ugly and painful flitted across his face, and he pushed it away before he followed Vex out onto the balcony. He rubbed his eyes before he unhooked his warhammer from his belt. When he spoke again, his voice was soft and neutral. "Derowen always preferred a place where she could see the whole battlefield."

She nodded. He waited for her to find a good lookout position. Somewhere where she could survey the whole square, while shouts and screams echoed around them.

As soon as she found the right spot, Wick took up position behind her, his warhammer loosely in his hands, to be able to protect her if the need arose. The staunchest of guardians. "Now focus on it."

"How?" Vex rolled the ring between her fingers. "Derowen must have summoned them when we were fighting. She was out of sorts and frightened. But she knew what she was doing, and I don't."

Wick closed his eyes and swallowed hard. "You're an archer. Focus on it like you would a target. Nothing else but you and the target."

"And the bow and arrow," she supplied.

He shrugged. "Like that, except with a ring."

Vex picked up the ring and slowly slipped it on.

Gems the color of thunderstorms, that's how Thorn had described the gems his sister had found in the depths of the mines before the ash walkers. Cloudy, stormy gems that had kept the cursed dead in the dark below, before they crawled out and tore through towns, upended families, killed travelers.

Vex didn't have experience with magical artifacts beyond the theoretical, beyond what her teachers in Syngorn taught her. She barely had experience with *magic*, beyond the slightest of powers that she felt in the nature around her. It was a kernel. A seed, nothing more. Some days in the wild, when she lost herself in the tracks she followed and in foraging what flourished around her, she felt an awareness of the magic of nature.

But she did know storms and the mines. She did know the feel of rocks and gems and raw power. She understood what death was supposed to be; she was a hunter, after all.

And she had experience with protecting people. She'd come to disagree with Derowen on so many things, but she didn't disagree with her on this: she wanted this strange, complicated town to thrive. She wanted Aswin to belong and be safe. Like Derowen had deserved to be safe.

She thumbed the ring. If Vax told her he believed in her, she knew she could do this.

"We'll talk when this is all over," she promised Wick before she turned her attention to the square outside. "I'll tell you everything we found out about Derowen and Culwen."

She twisted the ring around her finger and focused on the scene in front of her. Ash walkers crawled across the square and the wind rustled, blowing up clouds of dust and sand around them. The Shadewatch tried to push them back. The children in the inn had found or been given slingshots, which they used with abandon. The cursed dead fought hard, and the townspeople fought harder.

The rolling ash reminded Vex of the first night on the palisades, where she'd shot side by side with Culwen without even knowing who he was. Of Aswin, hiding out in the guard post to be closer to her mother. And of her own despair at the thought of Vax being a fight, a night, and a magic barrier away.

But he was here now, and this had to end.

She focused on the ring. The silver, warm to the touch. The clouds inside the gems that almost seemed alive. She stopped twisting it around and felt the warmth of the ring spread through her.

The air shimmered around her, and the wind picked up.

On the square below, some of the creatures stumbled and hesitated. A dwarven guard with a large ax hacked into one of them while Beryl took out another with her magic bolts.

Vex breathed in deeply and let the warmth of the ring spread through her. She felt the wind swirl around her, and she zeroed in on one of the walkers in the center, like she would if she were drawing her bow. She kicked her feet wider. She needed to ground herself well. She needed to be able to pull her weight.

Vex breathed until there was nothing left but her and the target. She breathed and *released*, targeting the ring's magic like she'd loosen an arrow. Like a bolt of lightning that she could send through the sky with unerring accuracy, because while she may struggle to hold a sword too heavy for her, *this* was how she fought. Hard, fast, true.

She aimed for one of the walkers, and it stopped dead in its tracks while the others around it continued to fight the guard tooth and claw. Right behind it, an ashen skeleton tore into one of the townspeople, while a young guard helplessly tried to hack away at it.

Vex shuddered. Fuck, she didn't need an arrow. She needed to find a way to push them all back.

She released the creature, and it went sprawling to the ground. She focused her attention on the ring instead, the shimmering of the stones. The storm, and a degree of power that took her breath away. She pushed. Away from Aswin, who'd tried to fight them all with a bow too large for her. Away from the miners' children, who'd gone from seeing their small group of survivors torn apart to ashen corpses attacking. Away from Beryl, who'd been kind to her for no other reason than that she could. Away from this fucking Shade Hall with all its fucking heartache.

Vex felt the tide turn. The ash walkers might prowl and attack everyone who got too close, but they were no match for an entire town fighting together. They were no match for her.

She imagined a barrier, and she waited for it to spring into life with lightning and thunder.

It didn't.

There was no flash in the sky. No bright, shimmering barrier that circled the palisades or spread out from the town square. No wave of magic that told the townspeople they were safe, or that eradicated all the cursed dead.

She panicked, at first. Certain she'd done something wrong. She could feel the connection with the dead, the ash, the silver, the tunnels that meandered through the depths below.

She pushed out again, *hard*.

Still, there was no flash. No grand gesture. Instead, there was simply quiet. There was the wind that tousled her hair.

The ash walkers stopped.

One by one, they began to disengage and retreat. A handful of them skittered in the direction of the miners' gate, back to the hills. The guards circled another group, working together to dispatch them with the help of townspeople armed with spades, shovels, and even a few slingshots. The cursed corpses pulled away from the Shade Hall. Away from Vex. She pushed harder—and before the guard could regroup and overwhelm them, they fled.

AND THE TOWN WAS SILENT.

The wind that cascaded around them picked up the ash that remained and scattered it far beyond the town. Back to the hills, until it re-formed again.

A breath, before members of the Shadewatch spread across the square to pick up their fallen comrades and help the wounded inside. A breath, before the townspeople disappeared back into their houses. A breath, while the children in the inn carefully celebrated, because someone had to.

It was the same potent sense of relief that Vex had felt that first night, and at the same time it was nothing like that. It was exhaustion and pain and grief.

And silence.

"Thank you," Wick said simply, because there was nothing else to say.

Vex took a step and stumbled. She sagged down to the floor, her back against the wall, while across the room Vax leaned against the wall, apparently having found his way to them. His wounds were bandaged and his pride was palpable. He mouthed an *I told you so.* She exhaustedly flipped him off.

She stared up at Wick instead. His light-gray skin was even paler, and the mourning lines around his face were so sharp they might as well have been cut with a knife. She twisted the ring around and around her finger, and with a rough voice that echoed against the emptiness outside, she told him everything she knew. From uncovering the notebook to her disastrous conversation with Derowen and everything she'd learned about Thorn and his miners. The survivors on the ledge. The stories Vax told her. The list of names.

Wick sat down next to her, and she told him about Culwen and Derowen's fear. The coin that the Shademaster had stolen on behalf of her brother, with the town and Wick being none the wiser.

"I trusted every single word Derowen told me," Wick said. He tried to elaborate and his jaw worked, but no words made it past his lips. Her heart went out to him. Despite everything, she couldn't be certain that he had nothing to do with this. But she believed he didn't. *Some people are more important to me than my own life, Wick, though neither of us would freely admit that.*

"She cared so much about you," she said. "You were her truest friend, and maybe that's why she wanted to protect you from what Culwen did to her."

"Besides, he threatened to hurt Aswin if she didn't comply," Vax added softly. "She wasn't blameless in this, but she was the victim too."

Wick didn't say anything. He turned toward the balcony, hands clasped behind his back. His shoulders trembled.

"I thought we were doing better. I thought we could *be* better. Derowen had such visions for Jorenn . . ." His voice trailed off, and his pain was so raw.

"She told me," Vex said, though she had to push the words past her lips, Derowen's other words still ringing in her ears. *It's how you tell the story that counts.* "And she succeeded too, in some ways. I've seen how much the people in this town care for one another. I see how at home Aswin feels here. None of that is a lie."

She recalled Thorn's words. "But it was also only ever true for some people."

Wick flinched but he didn't deny it. She reached for his hand and squeezed hard, and before she could stop herself, she pressed the ring into his fingers. "You know we came to steal it," she admitted. She glanced at Vax, who'd listened quietly and nodded. "We came to steal it because of what she did and who she got entangled with. But I think . . . you should keep Fracture here. Use it or find someone who will. Keep the ash walkers away permanently and finish what you started. For both of you."

Because if they did, this town was something worth fighting for.

Wick looked down at the ring. "I would give it to you in a heartbeat, but I don't know how to tell the people of Jorenn that they've lost both their Shademaster and the one thing that kept them safe."

"It wasn't entirely what kept them safe," she said.

"No," he admitted. He grimaced. "They believed her stories too."

"And the barrier. However she made it." She mulled it over. The flash and the theater were the tale she told too. Her visible power. They all served the same purpose of trying to distract people from what was really going on.

"Another one of Culwen's strange finds?" Wick tucked the ring into his shirt pocket. "I'll figure it out."

She looked out over the town square, where blood marred the dusty ground and the innkeeper's son was running around collecting arrows, while the Shadewatch healers were already busy with those too wounded to be carried in.

Perhaps she believed a few too many of Derowen's stories too. She understood wanting to cling to them, when reality amidst these hills was harsh and unyielding. "You'll have to tell them someday."

"At least this is a harmless lie." Wick sighed and got to his feet. "What do I do, Vex? I can make decisions, but I'm no leader. Not like Derowen was. I don't know how we can stay. I don't know where else to go. And this is all the home Aswin has ever known."

Vex swallowed hard, and she righted herself. She swung her bow over her shoulder and tugged her hair behind her ears, where she could feel her feathers. "Then you make it into the home that she would want it to be. You owe it to that little girl, and you owe it to the people who died to make it a haven for Derowen's schemes, when it should have been their haven all along. You tell them the truth."

AND VEX HAD TO TELL the truth too.

When the town square was scrubbed clean and the wounded were patched up by the healers, when the dead were counted and when the fight left the town, when Trinket finally found his way back to the twins, Vex went looking for Aswin.

Jorenn Village should have been a haven for a brave little girl too, but Vex knew it had been turned into a nightmare. And she knew she had to tell Aswin the truth.

Vex found her curled up in one of the chairs in Derowen's sitting room, two very uncomfortable guards standing outside. Aswin was staring at the wall with a forlorn expression on her face. It was equal parts confusion and grief, like she was aware something awful had transpired around her, but her brain refused the overwhelming horror of the situation.

Vex knelt down in front of her. "Aswin."

The girl didn't reply. She bit on the nail of her thumb.

"Darling," Vex tried.

The girl slowly turned to her, her large green eyes older than they had been. It made Vex want to scream her own rage. It hurt to see her like this. It was unfair. But she knew fair had very little to do with the choices people made and the consequences others suffered. She just wanted Aswin to survive and make it through to the other side without losing too much of herself. Not like she sometimes felt she had.

When Vex reached out to take Aswin's hand, she inadvertently flinched back. Vex simply grabbed onto the armrest of the chair and kept a space between them.

"It hurts," the girl muttered.

"I know it does," Vex said softly. "And I'm sorry."

"I want my mama to wake up." Aswin wiped at the silent tears running down her cheeks and nose. Earlier that day, she'd screamed and sobbed but even in her exhaustion she couldn't stop crying.

Vex wanted to brush her tears away too. She wanted to hold her and tell her everything would be all right, but instead she breathed in deeply. "Remember what I told you? Remember what you told me out on the square?"

"If you just keep fighting, no matter how scary they are, the monsters can never win," Aswin mumbled.

"Exactly." Vex swallowed. "I was wrong, darling. The truth is, sometimes the monsters do win. Sometimes, no matter how hard you fight, it won't be enough. And it hurts, and it makes it real hard to be brave."

"I don't want to be brave today." Aswin curled up further, her knees pulled up all the way to her chin.

"Then you don't have to be. No one knows how to be brave all the time. But do you know what?"

"What?"

"Even if the monsters won today, they won't win every day. And maybe it feels almost impossible to be brave now, but you're not alone here, darling. When you're scared or sad, Wick can help you, just like you can help him too, because sometimes it's easier to be brave together. When you think you can't, you can still try. And then, I promise you, one day the monsters won't win. Because even though daylight doesn't stop dragons, someday *someone* will, as long as we fight for it."

"And ash walkers too?" Aswin asked with a small voice.

"And ash walkers too," Vex said softly. She lifted the chain with the small copper bear figurine over her head, and slowly placed it around Aswin's neck instead. Aswin grabbed the bear. Her emerald eyes scarcely focused on it, as she turned it this way and that, and eventually, she wrapped her small fingers around the chain and held it close.

"Will you be brave too?" she asked, looking up at Vex. "When you're scared?"

Vex didn't quite meet her eyes, but she stared at the copper bear instead, at the way it bounced against Aswin's hand, and every single facet and maker's mark as it caught the light, and in it she saw a little girl on a bear with a bow that was far too tall for her, a talented craftsperson with curious eyes, and two young half-elven twins fighting monsters in a horrible poachers' camp. And she smiled.

"Of course I will," Vex promised. She could try to be, at least.

CHAPTER 41

The guards Vax had seen at the gate when he sneaked in were gone, dismissed by Wick. Vax briefly wondered how many stealthy girls like the one he'd seen on his way in had taken advantage of that opportunity, of being able to walk out instead of sneak out. Not any of the smugglers in the Shademaster's employ, but apprentices and messengers and thieves, each of them hankering for adventure, for something more or something better.

The unconventional path he'd followed, across ridges and rocks, looked a fair bit more dangerous by daylight, but today, they could simply follow the mountain path toward the large boulder near the entrance of the mines. While Trinket led the way, Vax stayed close to Vex.

He nudged her softly, and she glanced over and smiled.

When they left the town behind, Vax looked at Wick. Vax had only crossed paths with the half-giant once before everything fell apart, but between that and Vex's stories, it had been enough to see how his gentle demeanor and his teasing words had made way for a heavy responsibility and a deep grief that only let up whenever Wick was with Aswin.

Right now he kept his eyes on the boulder ahead, and the half-elf who stood next to it.

Thorn leaned heavily against the rock and stared out at the town below. He'd have new scars to show for his brush with death, and he looked wan and exhausted, but he was here. In the end, that was what mattered.

Vax knew Thorn and Wick had spoken. Carefully, cautiously, comparing notes and stories, guilt and pain, comparing the Jorenn Village that was and could be.

Wick had released the survivors and captives immediately after the fight, while he'd given Thorn a place to recover in the Shade Hall, much to the discontent of many of the guards there. Sencha had stayed to look after Thorn those first few days—because she didn't trust the Shade-watch with her foolish boy, she'd said—but Faril had led the others back to the cavern without hesitation. Freedom felt like a trap to them. Both they and the townspeople were mourning their own losses, and they needed to be able to do so in peace.

Thorn had been the last who stayed. Until today, when he'd invited the twins and Wick up to this boulder. When they walked closer, he took a deep breath and tenderly traced a spot of stone. "I wanted to say good-bye."

"To us?" Wick asked, his voice oddly stricken.

"To my sister," Thorn said. "And to you too."

The boulder next to him was full of names. Carved into them, mag-ically burned into them, even shaped into the stone. Vax walked up to it and traced names shallowed by age and weather. Names that crossed others or existed on different levels, with paints that bled over carvings.

"When we still worked the mines, we left our names here," Thorn explained. "Every single one of us, on the first day we went down below, gave our names to the rock, so the mines would recognize us. My own is somewhere on top, because I wanted no one else to be able to reach it. Anissa's is right here."

Vax took a step closer and, when Thorn nodded his permission, looked. Anissa's name had been carved deep into the stone, the letters so neat, it had to have been done by magic. The deep letters were filled with small pieces of rock in all colors, slivers of gems, shards of glass, and sand to fill the spaces in between. It was chaotic, and well loved.

"I have to go back to my people," Thorn said. "I thought it was time I left her here. She's been with us long enough."

"You and your people are welcome back in Jorenn," Wick said with a sense of urgency. "I'd see to it that you are safe. It'll be a long path for all of us, and not everyone would agree, but we can be more than our worst decisions. I cannot bring your loved ones back, but I can offer you homes and protection. While we both have pasts to reckon with, I want us to be able to look to the future and learn."

"We don't want to come back," Thorn said immediately. He hesitated, and amended, "At least I don't think so. We carry the weight of too many empty homes too. But I will take your offer back to the survivors." He traced the name once more, and straightened. When he took a step away from the boulder, he looked more at ease than Vax had ever seen him. "Perhaps some of them wouldn't mind."

"When will you go back to the cavern?" Vax asked.

Thorn glanced at the sky overhead, the uneven layer of clouds and the patches of sunlight, before he met Vax's gaze. "Today is as good a time as any."

"Then perhaps it's time we travel back to Westruun too, don't you think?" Vex asked, with a smile to Vax. "We can see you safely there first."

Thorn smiled at her with appreciation. "I'd like that."

"I'd like that too," Vax admitted.

"I wouldn't," Wick said. He kept alternating between staring at the boulder and looking over the town that spread out in the embrace of the hills. Now he met Thorn's gaze. "But I understand it. In your place I would have left days ago. I'm grateful that you stayed and helped me figure things out." He rubbed his face with a large hand. "Gods, rebuilding this town terrifies me, and I'm not sure I'm the right man for the job—"

"You are," Thorn interrupted him, his tone brooking no argument.

Wick winced but acknowledged the words. "Thank you. I'll try to live up to that."

"Besides, I'm still here. Your guard knows where to find me, should you need me."

"Let's find a way to make this place better than our mistakes." Wick held out a hand to Thorn. And Vax couldn't help but wonder if this would mark a new beginning for them both, if something good could come out of this nightmarish place, or if in time they'd forget and go back to the way things were. The town above and the town underground, and a fracture between.

Thorn hesitated for a small eternity, then he reached out and clasped Wick's forearm. "Tell your miners to continue the custom. The hills should know them too."

VAX KICKED AT A PILE of ash, and in retaliation, it didn't move. The gray and somber hills around them were as colorless as they had been the first time they both had laid eyes on them, but the difference was that they now knew what lay beneath the shroud that blanketed the place.

When they reached the shadegrass meadow they'd found on their way out of the mines, Vex stood at the edge for a long time, staring down at Jorenn Village in silence. Vax wasn't sure that either of them would ever want to come back here.

He turned to the stack of rocks she'd placed as a way sign and tried to figure out exactly what they meant and how to read them. She'd tried to teach him survival skills on at least a dozen different occasions, but to no avail. He recognized the pattern, but not how to interpret it.

He picked up one rock and replaced it again. Then another.

"You know, I can just tell you where the bloody notebook is." Vex's voice held tired amusement, but amusement nonetheless.

He wasn't so easily swayed. "I have to be able to figure this out somehow. Isn't this supposed to be easy?"

He picked up another rock, and she chuckled.

At the edge of the meadow, Thorn laughed too, a rich, musical sound that Vax realized he'd never heard before. "I'm glad it wasn't the lack of fresh air that made him so stubborn. I was beginning to feel responsible."

"Oh no, he's always been like that," Vex supplied generously.

Vax turned around. "If you two need a moment to discuss me, I can hide out in those underground passages again."

"If you can find the way," Vex suggested cheerfully. She walked over and knelt down next to him, removing another set of rocks and digging at the fresh earth underneath. Within an instant, she was plucking at the fabric of his cloak.

Vax smiled ruefully and looked over his shoulder at Thorn, who smirked. "I can't believe you found a way out here. Even I didn't know it existed, and we've spent generations exploring the caverns and ways. I'm excited to find out where it leads."

Vex pulled up the cloak and unfolded it. A blush crawled up to her cheeks. "I guess I'm good with underground spaces."

"Better than your brother." Thorn wiggled his eyebrows at him.

She cleaned the notebook and tossed the dirty cloak at Vax. "Believe me, I know."

"Cute. Both of you." Vax caught the cloak and dusted it off before slipping it on despite the streaks of mud and soil. It felt cold and uncomfortable, but it was also a decent reminder of Westruun. Of getting back on the road.

Thorn winked at Vex. "If only I'd met you first, I would've known I got the lesser end of the bargain."

"I do like him." Vex's laughter rolled across the hills, her blush ran deeper, and it made this desolate place look brighter for a moment.

"You would," Vax grumbled, without any real force behind it.

The teasing made them all feel better, but Vax couldn't deny the note of finality to Thorn's words, especially when the miner walked over to the side of the hill where a narrow passage led back underground, and ran his fingers over the stony surface.

He'd move on, and he was right to.

"Where will you go?"

Thorn pulled up one shoulder in a half shrug. The other arm was healing, but he hadn't regained full movement yet. The Shadewatch healer doubted he would, given how extensive his wounds had been. "Away." He nibbled at his lip. "I'm not trying to be secretive and keep it from you. I simply don't know yet. I don't think anyone will make their home in Jorenn again, but I have to talk Wick's offer through with everyone who went back to the cavern." He sighed. "After that . . . We'll see who's left, what we can do here while we stay, and who will want to take us." A bottomless grief opened up in his eyes when he tried to smile, and some of his anger slipped through. "Easier to find a home though. Now that there are only so few of us left."

"Thorn . . ." Vax reached out a hand, and the other half-elf flinched away from it.

That same mask of pride and determination he'd seen so many times over the past week closed over his smile. "Don't. Don't give me your pity or your guilt. Remember what I told you about Emryn? *We made our choices.*"

Vax grimaced. "Foolish bastard."

"Apparently so." Thorn's shoulders dropped, and some of the tension leaked out of his stance. "It would've gone wrong sooner or later. You being here . . . made it better. And easier to bear for a little while."

"You're a good man," Vax said, meaning every word of it.

Thorn smirked, but the intensity in his gaze cut through Vax. "Sometimes."

"Anyway." Vax looked away, and woke up the snake belt that he still carried. It had remained with him after the fight, and he hadn't yet thought to give it back, nor had Thorn asked for it. "You shouldn't wander around the hills alone. It's dangerous. You'll want this, I'm sure. To keep you company in mines so deep the light won't reach." He held out the belt to Thorn.

Thorn stared at him like he could look straight through him. "Keep him. I think he may be done with deep mines for a while too."

The snake circled up and around Vax's arm, staring between both of them, like he could understand what they were saying. "Are you sure?"

"I do actually know my way around most of these passages. If I need company for my glum monologues, I'll talk at Sencha for a while. Tell her it's your fault." There was a sparkle in Thorn's eye. A challenge too.

"I'm sure she'd appreciate that."

Thorn wrapped a hand around Vax's neck and pulled him closer, and his kiss said everything his words couldn't. Behind them, Vex groaned, and with his free hand, Vax flipped her off. He felt Thorn's smile on his lips.

When they broke apart, some of the color had returned to Thorn's exhausted face, and he stepped back. "Thank you." He glanced at Vex. "Both."

She winked at him.

"Be careful, okay?" Vax asked when Thorn walked over to the narrow, jagged opening in the hillside that would lead him back underground. "Be safe."

Thorn stared up at the sun, letting the bright light wash over his face and relax his posture. When he turned to the cave in front of him, taking his first step back into the dark, the deep longing on his face was like a gut punch. "Aren't I always?"

Vax shook his head and gave the only possible reply. "Give Sencha my love and tell her to take care of you."

"I will do no such thing." Thorn laughed and with that, he let the hill swallow him. They heard his footsteps echo briefly. He whistled a cheerful tune that grew fainter with every passing step.

And then it was gone.

Vax stood staring at the jagged cave for a while. Then Vex walked up next to him and nudged him. She was still holding on to the notebook, which she handed over to him. "Where to next?"

"I still have a meeting with the fucking Clasp." He sighed. That was one meeting he wasn't looking forward to.

"You know," she said. "I told you so."

"I'll never hear the end of that now, will I?" he asked.

"Never is a long time, brother," she mused. "But give me another year, at least."

He elbowed her. "As long as you need."

He pocketed the notebook, held his sister's hand, and together they followed the path down the hill to a narrow stream where Trinket was unsuccessfully trying to catch a fishy meal, toward the valley where horses would be waiting for them, courtesy of Wick's Shadewatch, and from there toward the Blackvalley Path back to Westruun.

And as they made their way down, around them the wind picked up. The clouds overhead dispersed, and beams of hesitant sunlight peeked through the cover, illuminating the ashen figures that swirled around the meadow. They danced over the shadegrass, rolled along the hillside, and scattered and re-formed endlessly.

EPILOGUE

"Spireling Culwen is dead." Vax held the notebook out to Spireling Gideor, his face impassive. Despite the daylight hour, the office was lit only by magical means. There were no windows here through which an enterprising thief might try to gain entry, and the shelves and cabinets loomed darker than they had in his recollection. Vax ached for the daylight. Magically lit rooms belonged to another place than this vibrant, loud city.

The dwarf in front of him didn't flinch. He only tilted his head ever so slightly. "I don't believe this is the ring I asked for."

He wore a velvet doublet underneath a loose coat, both in a dark mossy green. Silver beads were braided into his beard, and he ran his fingers over his chin. He seemed intrigued rather than angry, but that didn't make him any less dangerous.

"This notebook will show that the former Shademaster of Jorenn Village traded with her brother—that same Spireling Culwen—off the books. She skimmed from the town's treasure; he did from the Clasp's. That *was* what you wanted to prove, wasn't it? And you couldn't have me marked as a Clasp member because it means plausible deniability?" Vax already knew the answers to those questions, but he needed to have them spoken here. He needed the other man to know that he understood what had happened.

Spireling Gideor accepted the notebook and leafed through it, going back and forth to consult the cypher the twins had added over the course of the trip back to Westruun. He managed to keep a straight face, but Vax saw interest spark in his eyes. He closed the notebook again and tapped it against his palm. "It's an interesting choice, my friend. Bold too, I must add. Tell me, what happened to my esteemed colleague?"

"He found himself on the wrong end of a dagger," Vax said flatly. Then he squared his shoulders and met the spireling's steady gaze. "I thought we had an understanding, but it seems he valued his own needs more."

Gideor raised his eyebrows. "Over those of the Clasp?"

Vax snorted. "The notebook tells you that plainly enough. He valued his own needs more than the needs of those closest to him. The needs of a town." Perhaps it was the grief or the exhaustion of this supposedly simple heist, but he leaned forward and his voice dropped. "Is that what your Clasp does, Spireling? Teach people to betray each other for power and coin?"

Spireling Gideor sighed. He opened a drawer in his desk and slid the notebook inside. "Betrayal is a part of life. It's not something we have to teach, because it comes naturally to most. Instead—though by your tone I hear this may surprise you—it's something we discourage. A lack of trust is terrible for business."

He got to his feet and Vax tensed, but the spireling simply walked over to one of the bookshelves. He picked up a wooden doll with emerald eyes and carefully turned it around, letting the gems catch the light and send green flecks dancing across the walls. "We understand the value of both safety and conflict, for both can be profitable. We do not trade in unnecessary chaos or selfish violence. What we do, we do for the betterment of all. And lest you forget, that includes you too. We have an understanding after all."

He placed the doll back on the shelf while Vax slumped in his chair, all too aware of the shackles of this understanding. It had seemed like a trap before, though one sweetened with the promise of stability. But when he looked at the dwarf in front of him, he couldn't shake the image of Culwen running Derowen through, of Thorn nearly dying, of so many lives derailed by the influence of a handful of smugglers under the Clasp's banner.

"I fulfilled my obligations to you," he managed. "I did what you asked me and more. You protected my sister. I rid you of a traitor. We'll call it even."

It was a bluff, of course, and Gideor laughed. He casually walked around Vax, observing him from all sides like some kind of prized possession. He didn't bother keeping himself between Vax and the door, because they both knew Vax wouldn't make it past the threshold.

Instead Gideor tented his fingers and looked at Vax long enough to make him uncomfortable. "From outsmarting our trackers to taking it upon yourself to change an assignment to bargaining with me, and all before receiving your brand. You could go far in our organization if you so wish. You have the talent and the skill, if you don't let your heart get in the way too much."

It was a backhanded compliment if Vax ever heard one, and his distaste must have shown, for the corner of Gideor's mouth pulled up. "The deal still stands, of course. You did not, in fact, fulfill your obligation to me, since the contract was for a ring not a notebook. But given the extenuating circumstances, I'm willing to overlook that. Let it not be said that I'm not considerate." The spireling walked over and knocked on the door, inviting into the room the same half-orc who'd stood watch the first time he'd visited. The half-orc didn't say a word, and simply crossed his arms.

Spireling Gideor curled a finger and gestured Vax to rise. "And since I am a considerate man, I also understand you wanting to spend time with your sister. In fact, I applaud it. Family is important, after all, and I would not wish to deprive you of that in the slightest."

There was no hint of a threat in his voice, but that didn't reassure Vax in the least. He hadn't forgotten how easily Spireling Gideor had threatened Vex last time, and he was sure the spireling hadn't either. He got to his feet and grudgingly came closer. "But you want me to be at your beck and call?"

"Not in the slightest, my friend." Gideor motioned for the half-orc to fall into step with Vax, and he did so without hesitation. "I know where I'm not wanted, and reluctant members are a danger to all. For now, I only want your oath and your mark, and then we'll call it even."

The half-orc's towering presence and Gideor's smooth words combined spelled danger, and Vax considered running, though it would've been a foolish endeavor whichever direction he chose. "That hardly sounds even."

"That was what you agreed to," Gideor reminded him. He spread his hands wide. "Think of all of the benefits. We are not all bad, Vax'ildan, even though you may believe so. We can do so much good for you and your sister. Isn't that true, Kal?"

The half-orc grunted. "Sure, boss."

Vax considered that. "You'd let me use those benefits without asking for anything in return? What do you gain from that?"

Gideor smiled, comfortably amused by Vax's questions. He reacted to him like a teacher would tolerate a willful but talented student. "We hope to gain your trust. Like I said, betrayal is all too common to many of us, but an organization such as ours cannot flourish if we do not trust one another. We cannot be successful without loyalty. So if you need time to find those feelings within yourself, we are of course happy to provide that. You understand what it's like to be a thief. We are a very patient people."

Those last words were many things. A warning. A reminder. A statement of fact. But when Gideor reached out his hand to Vax, he saw no duplicity in the spireling's eyes. It was as genuine an offer as the man could make him. Not based on any threats to his sister, but simply on the understanding that they'd made a business deal. And while trust might be a hard sell—perhaps even impossible—this was the best of both worlds.

Vax hesitated for a second longer. He could've elected against coming back here. They could've traveled east, through the Dawnmist Pines, or west, over the mountains. But he didn't want to keep running.

He shook the spireling's hand. "Is there some kind of fucking ceremony to this?"

"Do you want there to be?"

He didn't. "Just get it over with."

"That's what I assumed. Besides, we're short a spireling." With that, Gideor gestured at the door and led the way out of his office, down the hallway with its tapestries, and toward the staircase.

While the building was quieter during the day than it had been at night, people still milled around, deals were being made, and Vax felt the walls around him keenly. He kept his head high when Gideor and Kal led him up a winding flight of stairs, instead of down toward the Clasp-owned tavern, and toward a small chamber with a stained-glass window that provided him with a bird's-eye view of Westruun. The Clasp symbol made up the center part of the window, and the light that streamed through cast the room in dark blues and reds amidst the pale afternoon sun.

It offered a very similar perspective as the room opposite Shademaster Derowen's office, but the city that stretched around them was grand and colorful, and though Vax didn't doubt it was equally full of selfishness and greed, here at least he understood the rules. He could find his sister in a heartbeat and they would take on the world together instead of finding themselves at opposite ends of a struggle.

"The view is a good reminder of the world we live in," Gideor said from behind him. "We thrive if civilization—of some kind or other—does too. We are loyal to our members, but we are not ignorant of those around us."

"As long as it serves your own purpose," Vax said.

The spireling coughed an amused laugh. "We can be charitable, but we are no charity."

Vax didn't reply. He kept staring out the window, at the city and the world beyond.

"Will you swear your loyalty to us?"

Vax turned. Gideor opened up a glass cabinet that held the branding iron with the Clasp symbol he'd seen on so many members' shoulders. He clenched his jaws together. "I will."

Gideor turned over the iron in his hands. It looked almost like a seal used for wax; small enough to be held in one's hand, but big enough to leave a tangible scar. Gideor smiled at it fondly. "This mark means we can call on you in times of need, and you may not refuse. It means you can call on us in times of need too, and we may not refuse. Consider that. We can be your family too."

The words barely registered, because the branding iron began to glow in the spireling's hand, and the air around it rippled. Vax stared at it in rapt—and horrified—fascination. "I don't . . ."

"No, I know, you have your sister. Regardless of what you may think of me, I would never wish to come between that and I regret that it was necessary to do so to convince you." Gideor stepped closer to him, and the glow from the iron illuminated his face, highlighting the lines around his mouth and eyes, the scars along his jaw, and the ruthlessness in his gaze. "All I want to do is remind you that family can take many forms. And you may have one here, should you want it."

He didn't. He would never. He wanted a place to belong, but this would not be it.

Kal offered Vax a piece of leather to bite down upon. He swallowed hard and shook his head. He took off his cloak, pulled off his shirt, and faced the window. "Until then?"

"I wish you luck, my friend. Genuinely." With that, Gideor pressed the brand between Vax's shoulder blades.

VOICES RANG THROUGH THE MARKET Ward of Westruun. Merchants praised their wares, every single one of them trying to draw attention to themselves. Children were playing and pickpockets were hard at work. A young girl escaped her older sister's notice and ran toward a stall full of baked goods. A one-eared dog zigzagged through the crowds and a young elven boy ran after him, using a pair of crutches to propel himself forward. And although it was too early in the day still for patrons to frequent the cheap-looking taverns, that didn't stop the ones who simply claimed late morning as a bright continuation of night.

The city was, Vax'ildan Vessar decided, obnoxiously loud and contentedly alive. It wrapped itself around him like a cloak too often worn. Patched and dirty and torn in places, but no less comfortable. It chafed along the brand on his back, but the uneven cobblestones underneath his feet were easy to follow and teased a swagger into his step.

Especially when he noticed a half-elf with messy dark-brown hair and deadly weapons in front of a bowyer's stall. From a distance, observers might be forgiven to think his sister was all harsh angles and raw edges, proud and untouchable. He saw the smile that teased at the corner of her mouth. The gentleness in her eyes. He saw her fierce courage and her intelligence and her heart. And he definitely saw the faint blush on her cheeks when she haggled with the woman behind the stall.

He grinned.

He knew that they might not have a place yet where they could easily fit, where they could find a space that was made to include them and where someone cared that they returned safely if they got lost. But maybe someday.

For now, he couldn't wait to get out and keep traveling on.

He walked up to her and nudged her with her shoulder. "Am I interrupting something?"

Vex gnashed her teeth. "Yes."

The bowyer, a young woman with an easy smile and sparkling eyes, arched an eyebrow. "Didn't realize there were two of you." She had a spread of beautifully carved quivers lying in front of her, alongside the usual gear, and with a sideways glance at Vex's similarly decorated quiver and the fact that she wasn't holding any archery equipment, he realized he *had* interrupted something.

The bowyer spotted a customer who perused her rack of bows, and with a hint of disappointment, she shook her head. "Duty calls." Before she walked over to the customer, she winked at Vex. "Next time, I do demand drinks."

Vax bit his lip to keep from smiling when his sister watched the bowyer with a curious expression, before she turned around and stalked away, muttering something about *brothers* under her breath.

He jogged to keep up. "Next time, eh?"

"I was waiting for you. I got us supplies for the road, but when you took forever, I spotted Fida and I needed something to distract me," Vex snapped. She scanned the street around them for anyone who might be able to overhear what they were saying, and she softened slightly when she turned to him. "How did it go?"

He flexed his arms, and the skin around the brand pulled painfully. "Well enough. I'm sure I'll have business here again, but not right now."

They'd agreed before Vax went in to meet with Spireling Gideor that they'd only stay in Westruun for that meeting. Unless the Clasp demanded he'd stay—and he probably wouldn't have even if that was the case—they needed a change of scenery. They needed other places. "We can stay if you want."

She shook her head. "We'll come back, I'm sure. For now, I've had my fair share of cities and towns."

He thought for a moment her eyes darted in the direction of the bowyer, and she took her archer tab from her quiver, twisting it around her fingers. "So. Where do you want to go next?"

"Not Emon," he said immediately. He'd thought about it when Gideor tended the brand. "Let's stay clear of places with a Clasp presence for a while."

She smirked. "Isn't that everywhere?"

"Hush." He elbowed her. "I'd rather be far away from all of this for a while."

They slowly meandered through the Westruun streets, with their backs toward the tall outline of Gatshadow, looming over the city. They sidestepped a merchant with an unruly cart full of equipment, and watched a messenger on a horse speed by.

"That half-elven scout at the encampment mentioned Kraghammer, but I've had my fill of underground adventures for a while. I've heard wild stories about Shadebarrow, we could go explore that? Or head back to Kymal." He didn't have a particular preference. He amused himself with flinging options at his sister.

Vex rolled her eyes. "We can spend unnecessary coin to buy a map, throw one of your daggers at it, and see where it ends up."

He slung an arm around her shoulders and winced at the stab of discomfort that crawled along his back. Even so, he pulled her close. "I don't care."

"As long as we're together?" she teased.

"As long as it doesn't involve any more people branding me."

She placed a hand on his and held him close, and he could feel her thoughts turn inward. She tensed, but after a moment she plastered on a smile. "Let's go to the Lucidian Coast," she suggested. "I'm tired of mountains."

"It's a surprisingly unterrible idea," Vax said.

She stepped on his foot.

He didn't let her go. "I like it. It's new. I don't know what we'll find there. We'll spend some time exploring. I may be able to find work near Stilben. Stay there for a while." It would be entirely different from what they were used to, and that was exactly what they both needed.

"I don't know what we'll find there either," Vex admitted. "But that's the fun of it."

"Always," he promised.

She finally, truly, smiled at that. "And no matter what happens."

Under the watchful eye of Gatshadow, the city changed around them as they got nearer to the gate that would lead them back to Trinket and farther south. The buildings in the Market Ward were all bright and meant to attract customers, but closer to the outskirts of the city, nearer the gates, the houses were humbler. These were the homes of people who lived their lives between the city walls, where notches in the walls showed children growing up, where space was made to fold in newcomers, and where the stories told by wandering strangers were endlessly retold.

Vex and Vax passed them by, together, and they kept on walking.

—⟨ ACKNOWLEDGMENTS ⟩—

I t's an honor, a joy, and absolutely terrifying to take beloved characters and craft a new story for them. Liam and Laura, thank you endlessly for entrusting me with the twins. Maybe someday, I'll tell you how much these characters mean to me. But until then, I hope I did them justice and I hope this book says it too.

To everyone at Critical Role, thank you for making this such a delightful project to work on, with excitement, wonderful notes, and the high level of care for this world and the stories in it. Thank you for all of those stories.

Many, many thanks to Elizabeth Schaefer, for being the guiding light of this book with insightful edits and excited flailing, and everyone at Del Rey, for making it look spectacular.

To Nikki Dawes, for a glorious cover. And Andy Law, for a stunning map.

To Suzie Townsend, Dani Segelbaum, and everyone at New Leaf for keeping me going. To Jennifer Udden, for making that first connection.

To Diana Sousa, for putting up with my cryptic hints and only being slightly extra about them. (And for being a wonderful friend and a super talented artist.) To Fox Benwell, for a shared love of fantasy, found family, and adventures. And to Francesca Zappia, for introducing me to Critical Role in the first place.

—⟨ ABOUT THE AUTHOR ⟩—

MARIEKE NIJKAMP (she/they/any) is a #1 *New York Times* bestselling author of novels, graphic novels, and comics. Marieke is a storyteller, dreamer, globe-trotter, and geek. Before pursuing her lifelong passion for writing, she majored in philosophy and medieval history. She loves to go on adventures, roll dice, and daydream. She lives and writes in Small Town, The Netherlands.

mariekenijkamp.com
Twitter: @mariekeyn
Instagram: @mariekeyn

CRITICAL ROLE is one of the fastest-growing independent media companies in the world, starting as a roleplaying game between friends and evolving into a new kind of organization dedicated to storytelling, community, and imagination. As Critical Role continues to expand the unique universe it has created, with complex stories set in an ever-evolving world, it also continues to create more ways to experience Exandria, including books on the *New York Times* Best Sellers list, comic books and graphic novels, collectibles, tabletop and roleplaying games, podcasts, live events, and a highly anticipated animated series, *The Legend of Vox Machina*, airing exclusively on Amazon Prime Video. With an original cast of award-winning veteran voice actors who are also co-founders of the company, including Matthew Mercer, Ashley Johnson, Marisha Ray, Taliesin Jaffe, Travis Willingham, Sam Riegel, Laura Bailey, and Liam O'Brien, Critical Role is committed to ensuring anyone can discover its stories, characters, and community.

critrole.com